FOR THE LOVE OF POLITICS

In accordance with Australian copyright laws (1968) the scanning, uploading, and electronic sharing of any part of this book without the permission of the publisher constitute unlawful piracy and theft of the author's intellectual property and can incur legal action. If you would like to use material from the book (other than for review purposes), prior written permission must be obtained by the publisher who can be contacted at wild.dreams.publishing@gmail.com. Thank you for your support of the author's rights.
This book is a work of fiction. References to historical events, real people, or real locals are used fictitiously. Other names, characters, places and incidents are the product of the author's imagination, and any resemblance to actual events, locales or persons, living or dead, is entirely coincidental.

Wild Dreams Publishing
A publication of Wild Dreams Publishing
Traralgon, Vic
© 2018 by Wild Dreams Publishing
All rights reserved, including the right of reproduction in whole or in part in any form.
Wild Dreams Publishing is a registered trademark of Wild Dreams Publishing.
Manufactured in Australia.
All rights reserved.
Cover © Bella Emy

A WHISPER OF WINGS 10
ONE 12
TWO 18
THREE 26
FOUR 28
FIVE 30
SIX 34
SEVEN 40
EIGHT 44
NINE 46
TEN 50
ELEVEN 52
TWELVE 56
THIRTEEN 60
FOURTEEN 64
FIFTEEN 66
EPILOGUE 70
NOT JUST POLITICS 72
THE LOBBYISTS DILEMMA 88
THE GIFT OF FORESIGHT 100
PROLOGUE 102
ONE 104
TWO 106
THREE 108
FOUR 110
FIVE 114

SIX	118
SEVEN	120
EIGHT	122
NINE	124
TEN	126
ELEVEN	128
TWELVE	130
THIRTEEN	132
FOURTEEN	134
FIFTEEN	136
SIXTEEN	138
SEVENTEEN	140
EIGHTEEN	142
NINETEEN	144
TWENTY	146
TWENTY-ONE	148
TWENTY-TWO	150
TWENTY-THREE	152
TWENTY-FOUR	154
TWENTY-FIVE	156
TWENTY-SIX	158
TWENTY-SEVEN	160
TWENTY-EIGHT	162
TWENTY-NINE	164
THIRTY	166
THIRTY-ONE	168

THIRTY-TWO	172
THIRTY-THREE	174
THIRTY-FOUR	176
THIRTY-FIVE	178
THIRTY-SIX	180
THIRTY-SEVEN	182
THIRTY-EIGHT	186
THIRTY-NINE	188
FORTY	192
FORTY-ONE	194
EPILOGUE	196
THE SPINSTER OF INDIA	198
CHAPTER ONE	200
CHAPTER TWO	210
CHAPTER THREE	220
IMPASSE	232
-PROLOGUE-	234
-ONE-	238
-TWO-	248
-THREE-	252
-FOUR-	270
-FIVE-	286
-SIX-	288
RIVER	313
PROLOGUE	315
CHAPTER ONE	319

CHAPTER TWO 327
CHAPTER THREE 337
CHAPTER FOUR 349
ELECTING ELLIE 353
ONE 355
TWO 361
THREE 363
FOUR 367
FIVE 373
SIX 377
SEVEN 385
EIGHT 391
NINE 397
TEN 401
ELEVEN 407

A Whisper of Wings
M. E. Giquere

One

Angel Wings

Wyatt

My hooded figure blended into the inky canopy of darkness as the stars align flickering like fireflies hidden in the night.

Iridescent angel wings lit a path in the twilight causing me to squint. A vision of beauty hovered above for seconds maybe minutes. It was like a spaceship claiming its territory. As quickly as this spheral illusion appeared, it disappeared into the still of the night . . . leaving me breathless . . . wondering if I'm caught between two worlds . . . theirs and ours.

Dream?

Reality?

I'm not sure.

A safe haven between dusk and dawn begins in darkness and awakens as silhouettes give way to the sun peeking over the horizon. My only existence since the fatal car crash that claimed my families lives years earlier. Shadows of demons tightly woven in a web of my past flirt with my senses.

Present day I'm running for a second term as Senator from California forcing me to stay low key as much as possible in between rallies and guest appearances on the nightly talk shows. And, of course, my frequent trips back and forth to DC. Supporting a yes or no vote, for or against, on the floor.

"Good morning, Senator," echoed.

"Good morning guys," as I grab a coffee from Starbucks and pick up the latest edition of the paper on my way back to my empty space I call home. I take the elevator to the penthouse . . . thanks to the trust fund my parents left me. Just inside the foyer I place my hoodie on the rack and glance at the scattered photos of my family lining the wall from happier times. A day doesn't go by without memories flashing in front of me. Paralyzing my thoughts in place.

Reminding me of the special way Mom and Dad looked into each other's eyes, said they loved each other and sealed it with a kiss before starting their day.

My younger sister Dr. Maggie La Blanc's bright future ended along with theirs on that fatal day. Derek, my twin, best friend and only brother was driving on a rainy, slippery road leading down into the Hoover Dam on a cross-country vacation.

Derek's car veered into the guard rails that separated the road from a twenty-foot drop.

In an instant my entire family was taken from me. A void that swallowed me in grief.

How does one go on from there? They don't. Time heals nothing. Who ever said that obviously hadn't encountered a devastating loss. You learn to live each day that's handed to you, but as I said, time heals nothing. Bit by bit. Piece by piece. The heart tries to heal itself.

Miss Catherine is busy making breakfast when I sneak up from behind, blindfold her with my cool hands and give her a heads up that I'm back.

She yelps, "Brr," slapping my hands away as we both laugh.

"Smells awesome. How's my barista girl today? I'm starving. I'm headed for the shower then up to my office."

Miss Catherine was just that, a Miss.

Single . . . easy on the eyes. Strawberry blonde hair like my mom's that twisted down past her shoulders ending at the middle of her back.

Her smile lights up my world on a daily basis with the biggest and I mean biggest, emerald-green eyes that freeze me in place first thing each and every morning.

Unattached. But for the life of me, I can't figure out why.

I think. I never did ask. But she doesn't wear a ring and there's never been mention of a husband during our endless marathon talks while sharing a vino.

She's been my saving grace since the accident. I can be myself with her, no pretense, no Senator La Blanc, just me letting my guard down. Airing my feelings without judgement.

"Good morning, Wyatt, how was your run?" Shooting her inquisitive look my way.

"Invigorating, as always. Thanks for asking." I place the folded newspaper on the counter and keep walking.

"Breakfast in ten." She yells.

Well, scratch the office for now. I step out of my jogging pants and pull my jersey over my head leaving a trail across the bedroom's white marble tile before stepping into the overhead jets of the pinging shower. I whip my head back and ponder the thought of a whisper of wings that shook my world only moments ago.

I glance at the morning paper facing up when I plank my butt down at the counter. Carter Grand's editorial headline of the day. "La Blanc is at it again." I shake my head and push it aside until after my first sip of my joey.

"Many voters slash constituent's think of Senator Wyatt La Blanc as a nonconformist. Always thinking out of the box and crossing party lines."

Well, I couldn't ask for a better campaign boost. "Thanks, Carter." Shooting a high-five in the air.

"Others paint him as a free-spirited politician. Well, once again they were 100% correct as he formed a tri-partisan committee for women's rights across the board. State by state engaging the political agenda as excitement builds."

Carter keeps giving. I should hire him as my campaign manager. And he doesn't stop. He's quite the feather in my cap.

"Equal pay."

"Equal job opportunity."

"Equal say in the political arena."

What better way to jump start my morning, a cup of coffee and a step closer to another six-year term.

I walk in my office that housed a circular conference table . . . with twenty-four black leather chairs peeking over. Monitors lined the wall bridging the latest news from one station to the next across the world.

I live a sheltered life behind these doors to the outside world.

A shell of an existence at times.

After a full day of non-stop business meetings and a late dinner with my smart, capable assistant Izzy Thompson. I crash for a few hours before my early morning jog along the path of the Pacific Highway following the ocean's shoreline of Laguna Beach.

I relish the peace and serenity the early morning hours bring. Always trying to quill the nightmares that have pattered my existence since the crash. This time, my trail was lit by several angels scurrying across the heavenly skies with the billions of stars as their canvas lighting the way. The oceans turquoise tide kisses the pebbled sand as far as the eye can see. Peace personified.

I secretly watch from a distance as *Iris*, my name for her, with the bright-lavender angel eyes cocoons herself within the span of her wings before tucking them in by her sides.

She glides effortlessly over the skyscraper of the city out of view from the world as her universe silently speaks to my heart.

The billionaire Senator taken hostage by a fallen angel. That's even too farfetched for me to comprehend.

But not just any fallen angel with her shiny pitch-black hair gracefully touching her breasts . . . and a white satin sash cinched around the waist of a slinky lavender dress. My eyes were pulled to her alluring voluptuous breasts spilling out of the sweetheart neckline. Really? And, in a blink-of-an-eye, she faded into the skyline.

I've been known to be a lady killer, but an angel killer is not in my MO. Taking my thoughts hostage.

At dawn just before sunrise, I'm taken back by the movement of a shimmering object through the floor to ceiling windows of the penthouse.

When I walk out onto the balcony, a fragile *Iris* was perched on the edge of the railing taking my breath away. Her toes sprinkled with purple stardust.

Unable to breathe . . .

I still myself in place . . .

I absorb the glorious sight of the most *enamored* creature I've ever seen as the rising orb blanketed the horizon behind her.

"Hi," she whimpers slightly above a whisper. Hiding behind her sad violet eyes . . . overflowing with emotions and crocodile tears.

My eyes hold hers in place as I slowly move closer and take her fidgeting fingers in mine. "Now, what's this?" Ever-so-gently wiping each tear as it releases itself caressing her pale cheeks.

"Where do you come from, my beautiful *Iris* with the angel eyes?" Finally a resemblance of a smile nudges across her lips.

"Iris?" Tilting her head to one side in a shy gesture. "I come from the heavenly galaxy many light years away." Talking softly through her tears.

I ask. "Are you lost?" In a nanosecond I watch her transcend into the early morning skies as disappointment shadows my sadness. She turns my world upside down and inside out and disappears like a soft violet glow into the sunlit day. I jam my hands in the pocket of my PJ drawstring bottoms and watch as *Iris* becomes a speck in the sky. "Go away world" I shout out loud as the ring tone from my cell distracts me.

When I glance over it's my 9:30 appointment here in the penthouse. I'd better hurry.

#

Angels Amongst Us

Wyatt

"Yes . . . no?" Still questioning myself.

"Wyatt, breakfast is ready." Miss Catherine's voice echoes through the intercom of the penthouse.

Disappointment follows me from room to room. I take a seat at the kitchen island where Miss Catherine has a large juice set out for me and take a sip before saying, "Good morning Catherine."

"Good morning, Wyatt. Eggs Benedict, your favorite," as she sets her creative presentation in front of me for my eyes to salivate on.

She's right about that. Raising my mood up a notch. "Thank you."

"Did you opt out of your morning jog?" She asks.

Well, I was temporarily distracted by a fallen angel, named Iris. You do believe in angels, don't you? Now how bizarre would that sound if I actually said that. I'm even having a difficult time wrapping my head around the reality myself.

The penthouse elevator dings on the ground floor as I watch Gabi, short for Gabrielle on the monitor step in. She's VP of the multi-billion-dollar marketing business La Blanc Inc. I inherited from my dad and my number one campaign advisor. Even though she knows she's being monitored from every room of the penthouse, she goes through the same routine each and every day.

Knowing full well she sexually turns me on before my day starts. *Lipstick covering her pouty lips . . .*
Mascara outlining her cobalt eyes . . .
Spray of breath mint . . .

Combs through her blonde wavy locks that grace her shoulders… Straightens her pencil skirt hugging her thirty-one-year-old figure
Checks out her Christian Louboutin's in the mirror . . .
You get the drill . . .

"You're late." Checking my watch as the doors to the elevator open. My arms spread eagle from end to end.

"Well, by the lack of attire, I'd say, I was early." Dragging a freshly manicured nail down over my six-pack. Gabi kisses my cheek . . . laughs and pushes by me.

"Tease."

"Who me??? Tease. Takes one to know one, my blonde hombre with the blue eyes. Greeting me half naked." A grin emerges from deep inside.

"What did you expect?" Yelling back at me as she continues up to the office.

I check myself out in the mirrored elevator doors. Smile a Cheshire grin and head to the bedroom to get dressed for the day. Bare chested with draw string bottoms. See what *Iris* does to me. All reasoning escapes me, shaking my head. "Blonde hombre. Really?" You have that 9:30 appointment, Wyatt.

Focus!!!

Iris is from a heavenly galaxy and you're from earth. Reminding my wavering mind, the realty of the situation. I'm more than likely caught in a vortex of a paralyzing dream state unable to free myself of its hold on me.

The intercom dings. "Wyatt, your 9:30, Landon Ferguson, is here." Bringing me back to the here and now.

"Offer him a cup of coffee, Gabi. Remember he takes it black. No sugar." Kibitzing with her.

"Funny!"

"I thought so." Gabi's an easy target to poke fun at. "Did I tell you how stunning you look this morning?" Buttering her up for a romantic dinner here in the penthouse and the after-party in the bedroom. "And was that a new fragrance that teased my senses as you swished by earlier?"

"No to the first question. Yes, to the second. Christian Dior will be happy to know his latest perfume meets with your approval."

Corporate meetings monopolized most of the afternoon.

Memorable moments with *Iris* float in and out of my mind pulling my full attention away from the power point presentations of the day.

I find myself looking forward to seeing her again. But when is the question?

Guilt runs rapid between my affection for Gabi and my desire to spend time with Miss Angel Wings.

More than likely we won't cross paths again.

For God sake, Wyatt. One's from a heavenly galaxy far away and the other has her two feet securely grounded on this planet.

Guilt shouldn't even enter the equation.

Fantasy versus reality. Maybe I want both.

I send Gabi a text. 'Give Miss Catherine a heads up as to what you're craving for dinner. Looking forward to stripping you out of that sexy pencil skirt that hugs your butt.' Click send.

'Looking forward to your sexual assault of my butt. Maybe I should tell Miss Catherine to go home early and skip dinner.'

'No. No. No. We'll need our strength. Don't forget to tell Miss Catherine we'll be needing a couple bottles of our favorite wine.'

I grab the iron poker next to the fireplace and stoke the logs with one hand and bring a goblet of wine to my lips with the other.

I watch Gabi slither herself up between my legs, unbuckle my belt and with an open invitation does what she does best. Challenges me.

I tug her pencil skirt down over her hips and smile as I reach my hand in between her G-string and the softness of her velvety sheath. Envisioning a blossoming blush.

She throws her head back and moans like a baby. With every beat of her heart I fall more and more in love with her. Or is that the alpha male surfacing with the touch of her fingers encircling my boxers?

I pause . . . lingering at her sex. I massage the sensitive bud between her lips as I slowly drive her out of her ever-loving mind. "More?"

"You mean there's more?" She murmurs. Jesting with me.

She has no idea. "Gabi, unbutton your blouse." Panting across her lips as my tongue captures hers in a torturous twist. There's something seductive about a woman disrobing in front of me. The first three buttons teasingly release her caged breasts.

Salivating as my mouth aches, vying for my assault as my hands encapsulates her breasts pulsating against my touch.

Then the final unveiling . . . my uncontrollable navel fetish as my genitals twitch. Gabi tucks a thumb on each side of her pencil skirt and steps out modeling only a black lace G-string. Just the way I love her, nude and heart racing sensual.

I grab both sides of her waist and crush her to me. Mouth to mouth, skin to skin, the rhythmic beat of our hearts. "How about we finish what we started in the shower?" Breathing heavily. I scoop her up in my arms and carry her into the snail shower where I made love to her over again until there wasn't a breath left between us.

She was like a "pro" in a brothel with the skilled hands of a surgeon. Gentle, precise and calculating.

I wrap Gabi's hair in a towel and knot another one at her breasts, kiss her neck and pat her butt sending her off towards the bedroom while I finish brushing my teeth.

The word "HI" was written in the steam of the mirror. Cute. Wiping it away with the palm of my hand before Gabi sees.

"Jesus, *Iris*, you just can't barge in here whenever you feel like it and play private eye," I whisper, spinning in place to find her.

"If I didn't know any better, I'd say you were acting like a jealous woman," talking into thin-air. My eyes were everywhere, searching for a sign, any sign of her, but I was met with an emptiness.

"*Iris*, stop playing these games." A not so vivid reflection popped up in the mirror hiding in a veil of a shadow.

She was holding one finger to her lips, telepathically saying 'hush', looking like the sweetest angelic creature that she was.

"Gabi will hear." Inhaling slowly as I turn to face her.

"Then what?" Taking quiet breaths.

Or maybe that's it.

She's deliberately trying to sabotage my relationship with Gabi? "This can't happen again," softly speaking. "*Iris*, there're boundaries."

"Boundaries?" she asks in a naive tone of voice fluttering her poetic eyes.

"You know exactly what, I mean, *Iris,* stop playing the innocent card with me." Touching the tips of her fingers in a gentle, quiet gesture.

"Wyatt, if I didn't know better, I'd say you have a secret mistress hidden in the walls of the penthouse."

Gabi wrapping her arms around me from the back. "Does she have super powers like this? Teasingly manhandling my family jewels that instantly come alive with her touch while *Iris* disappears with a distant thought back into the Universe. Her behavior is becoming somewhat predictable and inevitable.

"Two women with the same magical powers. I think not." Trying to defuse the fiery heat of jealousy spewing from her eyes as I try turning a blind eye to my feelings. "It's horribly late and we both have a tight schedule tomorrow, Wyatt, let's get some rest," as she turns the covers down for me to join her.

"You, Mr. La Blanc, have an early flight to DC and a quick turnaround to do the Jimmy Kimmel show for tomorrow night's broadcast."

When I slid in beside Gabi's velvety skin, a spark of energy ignited between us and sleep became a distant second.

The visual of Gabi's hands above her head aching to be handcuffed to the bed was a definite turn-on. She let out a whimper as the coolness tightened around her wrists, enjoying her squirm as I marvel at her flawless skin. The softness of her breast to my touch as my thumb massages her hardened nipples.

The way her tongue outlines her perfect lips, taunting me before twisting into the folds of her mouth. "Humm," she breathes like one continuous echo in the room.

I push her knees apart, slide the vibrating ring in place and enter her slowly, filling her as she withers underneath me letting me know she's all mine. "Jesus, Wyatt, deeper. Oh, God deeper," spreading her legs apart even more. Wiggling in place. Taking all of me with a ring of vibration encircling us. Gabi's eye shoots open with the low buzzing sound of the vibrator teasingly stroking her navel. I tip-toe down further resting it on her sex listening to her shallow breathes of excitement.

I continue slow agonizing thrusts imprisoned within her till we both come with a vengeance of brutal passion.

Lost in warm spasms encircling us. I release her hands and lift her to my lap covering us both with a satin sheet, sink into the mattress and enjoy the emotional moments skin to skin after making love.

Thunder roars bringing with it a gusty wind and lightning, crackling and snapping across the rain filled sky destroying anything and everything in its path. Saguaro cactus tall in stature split in half as the lightning goes to ground.

I wander down the middle of the slick pavement past a sea of cars piled into one another. Bodies everywhere. Stop. Horror rushes over me. "Mom, Dad, Maggie," I scream.

They were crushed under the hood of the car on impact and Derek dead at the wheel. I call out to them again in hopes that's it's only a nightmare I'll wake from and life will be normal again.

"Oh, God, no," I cry out. I awake with a jolt, in a pool of sweat like the nightmare before and the one before that. The tragic crash that took my family still haunts me.

I'm holding on by a thread.

Just trying to survive a life without them.

I untangle myself from Gabi and leave her curled up sleeping like a baby.

Lost in thought I take a quick shower and mosey up to the office. I browse through the notes Izzy left face-up on top of the desk from the night before. When my right hand doesn't know what the left hand is doing, I rely on Izzy with the auburn hair and fiery eyes.

Repeating the same words Dad always said about her back in the day.

Dad called her by her given name Isabelle but Izzy is more personal. She has tweaked my day, minute by minute, from leaving DC to the second I need to be back stage in preparation for the Kimmel show.

Iris, Iris, Iris. What to do about my dangerously beautiful *Iris*. She's become quite the stalker, leaving me feeling like I'm cheating on Gabi whenever she makes an untimely appearance. What the hell? I ask myself with my elbows resting on the desk.

I pull my fingers through my hair in desperation of this hold she has on my heart as Gabi grows more and more suspicious as time goes by.

Robert my driver beeps in. "Mr. La Blanc, your flight to DC leaves in two hours."

"Really that soon? The time got away from me, Robert. Thanks for the heads up."

"See you downstairs in an hour, Mr. La Blanc."

"That you will, that you will" and disconnect.

I pick up my briefcase and hurry downstairs to have breakfast with Gabi.

When I walk into the kitchen, Miss Catherine is putting the finishing touches on a magnificent spread, as always. I give her a wink and plank myself down at the counter and swivel.

I watch Gabi close the distance between us with a cute slash sexy wiggle in her stride.

She greets me with a not so gentle kiss and slams her tongue down my throat.

"I hate when I wake up and you're not sprawled out beside me."

"Well, you don't have to be so hostile." Slamming my tongue back in stride with hers."

Three

In My Words

Iris

I don't even know his name, but his manly presence branded my heart.

On this spectacular night just before daybreak, my seraph wing span carried me above the Pacific shoreline. It was even more beautiful in the early twilight hours as I playfully swished closer to the waves that caressed the ocean floor. And in a nanosecond descended into the early morning horizon.

The sky was filled with an aura of magnificent dancing colors of several shades of yellows, deep oranges encircling an orb of red.

At first glance, his ocean-blue eyes glistened like jewels against an olive complexion and dirty blonde waves of hair hanging loose around his face. His taut 6'3 surfer boy frame took by breath away.

Separated by death was the beginning of my heartbreak and shell of an existence.

Flashing back to a year ago, I was involved in a fatal car accident. I died on impact as I watched in horror. My earthly body slowly rose to another dimension of being as I stood by helpless. I was a spectator witnessing first responders and Medics saving lives. Red lights flashing . . . sirens blasting . . . survivors scurrying to lend a helping hand. When they placed me on a gurney and covered my face with a light cloth, I panicked.

"No. God no. No." I yelled, screamed and cried.

But no one answered. I screamed louder but again no one heard. Then the medics continued on to the next victim as I watched in horror. I couldn't catch a breath. I tried and tried again to no avail.

Is this death?

Another dimension of reality?

Am I in heaven? I repeatedly questioned the validity of this new existence.

Not good.

Not bad.

Just different as I floated above the chaos listening to the deafening screams of sobbing parents, husbands, wives, children searching for their love ones.

The last thing I remembered I was traveling east on the 1-10 towards Denver. Singing along to Celine's Power of Love with my 13-year-old son Lance in the passenger seat busy texting on his smart phone.

A tractor trailer west bound lost control and crossed the highway taking out seven cars and lord knows how many lives.

Lance was missing, and I was dead. Our lives turned on a dime.

I searched for some sign . . . any sign of him.

A year had passed and my futile attempts to find my son was closing in on me.

Casanova's caring eyes held out new hope. Guiding him to another six-year term as Senator was my earthly mission. There was a power bigger than both of us that led me to him, hoping to find my son Lance in the process.

What I didn't know was how madly in love with him I was.

But, after all, we are soul mates that have lived many lives together.

Butterflies

Wyatt

A yellow *butterfly* . . . flutters its delicate wings through the open window hovering near the edge of my desk distracting me from my morning conference call. An unusual sight to witness this many floors up. A repeat of yesterday's butterfly gracefully letting its presence known while Gabi and I were having breakfast. I glance up and peruse the office for any signs of *Iris*.

Out of my peripheral vision, a butterfly emitting colorful hues of lavender and blue cast its shadow near my eye. I watch the delicate, iridescent wings dance amongst the rose petals . . . paused for a second, posing like a porcelain statue. Fitting for the cover of National Geographic's.

Iris's presence was a powerful force as the fragrance of rose petals from the morning dew clung to her angel wings . . . In a blink of an eye she appeared out of nowhere. Like a magician's wave of his wand.

"Hi," I whispered, gazing into her eyes that shimmered like crystals of amethyst.

"Hi," she whispers back . . . from the corner of the room.

"I don't think I properly introduced myself. I'm Wyatt." Almost forgetting to breathe.

"Come closer." Her wings opened ever so gracefully as she glides herself closer like a whisper of a breeze. Her angelic presence was beyond description. She was soft spoken and alluring.

What do you say to an angel? Standing there tongue-tied.

Do I wait for her to speak?

I'm speechless in the presence of a woman.

This has never happened. Laughing at myself.

But, she's not any woman. She's an angel.

Gabi's voice echo's along with her stride as she walks around my desk and takes the liberty of sitting on my lap. Her scent from this morning's shower still lingers as I devour her delectable mouth as a ping instantly lands in my groin.

"I heard voices." Gabi's quizzical nature questioning me. "Wyatt, you seem preoccupied the past couple days. Want to share?"

"There's nothing to share. Now scoot." I pat her on the butt and wave her on.

"Can we finish this conversation later, Wyatt?"

"There's nothing to finish, Gabi. Turn your cute little butt around and let me get something done. What time are the Larson's scheduled?"

"Within the hour." She shouts back as she sashays out the door.

"Like I said, this conversation is not over."

It's Gabi's unprofessional way of giving me the finger. Holding in a laugh.

Iris silently reappears after Gabi exits through the door of the office.

This time a brazen *Iris*.

A not-so-timid *Iris*.

If I didn't know better, I'd say a jealous *Iris*.

She was a pinch of sass and a splash of class.

"Why are you here?" Her skin was as smooth as a porcelain doll as I tip-toe down her cheek with the back of my fingers.

"Why me?" Lifting her chin.

"With the millions of people in the world." Holding her gaze to mine.

"Why me?" Pecking her lips on mine. Iris looked into my eyes. Her gaze delved deep in my heart as her words brushed softly into my ears.

"You looked like a wounded soul caught in a pre-dawn trance . . . with the placid ocean stretched out in front of you.

When the shimmering rays touched the horizon I was lost in your spell and forever tangled with your soul. So why not you?"

Five

My Heart's in Jeopardy

Iris

A white spectacular baby grand piano sits in the center of the grandiose room. Azure ocean views and white sandy beaches peek into the floor to ceiling windows. Furious sounds of waves crashing into the boulders below echo in the wind knocking against the panes of glass.

My heart flutters like a living breathing person as I watch Wyatt's fingers dance across the ebony and ivory keyboard. He was drop-dead gorgeous . . . wearing only a pair of torn jeans as his bare feet tapped the pedals. I nestle myself next to him on the stark white leather bench tucking a wing into his side . . . resting my fingers on his.

Forgetting for a moment I'm an angel as my attraction to Wyatt pulls at my heartstrings.

But the sad reality is I am. But only if I weren't. Questioning my own existence.

"Why so sad?" Witnessing a melancholy expression on his face. He didn't answer, turned the page of the sheet music and continued to tickle the ivories to a slow tempo of a whisper. Lost in a meditating trance. Eyes closed, shallow breathing.

Finally, he paused and said. "Certain melodies stir fond memories," engaging with my eyes.

"Playing a duet with my mom at her infamous dinner parties with the stars peering in while watching God's paintbrush create the sky."

He takes a deep breath and breathes a heartfelt sigh reminiscing about happier times.

"The Milky Way galaxy always spiraled out in front of us with zillions of planets circling around."

Breathing in a moment of silence I reply, "I'm sorry." Leaning my head on his shoulder. He was withering in front of me.

"Me too!" And continued transitioning into Beethoven's Piano Sonata No. 14. Leaving me spellbound. With his eyes closed, his long masculine fingers moved with determination and grace caressing the keys.

My eyelids were heavy with emotions as I lost myself in the rapture of the notes.

"Beethoven . . . a favorite of mine. Do you mind?"

Wyatt nods. A shocked nod.

Witnessing my fingers hug the keys as I play along. I could feel the heartbeat of the music as the harmonious sounds encircle the room. Echoing from wall to wall, floor to ceiling.

Wyatt leans in. "An accomplished pianist, I see."

Smiling the biggest smile. Our duet . . . took us to another level of consciousness. My delicate fingers hurried along the keys keeping in sync with the lightning pelting across the darkening skies.

"Your mother's presence was bigger than life vying for her son's attention, sandwiched in between us."

Wyatt laughs. "I felt her, too. Thank you. *Iris*, I can't seem to wipe you out of my head or my dreams. Or do I want to?"

"I know."

"Of course you do. Several days went by.

It was like you disappeared off the face of the earth taking with you a sliver of my heart."

"I know."

"You were spot-on. The connection between us is surreal. The missing half of my soul."

"I know."

"I lay awake staring out at the galaxy of stars that are like vivid chips of light reflecting back to earth, wondering where my angel is.

I reinforce my nervousness knowing you're out there somewhere, but where? I keep asking."

"I know."

"One by one, *Iris*, piece by piece, you have a way of gluing all the missing links of my life back together again."

Lightly brushing up against my fingers with his. Feeling a not-so-subtle surge of intimacy.

"You have become my calm before each storm." Shooting his intriguing eyes of lust into mine. "The only thing missing, *Iris,* is you."

"I know."

Wanting him to make love to me like he has done so many times in our past lives. But, he hasn't been privy to that, as yet.

"Jesus, *Iris*, what choice do we have?"

I shrug, lost in the foreplay of his words.

My heart begged me to press my lips to his and put us both out of our misery. But instead. I kiss his cheek and disappear in a cloud of sadness hearing Gabi's distant footsteps narrowing in. I love Wyatt, I loved him before I knew him, before I met him.

California Senators Race

Wyatt

"This is Wyatt, your charismatic Senator from California. Leave a message. Or I won't call you back."

"Wyatt, stop cherry picking your calls. I'm melting at the sound of your voice."

She's right about that.

I've been letting my calls go directly to voicemail, inundated with speaking engagements since the polls closed.

It's a necessary evil.

Seductive on the phone. Seductive in the bedroom. That's my MO.

"Color me horny, Wyatt."

How does she do that? Always hijacking my thoughts.

Gabi is stunning, as always, when she struts through the doors of the Ritz- Carlton convention hall on the arm of the Secret Service. My heart beats faster at the sight of her dressed in white against her tan skin. Putting me in a hypnotic state of arousal. The way the white fabric clung to her curves as she walked was like it was designed only for her.

I make my way through the crowd zooming in on her sexy persona.

An arm stretches out in front of me. "Congratulations Senator La Blanc. The districts are starting to report the voters, choice. Clearly another six-year term is yours."

"Let's not jinx it, Liam. It will be hours before the race is called. Keep our fingers crossed my lead continues to hold." Slapping him on the back. But my eyes were focused on Gabi as I closed the distance.

I intertwine Gabi's fingers with mine slowly taking her in my arms, "Speaking of horny. You aced it." Whispering near her lips before drowning in her eyes. A powerful aphrodisiac as we share an intimate moment in the midst of thousands of people.

"Well, aren't we the handsome one tonight, Senator La Blanc." Twisting her fingers through my hair.

"God, I love how your dishwater blonde curls trim your sexy blue-eyes." Her words have a way of undressing me.

"It's enough to make a girl wonder what's under that stunning, form-fitted navy-blue suit of yours."

Rubbing up against my hardening length as she eases her tongue into my parted lips, exploring the deepest part of me. Gabi puts the F in foreplay as bolts of lightning shoot through me.

"Looks like the thirty-six-year-old heart throb of Cali just stepped out of GQ." Crinkling my lapel in her fingers.

"Well, what do you say we sneak upstairs for a minute and check it out beautiful." She has the voice of an angel when trying to seduce me. "We won't be missed in all this chaos."

"I only wish Wyatt, but you have responsibilities."

Now she tells me. "We can't be giving into our sexual cravings on a whim." What a freakin' tease. She doesn't waste a second sliding her rebellious tongue back in stride with mine trying to harness my crazy thoughts of having her right now.

I heist two glasses of liquid courage from the waiter's tray handing one to Gabi.

Guilt comes knocking knowing Gabi has to share a piece of my heart with *Iris*, as our unrequited love stays hidden between her world and mine.

The convention hall was jammed with excited staff members and screaming supporters holding up La Blanc banners and signs.

Still, the race was too close to call even though I had a three-point lead. I felt a royal flush course through me like a winning hand at the poker table as my eyes were drawn to the far corner of the hall where *Iris* hid in the shadows, unnoticed to everyone but me.

Hopefully sharing in a night of jubilation. She was cocooned inside the span of her wings barely recognizable to the outside world, but to me she was the most beautiful gift of the evening.

My saving grace from another life that has crossed over to help me overcome the stumbling blocks of an existence without her. With every step I take along the way, with every breath I breathe, beyond this life into the future dimensions of past, present and future, *Iris* watches over me.

The next two hours dragged by in slow motion keeping Gabi and me on the edge of our seats. A nail biter to the bitter end. With *Iris* never far from my thoughts or straying from my peripheral vision longer than a second.

CNN . . . Breaking News . . . "California's Senator Wyatt La Blanc, as expected, wins another six-year term." Anderson Miles pointing to the final numbers.

"No surprise here." Everyone in the convention hall vaulted to their feet. High-fives shot into the air. Deafening cheers echoed like one continuous air-splitting hurrah.

Within the hour challenger, William Monroe called to congratulate me just minutes before he formally conceded the race from California's Convention Center.

Celebrating my win with Gabi by my side is an extra bonus. I spread my fingers at her waist from behind and pose for the first click of the cameras.

Finally I was able to put an end to the turbulence in my stomach and the nervousness that channeled through the room the past few days. Giving way to sounds of Dom Perignon . . . popping and the bubbly champagne splashing into the fluted glasses generously being passed around.

I looked back to find *Iris*. She was gone. I panic. My heart froze in place.

She touched my life, my heart, my soul, in so many ways I stopped counting. It's unthinkable that I wouldn't see her again.

A soft breeze touches my cheek, my lips. *Iris* is that you? I silently ask.

"See you around, Wyatt Earp," whispering near my ear as a butterfly flutters by teasingly playing with me. "Tyron Miller taps the mic once and then again quieting the room. Wyatt, you're needed up here on stage." And the crowd goes insane. "Wyatt, Wyatt, Wyatt," chanting my name as I take to the stage hand and hand with Gabi.

"Wyatt. Wyatt. Wyatt." Bringing my hands down to quiet the crowd. "It was a sad but proud moment in American History when Civil Rights activist Rosa Parks refused to move to the back of the bus and paved the road for a better America for each and every one of us here tonight." Screaming above the cheers.

"She was a symbol of courage, strength and perseverance." La Blanc sign's speckled throughout the crowd. "Which empowered women to march in the streets protesting for the right to vote." I was wired-up. "Years later, it was Gloria Steinem's impact on generations to come as she headed the Women's Liberation movement of the "60's."

Raising my voice to be heard above the roar of the crowd.

"Let's take a moment to honor the brave men and women that came before us. This night is for them."

Fast forwarding, as Senator-elect I was sworn in by the Vice President to swear or affirm that I will "support and defend the Constitution of the United States against all enemies, foreign and domestic, that I will bear true faith and allegiance to the same."

"Congratulations, Wyatt," President Preston Gray extending his hand as I walk through the doors of the Oval Office as an invited guest. He gestures for me to take a seat across from him. Preston Gray is a seasoned politician, late fifties, stands approximately six-four. Known as a lady killer back in the day. Working on a string of marriages to his credit or lack of, but you wouldn't know it with an entourage of extra marital affairs hanging around his neck. It's like the devil took his soul. Silver specs of gray metallic twisted through his ebony hair accenting his charcoal eyes of deception inside and outside of 1600 Pennsylvania Avenue.

The Oval Office brings with it an aura of times gone by. Flashes of John Hancock proudly signing the Declaration of Independence echoed from the walls of the West Wing.

Widely credited Betsy Ross pictured making the first American Flag.

Imagining the feeling of pride, President Abraham Lincoln felt signing the Executive Order for the Emancipation Proclamation of 1863.

Picturing the signing of The New Deal during The Great Depression.

Paving the way to this great nation as history played out in my mind hijacking my attention from President Preston Gray sitting across from me. A feeling of empowerment, entitlement and inspiration washed over me as I listened to the inner voices of past presidents and activist, speaking to me.

I felt *Iris's* presence as a shot of adrenaline spiked through me. I knew at that moment the presidency was within my grasp.

You're freakin' brilliant, Wyatt, freakin' brilliant.

A secret I'll keep hidden till the right time unveils itself. This is political madness in its broadest form.

Preston walks out from behind his desk.

"Wyatt, let me walk you around the West Wing."

Waving me on to follow his lead as he continues to hijack the soul of the political playing field.

Seven

Love is in the Air

Wyatt

    On the four-hour plane ride back to California, I start mapping out a strategy for the presidency and sweep Gabi off her feet with a proposal of marriage. We've put the inevitable off long enough. We love each other. What are we waiting for? I send Gabi a text. 'Call and make a 9:00 reservation at *Harmony's*. 'I'm always up for a romantic evening.' Scrolls back across the screen.

'Wear something sexy. I love my women braless. And stuff the G-string in your evening bag. I'm already horny.'

'Any more requests, Mr. La Blanc, while I grab my vibrator?'

"No! I want you to save every ounce of you for only me.

No vibrators, no touching yourself. The build up to an explosive night of sex.'

'Jesus, Wyatt, you never play fair.

You've got me all-hot and bothered. Now what?'

'Hot and bothered. Wow! Stay that way and I'll meet you at nine. Our special table tucked in the corner. If you arrive before me, order our favorite bubbly.'

'Wyatt, the lines are lighting up, I have to go. Love you.'

    I walk into *Harmony's* a few minutes early and have the maître tuck my note between the white roses that adorn our table and order a bottle of champagne.

The spectacular views of Laguna Beach sprawled out in front of me was mesmerizing, stilling me in place while I wait.

The setting for a proposal couldn't be more beautiful. Afterwards a romantic stroll along the beach will be the frosting on the cake.

That is if she says yes.

My heart stops. Watching Gabi strut through the double glass doors of *Harmony's*. Jesus, Mary and Joseph. She was a vision. Emerald-green from head to toe tinting her blue eyes green that turned me on even before she touched me. I stand and wait for The Secret Service to escort her to the table as my insides turn to mush in her presence. "Gorgeous, hi," leaning into her. Forehead to forehead.

"You take my breath away, but you already know that." Sliding the back of my fingers down her cheek. I take her hand and pull her chair out. "Madam." I kiss her cheek and whisper near her ear.

"Naked may have been a bad decision on my part." Shooting her my cocky grin.

She gives me that torturous grin of hers. "Is my nakedness too much for you to handle big boy," as she tip-toes down the velvety skin of her cleavage with her index finger that ends at her navel and slowly but teasingly tip-toes back again.

"Wyatt, I love how you touch me with your eyes." Salivating at the wonders of her.

"And kiss you with my eyes," zooming in on her luscious lips.

"That, too." Nipping and licking across her bottom lip to the familiar melodies of the 20's.

"And seduce you with one touch. A highly visualization technique I've mastered." Scanning her plunging V.

"This will give me a chance to sharpen up on my fantasizing skills."

Gabi places my quivering fingers at the opening slit of her dress and nudges them up and over her pulsating smooth sheath. "You can't ask me to sit across from you, Wyatt, in the buff without touching me," as she nudges her legs apart ever so slightly, inhaling deeply. "Now can we, Mr. La Blanc?" Moaning as she dismantles my heart in the grand scheme of things.

"Senator," the waiter standing over us holding a bottle of champagne wrapped in a white linen cloth. Nonchalantly untangling ourselves.

"Please." Both smiling from embarrassment as an aubergine blush rises in our cheeks. Gabi intertwines her hand in mine holding the fluted crystal glass to by lips.

"To the love of my life," saluting to the first toast of the evening.

"And mine." Undressing her with my eyes. An occupational hazard of mine.

"Open your card." Pointing to the flowers.

"What's the occasion, Wyatt? A reward for sitting here naked as a jaybird so you can fondle me throughout our fine-dining experience? Foreplay before taking me?"

"Something like that." Sliding my hand from her knee to the inside of her thigh. Listening to her gasp. As one continuous rhythm of moans escape, "I'd say I hit a home run."

She plucks the note from the petals of the white roses overflowing with emotion as her fingertips caress her name.

A silence filled the air around us as I watch her eyes scan the written words I carefully orchestrated hours before.

Tears escaped from the corners of her eyes and crept slowly down her cheeks. Gabi, I have loved you from the moment you stumbled into the penthouse. Maybe even before. At that moment I knew, but it took a while for my brain to catch up.

I want to fall asleep each night entangled in your web and wake up with you wrapped around me each and every morning. Marry me.

Gabi was speechless. I reach inside my lapel pocket and flip open the purple velvet box.

She brings her hands to her mouth and gasps for a breath. I guess I can clearly say I swept her off her feet and pulled off the surprise of a lifetime giving her a moment to adjust to the magnificent diamond set in platinum. She continues to remain tongue-tied as I slide the ring on her finger. Gabi's electric-blue eyes ricocheted into the diamond's luster blinding her in place.

Finally a string of yeses escapes. She reaches under my zipper and teasingly fondles my rising shaft.

Parts my lips with her tongue continuing the assault of my genitals. "My reward for marrying you?"

"Well if you put it that way. That would unequivocally be a yes." Skimming my thumb up over her sex.

"Now can we have dinner? I'm famished."

"Yes! Only if you promise to walk the beach. Skinny-dip in the ocean. And make love to me under the billions of stars and the full moon."

"I think that can be arranged." Tightening my grip at her waist. I breathe softly against her hair leaving gentle kisses.

The ocean was beautiful this time of night with the waves splashing against our skin as we paddled further and further from the beach on a bright-yellow surfboard we snatched from the 'Beach Bum Shack' along the boardwalk. Free-spirited. Wind rustling through our hair. Catching an enormous wave bringing us within a few yards short of the shoreline.

The deserted beach held promise. I grab hold of Gabi's waist and walk hand and hand along the beach with the water swirling at our feet before settling under a beachfront palapa. We borrow an oversized towel and snuggle into each other. "Wyatt, this has to be by far the happiest day of my life."

"Gabi, lets elope."

"Really?"

"Really! Or a small ceremony next weekend here on the beach? What do you say?"

"Well, you're full of surprises tonight, Mr. La Blanc." Guiding me into the warmth of her private sanctuary reserved only for me.

"You could ask me anything, Wyatt, cocooned around you and the answer would be a big-fat-yes." Squirming underneath me.

"Beach? Elope? What's your poison?"

"Jesus, Wyatt," lifting her butt to meet my compelling climax.

She's a powerful aphrodisiac to be reckoned with.

"Let's fly to Greece for a few days. Get married. Make love on all the Grecian Islands till there's not an ounce of breath left between us."

Eight

Soulmates

Iris

I was blindsided by Wyatt's proposal to Gabi. Jealous, sad and crushed.

But for now she holds the bragging rights as Mrs. Wyatt La Blanc. I gave Wyatt the space he needed while they honeymooned in Greece. But the pain was unbearable knowing he unleashed his sexual desires on Gabi, ravishing her with his godliness and not me.

"Iris?" Wyatt startled by my presence.

"Wyatt," taking his hands in mine as I quietly speak.

"Someday in the distant future you will join my world. We are soul mates and we'll be reunited in our next life as husband and wife." The dam in both our eyes burst "Vivian, our daughter," will be the apple of your eye, wrapping you around her little finger." His eyes reflected the shock that radiated from his soul. I could hear his heart explode in his chest, as every emotion of his being surfaces. Wiping each other's tears from our cheeks. "Leonardo Junior, a spitting image of his dad, will pull at my heartstrings just like you." Kissing him ever so gently. "I can't wait for you to meet them."

Wyatt crushes me to him. *"Iris my beautiful Iris,* how do you know our future?" Our tears mingling against our cheeks.

"I just do.

We have loved each other in all our lifetimes." Wiping his sobbing tears away. "Wyatt don't cry. In our next life we will search and search for twenty-four years before we find each other."

"Jesus, *Iris,* those lavender eyes of yours always turn me into mush," as he brushes a strand of hair from my face and kisses the lids of my eyes.

I lean into his palm. "When we finally cross paths the missing piece of the puzzle will be complete, but until then."

Resting my forehead on his. "This is my promise."

"Feel my presence from a distance as I guide you back to me, Wyatt."

"Feel the tips of my fingers glaze yours as you stroll along the shoreline in the early morning hours and I plant delicate kisses on your lips ever-so-gingerly as the wind brushes across."

"Feel the splendor of my fingers dance along the keyboard as you play our favorite concerto."

"Search for my smile in the moonlit skies. Wave 'Hi' and blow me a kiss. I promise Wyatt to wave back with a 'Hi' and more kisses than you possibly could catch in a lifetime."

"Be the best that you can be while you travel the open roads of your journey called life." Inching myself several inches off the ground with our fingertips still touching. "Continue to fight for the underdog, Wyatt. Soon you will be the most loved, respected, powerful man on the face of the planet as the world opens at your feet." I levitate to the height of the balcony's railing and hover for a few seconds. A Monarch butterfly flutters its wings and lands in the palm of my hand, pauses and moves to my shoulder.

Nine

Iris's Presence

Wyatt

I take a shallow breath and breathe, *"Iris,* don't leave," I whisper. "Please!" I beg clinging on to the tips of her fingers. Her lavender eyes illuminated with silver tears against her porcelain skin that whispered a sadness piercing my heart.

But she ignores my plea. Her delicate wings feather out ever-so-slightly as my insides plummet.

Panic may be a better word for the feelings coursing through me at the moment.

I was sad knowing I may never see her again. Gabi's footsteps and voice drew closer as *Iris* and I were saying our tearful goodbye.

"See you around, Wyatt Earp." Smiles and sets off into the sunset. Metaphorically speaking. I stepped back and wiped my tears from my cheeks before wrapping Gabi into my side.

"Mr. Wyatt La Blanc."

"That would be me. Mrs. La Blanc."

I became good at living in denial, plunging the memories of *Iris* to the back of my mind.

Two years later the presidential race is well on its way. *Iris's* prediction is right on target. I clinched the nomination against a handful of constituents and now will face-off with my opponent incumbent President Preston Gray.

Where are you my beautiful *Iris*, I miss you. I miss us.

Wrong or right she managed to get under my skin, inside my mind and deep in my heart. Speaking quietly hoping *Iris* can hear. "Gabi and I had our first child. A girl. We named her Iris, but we call her Angel. I bet you already knew that? She stole my heart while still in the womb. I never knew how much you could love someone until I held her in my arms. I can't help feel like I still carry a piece of you with me every time she smiles, or our eyes engage. Are you sure your soul left?" Feeling the portal to our souls will always stay connected.

At that very moment a butterfly flutters its wings on baby Angel's tiny hand where she lay sound asleep. Answering my question. My head did a one-hundred-degree spin hoping to see *Iris*.

I whisper. "Give me a sign."

And she shoots back a subliminal whisper, 'I just did.' A whimsical touch brushes down my cheek.

"See you around, Wyatt Earp," whimpers across my lips. I could feel her breathe a breath of sadness. *Iris*, is a splash of mystery around the edges laced with an aura of danger. Just like I love my women. She's a breath of fresh-air still playing head games from the other-side.

Preston Gray is like a smorgasbord to the press like a mouse trap is to a mouse. At times snuggling up to the media is like sleeping with the enemy, forever challenging the truth-meter. Preston is notorious for using highly irregular tactics. Better known as dirty politics. Always painting a tainted picture with lies of deception. The press, TV news networks and late-night hosts make him accountable for his daily tweets and outrageous demagogue practices. If that's the way you want to play Preston Gray? Bring it on. Gloves off. Game on.

Unlike President Preston Gray, I try being the voice of reason as we campaign across the country.

Wyatt La Blanc's motto is, 'Transparency' all the way. Truths verses falsehoods.

Each and every day we wake up to Gray bringing it up another notch of craziness. Shaking my head as I take Gabi's hand and push through the doors of Miami's Convention Center just before I climb the steps to the podium. The screams from the deafening crowd was like music to my ears. Giving me a high without the drugs. Pure adrenaline. I look over at Gabi and wink.

She winks back, throws me a kiss and mouths the words, I love you, Earp.

Well that threw me off my game. Where the hell did that come from? I peruse the crowd for signs of *Iris*. Not funny!

Russians interference in the election is foremost on my mind as I tap the microphone to get everyone's attention to take a seat, sensing *Iris's* ghostly presence. "Thanks Miami, we love you."

"Our agenda is solid paving the way to the White House.

Are you with me?" I yell. "Are you with me?" Signs shot up into the air as my supporters sprung to their feet.

"We have a platform of issues I'm here to discuss." Raising my hands in the air to quiet the overlapping chatter. First and foremost. "Russia tampering with our democratic system of voting.

Spying on our citizens. Meddling in the e-mail hackings." Shouting over the noise.

"And if that wasn't enough, assault weapons are on the table. Increasing the age limit to 21 and steeper background checks."

Raising my voice several decibels trying to compete with the overlapping cheers.

"Let's not forget we are a nation of laws always protecting the 2nd. Amendment. The right to bear arms."

Everyone leaped to their feet in agreement. Chanting, "Fast Forward to Equality." My logo from the get-go. "Let me make myself perfectly clear. At the moment DC is the nation's most depressed area." Yelling over the crowd. "The White House is scrambling to pull its likeability numbers up, out of the dumpster, as the shakeup inside the walls at sixteen hundred continues." Darrell my campaign manager leans in. "La Blanc, your poll numbers are climbing as we speak." Slapping my back. "You aced it tonight."

"Thanks my friend we're right on schedule," shaking his hand. "Another feather in our cap."

I step back and tuck Gabi into my side. Kiss her hard then ease to her cheek and walk back and forth across the stage both waving into the crowd. "God, you're beautiful. The crowd loves you more than me. Maybe, I should choose you as my running mate?" Enjoying a private moment of intimacy and foreplay on stage leading-up to having her naked at my feet. Making love to my wife is number one on tonight's bucket-list. God, she smells and feels like a million bucks.

"Let's get out of here before I take you right here."

"So this is how you get-off night after night." Being her usual smart-ass.

The Secret Service clears a path through the crowd of screaming, energized men, women and children.

Stopping to shake hands, sign autographs and a handful of selfies.

The limo driver pulls up to the back entry of the hotel and we're whisked away.

Gabi climbs onto my lap, unzips my zipper, hikes her dress up and seduces me with only a tinted shield dividing us from view. And a motorcade of Secret Service on both sides.

"Mrs. Wyatt La Blanc, what do you think you're doing?"

"Seducing my husband. What does it look like I'm doing?" Capturing my tongue with hers.

"Foreplay before the finale?"

"I guess you could say that." She laughs. "You beguile me, Wyatt."

"That's what they all say." Kibitzing with her. And take her as mine in the backseat of the limo.

Ten

The Final Debate

Wyatt

CNN's Anderson Miles narrates the third and final debate:
Live from New York. President Preston Gray walks onto the stage from the left as I enter from the right meeting with a not-so-friendly handshake somewhere in the middle before taking our rightful places at the podium. "President Gray and Senator La Blanc, welcome." Anderson wearing somewhat of an intimidating face.

"You each have one minute for your opening statement."

Preston starts out of the gate by praising his accomplishments of his first term in office. Always patting himself on the back. When he walks back to the podium, a group of his constituents clap while the others in the audience moan in agony.

"Wyatt, you're next." Anderson shaking his head in astonishment of the lack of restraint Gray exemplifies.

"Thanks for having me, Anderson and let me start out by quoting FDR." Taking a step forward.

"The test of our progress is not whether we add more to the abundance of those who have much; it is whether we provide enough for those who have too little." Gripping the podium. "Values I'm proud to live my life by and campaign on."

Anderson asks, "Mr. President, will you share your feeling on The Women's March with the millions of viewers across the world."

He looks directly into the camera, "Women have all the rights men have. I personally don't see the problem." Muffled claps mixed with a long roar of anger.

"Same question, Senator."

"I have a different take, Anderson. Behind every movement young people are at the helm. Leading the world across the finish line." Shooting a high-five in the air. "We have been waiting for you."

Preston gets in my face. "These teenagers or whatever they call themselves are nothing but terrorists."

"Is everyone a terrorist that doesn't agree with you, Mr. President?"

Preston comes back with, "I resent your implications, Wyatt."

I turn to face him, shoot him the look and reply, "Well live with it and stop lying at every corner. You make more crap up. It's getting old." Pulling my freedom of speech card out of my ass.

"You're nothing short of a bully on the school playground." Wounding him like a scorpion's fiery sting. "Times up, gentlemen. You each have a one-minute closing statement." With that Preston collects his notes, steps down from the podium, turns and gives me the finger of affection, pausing, before walking off the stage. "That's why you're slipping in the polls, Preston. I don't see another four years for you. Deal with it and walk while you can save face." Shouting after him. "What you lack in couth, Preston, you make up for in stupidity." Rolling my eyes at the audacity of this person who calls himself a president.

"May, I take this opportunity to quote Martin Luther King Jr. during the Civil Rights Movement . . . I've been to the mountain top and If you can't fly then run, if you can't run then walk, if you can't walk then crawl, but whatever you do you have to keep moving forward. Powerful!"

After a grueling hour and a half of Preston's outrageous behavior, or should I say lack of, every major network capitalized on the president's temper tantrum. Thanks, Preston, you just handed me the third debate on a silver platter.

Eleven

The Latest Polls

Wyatt

"Senator Wyatt surges ahead in the polls after last night's Miami rally.

The largest crowd ever with over twenty-five-thousand plus attending and millions of TV viewers."

Gabi rolls over snuggling into the warmth of my morning erection. Takes the remote away and clicks off.

"Hey!" Well, if she isn't the feisty-one. "Is this any way for the future First Lady to be acting?" Taunting her before taking her.

My cell dings on the nightstand. Gabi reluctantly holds it up for me to see. "Toss it here beautiful."

Well that's a deal breaker if there ever was one.

"Oh will you stop with the notorious fake tears." I glide my hand up between the middle of her thighs, smile and say hello to Parker. "Don't move," I whisper near Gabi's ear as my hand travels north and lands at the junction of her bare essentials.

"Parker, I'm all yours." Now that's a little white lie staring down at Gabi laying there naked as a jaybird.

"I need to make my VP choice today, Parker. Have the list of my top picks on my desk in 45 minutes."

Women from California to New York, Hawaii and Alaska will be pleased to know all three are overqualified women that come with the highest credentials. More than likely bringing with her the Midas touch of a woman. Trisha knocks on the door.

"Can Angel and I come in? She wants to see her mommy and daddy."

Gabi and I scramble to pull the comforter up, prop our pillows behind our neck just in time for Angel to jump up on our bed and join us for our ritual of morning hugs and kisses. I plant a kiss on both of their foreheads and head for the shower. "See my girls downstairs for breakfast." And blow kisses their way.

Holy shit! Finally a message from *Iris*. 'Wyatt Earp,' was scrolled in the mirror for the first time in over two years. Now she's freakin' me out. "*Iris,* you have to stop sneaking up on me. You place my heart in jeopardy every day. Loving you, but in love with Gabi. I thought that's what you wanted for me?"

A very beautiful *Iris* was staring back at me in the mirror's image as her white florescent wings span the length of the room. She cups the palms of her hands together and when she opens them an exquisite Monarch butterfly flutters its wings as she sets it free. In a blink-of-an-eye she was gone. A bittersweet moment closing another chapter as a sadness wipes over me.

Gabi wraps her arms around from behind and reaches her hand inside the towel that was knotted at my waist. "Humm! What do we have here?" Lust pinged, adrenaline spiked. The biggest and I mean biggest mischievous smile crept across her lips when I turned. Her eyes crinkled at the corners and the sweetest, sexiest dimples dip in her cheeks. Gets me every time.

"Wyatt, my mysterious Wyatt, who are you talking too? A ghost?"

Shit, if she only knew. She'd lock me up and throw away the key. And my political aspirations would be flushed down the drain for a lifetime. Even *Iris* couldn't dig me out of this mess.

"You know me," as she continues massaging my genitals I coach her into the cascading spray of the overhead nozzle. "I have a habit of talking to myself. A vice I picked up somewhere along my thirty-six years on this earth." Enjoying the way she touches me.

"Just as soon as Trisha baths Angel and gets her dressed, she'll join us for breakfast before we lose ourselves in the politics of Daddy's day."

"Hush!" I nudge her thighs apart, cage her arms to the wall, slip her the tongue and listen to the sounds of her orgasmic pleasure pulsating through the air that we breathe. "Wyatt." I release Gabi's arm and guide it down to her pulsating sanctuary. "Wyatt."

"I love watching you touch yourself." Placing my hand over her sizzling fingers.

"You can do this baby." Securing one hand to the tile wall beside her. "And don't tell me you're not enjoying the thrill of it all."

"Jesus, Wyatt, touch me." Gabi cries out. The buzz from the vibrator startles her and she backs away ever so slightly as the coolness touches her skin.

A second later she's begging at my feet. The scent of coconut lingering in the air from her damp hair. Gabi snatches the vibrator from my hand and runs it up between my thighs as I gasp for a breath and spread her knees before pleasing her.

Twelve

Over the Finish Line

Wyatt

The race to the White House is on:
Breaking News . . ." The heart-throb of Cali, Wyatt La Blanc, choses a woman VP as his running mate. Not just any women, but a woman with a lethal combination of brains and beauty." And backs it up with a video of Stormi Lawrence the reigning Mayor of Kentucky being interviewed on this morning's 'Today Show.' "Can't help but wonder how Mrs. La Blanc is handling her husband's choice?" Shit! They just love to stir the pot of negativity.

"Pay no attention to the gossip, Gabi. It comes with the territory."

Gabi's usual upbeat personality went into hiding. "Hey, beautiful, want to share?" Raising her puppy dog eyes to mine. Knowing full well what's on her mind. But we need to talk and clear the air.

"Wyatt, I hate to play the jealous wife here, but I immediately questioned the obvious."

"Gabi, honey, I'm not sure what you're referring to but I'm sure you're going to enlighten me." Putting the TV on pause.

"Her attraction to you. That's what." Stormi's lit a fire under her ass. Shit! "And stop denying the unsubtle ways she undresses you with her eyes whenever you walk in the room. She's like a giddy school girl with a crush. It's embarrassing."

"Gabi?"

"Don't Gabi me. The ravishing VP working her way up to mistress." Storming out.

Several months down the road, Stormi and I had rallied across the country making several campaign stops a day covering all 50 states.

One more stop heading into tomorrow's vote. Destination Alabama on the eve of the election.

Stormi, her husband Gideon of twenty-years and yours truly with Gabi wrapped into my side climb the steps to the plane. We turn, wave to the crowd that's cheering us on at San Diego's International Airport just minutes before take-off in our private plane, fueled and ready.

Senator James Olson of Alabama hands me a megaphone seconds before Stormi and I lock our hands in the air and step up onto the podium.

"Alabama, we can't hear you." Yelling over the deafening sounds. "Louder." Fueling the fire. The thunder of voices echo through the crowd of over fifty-thousand cheering voters camping out overnight to cast their votes. Thousands more took to the streets watching from the large screen monitors outside.

We were stalked by a mob of reporters as the four of us duck into the limo that would be taking us back to the airport we had just flown into hours before.

This time Alabama to California. The polls open bright and early so we can cast our vote before flying into The Big Apple's John F. Kennedy International Airport to await the results.

Hours after Gabi and I cast our ballots, we were spirited into the city that never sleeps. Smell of fall still lingering in the air. Energized and ready to party.

The festivities will begin and end in Central Park. Win or lose.

We check-in to the 5 Star Ritz-Carlton New York, Central Park with the charm of a prime midtown Manhattan address with unrivaled skyline views. I couldn't wait to undress my wife and make love to her in the final hours before they close the polls here on the East Coast and hopefully seal it with a win.

Gabi and I strolled the streets of New York in awe of world-renowned Times Square and the skyscrapers touching the clouds. Not without the Secret Service, however, breathing down our necks, but it comes with the territory.

We occasionally stopped to connect with the endless crowds that lined the streets. Cameras waved in our direction hoping for a selfie. Gabi was a genius when it came to taking selfies so I just sat back and smiled. She was a breath of fresh air as the autograph seekers along the streets of New York yelled her name.

Next a romantic carriage ride around Central Park snuggled under a cozy blanket with the love of my life curled into me.

"You light my fire, Gabi, you always have." Placing soft kisses on her hair.

"Wyatt, I have loved you in so many ways; I've stopped counting."

"You're the air that I breathe every hour of every day." Bringing my lips to hers.

"And thanks for giving me the greatest gift of my life, our daughter Angel." Captivated by Gabi and the late autumn splendor.

We ended our afternoon with a leisurely lunch at The Tavern on the Green, the icon landmark nestled in a bucolic setting with nothing short of an amazing fine dining experience.

I reach across the table and intertwine my fingers in hers. "Thanks for supporting my dream. Our lives are about to change."

She challenges me in a lustful stare, "How about an interlude to sex for starters?" The words of a predator coming in for the kill.

"Just a small token of your appreciation." Gabi slides her foot up between my thighs as she savors the spear of asparagus at her lips. Twirling, licking, biting, "You on?" Upping the tempo of her glorious foot massage.

Is she f**king kidding me! Of course I'm on.

Turned on at the moment. "If you keep this up Mrs. La Blanc, Congress will start impeachment proceedings first thing in the morning."

Well no surprise here, coming back with one of her infamous smart-ass comments. "Well worth the risk, wouldn't you say?

Sometimes, many times, Gabi knows me better than I know myself.

"Let's get out of here so I can bury myself inside you for the afternoon." I reach for her hand. Smile, taunting her with my seductive words as we're escorted to our limo parked outside.

Shit! I'm not the only one turned on at the moment. Gabi, hikes her dress up, stuffs her G-string in my lapel pocket and straddles my hips. "Jesus, Gabi, what the hell, do you think you're doing?" My words fall on deaf ear as she releases my explosive length and quickly mounts my glorious package just for her.

"Sit back and enjoy, Mr. La Blanc," diving her tongue into the crevice of my mouth. Within seconds we came with a force of nature, spilling into one another.

"Gabi," swooshing the wild strands of hair off her face. "What's up with you and the limos lately?"

"I guess you could say I officially have a limo fetish." Scrambling to put herself back together from her crazy over-the-top assault of my genitals with the Secret Service riding shotgun. "I don't see a problem with that. Do you?"

"Well now that you ask, I can't say as I do."

"I love living life on the edge with you, Wyatt. Always looking around the corner for the next high. I hope these moments of excitement we share never end."

Somedays she's like a tropical storm. Teasing the beach with light breezes that suddenly push the waves higher and higher til there's only a raging Sea of unbridled fury. I love that about her. "We need to get ready for tonight's celebration. And put our overzealous sexual appetite on the back burner until after tonight's festivities."

"Oh, no you don't, Mrs. La Blanc. I have plans for you when we get back to our suite." She gives me the grin, the over-the-top grin and I know she's mine for a while longer.

I plan on taking her in every room, leaving just enough time left over for a shower.

Thirteen

Central Park

Wyatt

My announcement of wanting to celebrate my victory in Central Park came as a shock just weeks before the elections.

Heightened security of law enforcement and intelligence officials were quickly put into place.

The campaign staff is gathered around the big screen TV when Gabi and I strut into our suite at The Ritz-Carlton. The buzz in the room is deafening competing with MSNBC's, Rachael Maddow, broadcasting live from Washington, DC.

Maine, New Hampshire and Vermont will be the first polling centers to close at the top of the hour. In the meantime, the guys and gals were keeping the pizza delivery guys busy and happy as the tips padded their pockets.

The limo pulls up into Central Park alongside the stage where the first band of the evening was in full swing. The crowd goes wild as Bruce Springsteen bursts out with 'America' and thousands chimed in.

Anderson Miles from CNN announces, "The race to the White House is too close to call," from the limo's TV.

"An estimated quarter of a million people jammed Central Park and thousands more took to the streets and the surrounding areas waiting with baited breath."

CNN, Fox, MSNBC and tonight's concert was broadcasting live on the TV monitors placed here and there throughout the park.

A no-fly zone was imposed with only police helicopters overhead with Secret Service personnel and thousands of army police on the grounds. We were protected behind large bullet proof shields of plexiglass, some as tall as fifteen feet and twenty foot wide. Similar to the ones constructed for Obama's election festivities held in Chicago's Grant Park with backdrops of the American Flag spaced here and there.

President-elect Wyatt La Blanc's face flashed across every TV monitor in the park. The crowd was electrified.

With Angel's arms wrapped around my neck and Gabi tucked into my side we walked out onto the stage. "Daddy, look!"

A cluster of butterflies danced on her fingertips gracefully fluttering their wings, protecting her, loving her, loving me.

I turned to Gabi and shouted. "Bucket list complete." She leaned in, kissed Angel's cheek then without caring who sees brought her lips to mine. Sensual and seductive in front of the world. Stilling me in place for a moment before reaching for the mic. I yell. "Hello, New York." The crowd chanting, "hello, hello" back. "Hello, California." Screams echoing, "hello!" back. "Hello, Hawaii, hello Alaska and every state in between, hello."

People shouted from their rooftops and were suspended from balconies. Banners with red, white and blue bold stripes flapped in the wind that hung across hundreds of entrances surrounding the park. A humbling sight. "Martin Luther King Jr.'s 'I Have a Dream' is appropriate tonight." Gabi and I took hold of Angel's tiny hands and raised them in the air bouncing her on my shoulder. "Well, I had a dream, America had a dream." Choking the tearful, emotional words out. "Thank you. And God bless America, thank you."

I looked out over the thousands of people sitting in clusters sprawled out on blankets, others perched on tree limbs holding, 'Flash Forward to Equality' signs and waving American flags in the air. "Stormi and her husband Gideon joined Gabi, Angel and I on stage energizing the endless roar encircling Central Park.

Breathing in the jasmine scent of her hair, Gabi looked the part of the First Lady wrapped in a cobalt-blue mini dress bringing out shades of ultramarine in her eyes, accenting with matching Christian Louboutin's blue strappy heels.

Smashing! Cornering the market on sexy. We took our seats in anticipation of the concert of a lifetime.

The stage went pitch black as a hush of silence whispered in the air.

Blinding spotlights on either side of a winding staircase climbed in anticipation . . . focusing in on Cher. She stood there larger than life bedazzling the crowd with her iconic flare of fashion gracing us with her presence dressed in all white. She stepped out from the shadows and took the first step down, followed by Dianna Ross who put the S in sassy and Celine a close third walking through a maze of fireworks that shot in the air. Bruce Springsteen stormed the stage from the side accompanied by Keith Urban, Elton John and Neil Diamond singing Born in America. A musical shout-out to the USA.

"Wyatt. Wyatt. Wyatt." Bruce Springsteen shouts above the crowd climbs down off the stage and places a mic in my hand. "President-elect is joining us on stage." Lost in the thrill and excitement of the night, I was revved-up as I climb the steps. "Wyatt La Blanc on piano, Keith Urban on guitar." With Bruce strumming his guitar playing to a pumped-up crowd jamming with Neil Diamonds 'Coming to America.'

Fourteen

The Vetting Process

Wyatt

The months following the election:

Priority number one. Putting a cabinet in place before Inauguration Day.

Stormi and I spent hours overseeing the vetting process along with members of my loyal staff and constituents that will be following me from the California office to the West Wing.

At the end of the day Gabi, Angel and I get to spend the evenings together as a family here in the penthouse preparing mentally for the move to DC. Out of the blue Gabi says, "Wyatt, Stormi is one gorgeous woman." Where the hell did that come from?

"And your point is?"

"You'll be working side-by-side with her for the next four years possibly eight."

"And?"

"Look at her? She's a blue-eyed bombshell who has her claws in you already."

"I thought we were on the same page here, Gabi. We both wanted a woman on the ticket."

"I did, but not one so striking."

Laughing out loud.

"Yes, she is a blonde bombshell. Your words not mine. But I'm in love with this blonde bombshell. Deal with it."

"I ran on equality for woman. And I put my money where my mouth was."

"You've made women proud, that's for sure. But seeing the two of you on the front page of every rag and newspaper on a daily basis doesn't make for a secure wife. Just saying."

"Jesus, Gabi, I thought you liked her as much as I did. And yes there is no denying she's striking but she's also smart, an Oxford Rhodes scholar. Let's not forget she spent the last few years as the Mayor of Kentucky."

Sneaking up from behind branding her with my hand at her point of entry.

"And your point is?" Repeating myself. Knowing where this jealous tantrum is leading.

"Dangling the sex card in my face isn't going to work this time, handsome."

Want to bet, I'm confident it will. "Oh, will you stop." Sex card is that what she calls it? Jealousy becomes her. "She comes with an endless list of qualifications, Gabi, you know that. But at the end of the day she's not you." Or *Iris* as I continue to keep this highly guarded secret.

"Well, Wyatt, tell her that." Where the hell did this come from?

"You're joking, right?"

"She hangs all over you like a clinging vine and like all men you eat it up." Shooting me daggers of jealousy.

"Stormi wilts with your every word, like you're some kind a God."

"Well?" Teasing her. "My God-like qualities gets them every time." Cocooning both breasts in my hands.

"I'm serious, Wyatt."

"I know you are. That's what makes it so laughable."

"Someone forgot to tell her that you're my God. I'm this close to telling her to keep her hands to herself." Waving her hands in the air without letting up. "Notice how she takes the liberty of touching your hand, sliding her arm around your waist and rubbing her hand up your arm whenever it pleases her."

"Gabi, really?" Taking her in my arms. Reassuring her, kissing her, hiking her skirt to her waist, running short of a breath of air. I yank her G-sting to shreds embedding myself deep inside the warm folds of her blush. Riding her like a dog in heat. Keeping her jealousy under wraps for a while longer.

"Better?"

"I think so." Taunting me. "You just put a Band aid on my heart. Even though you always leave me utterly breathless."

Fifteen

Whispering Walls

Wyatt

Earlier today I felt the shadowy presence of Mom, Dad, my sister Maggie and brother, Derek standing beside me while I placed my hand on the Bible and took the oath of office as President of the United States of America. Our limo pulls up into the long circular driveway at 1600 Pennsylvania Avenue. What a rush. I turn to Gabi, bring her knuckles to my lips, then my cheek and pause for a few seconds to compose the nervousness coursing through me.

"First Lady Gabi, today I start the journey of the presidency with you and Angel wings by my side." Choking up. My special nickname for her. We sat in silence before the driver helps Gabi out first, then myself. Hand-in-hand we climb the steps leading to the White House where President Preston Gray and First Lady Cynthia are waiting our arrival.

Gabi and I took a tour around the West Wing before climbing the stairs to the residence. I lifted her into my arms and carried her over the threshold, kissing her hard and long.

"Hummm, Mr. President, you're so bold."

"You bet I am Mrs. La Blanc slash First Lady," squeezing her butt.

When we looked up we were greeted by the staff . . . each one grinning from ear-to-ear while welcoming us to our new home. Hopefully for the next eight years. "So busted," I whisper.

"Wyatt, I'm going to tuck Angel in for a nap. I'll be back before you have time to miss me."

The view of DC's landscaping from the residence was filled with an aura of history stretched out in front of me. I could almost hear the gusty wind whistling through the barren branches.

Warm hands blindfold me from behind as I breathe in a familiar scent of coconut and *Iris*. *"Iris?"*

When I do a 360, *Iris's* angel wings are on the floor. She was a vision of beauty as I watched her lavender dress cascade down to her feet leaving me breathless.

Her violet eyes shot through the lashes that framed her eyes silently begging me to kiss her, touch her, make love to her. My insides turned into several shades of wanting her as the softness of her lips quivered on mine as I hardened against her. "Humm, you taste and feel just like I remembered."

"And you," tapping her fingers down over my six-pack, slowly, but teasingly circling my navel just seconds before reaching in between the layer of fabric that housed my arousal.

"Jesus, Iris," I moaned as her lips parted letting me into the warmth of her folds.

Jolts of lightning bolted through me. I nudged her legs apart further and further until she took all of me into her fiery portal. Screaming my name.

"Wyatt. Wyatt." Gabi jarring me awake.

Dream?

Reality?

I'm not sure. What the hell just happened here?

"I'll be back in a jiffy, Gabi, I need to take a quick shower."

"Can I join you?" Wrapping her arms around me. And I walk away without answering. Leaving a wounded Gabi standing there.

I need a moment alone to clear my thoughts.

"*Iris,* there are times like this, I miss you," I whisper. Washing the sexual need for *Iris* down the drain. 'I miss you too,' was scrolled on the bathroom mirror. Her infamous prank. *Iris's* cheeks were sprinkled with tears as her nude reflection stares back in the full-length mirror. She stepped into her lavender dress, cocooned herself within the span of her wings, threw me a kiss and smiled, taking a huge chunk of my heart as I watch her blend into the clouds.

Iris leaves me with an emptiness knowing it's unlikely I'll ever see her again.

I have to question myself again.

Dream?

Reality?

I'll never know.

Three months into my first one-hundred days. Every thing's going according to schedule. My numbers are breaking records. Holding at seventy-one percent. Unheard of ever!

The people love me, they're crazy in love with Gabi and they've fallen deeply in love with little Angel who just turned two.

She's spunky, full of sass and knows exactly what she wants and how to get it. The whole package. If I didn't know better, I'd say she was *Iris's* daughter not Gabi's. All that was missing was a pair of angel wings and a mascot of butterflies.

Now for the christening of my mahogany desk enveloped in the Oval Office. "Gabi, put something sexy on. Are you ready for crazy and wild?"

"Always."

"Meet me downstairs in twenty."

Looking around to see if *Iris* is lurking somewhere in the shadows.

I stood cocooned in centuries of nostalgic moments like an echo chamber of the past, present and future. Infringing on the minds of world leaders as some stood the test of time . . . while others did not.

The tall stature of the Washington Monument's reflection gave a credence as I start plotting a bestselling novel capsulizing the next eight years.

68

Epilogue

Wyatt was startled from his thoughts as the late afternoon sun shimmered on the wall of his office as his daughter came running through the house yelling. "Dad, Dad. The butterflies are back." She ran like a child of five though she would be twenty in a few months.

Wyatt's heart gave a leap as his eyes clouded with tears. The last time they had seen butterflies had been at Gabi's funeral five years ago when the cancer had taken her.

Just before the casket was lowered into the ground, he had put his hand on the coffin to say his last goodbye. With a force to reckon with, the sun had broken through the rain-filled clouds as a melody of tiny wings rode the breeze. Hundreds of butterflies hovered over the grave. One landed on his hand like a gentle kiss of comfort and his heart jumped as a vision of *Iris* rose from the tiny fluttering wings. They looked at each other for a minute seeming to have a silent conversation. He smiled at his reflection.

Iris's luminous, wide open orbs were a deep shade of amethyst reflecting back a smiling Gabi cocooned in a pair of angel wings standing alongside a handsome young man. A spitting image of his mom, *Iris*. He remembered thinking his grief-filled mind was playing tricks because just as suddenly, she was gone.

Dedication

I'm beyond excited to have my grandson, Hunter James Luck highlighted along with his grandma on this anthology.

I am M.E.Giguere. A proud grandma.

NOT JUST POLITICS
Tanya Deloatch

Coming fresh off a landslide win in the election of the President, Federal Republic of Nigeria; the celebratory dinners, press conferences, and meetings were finally winding down.

Chimdi was eager to return to the plans he had initially made for his farming business. It was an exciting and rewarding time to be a Nigerian businessman and successful political campaigner to the office of the Presidency.

Closing this chapter, Chimdi was now refocusing his energies on visiting the United States and campaigning for his own professional goals.

He returned to his home compound, showered and began to follow up on emails. Cassava farming was beneficial, not only in Nigeria; but could be in the United States as well, especially if Chimdi could convince the Agricultural Commissioner of the State. Scrolling through the messages, his attention was directed to a response he was waiting on from the State of Georgia.

The letter reads:

Thank you for your interest in obtaining farmland within the State of Georgia. Unfortunately, we are not able to provide funding or any type of joint partnership at this time. We are not able to obtain approval from the State of Georgia taxpayers without confirming any type of return on the investments that would be needed. Please accept our best wishes going forward, as we extend you much success with Cassava Farming...

Blah blah blah, Chimdi mumbled to himself as he closes the message without reviewing it further, discouraged, but continuing to scan through more emails. He stumbles upon a new, unread message that appears to be hopeful. It is from the Commissioner of Agriculture for the State of Virginia. He double-clicked to see the entire scope of the message. The letter reads:

Dear Mr. Owhorji,
We are excited to learn more about this Cassava farming project. At this time, we would like to extend an invitation for you to visit and share more about the possibilities of expanding Cassava Farming here in the great State of Virginia...

Without reading any further, Chimdi pressed the button to print out the entire contents of the email. Elated about the new possibilities, he was now making plans in his head and ready to embark on his first trip to the United States by way of the state of Virginia. Gathering up his presentation notes, he started to research sites to review and create a travel itinerary within the next few days. Simultaneously, he sent a group text message to his confidant Uche along with business partner, Chuks, to advise them of the great news. No longer would they feel like hostages in their own home country. Cassava farming could become a phenomenon and global economic goldmine for them, if they could share their business plan, projections and expectations of the various uses of Cassava with the governing body for the state of Virginia. Consulting with Chuks about business by text was too limiting; Chimdi decided to place a call to him and celebrate their potential success by telephone.

Chuks was just as excited upon receiving the phone call. His sights were already set on the beautiful beaches, taking in the culture and cuisine of the United States and making purchases for goods that his family might enjoy. They joked and simultaneously said to each other, Uche will of course be ready to meet some of the gorgeous American women he had seen on television but had only dreamed about. During the call, the two men laughed and reveled at the idea of their upcoming adventures in America. Chimdi reminded Chuks that they must focus on the business at hand. Romance for Uche, if anyone, would have to wait. Plus, Chuks already had a wife at home to say his goodbyes to and get welcomed back home. Chuks also had three daughters at home and a baby boy on the way, so his visit to the United States would probably be a brief one. Uche and Chimdi would remain in the States as long as they needed to in order to convince the governing body that Cassava farming was the next best thing. Over the next few days, preparations were made to travel from their homeland of Nigeria to the land of new beginnings in the western world. The itinerary needed to be created and handled accordingly, so Chimdi had the luxury of communicating via email with the Commissioner of Agriculture's Assistant, Ms. Tia Terrell.

With so many travel connections and destinations, plans had to be set up smoothly, the emails soon turned into calls via Skype. The accents were challenging for both Chimdi and Tia initially, but he seemed to enjoy her southern drawl and she found his English-speaking dialect very intelligent, attractive and inviting. Even though she was very professional in her conversations, Ms. Terrell was actually looking forward to meeting this Mr. Chimdi Owhorji from Nigeria; upon his arrival in the States.

Excitement poured from Chimdi, Uche and Chuks as they packed, gathered their business plans and assembled in Abuja, Nigeria to board the first of many flights. With proud families seeing them off, the three homegrown well-educated Political Science majors who done good were well on their way to show the world the benefits of Cassava Farming. Not only would Chimdi and Chuks utilize the skills that they have learned with Cassava farming in the political arena, but Uche would chime in with their life experiences and lessons as well. They made a perfect team, just as they had in the strategic, winning political campaign.

The first leg of their trip would be several hours. As soon as Chuks boarded the plane, he packed away his carry-on bag and settled into his window seat. He proceeded to lounge back and make himself comfortable. Chimdi and Uche, on the other hand, were far too excited to sleep. Neither had they ever traveled to the United States, so the adrenaline was high and they were eager to get there and make a difference.

No sooner than the flight attendant finished her speech about safety and in-flight expectations, Chuks was already well on his way to slumber. Chimdi had convinced Chuks to change seats so that he could appreciate the serene views of the clear blue skies and the miles of soft, billowing clouds across the skyline as their journey began. Meanwhile, Uche was enjoying his luxury aisle seat, complete with flight attendants passing by every few minutes assisting other passengers. Despite Chuks's continuous snoring, Chimdi loved watching the beautiful and peaceful skies turn from day to night. He peered down to see the landscape of the countryside below and relished in the picturesque views of the tiny cars moving and a group of bright lights in the apparent cities below. Yawning, and peering over at Chuks, who was still blowing the roof off the plane with his snoring, Chimdi finally joined in and dozed off for the remainder of the flight. Uche soon followed in slumber after watching the closing credits of the in-flight action movie.

    Hours later, their first flight ended upon descent into the United Kingdom. Chimdi peered out the small window to see light raindrops falling, green short cut grass and the withering concrete of the airport runway. The pilot proceeded to speak into the intercom, letting all of the passengers know the time and temperature, as well as thanking them for flying the friendly skies with them. After arrival and retrieving their things from the baggage claim, Chimdi and Chuks checked in with their families to let them know that the first leg of the trip had been successful. As Chimdi ended the call with his family, his thoughts went to the current time in the United States. He wanted to reach out to Ms. Terrell to advise their current status, and also let her know that they were excited to meet with the governing body in Virginia within the next few days. The broad smile that came across his lips gave him away, and Chuks immediately knew who he was speaking with.
    Since there was a six-and-a-half-hour layover, Chimdi and Chuks decided to enjoy fish and steak dinners along with beer in the airport restaurant and discuss their upcoming meetings in the States. Before leaving, they watched a few sports events in the airport before walking to their designated gate for departure. The next few flights would prove to be similar to the first one and the excitement of travel wore off quickly for Uche, Chimdi, and Chuks. They would be glad when they ultimately reached their final destination on U.S. soil.

Eventually, they arrived in Richmond, Virginia to their awaiting host team led by Ms. Tia Terrell. The group was holding signs welcoming them to the great state of Virginia. Upon first sight of their small entourage, Ms. Terrell easily knew which of the three gentlemen was Mr. Chimdi Owhorji. He had a natural glide when he walked. His head was held high, shoulders leaned back and a broad look of confidence, intelligence and style. His bright smile was infectious.

Everyone greeted each other cordially with handshakes and hugs, then proceeded to exit the airport to the awaiting vehicles. Tia and Chimdi seemed to hold each other's gaze, hugs and hand holding longer than anyone else in the group. No one said anything, but the apparent attraction between the two was unmistakable. Chuks, Uche and Chimdi soon arrived to their upscale accommodations for the next several weeks and said their goodbyes to their hosts until morning. Everyone needed a good night's rest because the next day would be filled with introductions, meetings and presentations to the governing body of Virginia.

In true customary fashion, the welcoming entourage led by Tia Terrell met the Nigerian gentlemen as soon as they arrived to the government offices for the first meet and greet session. The leaders of Virginia were immediately impressed with the pleasantries and cultural traditions such as wardrobe the men wore for business functions. Their attire was rich in colors and matching headwear, draped in fine handsewn materials. *The Associated Press* and other media were elated to take photographs of the three Nigerian men who were not only successful politicians, but businessmen as well.

After such introductions, the Commissioner of Agriculture, took his seat alongside Uche and Chuks. Chimdi took to the podium and began to share his background with the leaders of Virginia. Ms. Terrell watched on in pure admiration as Mr. Owhorji was now passionately expressing his efforts to bring Cassava farming to the United States and boost economic growth around the globe. His delivery was masterful and his approach undeniably powerful. This intelligent, thinly framed man was quickly becoming a gentle giant in his appearance before the

Agricultural committee. Ms. Terrell paused her gaze from his speech, as a staff member interrupted her for an important phone call.

Even though she missed the ending of his words, Mr. Owhorji had certainly made an impression on her...and by the thunderous claps in the meeting room, other constituents agreed. He had not only arrived but was fast becoming a worthy and charming role model of what the Nigerian culture is truly about. He was no stranger to hard work and his educational level was superb. This man was the complete package; a businessman, respected by all persons and a potential political tycoon in the making. At least according to Ms. Terrell, but she would keep her thoughts private, at least while in the workplace.

As she returned from her office, she glanced over at the podium. Mr. Owhorji was now engaging his audience in a Q&A session. Briefly, he locked eyes with her and gave Ms. Terrell a teasing wink and smile. She blushed and turned away quickly. He had the entire room smitten with his ideas of growth, prosperity, and development. He also had Ms. Terrell smitten with other possibilities. The first day of business proved to be a successful one— all of the days that followed were as well.

Ms. Terrell and her team made sure to make Chimdi, Chuks and Uche more than comfortable during their stay in Virginia. They introduced them to as much of the culture in Virginia as they could whenever there wasn't meetings or sessions to discuss business and daily operations of Cassava Framing. Though Chuks and Uche seemed to be less interested in spending time at movies, plays, museums and such, Chimdi enjoyed every moment he spent in the presence of Ms. Tia Terrell and made it no secret. Chuks and Uche teased and reminded him that they are supposed to be focusing on business. Chimdi chuckled and said that he was mesmerized by Tia, she had captivated him from their very first meeting. It was just something about her, something beautifully necessary to his life. Chuks and Uche looked at each other, laughed and realized that it was Chimdi who had fallen for an American in just a matter of weeks.

The remaining business meetings went well and an alliance and new partnership was formed. The following fiscal year would bring the Nigerian businessmen back to Virginia in order to break ground and begin their successful venture and expansion of Cassava Farming in the United States. While this was great news for everyone involved, it was heartbreaking for Tia and Chimdi to realize that he would no longer be in the country. He vowed he would keep in contact with her from Nigeria, until his return. Tia hung onto every word as she looked up into his beautifully deep, chestnut brown eyes for the last time. His final boarding call for the departing flight was called, Chimdi embraced Tia with all the love he could muster and said farewell.

A few evenings later, Tia was leaning over to turn off the light and enjoy the plush comforts of her bed. Her cell phone began to light up and vibrate. Wanting to be with him, wasn't out of lust or need, but the desire to share the same space and breathe the same air. Becoming discouraged was not an option, but feeling the increasing distance caused her heart to crack into little pieces. Tia answered the call on the third ring. On the other end of the receiver, his melodic tones sang to her ears...*I'm about to go to sleep, but I'm missing you. Missing your voice, your laughter and missing the way you say my name. I'm missing your arms around me, missing my legs around yours. I'm. Just. Missing. You. I hope you are missing me too.*

His words always created an immediate smile to form on her lips, and the way he spoke so eloquently to Ms. Terrell continually made her blush. Rubbing her eyes and remembering their goodbyes at the airport. Her sleepy thoughts deferred back to his smiling eyes and beautiful words. Reminded of their call, Tia generously replied, "Of course, I'm missing you too Mr. Owhorji. Loving you is the one constant thing that keeps me together while we're apart."

That would be the first of many phone calls, video chats and conversations between Tia and Chimdi as a couple in love.

Despite the challenge of the distance between them, they were in constant contact on a daily basis. They introduced members of their family to each other and sent silly pictures, romantic words and small gifts to each other over time. The holidays and seasons went by swiftly and soon Chimdi, Uche and Chuks were returning back to Virginia with a Nigerian team of Cassava farmers to set up and break ground on several parcels of land throughout the state.

Excited about their new joint venture, Chimdi invites Tia to one of their newly designed cassava farms. Upon her arrival, they cut the ribbon collectively to commemorate the grand opening of another fruitful opportunity for the local and international farmers and their families. Chimdi then hands Tia a celebratory shovel to dig in alongside him on the row designated for the members of the founding partnership.

As she finishes applauding with the bystanders, Chimdi encourages her to use her shovel and lift the soil representing their new joint business venture. A little uneasy with her four-inch heels, Ms. Terrell presses firmly on the handle of the shovel and raises the dirt beneath her. As she begin to retrieve her shovel from the freshly raised land, she turns to her left to find Chimdi down on one knee with a flickering, sparkling rock of a ring in his hand.

With smiles from all around, the crowd that has gathered, pauses and takes in this new and interesting development. Eagerly watching and anticipating Ms. Terrell's response to the apparent and inevitable question of marriage. True to his ability to sell over an audience, Chimdi began to deliver these words directly to Ms. Terrell:

"You're my beautiful reflection,
A rare gem, the true diamond in my collection,
You will always have my protection,
My guidance and direction,
My love and affection.
Every now and then,
I see a glimpse of myself in you
It's a hint of a sparkle,
But it's the one thing I know that's true.

You're my beautiful reflection,
Encompassing a piece of my heart,
Shining through every experience,
You live life,
And loving you is living.
Will you allow me the honor of being the happiest man alive
By becoming my wife?"

   Without hesitation, Ms. Terrell stretched out her hand and graciously accepted the ring upon her finger. All while saying a resounding "Yes I will" through happy tears that didn't appear to ruin her makeup. The press, media and small crowd gathered rang into roaring applause and cheers. There was cameras flashing, and cell phone videos that captured glimpses of the entire event. Tia and Chimdi could see and hear nothing but each other, as they gave the media and press an eyeful when they solidified their engagement with a passionately romantic kiss.

   It was no longer just about business, the engagement between the American and Nigerian became national news. Time passed quickly, and there were several ceremonies to celebrate their marriage. First, the couple traveled to Nigeria and had a traditional marriage ceremony in Chimdi's hometown. This cultural experience was not only humbling, but exciting for Tia and her family. They had never been to Africa, let alone be welcomed in so graciously by their new Nigerian family. Tia and her family members were each adorned in the traditional native attire for weddings. The love no longer existed solely between Chimdi and Tia, their families were immediately enriched by their combined experiences. This was no ordinary love or marriage, it was the coming together of two families of differing cultures and beliefs, built on the love of two of their own.

After spending two weeks in Africa, Chimdi, Tia and their American relatives returned to the United States. There was yet another plush ceremony to celebrate marriage between the two. This time the festivities took place on the beautiful big island in Hawaii. While there was some press invited to share in their nuptials, Chimdi and Tia kept the affair intimate and the guest list small. They honeymooned for another week before returning to Virginia, and back to normal daily operations for the Cassava Farming business and conducting government sessions.

Arriving home early in the evening, Tia shook off the stresses of the day. It had been a long week and Friday could not have come fast enough. Placing her keys on the counter, Tia made sure the side entranceway to the garage was locked and made her way inside their cozy rancher. The corner lot had always felt inviting and she was glad to have so much room, but still, have neighbors close by.

Tia turned on the surround sound, the smooth tunes of Teddy Pendergrass filling the air and washed her hands before preparing dinner for Chimdi and herself. Being newly married, Tia and Chimdi liked doing nice things for each other. Tia was usually sweet and practical, picking up his dry cleaning or scheduling appointments; but tonight, she was taking a page from Chimdi's book by being extra sexy and romantic.

After carefully placing the pot roast, potatoes, carrots, green peppers and onions in a baking dish; Tia preheated the oven and set the cooking timer. Next, she decided to make a fruit, chocolate and cheese tray as an appetizer to snack on before dinner. She giggled to herself, thinking of all the naughty things she and Chimdi would do with the fruits. Tia placed the tray in the fridge to chill and decided to hop in the shower before Chimdi returned from his workday.

It was still early evening when Chimdi pulled into the driveway. He couldn't wait to kick his feet up and wind down with an ice-cold Miller Lite beer in front of the television. This was definitely one of the American beverages he had come to enjoy and appreciate. Opening the front door, the delectable aroma of dinner led him towards the kitchen to see what was cooking.

Meanwhile, Tia had just finished a hot shower that seemed to soothe every muscle in her body. Refreshed and relaxed, she reached for her plush terrycloth bathrobe and slid her toes into her matching slippers. Walking down the hallway, Tia hears the oven door close. She turns the corner towards the kitchen and finds Chimdi plucking a few seedless grapes off of the fruit tray in the fridge and a beer sitting on the adjacent island.

"Hey honey" Tia spoke up, startling Chimdi out of his grazing. He turned around to find her teasing him with bare shoulders, her supple breasts playing peek-a-boo and freshly shaven chocolate legs peering out from the bottom of her bathrobe.

"Whoa! Hey baby, I was just grabbing a little snack before dinner; but I see you have something else in mind." Chimdi smiled and greeted her with a kiss, then embraced her in a hug, inhaling in her warm vanilla body lotion. He wanted to take her right there in the kitchen. She looked invitingly delicious.

Tia flashed her girlish smile and suggested that Chimdi shower and meet her in the living room...and hurry up, she said. No need to say it a second time, Chimdi was on his way down the hall, peeling off his clothes along the way.

Tickled by his reaction, Tia checked on their dinner in the oven and turned on the warmer. Retrieving the appetizer tray from the fridge, along with the beer for Chimdi, Tia opted for a lemonade for herself. She picked up the universal remote, turned off the music playing and turned on the television. Not that she was interested in watching anything in particular, Tia casually flipped the channels and decided on a repeat episode of the popular show *Power*.

This was one of her favorite shows since she didn't watch too much TV. "Oh yeaahhhh," she said as she sat up on the couch when she realized this was the episode where the characters

Tommy and Keisha were finally going to get it in. Not that she needed any help getting in the mood, but watching the way Keisha rode Tommy, like he was a prize-winning stallion in the Kentucky Derby was right on time. He licked and kissed her caramel nipples as if he had hungered for them ever since he had known her. Keisha didn't know he got down like that, but she wasn't complaining one bit. She was loving it and enjoying every inch he was giving her.

Chimdi returned to the living room, finding Tia so engrossed in the on-screen lovemaking that he stood there for a moment before interrupting. He cleared his throat, and Tia jumped out of her gaze. She grabbed the remote and turned off the television.

"Baby you can watch your show if you want." Chimdi laughed and remarked to Tia.

"Not a chance." Tia said as she stood up to take off her bathrobe.

Chimdi helped her with that and placed the robe on the loveseat. She continued standing and he admired her body in the dimly lit room. She waited, allowing him to get comfortable on the couch first.

He wore a pair of shorts and his manhood pressed gently on Tia's leg as she straddled him and wrapped her silky-smooth chocolate legs around his. As she gazes into his eyes, he sees his image reflecting in hers. They start to communicate without words, lips eagerly meeting and inviting tongues to taste and seek each other. Their breaths become heavy and Tia begins to explore every ripple of Chimdi's massive chest with her fingertips.

Chimdi continues to respond affectionately by savoring Tia's neck, shoulders, and breasts. He tenderizes her nipples with his mouth, apparently, he caught a little bit of the television episode too. Tia pauses, enjoying the attention. Her nipples harden and she feels the wetness building between her thighs. She slides down and carefully pulls Chimdi's manhood out of the opening of his shorts. She begins to massage him with her tongue and proceeds to tease and tantalize him before completely deep throating and devouring him. Chimdi moaned loudly with satisfaction, his eyes were closed. Tia continued to lick and suck Chimdi's manhood until he could take no more. She was pumping her hand and sucking him off until he came. Gushing in the back of her throat, she swallowed every drop and smiled up at Chimdi.

He was already eagerly awaiting his turn to treat her. Tia leaned back into the opposite end of the couch and spread her legs open widely. Chimdi dove in towards Tia with intention. She chuckled at his look of determination, but that chuckle quickly subsided when he started to hungrily lap and lick her awaiting happy box. Tia moaned with delight, rubbing his bald head with her hands and enjoying the masterful skill of his tongue.

"Damn! Who's got time for bed when we can get it in right here?" Chimdi asked as Tia pulled him back in to her grasp.

They smiled at each other with their eyes, while acquainting themselves with each other's bodies as if they were making love for the very first time. Exploring and loving every touch between them, every kiss and every sound. No differences in culture, politics, countries or anything else could separate the love that existed between the two. There was no time for questions, business or politics; there was so much more to life. After all, the obvious meeting between Tia and Chimdi was *not just politics*.

THE END

Acknowledgements

Thankful to God, not only for the gift of writing, but the privilege of every opportunity He has provided in and for my life. I am especially grateful to my supportive parents, family and friends for the continuous encouragement to follow my dreams and fulfill my passion.

To my ABC girls, as always- you are my reason; everything I do is for you. Much love and respect to the man in my life who is truly the reason behind my smile, my biggest supporter and undisputed leader of my fan club.

Special thanks to all of my extended family and friends for purchasing every one of my published books: *Conversations from Her Heart", In Her Feelings", "Mixed Emotions", Whispered Thoughts, Reasons Seasons and Holidays*; and the excitement you share with me on this compilation of poetry inspired by my first main character, Lexi Taylor, in my first novel *"Love Takes Time – Lexi's Heart"*. Your continued support means everything to me and I value each of you.

If you are reading this book, thank you for purchasing it and I hope you enjoy it!

THE LOBBYISTS DILEMMA

S. L. Heinz

Ariana found the waiting room in Senator Falber's office to be sparse, but elegantly furnished.

The receptionist was a no-nonsense woman who looked like she had been in her post for some time. She was cool, efficient and professional looking. Not a showpiece, to be sure. She had assured the group of four the wait would not be long, since their appointment had been announced to the Senator, who was on the phone at the moment. Various politically oriented magazines and the daily newspapers were laid out in an orderly fashion on the end tables. Ariana found the chairs to be less than comfy and hoped the promise of a short wait would be kept.

She was dressed in a tailored, periwinkle blue suit with matching shoes and carrying a soft beige briefcase. The white silk blouse had a small ruffled collar peeking from the top and front of the jacket. She thought the outfit was subdued enough, but flattering to her auburn waves, green eyes and peachy coloring. Her make-up was carefully applied to be an enhancement but not flamboyant. In all, she was a knockout no amount of toning down could disguise, even though she was not totally aware of that fact. The other three lobbyists, all men, were certainly more than cognizant. Her beautiful coloring, lush but slender body and sense of style were undeniable, as were her intelligence and credentials. They had hired her to assist them in presenting information to the Senator with the hope he might be persuaded to vote "Yes" on the upcoming bill meant to increase funding for schools and ensure a living wage for teachers. It was now under debate in the House and they expected it would be brought up for a vote soon. When it arrived in the Senate, they hoped it would pass and so did Ariana. She was a long-term educator, having worked in many levels of the system on her way to her current position as a Professor in a branch of the State University.

The receptionist looked up as the door to the inner office opened and the Senator emerged, his hand outstretched toward the lead representative from the teachers' union, who had jumped up at the sight of him. Introductions were made and the four led into the inner sanctum. No one in the group could misread the lightening of the Senator's otherwise resigned expression when he got a look at Ariana or miss the rather lengthy handclasp he bestowed on her as they entered the room. Nor were they surprised when he seated her closest to him in the conversation grouping on one side of the room, away from the desk.

"Now I have been told you are here on behalf of the teacher's union, is that right?" said Senator Falber.

John Stane, the lead lobbyist responded, "Yes, Senator. We have come to give you some important information about the state of funding and educator compensation in your state."

Senator Falber, a bit distracted by Ariana's fragrance, answered "OK. Let's hear it." John opened his briefcase and pulled out a bound treatise, handing it to the Senator, who absently placed it on the floor next to his chair.

John said, "We had that prepared for you by Ms. Lewis, who has spent her professional life in the field of education and has done a study of the situation which now stands in your state. She is prepared to explain it to you personally and respond to any of your questions."

Hearing that, Senator Falber leaned down and retrieved the booklet, turning to Ariana, he asked "Boil this down for me please, Ms. Lewis?"

Ariana had not been unaware of the Senator's initial reaction to her and thought to herself *'How can I take advantage of his interest without compromising my personal or professional goals, here?'* She began by saying "Please, call me Ariana, sir." He responded with a slight turn of his body toward her. The vibes were unmistakable and Ariana found herself mysteriously drawn to do the same. This was not a totally new experience for her, having worked around men before who saw her not as a professional colleague, but as a sex symbol and someone to be disregarded for her knowledge. Senator Falber was walking that line pretty well so far---he had asked her for the information personally instead of eliciting more input from the men in the group.

Ariana gave him a brief version of her own Curriculum Vitae, which was impressive to be sure. She was not showing off but attempting to bolster the credibility of what she was about to tell him. She launched into her presentation, having retrieved her own copy of the written report from her briefcase, concluding with, "__To make a long story short, Senator Farber,"

He interrupted and said, "Ariana, please call me Mark..."

Suppressing a smile, Ariana said, "Of course, Mark. Now, according to the U.S. Labor Department study done recently, the median annual salary of all those in the teaching professions is $57,949. That is $3,000 less than other workers with bachelor's degrees; 56 % of teachers have master's degrees and that figure is $15,000 lower than other workers with the same degree, making a median salary of $72,852. You are probably aware also that most teachers are compelled to buy many of their own supplies and most of the textbooks they are furnished are hopelessly outdated! These teachers are expected to prepare our young people for future jobs, educate them in living skills, the English language, the history of our country and social studies, including how to be good citizens, vote responsibly and on and on. During their breaks, they are supervising the playground, leading physical exercises and after school, the safe dismissal process. They spend their evenings communicating with parents, grading papers and making lesson plans. Increasingly, their workplaces are becoming unsafe, both for their students and for them. They are expected to put themselves on the line for the safety of their charges too."

At this point, Ariana took a breath and Senator Falber took her hand, saying "My goodness, Ariana, you are passionate about this cause, aren't you?" The look in her eyes was so arresting to him, he couldn't look away. Continuing to hold her hand, he said, "I wonder if you would be so kind as to return tomorrow at the end of my office hours when I have had a chance to read this report in its entirety, so I might ask my questions of you?" Turning to the rest of the group, he asked, "Have any of you anything you want to add right now?" They all quite wisely demurred and were told they had no need to return the next day. The Senator assured them he was confident Ariana had the situation well in hand and he would give their petition his closest attention.

Reluctantly, after raising her to her feet still holding her hand, he released her and strode over to his desk. Picking up the phone and speaking to his receptionist about arranging her appointment for the next day, he looked into Ariana's eyes and winked.

Blushing, she followed the entourage out of the room and the office, accepting a small appointment card from the receptionist as she went by. She was a bit surprised by her reaction to the handsome senator but trying to remain unruffled.

"My, my, Ariana," said Tim Jones, one of the associates from the lobbying firm, "That was amazing! You had him at Hello, for sure. He probably didn't digest a word of your excellent presentation, but he sure was spellbound. I'll bet he reads it tonight while fantasizing about seeing you again tomorrow." All three of the men chortled at that, but Ariana was stone faced and said nothing until they reached the lobby.

Then she turned to them and stated "I'm not sure it is wise for me to see him again, or to continue to represent the teachers with you."

"WHAT??" Three voices in unison.

Ariana, sotto voce, said, "Not here, let's take a little walk." As they put a bit of distance between themselves and the Capital, Ariana outlined her concerns, which were resoundingly overridden by the three professional lobbyists. They told her this was exactly the kind of response to be taken advantage of and that it was up to her to decide how to set the boundaries as the situation developed. The goal, they said, was to find a way to ensure a positive outcome to the measure in question and she surely had Senator Falber's attention. They begged her to keep the appointment, appealing to her dedication to the cause. She told them she would have to think it over and they parted.

Meanwhile, Mark Falber paced in his office, fighting to quell his arousal. Ariana had awakened something in him that was not comfortable for him to face. He was considering seduction and betrayal of his marriage. Yet again! He had thought himself to have conquered such impulses after the last whirlwind seduction and close brush with disclosure. When he heard stories from and about other powerful men in government dallying with their interns or with women they met as they moved in Washington social circles, he had nothing but contempt for his own vulnerability and the risks to his famiiy and career because of it. Ariana's beauty, intelligence and passion for her cause had touched something in him he could not deny. He admired her so much and knew he would fantasize about making love to her. The question he asked himself was this: *'Is it dangerous for me to meet with her alone?'*

His thoughts went around and around about this.

He knew he could make an excuse and have the receptionist tell her he had no questions; he knew her treatise would be thorough and self-explanatory, making the case with well thought out arguments backed with facts.

He wanted to see her again, with every fiber of his being, but he knew it was for the wrong reasons. He also questioned whether he could consider the upcoming vote without thinking of those green eyes flashing as she made her quite convincing case. It wasn't the accepted position of his party, but he had children and personally leaned toward a "yes" vote. He could just tell her that and be done with it, avoiding the temptation to risk his own honor and hers. He was just too weak to do it.

Ariana too, wrestled with her conscience all night, going back and forth between her need to remember the cause for which she was working so passionately and the fact that, while she responded to Mark's interest, she knew he was a married man with a family and therefore, off limits for her. Could she maintain her integrity and simply plead her case with the facts, letting him decide how to vote, or would she succumb to the temptation to cross the line into using his attraction for her to influence his decision. Where might that lead her? To be honest with herself, she was attracted to him. He was a handsome, intelligent, powerful man who appeared to respect her intelligence. How much of that was an act with ulterior motives? He was no dummy, she knew and he would instinctively know respect is what Ariana wanted. Should she remove herself from the temptation even to try and turn it over to the men in the lobbying firm?

At last, she decided to attend the meeting, convincing herself she could keep it on a professional level, avoiding that delicious hand holding which had unnerved her more than she wanted to admit to herself. She had begun to imagine how it would feel to be in his arms, to kiss and be kissed 'S*TOP, Ariana*!' she told herself.

She dressed carefully and with an eye to looking as professional as possible in a navy-blue tailored shirt dress with long sleeves, pearl necklace and stud earrings, with navy high heeled pumps. She was still a knockout and she knew it. Carrying her beige briefcase, she approached the door to his waiting room. Suddenly, out of a door to the hallway, Mark appeared, taking her by the arm and steering her inside to his office before she could react. It was a surprise to Ariana to find herself looking into his eyes, with his hands on her upper arms, turning her to face him. Neither of them said anything for a heartbeat and suddenly his arms were around her, pulling her close and he breathlessly said "Ariana, I have been thinking of you all night---please may I kiss you?"

Ariana was shocked, not only at his actions, but at her reaction! She found she really wanted him to kiss her! She wanted to melt into his arms and feel the length of him against her core. Instead, she jumped back, crying out "Mark, please!"

He whirled and sank down on the sofa, head in hands. "Oh, God, Ariana, I don't know what came over me. When I saw you there, I just lost it..."

She paced to the other end of the office, looking out the window and said to him, "Mark, I agonized all night about whether I should come here today. Yesterday, I sensed the attraction you had for me and couldn't deny it evoked something in me I was uncomfortable with. I don't want that to influence what I came here to do, but I'm not sure..." She paused, turned to look at him and saw naked pain in his eyes.

"Ariana, I would do anything to rewind that moment and greet you with the respect you deserve. I'm not the kind of man who leaps out at women and grabs them, I promise. I'm so ashamed of myself. Can you please accept my apology?"

There was a silence growing long before Ariana said, "Mark, that means a lot to me and you sound sincere. I will accept your apology if we can be honest with each other and agree to no physical contact, for both our sakes." He nodded his agreement and Ariana sat down across from hm. She told him of how much dedication she had to helping teachers receive appropriate compensation and improve their working conditions. She told him she hoped they could return to discussing those issues and leave any personal feelings out of it. She told him she knew this sudden infatuation would subside, but the responsibilities each of them had, personally and professionally, would continue and the way they each handled those responsibilities would define them. Then she waited.

As Ariana watched, Senator Falber returned and Mark receded. He picked up her typed report and, with extreme professionalism, began to ask her detailed questions about some of the facts and assertions therein. She responded professionally and with confidence. Each of them had thoughts during this conversation that were as far away from what they were discussing as could be. As a matter of fact, those thoughts were all about what could have been if they were not the kind of people who inspired the growing respect each had begun to feel for the other. That respect could lead to a productive collaboration and serve the common good, thought Ariana.

Mark knew better. He wanted her more than he could bear. When they moved together toward the door, they shared a handshake which may have lasted just a beat longer than most and was the reason for their mutual eye contact, followed by turning toward each other.

Ariana was drawn into his eyes which were lit by a desire so strong she could feel a drawing in her breasts forward to him and sending warmth flooding through her body, erupting in moisture between her legs. She felt a bit faint and he used that moment to draw her to the couch where they both sank down, in each other's arms. Their lips joined frantically, with tongues intertwining. She tasted him and all thoughts were erased. His hand moved to her sensitive breast and his thumb rubbed the nipple, causing her to arch under his hand. She heard him groan and adjusted her body for more contact with his erection.

Mark was feeling so many things. Triumph was mixed with his arousal and he pushed away all thoughts of restraint. He kissed Ariana's neck and licked his way up to her ear, whispering, "Ariana, I have never wanted a woman as much as I want you right now." He was working the buttons on her navy shirtdress, trying to free those straining breasts. He wanted to see them, feel them and get his mouth on them as soon as possible. She was right with him and her breath was coming fast.

With the top buttons open, Mark pushed the dress aside and cupped her left breast with his right hand. Kissing her, he ran his thumb across, then under the lace covering her roundness, then pushed the lace aside and transferred his mouth to her nipple. Ariana was lost in his lust for her and had not the will nor the strength to stop him. Her own desire was overtaking her and she wanted more. She pulled away with the intention of getting his shirt buttons undone too. In that moment, she became aware of the surroundings. Here she was in Senator Falber's office, sprawled on his couch with her clothing undone and a part of her body exposed and wet with his saliva. Her lips felt bruised and she suddenly felt so disgusted with herself she pushed Mark away and sat up, re-arranging and buttoning her dress.

He was not quite keeping up with this turn of events, trying to cup her chin and kiss her again. Now, Ariana wrenched away and said "Mark! We can't do this! Too much is at stake!" He watched her rise and back away, holding out his arms to her and piercing her with those eyes, full of desire for her.

"Please, Ariana. Don't leave me. I need you now. I want you now!"

In spite of herself, Ariana hesitated, then continued to tidy herself. Looking away from him, she said,

"It is not about what you want or what I want, Mark. These moments of pleasure carry too much risk, for you, for me. I have always considered myself a person of integrity and have drawn a line about relationships with married men. You are a married man and as much as I am drawn to you, I won't do this." I won't deny, I wish things could be different!"

Mark's face hardened and he rose imperiously, stating, "Ariana, you came into this office yesterday dressed so provocatively, making your plea so persuasively, agreeing to return today alone and now you're playing coy with me. Do you still want my vote, or not?"

Aghast, Ariana looked at him with utter contempt. She said, "I'm sorry, Mark. I must have mistaken you for a man of integrity too. I came to appeal to your reason, your sense of fairness and your duty to do what is best for the largest number of your constituents. Teachers and the children they are charged with, make up a very large group of those constituents and they are the future of our country. I won't trade my integrity for your vote and I don't expect you to make your professional decisions based on my choices. Look to your own conscience!" With that, she turned and left the office, with him staring after her.

The dozen white roses delivered the next morning, with a plea for a "chance to redeem myself" brought Ariana to an ambivalence surprising to her. She was clear on the moral stance she wanted desperately to support, but the memories of those moments in his office, with his hands and urgently demanding lips on her body sent quivers up and down, straight into her suddenly throbbing core. She swooned on to the nearby sofa, her head thrown back with eyes closed. The feelings were overwhelming in a way she couldn't explain. Fantasies of what it might it be like if she met him raced through her brain and she allowed them to take her at full force.

When she emerged shaken from the experience, it was through a monumental effort on Ariana's part that she was able to get back into rational thought, enough to look more realistically at the consequences of giving in to these almost overwhelming emotions. Consequences to her personally, professionally and to her soul, as well as consequences to Mark, his family and already tarnished reputation. Especially in the days of "Me too," she would not be part of his downfall. She steeled herself and gave no response to his request. In the days that followed, Ariana had to exercise all her courage and discipline to keep from giving in to the urge to call Mark. She held steady. Gradually, she came to terms with her decision, knowing it was the right one.

A few weeks later, Ariana smiled as she read the bill had passed in the Senate, with Senator Falber's "Yes" vote making the difference.

The Gift of Foresight

Kris Lomonaco

Foresight – the ability to predict what will happen or be needed in the future

Prologue

Inquisitive, blonde-haired, blue-eyed Rebecca Andrews stole her parents' hearts when she entered the world on August 17, 1970. They had her quite late in their lives, her dad was fifty-two and her mom was forty-six. It was so completely unexpected, particularly because Anne had never been able to conceive.

Anne and David Andrews raised their baby girl in a quiet middle-class neighborhood in Littleton, Colorado. David had built the two-story, four-bedroom, two-bath home himself back in 1955. Anne wanted it painted a pale yellow, and pale yellow it stayed throughout the years. They were the only residents in the Columbine West development for a long time and liked their quiet life. Eventually, of course, other lots were sold, and houses were built. Beautiful white-barked aspen and forty-year old cottonwood trees that provided shade from the hot Colorado sun, were cut down. The views of the Rocky Mountains became limited, but the sunsets were still spectacular with their streaks of purples and pinks. However, in 1969, with the news she was expecting, Anne was happy there were neighbors with children for her child to play with.

Rebecca was bright and happy, and she loved to learn. Her light blonde hair had turned a more honey-blonde color as she grew older. Her eyes stayed a startling shade of blue that took on a sparkle when she laughed or when the light caught them just right, but it was her love for learning that shone through the brightest. Over the years her appetite for learning grew. Books and notebooks were strewn about her room. The library, with its endless stacks of research books, was her favorite place to go on a Saturday morning.

Rebecca was chosen as valedictorian for the 1988 graduating class from Columbine High School. Her parents were so incredibly proud of their smart, determined, lovely daughter. She went to the University of Colorado at Boulder where she majored in political science and minored in business marketing and management. She didn't date very often during high school or college, not wanting anything, or anyone, to interfere with her desire to work behind-the-scenes in the game of politics. She studied hard, earned excellent grades, and graduated with top honors in 1992.

Right after graduation, Rebecca applied for an internship with Colorado's much-admired democratic Senator Thomas Vianese. Her transcripts and stellar resume landed her an immediate interview. She interned for three years and then Senator Vianese hired her as his assistant. Rebecca worked in the Senator's office in Denver near the gold-domed Capitol building. She commuted daily from her home in Littleton. For several years it had been a twenty-minute drive, but soon the traffic increased and her commute time increased as well. Her parents had had enough of the traffic and the winter weather and decided to move to Scottsdale, Arizona. They sold their home, and Rebecca rented a small furnished apartment in Denver.

Rebecca thrived at her job. Her quiet intelligence and willingness to work hard were a winning combination. But most people just saw her beauty. She felt she had to continually prove her worth as the assistant to a powerful lawmaker. In 2000, a new Senator was elected from the state of Colorado. Democratic Senator Paul Michaels asked Rebecca to stay on as his assistant, however, he wanted her in Washington. She had loved the idea of working in D.C. and quickly agreed to the position.

Rebecca had no desire to run for office. She felt her knowledge and skills were best used to help further the agenda of the Senator. If she had only had the foresight to see where the political world was headed, she may have created a different path for herself.

One

Rebecca angrily tossed the remote at the television. Every day, every single day, the current administration pissed her off. She wanted to change the world, but she didn't have the power. Not yet anyway. She jumped to her feet, picked up the remote, and turned off the television. She rarely watched the nightly news anymore but tonight was an exception. It actually seemed as though this might have been a day with no major fuck-ups. She was wrong. Thankfully, it was Friday and she had a couple of precious days to herself. Rebecca refused to watch any of the news shows over the weekends. She couldn't stand to hear the arguing and talking over each other that inevitably engulfed the participants. The spewing of lies and vitriol was unnerving.

Rebecca's apartment in Washington, D.C. was her sanctuary, her safe space. It was neat and tidy with everything in its place. Tumult was all around her at the Capitol and her home needed to be relaxing and inviting. She had found this place eighteen years ago when she came to D.C. to work in Senator Michaels' office. The old corner building in the Anacostia neighborhood had caught her eye immediately. Its curved floor to ceiling windows, quoined corners and stark lines appealed to her. There was a vacant apartment on the second floor over the Anacostia Bar and Grill and Rebecca rented it immediately. The ten-foot high ceilings were covered in tin tiles painted white. All the heavy beams and woodwork were original to the building and were coated in many layers of white paint. Rebecca had the landlord paint the walls a dove gray and had a slightly darker gray carpet installed throughout most of the four-room apartment. In the kitchen and bathroom, they had installed black and white ceramic tiles which she chose to have laid in a diamond pattern. She adored the simple, sleek look of her home. It brought her comfort, a comfort she needed after a week of dealing with politics.

Rebecca sat back down on her shabby chic white sofa and rested her bare feet on the coffee table. She shook out the tangled curls of her long, honey-blonde hair and leaned her head back against the cushion. Rebecca only wore her hair loose at home. At work she was all business with her hair up and her clothing impeccable. Her five-foot ten-inch frame carried her one hundred and twenty pounds quite beautifully. Her striking, pale blue eyes shone brightly with flashes of light when she smiled, which didn't happen very often anymore. Most of the time now, her lips were slightly parted, with her perfect top teeth partially revealed. Neutral. No hint of a smile or a frown so as not to convey any agreement or disagreement when she was at the Senator's side.

It was important to make sure no one had any ammunition to use against him, or her, when it came to the Senator's reputation and his political agenda. Lying and deceit had taken hold in the Congress and Rebecca was determined to keep it away from his office. A neutral countenance was the best defense.

Two

The years in D.C. had passed swiftly for Rebecca, with Senator Michaels being in the majority, and the minority, under three presidents. Her influence and capabilities expanded, but she had remained out of the spotlight, by choice. Rebecca loved her job and had been content in knowing she was well-liked and well-respected within the circle of power, but she had also liked her privacy. She had heard the rumors whispered behind her back, the questioning of her sexual orientation, the speculation as to why she was alone at her age. It didn't bother her to keep them all guessing. Her reasons were none of their business.

This particular Friday night, Rebecca let her mind wander. It was amazing how her perspective had changed over the last few years. She had always been a quiet person, not shy exactly, just reserved. But now, she felt a restlessness, a discontentment. She wanted more. A woman's place was not supposed to be in the shadow of a man. Her place is alongside of him, his equal. It was time to come out of the shadows, to have a voice, a loud voice, and be a part of making some meaningful changes for the country. Ever since the massacre at Columbine High School on April 20, 1999, she had hoped for some common-sense gun control laws to be enacted. So far, there had been nothing substantive done to prevent the mass murder of children in the schools. Now it could be her chance to push for reform.

Rebecca was excited about being asked to take Senator Michael's seat when he decided to step down. She had been worried, though. She knew a candidacy for Senator would invite scrutiny. Everyone knew that you didn't reach the age of forty-eight without there being something in your past that might become a roadblock. Clearly, the public in general is very forgiving of a man's past, but a woman is held to a different standard, a higher standard. She saw it every day in the Capitol. Rebecca had pushed the worry aside. She told the DNC chairwoman she would run. She told Wyatt she was running. It was her time.

Oh, Wyatt. Rebecca closed her eyes. *If only we could have foreseen the future.*

Three

Rebecca had met Dr. Wyatt Benjamin three years earlier in the city of Kathmandu, Nepal, in May of 2015. He had been on a humanitarian mission and, in a sense, so had she. Senator Paul Michaels' wife, Vyshali Bista, who today is a sixty-three-year-old, raven haired beauty, was from Kathmandu. She had emigrated to the United States with her parents when she was thirteen years old. She had remained spiritually and culturally connected to her birthplace and went back to Nepal every year to see her extended family and friends.

Vyshali had been awakened very early the morning of April 26, 2015 by a buzzing cell phone. Several of her friends in Denver had texted her to express their concern and sympathy. There had been a devastating earthquake in Nepal and they hoped her family was safe. She had immediately turned her television on to CNN and was horrified. She had called her husband, Paul, at his office in Washington. She told him the news and said she wanted to go to Nepal on the first flight she could get. He had insisted she fly into D.C. He wanted his assistant, Rebecca Andrews, to accompany her from D.C. to Kathmandu. Senator Michaels tasked Rebecca with not only keeping Vyshali company, but also seeing what kind of aid the area might need so he could present a proposal to Congress to appropriate funds. It was part of her job to do this for him, but this time it was far more personal.

Vyshali flew from Denver International Airport to Reagan National in Arlington, Virginia. The Senator and Rebecca were given special passes to allow them to meet Vyshali at the gate. She emerged from the jetway dressed in a traditional Nepali *kurta suruwal*. The flowing deep purple pants were cinched at the ankles. Over these she wore a beautifully vivid yellow and purple patterned blouse and matching scarf that she had draped over her shoulders. Rebecca felt less brilliant in her navy-blue pantsuit and white silk blouse. Vyshali broke into a smile when she saw her husband and hurried into his arms. He was so much taller than his wife, his six-foot four-inches to her five-foot two-inches. They hugged for a long time, Vyshali's shaking shoulders being soothed by Paul's comforting hands. He rested his cheek on her head, his receding white hair in stark contrast to her long, black braid.

A sadness crept into Rebecca. She had lived most of her adult life as a proper, strong, capable woman. She hadn't dated since she was thirty-five, preferring her own company. But now, with a journey ahead of her which was full of unknown dangers and experiences, she was sad to be alone.

The cart that Paul had arranged to take them to the international departures lounge arrived and they climbed in. The two-hour layover was much needed by Vyshali. She was able to freshen up in the private ladies' room of the VIP lounge. Senator Michaels had ordered a light snack of fresh fruit and cheese with crackers for the three of them. He had some last-minute instructions for Rebecca which she added to her iPhone, her iPad and also wrote in her notebook. She was thorough and efficient, two traits that made her a valuable employee and the perfect person for this mission. The Senator had purchased first-class tickets for Vyshali and Rebecca and they were called to board first. They stood up and Rebecca was taken by surprise when the Senator wrapped his arms around her in a hug.

"Please, take care of yourself and be safe. Take care of Vyshali for me. I love her dearly." He whispered hoarsely.

"I will, Senator Michaels. I will." She assured him.

Rebecca was surprised as tears prickled and then formed at the corners of her eyes. The Senator never showed much emotion and neither did she. They were all business in their dealings with each other, but the depth of his feelings for his wife became too much for her.

Rebecca watched as Paul took Vyshali into his strong embrace and whispered, "*Ma timilai maya garchhu*. I love you so much." They shared a loving kiss after which Vyshali turned to Rebecca and said, "Let's go, my dear."

Four

It was an incredibly long trip which took them to Delhi, India, where they landed at Indira Gandhi International Airport. The two women, one tall and light, the other short and dark, were quite a sight as they hurried to the next terminal.

"Rebecca, please. I must stop to catch my breath," Vyshali panted.

"I'm so sorry, Mrs. Michaels. We have to make this flight. It's the last one until tomorrow afternoon. Please hurry," Rebecca urged.

Vyshali nodded, drew in a deep breath, and continued on. They finally arrived at the gate just as the announcement was made to board. As soon as the door was opened, the hot, humid air, thick with jet fuel fumes, assailed their senses. Twenty-five anxious people walked single file through the shimmering heat waves rising from the tarmac. They climbed the steps to the plane and took their seats. An attendant pulled the door in place and secured the latch.

The propellers on the twin engine plane turned, sputtered, then stopped. Rebecca and Vyshali looked at each other with fear in their eyes. It was a short eighty-minute flight to Bharatpur, Nepal, but Rebecca wondered if they would make it on this plane. After a couple false starts, the propellers sprung to life and caused the plane to vibrate violently. Rebecca and Vyshali, seated on opposite sides of the narrow aisle, held tight to each other's hand. Vyshali closed her eyes and prayed silently. Rebecca looked out the dirty window as the plane turned towards the end of the runway.

"Mrs. Michaels?" Rebecca raised her voice loud enough to be heard over the roar of the engines. "We will be taking off now. Are you okay?"

Vyshali opened her dark eyes and looked into the clear blue eyes of the wonderful woman who agreed to come with her on this treacherous trip.

"My dear, Rebecca. Please call me Vyshali. We will be together for quite a while and I want us to be comfortable with each other. I'm exhausted but fine. I'm very anxious to see my aunt and uncle. I pray they were not hurt in the earthquake."

Rebecca gave Vyshali's hand a reassuring squeeze and turned back to the window. The land fell away below them as the plane slowly climbed into the early morning sky. The large buildings of the city gave way to farmland with light green pastures. Grazing animals appeared as small white dots and farm houses nestled in the protection of groves of trees. They passed several lakes and a river that wove its way through the countryside. It was beautiful and calming, and Rebecca closed her eyes.

The change in altitude startled Rebecca. She looked over to Vyshali who had her face pressed against the window. The scenery had changed a bit as the Himalayan Mountains dominated the horizon. Directly below, houses with roofs of red, blue and green perched on the wooded hillsides. As the plane came in to land, the houses were closer together and taller buildings came into view. There were fewer trees and the roads were heavy with traffic. The wheels touched down and the passengers exchanged thankful looks.

After getting off the plane, Vyshali and Rebecca went into the ladies' room to change into more suitable clothing for the last leg of their journey. Vyshali came out of the stall wearing a pair of tan pants and a pink blouse.

"Vyshali, you look great. I know you aren't accustomed to dressing like that, but you will be much more comfortable for the ride."

Rebecca, on the other hand, was glad to be out of her suit and into blue jeans and a white t-shirt. They rented an old, dark green jeep with no windows. Rebecca helped Vyshali into the passenger side and then hopped into the driver's seat. They left the airport and merged on to the main highway for the ninety-mile ride to Kathmandu. The air was humid but the slight breeze created by the jeep made it bearable. Vyshali pointed out some of the familiar sights.

"The river we just crossed is the Narayani. There are always dozens of ships carrying their cargo to port. Over there is the start of the Chitwan National Park. It was one of my favorite places to go, Rebecca. I loved watching all the birds and the sunrises and sunsets were always so beautiful. I used to go on jungle safaris with my friends when I was younger."

Vyshali became quiet as they began the climb into the passageway to Kathmandu. The road through the lush vegetation had become treacherous with damage cause by the earthquake. There was a lot of traffic in both directions and Rebecca had to drive very slowly. It took almost five hours to drive the ninety miles to Kathmandu. The closer they got to the city, the worse the roads became. Vyshali directed Rebecca towards her family home.

Five

The 7.8 magnitude earthquake had struck the Kathmandu Valley at midday on April 25. Houses and buildings collapsed in the city and for miles into the surrounding areas. The news had reported that tens of thousands had died immediately and millions were left homeless. Everywhere they looked there was destruction. Vyshali looked haunted and Rebecca imagined she was thinking about her family. The dirt roads, which before the earthquake, were difficult to navigate, became even more so. The paved roads had heaved and buckled and were virtually impassable. Rebecca pulled the jeep into the parking lot of a severely damaged office building which was near the Bista house. She and Vyshali lifted their overnight bags out of the back and went inside to see if they could find a restroom to change their clothes. The place was in shambles with window glass broken and plaster covered boards hanging from the ceilings. Vyshali got out of her traveling clothes and put on the *kurta suruwal* she had been wearing. It was important for her to be dressed appropriately when she arrived at her aunt and uncle's home. Rebecca would have preferred to stay in her jeans, but out of respect for Vyshali and her family, she changed into her pantsuit and blouse.

They climbed back into the jeep, anxious to get to the Bista house. As they made their way slowly up the road, the condition of the buildings they passed filled Vyshali and Rebecca with dread. Many of them had been leveled by the earthquake. Others that were still standing had been damaged severely and appeared uninhabitable. When Vyshali directed Rebecca to turn left on the next road, she brought the jeep to a stop and turned toward the scared woman. She took hold of Vyshali's hands. They were cold and shaking. Rebecca's heart ached for this poor woman who had no idea what she would find around the next corner.

"Vyshali, do you want me to go on ahead, alone? I promise I will come right back to get you."

"No. I want to see for myself, now, what has happened. Thank you, but please, let's keep going."

Rebecca could barely control the jeep as she dodged stones and bricks and inched them closer to the house.

"Oh my gosh!" Rebecca exclaimed. "Look at that house ahead. It looks almost exactly like my apartment building in Anacostia."

From this distance, the house appeared to be undamaged. Vyshali broke into a huge smile.

"That's my family's house!" Rebecca could only image her relief at finding the house still intact.

They pulled up in front and got out of the jeep. With a closer look, they saw there was more damage to the house than they originally thought. The brown plaster holding the stones had many cracks in it, and the rear portion of the house, not seen from down the road, had partially collapsed. The four concrete steps leading to the front entry were crooked and portions were crumbled. The tall curved windows had no glass in them and the second-floor balcony had been shaken loose.

Vyshali had taken hold of Rebecca's arm to steady herself. Her fear was returning with every stone she saw that was out of place. She leaned against the jeep, her back to the house.

"Vyshali, listen to me. This doesn't mean your family was injured. I know you're scared but you're not alone. I'm right here with you. Most of the house is still standing. That's encouraging, right?"

Vyshali took a shuddering breath and turned towards the house.

Nugah and Adita Bista had come out of their home when they heard the jeep come to a stop out front. They stood poised on the top step and watched the two ladies. They had no idea who the tall blonde woman was, but they recognized their niece in her pretty yellow and purple silk outfit.

"Vyshali! Vyshali!" they called to her.

"*Kaka*! *Kaki*!" Vyshali cried as she hurried across the driveway and up the steps. She gathered them into her embrace.

"Are you okay? Were you hurt?" Vyshali moved them back inside the house leaving Rebecca standing by the jeep.

Rebecca looked around her, shaking her head at the sheer magnitude of loss. It was nothing short of a miracle that this house was still standing. After several minutes Vyshali came outside.

"They are both well, Rebecca. They were not hurt, just shaken a bit. The house, as you can see, is damaged but still livable. You are welcome to share their home while we are here, of course."

Rebecca turned and pulled her large backpack and the overnight cases from the jeep. They went into the cool of the Bista home.

"Rebecca Andrews, this is my Uncle Nugah Bista and my Aunt Adita."

"It's a pleasure to meet you both. Thank you so much for your hospitality." Rebecca shook their hands carefully.

Vyshali took her case and went upstairs to her room. It was always kept ready for her whenever she came to Kathmandu. *Kaki* Adita showed Rebecca to a small room off the main living area. Rebecca unpacked the few clothes she had been able to bring and placed them in the two-drawer dresser. The three pairs of jeans, five t-shirts, three white, one jade green and the other navy-blue, five pairs of underwear and two bras, just fit in the space. The single bed was covered with a handmade, striped blanket with a white pillow leaning against the headboard. Rebecca laid down and closed her eyes. This was a very comfortable home away from home.

Six

Rebecca and Vyshali spent several days walking around Kathmandu trying to assess what was needed most. Rebecca took notes to relay to Senator Michaels when she talked to him. They went to search for Vyshali's friends who lived all around the city. They found that some were fine, some were hurt, and unfortunately, a few had died. One of her dearest friends, Priya Thapa, had lost her husband of forty years when their house collapsed. Vyshali insisted that Priya come stay with them at the Bista home.

Although the news reports that Rebecca and Vyshali had heard before they left home had been horrible, the reality of the earthquake was so much worse. To actually see what it means when thousands of people in one area die suddenly, and to hear the cries and moans of the injured, was heartbreaking. The aimless wandering of those left homeless throughout the region was very hard for Vyshali and Rebecca to witness. They felt so useless.

The American Red Cross had sent help which arrived two days after the earthquake hit. Doctors Without Borders also arrived on the second day and brought two hard rubber inflatable medical tents that were large enough to hold twenty beds each. They were set up on the east and west sides of the city. The Doctors Without Borders organization also supplied over six thousand family-sized tents which were set up outside the city and into the mountain villages for some of those left homeless.

A few smaller tents were set up for the teams of doctors and nurses to share as they rotated their time in the medical tents.

Packaged food and drinks were supplied to the medical staff. The Red Cross volunteers had a satellite phone hook-up. They tried to establish cell phone service and internet connections but, so far, were unsuccessful. Rebecca carried her devices and charger with her every day just in case. It was unsettling to not be in touch with anyone back home.

Seven

A little over a week after arriving in Kathmandu, Rebecca was walking through the streets by herself. Vyshali had stayed behind with her aunt and uncle and Priya. Rebecca had realized early on that she actually felt very safe here by herself. There was chaos, but there was no violence, no looting.

Many hundreds of people wandered about, some still searching for loved ones, most still in a state of disbelief. There was rubble all around her so she was stepping carefully in her running shoes so she wouldn't twist an ankle and fall. She had on her usual outfit of blue jeans and a t-shirt, the jade green one today, and her long hair was pulled back in a loose ponytail. She wore her backpack which held, among other things, the two precious bottles of water she bought that morning at the Red Cross tent. As she was passing a building that had partially collapsed, she heard someone calling out. She turned toward the sound and rushed over to see if she could help. Rebecca looked down into the steel blue eyes of a gray-haired old man. He was kneeling on the ground, covered with dust, and trying to get an injured young boy to lie still so he could help him.

"Please, Miss. You have to help me." He spoke perfect English and Rebecca squatted down next to him. "Hold the boy's head still." The boy appeared to be about ten years old or so. His face was covered with dirt and grime, and the man was trying to gently wipe it clean with a wet rag. Rebecca felt the bile rise in her throat as a large gash across the boy's face was exposed. She looked away.

"You have to pull it together and help me!" the man commanded. "Don't frighten this poor child any more than he already is. He might not understand what you are saying but talk to him anyway. His name is Imay. Just talk to him to keep him calm."

The boy's pants and shirt were in tatters and he had lost his shoes. Rebecca's voice was low and soft as she told a story to Imay. It was a nonsensical tale of pirate ships and buried treasure.

The boy visibly calmed as she spoke to him. The old man reached into a large brown satchel with creams and ointments, saline and pre-loaded syringes. He fished out a syringe and handed an alcohol wipe to Rebecca.

"Rub this on a spot on his bottom. He needs an antibiotic. It might sting him a bit so please, keep talking." The man liked to hear her sweet voice.

After giving Imay the shot, he tied a clean cloth in place across the boy's eyes. Rebecca cradled the child's head in her lap and watched as the man stood up. Her mouth dropped open as he rose up to his full six-foot two-inch height. He brushed the dirt and soot off his head to reveal wavy, dark brown hair to his shoulders. He raked his fingers through the top to keep it off his forehead. Rebecca realized he was around her age and not an old man at all. She giggled softly at the mistake she had made. The man knelt back down and scooped Imay up in his arms. Rebecca grabbed the satchel and followed closely behind him as he carried the boy to the Doctors Without Borders tent several hundred yards away. Once they arrived, he placed Imay on an operating table and ordered an anesthesiologist to put the boy under.

The doctor turned to Rebecca with a smile, extended his hand and said,

"Hi. My name is Wyatt Benjamin. And you are…?"

She took his hand, returned a smile, and said, "I'm Rebecca Andrews. Pleased to meet you."

Eight

After the introductions, Wyatt asked, "Rebecca? Would you stay and help me with Imay? All the other doctors and nurses are busy."

Rebecca started shaking her head no. "I can't, Dr. Benjamin. I have absolutely no experience." The very thought made her feel queasy.

"Please. I can guide you through the process. You can do this."

Rebecca looked into his steel blue eyes and realized she did not want to refuse him. As she looked away she quietly asked him, "What do you want me to do?"

Dr. Benjamin took her over to the shelves of linen. She took a blue gown and helped him into it. He did the same for her. His fingers brushed against the soft skin of her neck when he tied it and he felt the soft curls of her hair across his knuckles. They helped each other into masks and gloves and when Dr. Benjamin was told the boy was ready, he set to work.

He glanced at Rebecca way too often. The light from the overhead lamp created a halo on her hair. Her eyes were the most startling color he had ever seen, a pale blue that sometimes seemed almost clear when she moved her head just right. He saw that she was trying valiantly not to flinch as he cleaned and probed the wound, handing him the instruments as he asked for them. The beautiful woman he had enlisted to help him was distracting. He needed to concentrate on the surgery he had to perform, not on her. For the next couple of hours, he worked to suture the wound closed and save Imay's right eye.

Rebecca kept staring at this incredibly handsome man. His chiseled good looks, gorgeous eyes and tousled hair had captivated her. She had never been so affected by any man before. She felt her cheeks flush as the flames of desire, long ago put out, were ignited in her belly. She pressed her legs together as she enjoyed the feeling that crept down to her center.

After the intense surgery was over, Rebecca sat down on a nearby stool. She lowered her head into her hands and started trembling. Wyatt came over to her and touched her shoulder. She lifted her head.

"Rebecca, you did great." His voice was low and a bit raspy.

He offered her his hand and she reached up to take it. The touch, the warm contact of her palm with his, sent a tingle through her. The strength of his grasp surprised her after having seen how delicately he operated. She stood up next to him, her hand still in his, and tilted her head up to search his eyes.

There was a tremor in her voice as she asked, "Will he see out of that eye again?"

"I think so," Wyatt said with conviction. "Imay wandered into a building and fell into a hole in the floor. I heard his cries and went in to get him. A brick had been shaken loose and hit him in the face. I pulled him out just minutes before you walked by. Thank you so much for helping me with him."

"You're quite welcome, Dr. Benjamin." Rebecca reluctantly let go of his hand. "I have to get back to my friends' house before they start to worry about me."

She reached up to push his hair away from his forehead.

"Doctor Benjamin, you should have thought to bring something to keep your hair back."

"Ah, true. But if I had, I would have missed this, Rebecca."

Nine

Rebecca picked up her backpack and left the tent, feeling Wyatt's eyes on her as she walked away. She walked as fast as she could back to the Bista house. During the time they had been here, Rebecca had cleared a path in the street by pushing loose stones and dirt to the sides to form a border. It was so much easier now to get from the tents to the house.

Rebecca kept the intimacy of the encounter to herself, but told Priya, Vyshali and her aunt and uncle about Imay and the doctor who operated on him. They listened with great interest as she recounted the events.

"Rebecca? I'm going to try and reach Paul again using the satellite phone at the Red Cross tent. Do you want to come with Priya and me?"

"That would be great, Vyshali. I hope we can finally get through to him. I have a whole list of things to tell him we need for the proposal." Rebecca stood up. "I'll be right back."

Rebecca went into her room to change out of her shirt and bra. She brushed her tangled hair and pulled it back into a loose ponytail. Adita had given Rebecca a large brown jug of water a few days ago. She poured a small amount of the tepid liquid into the colorful ceramic bowl on the dresser and dipped a cloth into it. Rebecca washed her face and neck, under her breasts and her armpits. She rinsed and wrung out the cloth and tossed the water out of the window. She put on a clean bra and white t-shirt and she was ready to go.

The three women walked down to the Red Cross tent. Rebecca had gone in there every day, Vyshali a little less often. They knew all the volunteers and the volunteers knew them.

"You're in luck, Mrs. Michaels," Jonathan said. "We have a really good connection to the United States." He got a signal and handed Vyshali the headset.

After a few seconds, a smile brightened Vyshali's face. "Paul? Paul, it's me! Can you hear me? Oh, my dear husband, I miss you so much."

Priya and Rebecca moved away to give Vyshali some privacy. A few minutes later, Vyshali called out, "Rebecca? Come talk to Paul."

"Hi, Senator Michaels. I have a list of items that should be included in the proposal. Hello? Senator?" Rebecca handed the headset back to Jonathan. "We got cut off."

Vyshali thanked all the Red Cross volunteers and gave them a generous donation for allowing them to use the phone. Rebecca hung back as Vyshali and Priya started to walk back to the house.

"You two go on ahead. I want to talk to Dr. Benjamin and see how Imay is doing."

"Are you sure? It will be getting dark soon." Priya was always worried and on edge.

"I'll be fine, Priya. Dr. Benjamin will see me safely home before it gets too dark."

"Come on, Priya," Vyshali urged. "Rebecca will be in safe hands, I'm sure."

She linked her arm with Priya's and they headed up the path.

Rebecca caught the slight wink that Vyshali had given her. *Hmm*, she thought to herself. *Does that shy woman pick up on more than I give her credit for?* She watched with genuine affection for the two old friends as they walked away.

Ten

There was a line of people at the door to the tent, perhaps twenty-five or thirty, young and old. No one had any apparent wounds, but as Rebecca got closer, she realized that all the older people appeared to be blind. Each one had a younger person accompanying them. Inside there was a different team of doctors and clinicians than there had been earlier in the day, except for Dr. Benjamin. He was still there and seemed to be in charge of this shift as well. All twenty beds were occupied and the people in them were also old and blind. Rebecca noticed a sign on the medical cabinet that had been wheeled into the tent. *"Himalayan Cataract Project"*. All these people were here to have cataracts removed. It was then she realized that Dr. Wyatt Benjamin must be an ophthalmologist, not a medical surgeon as she had believed.

Rebecca stood to the side of the doorway so she could watch the doctors work without being in the way. With great precision and efficiency, they prepared each patient, performed the cataract removal procedure, and placed a patch over the eye. As soon as one patient was done, they were escorted out and another came in to take their place. In a short time, the people were all treated and sent on their way.

One of the technicians saw Rebecca standing outside and motioned her to come in.

"Hi. May I help you with something?"

"That was incredible!" Rebecca exclaimed. "What is the *"Himalayan Cataract Project?"*

"It's a service that was set up several years ago to restore sight to the people of Nepal and India. Hundreds of thousands of people are blinded by cataracts with no means to pay for the necessary procedure. The blind are unable to work, or even care for themselves, and they become a burden on their families. Now, Dr. Benjamin, and others, travel all around the world to provide this service free of charge. It is a wonderful organization."

"I'm amazed. Truly amazed." Rebecca watched as the bed linens were changed and the instruments were placed in the autoclave to sterilize them. "I'd like to speak to Dr. Benjamin if he has a few minutes."

Wyatt had turned when Rebecca mentioned his name. He was smiling as he came over to her. He extended his hand to her and she firmly grasped it.

"Dr. Benjamin. I'd like to talk to you if you have some time."

The technician spoke up, "You go on ahead, doc. We'll finish up here before the next wave of patients comes."

Eleven

Dr. Benjamin removed his gown and tossed it on a pile of used linen. Placing his hand on the small of Rebecca's back, he escorted her out of the tent. They walked a short distance and he dropped his hand to his side. She wished he hadn't. She had felt the warmth of his hand through her t-shirt and now she felt the cold. Rebecca stopped and turned to face him.

"Dr. Benjamin? How is Imay doing?"

"Please, Rebecca, call me Wyatt. He's doing really well. He's staying with his family in a tent just on the other side of the medical tent. I sent a nurse over to check on him a short while ago. He was alert and not in any pain."

"That's great news." Rebecca was really pleased to hear this. A weariness had seemed to creep into Wyatt's eyes. She reached out and again brushed his hair away from his forehead. "You look tired."

He took hold of her hand and urged, "Come with me."

"Where are we going?"

"To my place. It's quiet and we can talk in private."

Without hesitation, Rebecca allowed him to take her to his living quarters, one of the tents that was set up for the doctors. He opened the door, gently pushed her in and stepped in behind her. Rebecca smelled a slight musty odor from the tent being closed up all day. Wyatt went over to a small folding table and lit the green Coleman lantern that was on it. It wasn't dark out yet, but the light was needed in here. Rebecca looked around the space, taking in every detail. There was plenty of headroom, even for someone as tall as Wyatt. Two cots were at opposite ends of the tent, each one a bit wider than the typical cots she had seen for camping. Two tables and two chairs were at the front of the tent, and a footlocker was next to a smaller door in the back wall. Three thick wooden poles were holding up the center of the tent, and a pole supported each corner. It was very sturdy and larger than she had expected.

"Where is your roommate?" Rebecca motioned to the second cot as she turned to him.

"I don't have one." His voice was deep and gravelly as he passed his hand over his eyes.

"I'm sorry, Wyatt. You must be exhausted. I should go. We can talk tomorrow."

She turned to leave and he stepped in front of the door. He locked his eyes on hers.

"Please, don't go. I want you to stay with me awhile. Sit. Let me get you something to drink." He went over to the footlocker and took out a bottle of juice for each of them. He handed one to her with an apology. "I'm sorry it's not cold, but it's all I have."

"Are you kidding? I haven't had anything but water for almost two weeks. This is awesome, really." She took the cranberry juice from his hand. He motioned to her to sit at one of the tables and he brought a chair over to sit next to her.

"What brought you back here this evening?"

No sooner had he asked the question than they heard someone calling to him. He leapt to his feet and threw open the door.

"Dr. Benjamin! Come quick! They need you in the medical tent!" The young girl who delivered the message turned and ran away.

"I'm sorry, Rebecca. I have to go. We'll talk tomorrow."

He ran after the girl before Rebecca could say anything more to him. She put the unopened bottles back in the footlocker, pushed Wyatt's chair back to his table and turned off the lantern. She closed the door after her and noted the #1 on the fabric above it. She smiled. *Of course, he is*. Rebecca was disappointed that she hadn't had a chance to spend more time with the sexy, intriguing Dr. Benjamin. The sun had gone down over the mountains and there was a chill in the air. She hurried her steps up the hill to the house. They would talk tomorrow.

Twelve

The routine of Rebecca's days in Kathmandu had changed when she met Dr. Wyatt Benjamin. Now she was eager to get out of the house to help in the medical tent. She loved being put to work, even if it was just to write down patient care instructions, comfort a crying child or hand out bottles of water.

This morning, the clinic was less hectic than usual. Rebecca was sitting at the table writing generic instructions for wound care. She watched Wyatt move with ease among the patients. He was quick with a smile and a soothing touch to a forehead. Her attraction to him had been swift and powerful, her desire for him surprising but welcome. Wyatt had caught Rebecca staring at him and he flashed her a sexy grin. She saw the want and need in his steel-blue eyes. He came over to her and leaned his elbows on the table.

"Rebecca, those can wait. I can't. Will you come with me?"

"Dr. Benjamin? Do you have a minute? I need you to look at this dressing." The nurse's question broke the spell.

The quiet morning gave way to another busy day and the moment was gone.

Thirteen

Rebecca's sleep was restless, filled with erotic thoughts of Wyatt. In such a short time he had unlocked something in her, a restlessness, a need for intimacy. She wanted to feel the strength of his arms and hands on her body, to feel his sensuous mouth on her mouth, on her breasts, his tongue teasing at her nipples, her clit. She imagined her legs wrapped around his trim waist, her heels on his ass urging him to take her. Rebecca's hands simulated the things she wanted Wyatt to do to her. Her climax was reached, but it was lacking in fullness. She was quiet and alone. She wanted Wyatt.

Rebecca bounced out of bed, anxious to get back down to the Doctors Without Borders tent. She put on a pair of jeans and a white t-shirt. She made sure her iPhone, iPad and charger, and notebooks were in the backpack along with a navy-blue t-shirt, some high-energy biscuits and a bottle of water for lunch. She left the house without waking the others and made her way down the hill. She stopped by the Red Cross tent first to say hi to the volunteers, bought some water, and then went to Wyatt's tent.

She knocked on the wooden door and called his name, "Wyatt? Are you in there?"

"Come on in, Rebecca. It's not locked."

She dropped her backpack next to the door and took a couple steps inside. He was still laying on his cot, his hands locked behind his head. He had a thin gray blanket covering him up to his abdomen.

"I'm sorry, Wyatt." She turned around. "I'll wait outside."

"Don't go, Rebecca." He threw the blanket off and in a swift movement came up behind her. "I thought about you all night."

He turned her around. All he was wearing was a pair of green plaid drawstring sleeping pants.

"You have no idea how much I want you. I want to kiss every inch of you, your eyes, your nose, the softness of your cheeks, your sweet lips." His voice was barely above a whisper with desire.

Rebecca felt as if every one of Wyatt's words was a caress, as if each carried a touch that she could feel on her skin. They reached inside her, bringing a heaviness to the lower part of her body. He pulled her against the hard length of him and it felt as if the barrier of their clothing had fallen away. His lips followed the path his words carved out for him. He kissed each of her eyelids, the tip of her nose, first one cheek and then the other, and finally brushed his lips against hers. That brief, sensitive contact left her wanting more, and she let out a soft sigh.

Wyatt pulled his head away and loosened his grip on her. "Becky, darlin', I wish I could take you right here, right now, but I can't. I have to get to the clinic."

Rebecca nodded in understanding. "I know you do. I'm not going anywhere. We'll have time later."

She reached up and ran her fingers through his hair and flashed him a brilliant smile. She bent down to pick up her backpack and turned to leave.

"You can leave that here if you want. It'll be safe."

"That would be great. Thanks. I'll see you outside in a few." She opened the door and went out into the soft sunlight of a gorgeous morning. *Oh, my gosh! That's the first time anyone has ever called me Becky...and darlin'.*

Wyatt placed his hand on the small of Rebecca's back as they walked to the medical tent. She loved this intimacy, the continuing connection that they had shared in his tent. The medical staff was changing shifts. The weary overnight doctors and nurses, and the alert, fresh faced day team, passed each other with nods and greetings.

The morning hours passed quickly for Rebecca. She reveled in her new-found usefulness. She knew they would be going home as soon as Vyshali felt comfortable leaving her aunt and uncle, but until then, she would be here, helping the staff and being near Wyatt.

Fourteen

At first no one moved, their minds unable to make sense of the fact that it was happening again. The ground was moving, and the noise of extended thunder was deafening, but there was little panic. As the bucking of the earth continued, it was as if a switch had been flicked on and the medical staff rushed to the patients. The lights hanging from the ceiling of the tent were swaying violently and threatened to fall. Wyatt and the rest of the team were covering the patients with extra sheets and leaned their own bodies over them to protect them. Rebecca grabbed a sheet and did the same for a frightened child in the bed closest to the door. A cabinet fell over and the trays with instruments went crashing to the floor. The thunderous roar from the earthquake was soon over and the ground seemed to settle back into itself.

Rebecca raised her head to look for Wyatt and saw he was tending to several patients. She turned her attention back to the child she had protected. Pulling the sheet off, she saw it was a cherubic black-haired girl who was maybe three or four years old. Her dark eyes were filled with tears and she started to cry out. Rebecca tried to keep the child calm by talking quietly to her, as she had with Imay just a few days before. A doctor came over to check on the little girl and Rebecca stepped out of the way. Again, she looked over to Wyatt and this time their eyes met, his full of concern and hers full of fear. She knew she could be of use in the clinic, but she needed to go check on Vyshali and her aunt and uncle.

She yelled a quick, "I have to go," and ran from the tent.

Fifteen

The epicenter of this earthquake was further away from Kathmandu. Still, in the span of only forty-five seconds, many of the buildings that had remained standing after the first quake were reduced to piles of brick and stone and wood. Some homes that were cracked before now crumbled into their foundations. The only saving grace was that tens of thousands of people had taken to the safety of the hills many days ago.

As she got closer to the Bista house, Rebecca started to panic. She saw that a couple more houses on the street had collapsed. She was carefully picking her way over the debris that was strewn about when she heard her name being called.

"Rebecca! Rebecca!"

She looked up and saw Vyshali and Priya gingerly making their way towards her. She silently berated herself for having left them that morning. They were covered in dirt and dust and their faces were tear-streaked.

Vyshali collapsed into Rebecca's arms. "*Kaka* and *Kaki* are dead," she wailed.

Rebecca held tight to Vyshali as her grief nearly overwhelmed her. Priya was sobbing, her head dropped into her hands. Rebecca felt she should have been more alert to the fact that the house was already damaged. She should have made them all leave it. She should have known there might be violent aftershocks that would make the house unsound. Rebecca blamed herself for not having the foresight to move them to a safer place.

The three women clung to each other as they made their way to the Red Cross tent. The people inside had been shaken, but they were already busy straightening up and making arrangements to get additional personnel and supplies to the area.

Through her tears, Vyshali pleaded, "Please help me. My aunt and uncle have died. We must take them from their home as soon as possible."

Jonathan came from behind the table and wrapped his arms around her.

"I'm so sorry, Mrs. Michaels. Please. Sit down. I'll help you."

Vyshali turned to Rebecca and implored her, "Please, go to your doctor and help those who can be helped. I know you will be safe with him and I will be okay with Priya. We will take care of my aunt and uncle and then go to the displacement camp where some of the people gathered before. Please, Rebecca. Go to him." She gave Rebecca a hug and turned to Jonathan.

Rebecca hesitated. She didn't think she should leave them here.

Priya seemed to have gathered her courage and declared, "I will take care of Vyshali. We will go to the west side of the city. Please, Rebecca, it's okay. Go help the others."

Sixteen

After saying her good-byes, Rebecca went to Wyatt's tent. She got a bottle of water to soothe her throat which had become extremely dry from breathing in dust. She took off her dirty t-shirt and bra, tossed them aside, and wet a towel to clean herself off. She put a clean t-shirt on and ran to the medical tent.

Even though it had only been a couple hours since she left him, Rebecca was anxious to see Wyatt and for him to see that she was okay. The tent was crowded with injured people and Rebecca immediately went to work. There was so much to do that she and Wyatt could only nod at each other throughout the day.

It was getting late and the next shift came in to relieve them. Wyatt and Rebecca desperately needed to get some sleep. Once they were outside the tent, Rebecca turned to him.

"My friend Vyshali's aunt and uncle died in the collapse of their home this morning," Rebecca said with tears in her eyes. "She and her friend Priya weren't hurt. They have gone to the camp on the west side of the city."

Wyatt put his arms around Rebecca and held her while she wept softly. He could feel her trembling and pressed her head to his chest. Her arms wrapped tight around his waist and he dropped his head to her shoulder. In a world torn apart by earthquakes, they found comfort in each other's arms.

They walked in silence to his tent. Rebecca started straightening up a few things that had been knocked out of place and Wyatt was leaning against a tent pole. He was watching her with half closed eyes, his arms crossed over his chest.

"Wyatt? About how many patients do you think you treated today?" Rebecca's voice was quiet.

"I don't know. Two hundred, maybe more. Why?"

"There are just so many of them. And you can't fix them all. You must get frustrated."

"I don't think about those I can't help, only those I can. It's how I keep doing this work year after year."

Seventeen

Wyatt watched Rebecca in the dim light, feeling a slow tightening in his groin. She had changed into one of his t-shirts and boxers to sleep in. Her hips moved sensually as she swayed to smooth out the blanket on her cot. He came up behind her and pulled her back against his erection. She molded her body into his embrace, the tension of the day starting to melt away. He trailed kisses down her neck and she felt the scruff of his unshaved chin on her shoulder. She reached back and placed a hand over his arousal, gently massaging him through his pants. He moved one hand under her shirt and ran his thumb along the underside of her breast before cupping it in his warm palm. His other hand went inside her boxers and covered her mound. Slowly, with gentle pressure, he moved his fingers to spread her lips and touch her clit, sliding them over and around the inside of her soft folds. They were each lost in the pleasure of the moment and languished in the mutual masturbation.

Wyatt bent his long fingers to enter her, moving in and out, timing the rhythm to her pulsing hips. The heel of his palm pressed against her nub and she softly called his name. He could feel her contract around his fingers. He cupped her sex and breast and held her firmly as she shuddered through her climax. He felt her grow weak and quickly moved his hands to support her. He pulled down the blanket and laid her on the cot. He waved his hand past his nose, breathing in her scent.

"Thank you, Wyatt." Her voice was low in the dark tent.

"My pleasure, Becky. My pleasure." He pulled the blanket from under her, covered her to her chin, and kissed her forehead. "Good-night, darlin'."

Rebecca murmured, "Good-night, Wyatt."

Wyatt went to his cot and laid down under the blanket. His erection was raging and he needed his own release. He started his all too familiar, solitary journey. He brought himself to orgasm quickly and fell into a restless sleep.

Eighteen

Rebecca started screaming, her arms flailing at something unseen. Swiftly, he moved to her, his hands catching her wrists and holding them above her head. He spoke softly to her, easing her out of her nightmare. She was soaked in sweat and breathing heavily, but her eyes were open and beginning to focus on him. The horror of the earthquake, pushed aside during the day, had invaded her sleep. He released her wrists and reached down to move the damp curls that had fallen across her face.

Wyatt knelt beside her. "Becky, darlin', it's okay. I'm here. You're safe now." His deep voice seemed to soothe her, and her breathing slowly returned to normal. He held her cold hands, warming them in his. The fear in her eyes slowly faded away and he laid down next to her. He stayed with her until she drifted off to sleep.

Rebecca stirred and stretched, the blanket falling away from her. Rolling to her side, she blinked her eyes open and looked over at Wyatt. He was standing next to his cot and she met his steel blue gaze. She sat up on the edge of her cot, her shirt dropping off her shoulder and her curls a tangled mess framing her face. She stood up, closed the distance between them with deliberate steps, and wrapped her arms around his neck. Rising on tiptoe, she drew down his head and placed her mouth against his warm, smooth lips. Slowly, she moved her head, brushing her lips over his, savoring the feel of them. The pleasure of the kiss caught at her and traveled down her body, creating a swelling in her breasts and arousing a soft, warm ache in her center.

The tip of her tongue teased at his lips, gently spreading them apart, gaining access to his mouth and tongue. Wyatt's chest tightened and he felt the rush of blood through his veins. He reached around to her lower back and drew her closer against him. His body was cool except for the heated area that rested against her belly with insistent hardness. He freed Rebecca from her clothes and she pressed herself against him. Wyatt undid the tie at his waist, allowed his pants to pool at his feet and then kicked them aside. His arms crossed behind her back and held her to him. His muscles contracted and in one swift movement he placed her gently on her back on his cot. He caressed her cheek, his thumb brushing the corner of her mouth and smoothing over her lips. He kissed her chin, the tip of her nose, her forehead.

"You are so beautiful, Becky," he said as he moved his hands over her soft breasts. Her nipples hardened at his touch and he bent his head down to take first one, then the other, into his mouth. He teased his tongue around each areola.

"Please, Wyatt. I want you inside me. Please."

Wyatt moved over her body and placed the tip of his cock inside her pink folds. He positioned his hands on either side of her. "Open your pretty eyes and look at me, darlin'."

She saw the passion and want in his steel blue depths. "Now, Wyatt."

With steady pressure, he inched his cock into her, feeling her inner muscles wrap around him, urging him deeper. He filled her and began a slow, steady thrusting, making love to her for the first time. Rebecca reached her climax and Wyatt pulled out to spill his cum on her belly. They laid together in the dawning light, their bodies entwined, staying in the moment as long as they dared.

Wyatt eased himself off Rebecca and stood tall beside her. He let his eyes wander over her, wanting every inch of her seared into his memory. Life was precious, and he knew he had to savor every moment of it. Her eyes went to his cock and she reached out to touch him. He took a step back.

"Later, Becky. We really have to get going."

"I know. I know." She stretched, clasping her hands over her head and spreading her long legs slightly apart.

Wyatt let out a low growl. "Oh, Becky. You aren't playing fair."

"What?" Rebecca laughed.

"We don't have time, darlin'. Get dressed."

Nineteen

They quickly got into their clothes. Wyatt took an apple juice and a couple granola bars out of his footlocker.

"What would you like, Rebecca?" His voice had already lost the sensual timbre.

She looked through the food and helped herself to a cranberry juice and a fruit bar. She turned to him.

"Wyatt?" Rebecca was tentative.

"Yes? What is it?"

"I went through an early menopause."

"That's good to know."

"Also, I'm healthy. You don't have to be concerned."

Wyatt laughed. "I suppose we should have had this conversation a bit earlier. I'm healthy, too."

Rebecca didn't mind that he came on her, but she wanted him to know it wasn't necessary.

They walked out of the tent and into reality. People were helping the injured get to the clinic. Many of them had broken limbs wrapped in scraps of clothing. Wyatt picked up a woman whose eyes were bandaged and carried her into the tent. Rebecca wrapped an arm around a teenage girl and helped her walk. People were sitting or lying on the ground on blankets, shawls, bedsheets, whatever they had. Others sat crossed legged on the hard ground. They were all waiting to be called into the tent to be treated.

After the first earthquake, as physically devastating as it was, people were still trying to find their way around and trying to recover. After this second one, it was as if the last vestiges of hope had been removed from their lives. They realized that they were in an extraordinarily vulnerable position in a very vulnerable country.

Twenty

It was an endless stream of humanity that passed through the medical tent. Rebecca was a welcome part of the team. Wyatt showed her how to do an eye-wash so she could be one more person to help with that care. She also gave shots of antibiotic and cleaned some minor wounds. Wyatt kept an eye on her as the day went on, wanting to make sure she was okay in her new role as medical assistant. About mid-day he came to her and took her hand, leading her out of the tent and back to his place. Instead of going inside, he showed her around back to where the latrines and showers were set up for the doctors. She was thrilled at the prospect of taking a shower.

"Thank you, thank you, thank you," Rebecca cried gleefully. She rose up on her toes and planted a huge kiss on his smiling lips.

"Go in the back door of my tent and get some soap and a towel. There is a bucket by the door. Bring out your dirty clothes. You can wash them as you are showering and rinse them in it. You have to be very quick, Rebecca. We can't afford to waste water. I have to get back to work. Enjoy!"

With that he turned and jogged back to the medical tent. Rebecca did as she was told and reveled in the first shower she had had since she arrived in Nepal. PTA baths were all she could manage at Vyshali's. She quickly washed her hair, her body and her clothes. She filled the bucket and dunked her bra, panties, t-shirts and jeans in the clear water to rinse them. She wrung the clothes out and hung them on a rope that was strung between two poles. Wrapped in a towel, she stepped carefully back to Wyatt's tent. Rebecca toweled her hair as dry as she could get it and pulled it back. She put on the boxers and t-shirt from last night. She only had the one pair of jeans, so she decided to wear Wyatt's sleeping pants, cinched them tight around her waist and rolled up each leg into a cuff. She slipped on her walking shoes and she was ready to go.

Wyatt looked up as she came through the door. A smile of appreciation and a slow nodding of his head was all he had time to greet her with. It was enough for Rebecca.

Twenty-One

Late in the afternoon, just as Rebecca and Wyatt were finishing up their shift, they heard a commotion outside. The doors burst open and four men carried an unconscious man into the tent.

One of the men breathlessly explained, "This is Pravin. He was trapped in his office building yesterday. All the rescuers, even his wife and daughter, had worked for hours and hours to free him from under a large piece of wood. Will you save him?"

Wyatt gently told him, "We'll try our best. He is badly hurt, but we'll do everything we can to save him."

Pravin's chest had been crushed. He was no longer breathing on his own and his heartbeat was fading. The doctors tried for almost an hour to resuscitate him but were unable to. Rebecca offered to tell the family.

The man's wife and daughter were sitting on the ground outside the tent. She knelt down and said, "Hi. My name is Rebecca. I'm so sorry but Pravin has died."

The older woman looked at Rebecca with a blank stare. Her teenage daughter started sobbing inconsolably.

"The doctors did all they could for Pravin. He was just too badly hurt. I'm truly sorry."

Rebecca was shaking as she stood up. She turned and walked away from them. Wyatt took her hand and they walked to his quarters in silence, each lost in their own thoughts. It had been an upsetting end to a very long day.

Wyatt laid down on his cot with his arm across his closed eyes. Rebecca stood watching him for several minutes, her eyes filled with tears. She went to him, knelt at the end of his bed, and took off his shoes. He watched her from under his forearm. She stood up and untied his pants, grabbed the fabric, and pulled them down and off. She went to the waistband of his briefs and peeled them off over his butt and his growing erection. He raised his arms over his head and she removed his shirt. He watched her with a smoldering look as she quickly got out of her clothes. She held back the tears as she slid her arms around his neck and molded her mouth to his. Urgency grew inside her, swelling her breasts as she pressed her hardened nipples against him. She lifted her knee across his thighs as his hands moved to her hips.

Rebecca straddled him, positioning herself over his cock, aiding his entry, enclosing the warm hardness of him. He filled her so exquisitely that the tears she had been holding back spill over her lashes and down her cheeks. He reached to brush them away and pulled her to him. She clung to the strong muscles of his arms as she rode him, feeling him throbbing deep inside her. Their mutual climax was sweet, and overwhelming. Wyatt rolled to his side, holding her as she wept quietly against his chest.

"There's so much death around us, Wyatt. With you I feel alive."

"Oh, my darlin' Becky," he whispered. "I love your strength, your kindness, your compassion. You have a place in my heart forever."

She snuggled into him and softly said, "I love you, Wyatt."

Twenty-Two

Something woke Rebecca out of a sound sleep. She reached out and found she was alone. She looked around the room and didn't see Wyatt. She guessed he had to go back to care for patients. She got up to put on her own t-shirt and panties but remembered she had left them on the rope line outside. She opened the back door and looked around to make sure no one would see her. She ventured out and went to get her clothes. She heard the soft splashing of water and realized someone was in the shower. It was Wyatt. He was just finishing up and was rinsing the last of the soap off his feet. He straightened up to shake the water from his long hair, running his fingers through the wet strands to separate them. His body was lean and muscled. His chest was bare, but a thin line of hair adorned his abdomen from below his navel to his cock, a nest of dark curls surrounded the base. Not wanting to be seen, Rebecca silently left the protection of the shadows and went back inside. She laid on her cot and waited for him to come in.

Wyatt's large form filled the doorway, a dark shape against the greater darkness of the night. Rebecca saw him glance over at her, but he went to his own cot. She quietly came over to him and knelt on the floor. He reached out to her and slowly stroked her hair. His breathing was ragged and a moan escaped his lips.

"Becky, my darlin', I want to make love to you again. I want to lose myself in you, to leave the horror behind and be transported to another place and time. But I can't. I need to get some sleep."

"Don't speak, don't move, just lay here quietly," she whispered. She placed her fingers gently on the curve of his shoulder. Wyatt slowly drew in a breath. She touched his nipples, circling, lightly scraping her fingernail over them. Her hand traveled down to his navel, sliding the pad of her finger around the indent. Inching the blanket down to his thighs, she saw he had been aroused by her touch.

She leaned over him and licked at the very tip of his cock, moving her tongue around the rim before she wrapped her lips around him. Her hand encircled his shaft and, with gentle pressure, stroked him upwards, pushing more of his rigid flesh into her mouth. She moved her tongue along the length of him and slowly pulled her head back, taking care not to let him completely leave the moist warmth of her mouth. Her lips tightened around him and she took his length in, a bit faster, feeling a slight raise of his hips as if he were urging her on. Again, and again, she drew him in and released him, loving the power she had to bring him to this hard, throbbing state. His rapid breathing and deep throated growl accompanied his climax. He never touched her, he never spoke to her, but the pleasure she received in doing this for him was all she wanted. Without saying a word, she covered him back up to his waist and padded back to her cot. A smile played on her lips as she wiped the corner of her mouth with her finger.

Wyatt's voice was low with emotion. "Thank you, Becky."

"This was my pleasure, Wyatt."

Twenty-Three

The following morning, Wyatt gathered a team to go into the hillside and help some of the people who had fled the city.

Their mission was both medical and humanitarian. They carried boxes of food, mostly rice and high-energy biscuits, water and basic medical supplies. Rebecca followed behind Wyatt, lifting her eyes to watch him as he led the small team up the road. His strong legs and taut backside brought a secret smile to her lips. Her mind flashed to last night when she had watched him take a shower. The water had dripped from his hair and trickled down his back, the drops washing over the top of his ass and disappearing. Rebecca shook her head to banish the vision and quickly lowered her eyes to watch where she was walking.

There were a few clouds in the gorgeous azure sky and lush greenery was all around them. The hills here seemed unscathed by the earthquakes. It was truly amazing, the dichotomy of utter devastation in the valley and the beauty in the mountains. There were hundreds of people on the road. They were all dressed in brilliantly colored clothes, journeying away from Kathmandu. One of the team members, a native of Nepal, explained that because they had lost their homes, and they could only take a few things, they chose to leave with the best clothes they had. They would wear them because they had nothing else and the clothes helped them feel connected to their lost life. They looked regal in their beautiful silks. They were on the road into the mountains because that was the safest place to be.

So many of the people had eye injuries, and Wyatt and his team took care of everyone they possibly could. They handed out food and bottles of water and soon emptied the boxes of supplies. The team went back to the tent, thankful that it was downhill after such a tiring hike.

They all got something to eat and one of the doctors came up to Wyatt. "Hey, doc, could you hang out here for a few minutes? I want to go over a strategy for tomorrow morning."

"Sure, Sydney. I'd be happy to." Wyatt looked at Rebecca and she nodded with understanding.

Rebecca turned to Justin, one of the nurses, and asked, "Is there any body lotion here that I can use? My skin is so dry from the dirt and dust and the constant hand washing."

"Of course, Rebecca." He took a couple of travel-size bottles from a basket and handed them to her.

"Here you go."

"Thanks, Justin. You're a life saver." She clutched her treasure and she left the tent.

Twenty-Four

Rebecca had almost finished putting lotion on her legs, lost in the thoughts of the day, when she heard the door open. Wyatt stepped inside and just stood there, his gaze soft as he watched her. His eyes followed her legs from her slender ankles to the gentle swell of her calves, up to the fabric of the boxers that covered the triangle of her sex. She was still for a moment as she felt the color rush to her cheeks. She lowered her eyes, rubbing the top of her thigh with the last dab of lotion. Wyatt went to his cot and got out of his clothes. He glanced at Rebecca as she bent over her cot to fold the blanket down.

In an instant, Wyatt came up behind her and pulled the boxers down. She stepped out of them and he drew her back to lean against him. She settled against his length, resting her head against his chest and wriggling her ass against his crotch. He suddenly grabbed her wrists and pulled her arms over her head, pressing her up against the wall of the tent. He nudged her legs apart with his muscled thigh and swiftly entered her. Bending his knees for leverage, he thrust deeper into her. Again, and again, selfishly wanting his own release. Rebecca was riding her own wave, matching his rhythm, tilting her hips to better accommodate him. He plunged deep, pulsating and then exploding inside her. She felt her own contractions around his cock, holding him in, milking his length. Wyatt wrapped his arms tight around her, holding her close until their spasms were over.

The sense of urgency had pervaded their lives, each one knowing this might come to an end at any moment. They never spoke of it, not wanting to give words to their fears. But, they should have had the foresight to do just that.

Twenty-Five

Wyatt had to go to a small settlement in the hills with three other doctors and two technicians. They had received word that several dozen people had sight-threatening injuries and were unable to travel down to the city. He asked Rebecca to stay back at the tent and help since they would be short-staffed. She agreed and was busy gathering up instruments to sterilize them when she caught a flash of bright color in the doorway. It was Vyshali. Rebecca rushed to her and held her in a tight embrace.

"It's so good to see you. Are you alright? How is Priya?"

"We are good, Rebecca. I have great news. Paul arranged for us to have transport out of here. We can go home now!"

Rebecca was stunned. It seemed to happen so soon. She wasn't ready to leave the clinic, to leave Wyatt. But she knew she had to go. Rebecca had promised Senator Michaels she would take care of Vyshali. Even though both she and Priya had urged her to stay with Wyatt the day of the earthquake, she had felt uneasy about it. Rebecca knew she could never allow Vyshali to travel home alone. She would never forgive herself if anything happened to her.

"When, Vyshali? How much time do I have?" Rebecca thought about Wyatt being gone for the next several hours. She didn't want to leave without saying good-bye and making plans to be together when they were home.

"There will be a small helicopter dropping supplies into some remote areas. They will pick us up on the other side of this medical camp where they are building the new water plant. They said they will take us to the airport in Delhi but we must go at once. I've brought our overnight cases from the house." A shadow of sadness passed across Vyshali's eyes at the mention of the home she would never see again.

"I have to stop at Wyatt's and grab my things."

"Okay, but please, we need to hurry. They won't wait long for us."

Rebecca picked up the cases and ran to the tent leaving Vyshali scurrying behind. She quickly gathered her few belongings and shoved them into the backpack. She looked around, tears stinging her sad, blue eyes.

"Hurry, Rebecca, I hear the helicopter! We have to go now!" Vyshali cried.

Rebecca walked out of the tent and let the door slam shut behind her.

Twenty-Six

The trip home seemed longer and was more tiring than when they had first come to Nepal. On the plane from Delhi, Vyshali told Rebecca about the last few days.

"The Red Cross took care of my aunt and uncle. They got their bodies and sent them to the temple that was set up to take the dead. The usual rituals were not adhered to because there were so many of them. The bodies were cremated in groups and the relatives were not allowed to attend. The potential for disease was too great and would be devastating for those who survived the earthquakes."

Rebecca noticed that Vyshali was talking as if she were discussing strangers. She made sure to not interrupt or interject any words of sympathy. Poor Vyshali needed to get through this in her own way.

"Priya and I went to a large homeless camp a couple of miles from you. We sheltered with friends and helped the injured at the Doctors Without Borders tent on the west side. There was also a Red Cross tent set up identical to the one on the east side. I was able to contact Paul the day after the earthquake to assure him we were alive and unharmed. He immediately set out to find a way to get us home. It took a couple days to make the arrangements, a lot of red tape had to be cut, but here we are."

Rebecca placed her hand over Vyshali's and patted it tenderly.

"What about you, Rebecca? What have you been doing? How is Imay?"

Rebecca took a deep breath and gave the condensed version of her story, leaving out the worst parts of her days and recounting the successes.

"It will be several more days before we know if Imay will be able to see. He is living with his parents in a tent next to the clinic along with another family with an injured boy. Wyatt is an amazing doctor. He and his team see hundreds of patients a day. They work so hard..." Rebecca's voice trailed off. Vyshali rested her hand on Rebecca's arm, understanding more than what was being said.

The two women relaxed back into their seats. Each one had her own thoughts and memories to deal with. The plane engines' hum lulled them to sleep.

Twenty-Seven

As they came off the jetway in D.C., Senator Paul Michaels was there to greet them. They had been gone about such a long time and the toll of separation was etched on his face. He clung to Vyshali for several minutes, not wanting to let her go. He turned his head to Rebecca.

"How can I ever thank you for taking care of my wife? This was above and beyond anything I ever expected. I am forever in your debt. Thank you seems so inadequate."

He let go of Vyshali long enough to give Rebecca a hug. This time, Rebecca allowed herself to hug him back.

A valet came up to the Senator. "Sir? Your car is waiting outside the terminal. I'll take care of the bags."

Senator Michaels draped his left arm over Vyshali's shoulder and took Rebecca's hand in his right. His joy at this moment was boundless.

They drove to Anacostia first. The driver got out, took the overnight case and backpack from the trunk, and insisted on taking them up to Rebecca's apartment for her. After she opened the door, he set them inside and took her hand.

"Miss? Thank you for bringing Mrs. Michaels back to us safely."

"You're very welcome, Terrence. Have a good night."

"Good-night, Miss."

161

Twenty-Eight

Rebecca wandered aimlessly around her apartment, touching this, moving that, fluffing the pillows on the sofa, re-folding the throw on the back of the chair. She checked to see if there was a cold drink in the refrigerator. A lemon-flavored water sounded good to her. She took several sips, enjoying the feel of the cold liquid flowing down her throat. Rebecca went into her bedroom and stripped out of her clothes. She slid between the soft cotton sheets covering her queen bed. It was good to be home, but she was so sad to not be in a tent in Nepal with Wyatt. Thoughts of him danced playfully in her mind just before she drifted off into a dreamless sleep.

Even though Senator Michaels told her to take a few days off, Rebecca needed to go into the office. She swept her hair up on top of her head and secured it with a comb. A dark green skirt and cream-colored silk blouse suited her for today. She slipped into her black flats, took a quick look in the mirror, and went downstairs to wait for the car to take her to D.C.

Rebecca surprised everyone when she walked through the doors at 8:00 sharp. She gathered the staff so she would only have to tell her story once. She was brief and to the point, leaving out many details, of course. She answered a few questions and then declared it was time to get to work.

Rebecca's secretary, Jeannie, a pretty young brown-haired girl, sat down in her chair and waited for instructions.

"Jeannie? I need you to try and reach the Red Cross emergency tent in Kathmandu. It is imperative that I get a message to Dr. Wyatt Benjamin as soon as possible."

"Isn't he the doctor Senator Michaels' wife asked us to reference regarding the appropriation of funds?"

Rebecca was taken by surprise. "Yes. That's right. Please try to reach them immediately. This really can't wait."

"Of course, Rebecca. I'll get right on it."

"Thank you, Jeannie." Rebecca went into her office and closed the door. She had no idea Vyshali had mentioned Wyatt to Senator Michaels.

Rebecca needed to talk to Wyatt, to explain why she left so suddenly. *If it wasn't for Vyshali, I would have stayed with you. Surely the clinic staff told you about the lady who came to the tent that morning. They told you about the helicopter, right?*

Perhaps it was because of her time in Nepal, her new awareness of eye care, that Rebecca decided to call her eye doctor and make an appointment. She had been having trouble reading and realized her arms were just not long enough. She was in luck. He had had a cancellation and was able to fit her in at 3:00.

Jeannie was having no luck reaching the Red Cross and Rebecca was getting nervous. It had only been a few days since she had seen him go into the hillside, but it felt like an eternity.

The stacks of papers on her light oak desk had been arranged according to priority. Rebecca started to go through them but she couldn't concentrate. She decided to leave early for her appointment.

"Jeannie? I'm going to leave now for my 3:00. Please keep trying to reach them."

"Of course, Rebecca. I'll call you as soon as I make a connection."

"Thanks. I'll see you tomorrow."

In the waiting room, Rebecca picked up an issue of *Cataract and Refractive Surgery Today* and flipped through the pages. She was surprised to see there was an article about the *"Himalayan Cataract Project"*. She scanned the article looking for Wyatt's name. She turned the page and there he was. Dr. Wyatt Benjamin. With his wife Caroline and their fourteen-year-old son Jack.

Twenty-Nine

"What the fuck? He's married?" Rebecca practically shouted in anger.

She got to her feet, shaking with disbelief. She thought back over the time they had spent together. They never talked about anything personal, really. There was never time. She hadn't told him what she did. Their days were filled with tragedy, hard work, and the sensual pleasure of each other's bodies. They never spoke of home. Still, he should have told her he was married. If she had known, she never would have fallen in love with him.

Rebecca left her appointment with a prescription for reading glasses. Her thoughts kept going back to Wyatt. Married, for fuck's sake. She hated to think he had used her to satisfy his own needs. That just didn't sound like him. Although, clearly, she had no idea who he really was after such a short time.

She went back to the office and placed both her hands on Jeannie's desk.

"You can stop trying to reach the Red Cross. I don't need to get a message to Dr. Benjamin after all."

Rebecca turned and walked out, leaving her bewildered secretary staring after her.

Thirty

Rebecca settled into her work. Senator Michaels had given an impassioned speech on the floor of the Senate following the second earthquake in Nepal. The proposal for relief funds had been approved by a unanimous vote. Rebecca was asked to chair the Kathmandu Relief Fund Distribution Committee and she accepted without hesitation.

The papers on her desk dwindled as the days went by. Late nights and early mornings became her new normal routine. The beautiful, oversized, light-blue sofa in her office became her bed many nights during those first few weeks back in Washington.

There was a lot of excitement around the 2016 election next year. Many names were being floated as possible candidates for president. The hope was for a flip of the congressional majority to blue as well as a continuation of a democratic presidency. That would keep the country on its forward path and ensure a continued implementation of the current president's agenda.

Wyatt faded from Rebecca's day to day life, but her nights still brought him into sharp focus. The hurt and anger had dulled but the loneliness and ache from wanting him had not. Perhaps with more time they would.

Thirty-One

The election did not go as the Senator's office staff had hoped. In general, across the country, there was a lot of disbelief surrounding the electoral process. The new president was making questionable choices for cabinet posts and to staff his administration. Rebecca didn't have a lot of free time to dwell on what might have been with a different election outcome. The glass ceiling remained intact. It was even more difficult being in the minority in this partisan Congress, but Senator Michaels continued to serve with honor and dignity. Almost a full year in and it seemed to have only become worse.

Everyone in the office was looking forward to the 2017-2018 holiday recess. Rebecca decided to stay in D.C., relax, read some books and binge-watch a couple of TV series that she had not been able to watch during the year. One day in early January, Rebecca's phone rang. She looked at the caller ID and was surprised to see it was Senator Michaels.

"Good morning, Senator. Happy new year! How was your Christmas?" There was a long pause.

"Rebecca? It's Vyshali."

"Vyshali, what's wrong?" Rebecca heard the concern in her voice.

"Paul has been ill, Rebecca. He came down with pneumonia shortly after coming home to Colorado and is not recuperating as fast as he should."

"Oh, my gosh, Vyshali. I'm so sorry."

"He will be returning to Washington when the session begins next week. Rebecca? He doesn't look well. I wanted to tell you so you would be prepared. You are very special to both of us." Vyshali's voice broke.

"Vyshali, my dear friend, thank you so much for calling me."

"I need to go, Rebecca. Good-bye."

"Good-bye, Vyshali. Give my best to Senator Michaels."

Rebecca stood staring at the phone. She was so upset by this news. Senator Michaels had never been really sick in all the years she had known him. The fighting in Congress had become difficult for him and he had been looking tired, but still, this was so unexpected.

The following Wednesday Rebecca went into the office. She was looking forward to getting back to work after the long break. She loved the structure and sense of accomplishment the Senate provided her. When she opened the door, she was not surprised to see her secretary already at her desk working. Rebecca smiled at the brown-haired younger version of herself.

"Good morning, Jeannie! How were your holidays?"

"Hi, Rebecca. They were really great. I went home to Blacksburg and caught up with my friends from Virginia Tech. How about you?"

"It was a quiet break, very relaxing. Jeannie? The Senator is going to be coming in later today…"

"He's already here, Rebecca," Jeannie interrupted. "He asked me to send you in as soon as you got here."

"Really? My, gosh. I didn't expect him to come in this early. Thanks, Jeannie."

Rebecca walked down the hall to his office. She hesitated a moment, staring at his door. She wanted to prepare herself for what she would see. She took a deep breath and knocked.

"Come on in, Rebecca."

"Hi, Senator Michaels. How are you feeling?" Rebecca started towards his desk as he stood up.

"He's doing fairly well."

Rebecca stopped and turned around at the voice behind her. She hurried into the open arms of Vyshali Michaels.

"Vyshali! I had no idea you were coming to D.C. It's wonderful to see you!"

The Senator came over and embraced them both. He truly adored these women.

"Ladies, please have a seat." He motioned for them to sit on the burgundy leather couch. He perched himself on the corner of his mahogany desk opposite them and said, "Rebecca? I'm leaving the Senate. You know how difficult these last few years have been for me. I'm worn out and I need to make a new path, one that includes spending more time with Vyshali."

"I completely understand, Senator. How…"

He raised his hand to stop her. "There's more. I want you to take over my Senate seat."

"You want…but I…are you…" Rebecca stammered, unable to form a complete sentence.

"I already contacted the Democratic National Committee chair in Denver, Mary Ellen Moore, and told her my intentions. Her exact response was, 'if Rebecca Andrews wants to run, we will certainly back her. She's a perfect choice.' You are a perfect choice, Rebecca. Please say yes."

Rebecca turned and looked into the soft, dark eyes of the only person who had an understanding of what had happened in Kathandu.

"Yes, my dear, you are perfect for this. You need time to be sure, but please, don't take too long to decide." Vyshali patted Rebecca's hand.

Thirty-Two

Mary Ellen Moore called Rebecca in early February. After talking about the nuts and bolts of a short campaign, the rallies, the interviews, and the special election itself, the conversation became personal.

"Is there anything in your past, or present, that can derail you? Any personal identifying that needs to be addressed? Any past lovers that need to be brought into the light? Anything at all?" Mary Ellen was professional, but inquisitive.

"Yes, there is," Rebecca said quietly. "I need to reach out to someone. I'll definitely give you my decision in a day or two."

After she hung up with Mary Ellen, Rebecca went out to talk to Jeannie.

"Would you please find a phone number for Dr. Wyatt Benjamin? It's important."

Again, Rebecca had caught her by surprise. A quick Google search brought up his website with two numbers listed. One was the office number and the other was probably his cell phone. Rebecca went back into her office and called the cell number from her iPhone, hardening her resolve for when he answered. It went straight to voice mail.

She cleared her throat. "Wyatt, this is Rebecca Andrews. I'm going to be running for Senator in a special election in November. I thought you should know because Nepal might become an issue." She hung up without even saying good-bye. Her hands were shaking as she set the phone on her desk.

Rebecca saw that Wyatt had tried to call her several times but she did not want to talk to him. He sent her a text message later in the day.

Hi, Rebecca. It is wonderful to hear from you. It's okay if everyone knows about Nepal. I will be in D.C. for a long weekend the end of February. Will you meet me?

Rebecca replied with a single word.

Yes

Rebecca placed a call to Mary Ellen Moore the next morning. "Good morning, Ms. Moore. Yes. I would love to run for Senator of Colorado."

Thirty-Three

The last Friday in February, Rebecca came out of her office shortly after lunch. "Jeannie? Dr. Benjamin will be arriving at 2:00 for a meeting in my office. Please show him in when he gets here."

A quizzical look came over Jeannie's face. "Of course, Rebecca."

Rebecca was nervous, her usual all-business manner threatening to abandon her. The time was going by painfully slow. At 1:45 Jeannie texted her that the doctor just walked in. Rebecca smoothed down her skirt and went to the door, hesitating a moment before she swung it open.

"Dr. Benjamin. How nice to see you. Please come in." She hoped there was no emotion in her words.

Wyatt stepped inside and Rebecca closed the door behind him, catching a glimpse of Jeannie with her mouth hanging open. Wyatt was dressed in a perfectly tailored navy-blue two-piece suit, a white cuffed shirt, and blue and white diamond-patterned tie. His hair was still worn long to his shoulders and his steel blue gaze bore into her. Without even thinking, she reached out and raked his hair away from his forehead. She stepped back from him and retreated to safety with her desk between them.

"Wyatt, please have a seat." Rebecca kept her voice formal and neutral. It was important that she not let her emotions intrude.

Wyatt stood by the white leather armchair in front of Rebecca's desk. "Please. After you." She remained standing. Wyatt looked confused by her cold reception. She was glaring at him.

Suddenly, her hands pounded her desk. "You're married!" she said accusingly.

"What? No. I'm not, Rebecca. I'm not married. And I wasn't married when we were together in Nepal." Wyatt's voice was firm.

Rebecca was reeling. *Why was he lying to her?* "I read about you. You are married, and you have a son."

"Was, Rebecca. Was married. And did have a son." Wyatt's voice had dropped low, a look of anguish crossed his face. "I can explain. Please. Let me explain."

Rebecca had to sit down. She was afraid her legs would fail her. She stared at him as he started to speak.

Thirty-Four

"My wife Caroline and I got a divorce in 2013 after fifteen years of marriage. She couldn't get used to being second to my career. Even after our son Jack was born, she was still lonely. My ophthalmology practice and professorship took up so much of my time. It was too much for her. There were no arguments, no slamming doors, just a cold silence between us for many years. We stayed together for Jack's sake, but eventually even he had had enough. He encouraged us to get a divorce. I moved out right after Christmas that year. Caroline liked the prestige of being Mrs. Dr. Wyatt Benjamin and she kept the name. She and Jack stayed in the house in lower Haight and I got an apartment near the University of San Francisco campus. We shared custody of Jack. The arrangement was perfect for us."

Wyatt stopped talking and took a deep breath. He looked over at Rebecca and she nodded her head for him to continue.

"After you left Nepal, I made arrangements to fly home. I knew you had come back with your friend, Vyshali, but you had never told me who she was, or even who you were. There just wasn't enough time. We never took the time."

Wyatt grew quiet again. He closed his eyes and gave a slight shake of his head.

"The day I arrived home in California, that very same day, Caroline and Jack were killed instantly in a car accident. I lost my boy."

Rebecca drew in a sharp breath. Tears pooled in her eyes and spilled over onto her cheeks. She sat motionless.

"After the funerals, I went back to Kathmandu. They still needed my help there. After a few months, the Doctors Without Borders team left the area, and I was adrift. I kept myself busy with my work, giving lectures around the world and going to conventions. I traveled often to Tibet, for months on end, working with the project and teaching others how to do cataract surgery. I turned my practice over to my partner so I could be gone indefinitely. Helping others kept me from sinking."

Wyatt had been pacing the floor like a caged tiger. He now gripped the back of the chair and hung his head. Rebecca's heart was breaking for him.

Rising slowly, she came from behind her desk and circled her arms around him. She leaned her cheek against his back and hugged him close. She had been so wrong about him. If she had only known.

Wyatt turned around and pulled her hard against him. His lips brushed over hers, tentative, searching, waiting for her. Rebecca's response to him was quick in coming. She tasted the moist sweetness of his lips and pressed against them with her tongue. He opened for her and she touched the grainy firmness of his tongue.

Wyatt pulled away from her. "Becky, darlin', please understand me. There has been no one else since you and there will never be anyone else. I love you."

Wyatt's words were like a cooling salve taking all the remaining hurt away. They held each other for several minutes, reconnecting, and she felt the last three years fall away.

The ping of Rebecca's iPhone intruded. Reluctantly she turned from him and checked her message.

"I'm so sorry, Wyatt. I have an important meeting in the Senator's office. Can you stay until I get back?"

Wyatt checked his watch. "No. I have to get back to the convention center and attend to some last-minute details for tonight's session."

Rebecca was disappointed. "Wyatt, I want to see you later. Would that be possible?"

"There's a dinner at 6:00 followed by talks from several speakers. I can probably slip out about 9:00. Where can I meet you?"

She heard and felt the familiar urgency entering their lives again.

"I'll text you my address. It's not far from your hotel."

Rebecca's hands were shaking as she typed it in. "I have to go. I'm so sorry, Wyatt. Sorry for so many things." She went up on tiptoes and kissed him good-bye. "Jeannie will show you out."

She turned and left the room, happier than she had been in years.

Thirty-Five

It was almost 9:30 when Rebecca heard the knock at her door. She answered it wearing a jade green t-shirt and blue jeans. His smile of appreciation assured her she had made the right decision. Wyatt had taken time to change out of his suit and had on jeans, a white long-sleeved pullover shirt and carried a jacket over his arm. As soon as Rebecca closed the door, he kicked off his shoes, tossed the jacket aside and scooped her into his arms.

"Darlin', I missed you so much." His voice was husky and full of emotion.

"I missed you, too, Wyatt. You have no idea how much."

He clasped his hands behind her back and pulled her against him. She could feel his erection, already insistent against her belly. She took hold of his belt and backed up into her bedroom, pulling him along with her, their eyes locked on each other. Slowly, Wyatt undid the button and zipper on Rebecca's jeans. He peeled them down her hips and off her legs, revealing pink lace panties.

"No boxers?" he said in mock surprise.

"No boxers. I hope you don't mind." Her mouth turned up in a shy smile.

"It really doesn't matter, Becky. You won't be wearing them long."

Wyatt knelt down and opened his mouth against the lace, breathing hot against her mound. He soaked the material as he licked her through it, using his tongue to push the edges between her lips. Rebecca placed her hands on his head for support and stepped her feet apart. Wyatt grabbed her ass and nestled his face under her, tensing his tongue and dragging it through her folds. She was so wet and tasted so sweet. Rebecca rocked against him as his tongue found her opening and made its way inside her. He felt her tremble, familiar with the path her orgasms usually take. He took her clit between his fingers, exerting pressure. She curled her fingers into his hair and she came for him, shuddering and bearing down against him. He moved his hands to cup her bottom and held her to his mouth until it was over. He slowly drew the panties down away from her sensitive nub and tossed them aside. He stood up and looked at her in wonder. He had never felt such a climax from her before. There was a look of pure joy on her face. He kissed her tenderly, holding her tight until he could feel her breathing return to normal.

"Wyatt, that was incredible," she whispered. "Thank you for loving me."

"My pleasure, Becky. I've only just begun," he promised her.

They made love long into the night until exhaustion claimed them.

Thirty-Six

Waking up late was a rare treat for both of them. Today there were no early meetings, no patients, there was no urgency. Wyatt didn't have to be back to the convention center until 5:00. Rebecca had shopped the day before and bought eggs, Canadian bacon, and a couple of whole wheat bagels and cream cheese. While Wyatt showered, she scrambled some eggs, put a hazelnut coffee pod in the Keurig, and heated the ham. She set the food on the coffee table and raised it up to make it dining height just as Wyatt came into the living room.

"It smells great in here. Thanks for making breakfast for us." He gave Rebecca a sweet kiss and they sat on her sofa to enjoy their meal.

Quietly they talked about Jack. Wyatt was so relieved to be able to talk freely, without hiding his emotions as he had with his colleagues. He was finally able to cry, and be angry, and admit he failed both Jack and his wife by not living his life with them with purpose. He had taken them for granted, assuming they would always be waiting for him when he came home. And when they were no longer together, he hadn't made enough of an effort to spend more time with Jack. If he had only seen how important it was, things might have turned out differently.

It was such a beautiful morning they decided to take a walk around Anacostia Park. There was a little chill in the air and the sun was shining in the cloudless sky. The geese honked and splashed in the cold water as Wyatt and Rebecca strolled by, arm in arm, talking, laughing, kissing. They had started as lovers and now they were becoming the best of friends.

They passed a couple of young boys sitting on the ground playing on their phones. Rebecca turned to Wyatt. "How is Imay? Did he get his sight back?"

Wyatt led her over to a black iron and wood park bench. "I have no idea, Becky. When I went back to Kathmandu after the funerals, he and his family were gone. The tent they had been staying in had other people in it. I asked around but no one knew where they went."

"Well, Dr. Benjamin, you are a brilliant surgeon," Rebecca said with a hint of sarcasm. "I'm sure he is doing great."

"I hope so." He pulled her close to him and kissed the top of her head.

They sat for a while and watched the people around them hurrying by.

"They need to slow down and enjoy their life," Rebecca said with the wisdom gained from knowing.

Wyatt kissed the top of her hand. "Darlin', one day they'll see."

Thirty-Seven

Rebecca met Wyatt in the lobby of The Courtyard Washington Convention Center. She loved this old stone building with its rows of tall arched windows. It had once been a bank and still had much of the architectural features of the past. The décor was more practical than elegant, but it was stunning.

"My God, Rebecca. You are gorgeous," he exclaimed as he kissed her on the cheek. "That little red dress is beautiful."

"Thank you. Although I love you in scrubs, this black suit is perfect on you," she said as she slipped her arm through his.

He took her overnight bag from her and gave it to the concierge to put in his suite and escorted her to the dinner meeting. They sat at a table in the back of the room and enjoyed a meal of herb roasted chicken, twice-baked potato and buttered broccoli.

"I have to excuse myself and go up on stage. I'm the announcer for tonight's speakers," Wyatt said as he stood up. "Maybe they'll talk fast!"

"I'm really looking forward to the talks, Wyatt," Rebecca said. "I want to learn more about what you do."

Wyatt kissed her hand and walked to the front of the hall. One by one he introduced the speakers, listened intently to their talks, and politely applauded when they were finished. His speech was the last one of the night. Wyatt's powerful voice was full of passion for his profession. He conveyed with eloquence how he felt about giving the gift of sight to those who thought they would never see again. He encouraged everyone present to find their own way to give back to their community, and the world, in whatever way they could. His words were met with thunderous applause. Wyatt came back to their table as the desserts were being served. He had a huge grin on his face. He loved his work and these meetings really invigorated him. He held out his hand to her.

"Shall we?" he asked as he brought her to her feet.

"Of course," Rebecca answered with a half-smile. "I take it you want dessert in the suite?"

The elevator took them to the eighth floor. Wyatt slid the key card into the slot and opened the double doors.

"This is lovely," Rebecca said as she crossed the living room to the sliding glass doors.

Wyatt leaned against the doorframe to the bedroom. "Would you like to sit out on the balcony?"

"No, not really. I've never seen the city from this point of view. It really is beautiful."

"There are cold drinks in the refrigerator in the kitchenette. I'm going to take a quick shower."

Wyatt went into the bedroom and noticed the down comforter on the king-sized bed had been turned down for the night. Rebecca's overnight bag was on the luggage rack with a fresh terrycloth bathrobe folded on top of it. He kicked off his shoes, took off his socks, and tossed his suit jacket on the chair next to the bed.

The white marble bathroom had a large shower and Wyatt reached in to start the water. When he turned around, Rebecca was standing there, comfortable in her own skin and displaying every inch of it. He unbuttoned his shirt and tossed it aside. He had started to unbuckled his belt when Rebecca knelt in front of him. She undid the button and zipper on his pants and slid them down and off his legs. Taking his cock into her hands, she slowly stroked the smooth skin. He marveled at how quickly she was able to arouse him. Wyatt reached down and raised Rebecca up into his arms. He sought her lips and hungrily took possession of them. He moved his mouth over the red lipsticked surface, tasting, then separating her lips with his tongue, insistent, demanding. He opened the glass doors to the shower and pulled her in with him. Carefully, he lifted her and placed her over his erection. She wrapped her arms around his neck and his hands went to her ass to hold her against him. As he started thrusting, she rose and settled on his cock. He could feel her tighten around him as he buried himself deep inside her. With a matched rhythm they moved in this watery cocoon.

"Oh, Becky," Wyatt gasped. He held her still as he shuddered through his climax. "I'm sorry, darlin'. I didn't wait for you."

"It's okay, my sweet. We have all night."

Sunday was another dazzlingly bright, crisp day. The crumpled linens and disarrayed pillows gave testament to the night before.

Rebecca and Wyatt, complete in their love, got up to welcome the morning. It was already late and rather than calling for room service, they decided to walk down F Street to the Founding Fathers Restaurant for brunch. They enjoyed their waffles with maple cinnamon syrup, scrambled eggs and applewood smoked bacon as they talked about their early lives, their families, their hopes and dreams for the future. They were so thankful for this unhurried time to get to know each other without any intrusions. They walked for blocks, sightseeing, window shopping and wandering quietly, hand in hand, through the rooms of the National Gallery of Art. It was almost 6:00 when they got back to the suite. While Wyatt started packing to go to San Francisco, Rebecca ordered room service from the Gordon Biersch Brewery Restaurant. They shared a meal of blue crab and artichoke dip with crostini, top sirloin steak with jasmine rice and fresh strawberries. They sat at the table on the balcony, looking out at the city Rebecca loved so much. Wyatt had arranged for two cars, one to take Rebecca home and the other to take him to Reagan National Airport. They said their good-byes in the privacy of his suite. Rebecca's tear-filled eyes tugged at Wyatt's heart as he kissed her forehead, her eyes, the tip of her nose and her quivering lips.

"This will be a very short separation, darlin', I promise."

"I'm going to miss you so much. These days have been so wonderful. I wish they didn't have to end."

"Becky, we will make this work. Email me your itinerary for your trips to Colorado. I will coordinate them with my schedule."

"Wyatt?" Rebecca's voice was unwavering. "Whatever I can have of you will be enough."

"I love you, my darlin' Becky."

The knock at the door startled her. Wyatt opened it for the valet.

"The cars are downstairs waiting to take you to your destinations." He took their bags and they crossed the hall to the elevator.

Thirty-Eight

April 7th was the first opportunity Rebecca had to hold a rally. The sky was a pale robin's egg blue with a few fluffy clouds dotted in, and the mountains displayed their shimmering snow-covered peaks. Rebecca took the stage in Civic Park in downtown Denver, across from the Capitol building. Colorado had never elected a woman Senator and she was determined to shatter that particular glass ceiling. The sound system was checked and Rebecca stepped to the podium. A journalist from the local magazine *5280* was waving his hand frantically a few rows back from the stage.

"My gosh! You sure are eager. Go ahead and asked your question."

"Why have you never been married? Why have you never been romantically linked with anyone? What are you hiding from us?"

The questions were rude and accusatory, but not unexpected. Rebecca took a sip of water to clear her throat. She decided now was the time to get out in front of the story she knew the media was sure to uncover.

"In 2005, a #MeToo moment in left me traumatized and distrustful of men. I didn't want to date for a long time after it happened. The man has since passed and I see no reason to name him and upset those who loved and cared for him. I wish that I had had the foresight to realize how important it was that I speak up at the time it happened. I wasn't strong enough back then, but I am now. I will champion any woman or man who has had to endure unwanted advances and sexual exploitation."

The crowd cheered, and Rebecca knew she had made the right decision. When the applause died down, she continued.

"Three years ago, there were two devastating earthquakes in Nepal. They struck about two and a half weeks apart. I was there when the second one hit."

Before she could go any further, there was a commotion in the crowd. A tall, good-looking man, dressed in a pair of tight jeans and a white long-sleeved shirt, made his way to the stage. With a smile, Rebecca moved a step to the side as he took the podium.

"I'm Wyatt Benjamin. I fell in love with Rebecca Andrews in Kathmandu, and I love her still."

His voice was deep and rich. She had heard it giving orders which brooked no argument. She had heard it in laughter and passion and intimacy. Now she listened as he spoke to the crowd, telling of their encounter in Nepal, without apology, without excuses. She watched him with love and admiration as he shared their story, only omitting the most intimate of details. When he was finished, she reached out to him and raked her fingers through his hair. He kissed her tenderly and her supporters in the audience roared their approval.

Thirty-Nine

Wyatt was able to see Rebecca again in mid-July for another rally in Colorado Springs. He had caught an early flight and Rebecca was waiting for him at the airport. Wyatt gave her a hug and a quick kiss.

"You look beautiful, Becky. What's with the hat?"

"You'll see." She linked her arm with his and they went to the parking lot.

At the end of the first row, a shiny, black 1965 Mustang convertible gleamed in the morning sun.

"Wow! That is a sweet ride."

Rebecca laughed and dangled the keys in front of him. "Would you like to drive?"

"Are you kidding? This is great!" he snatched the keys from her and opened the passenger door for her. He went around to the driver's side and slid behind the wheel. "This is perfect, Becky. Let's go!"

Pike's Peak was visible on the Front Range of the Rockies as they drove to the Garden of the Gods Park. The road wound through red sandstone rocks of every imaginable shape and size.

"Wyatt. Look over there to your left. See that large rock balancing on a single point? Isn't it amazing that it doesn't tip over?"

"That's incredible. Oh, look down there. It looks like a giant decided to play chess with those rocks shaped like pawns."

Around every curve there were flowering bushes and trees that were growing out of the rocks, defying the laws of nature.

They spent the morning sight-seeing and stopped for a quick lunch at a roadside café. The rally was at 2:00 and Rebecca was eager to get there.

The Colorado Springs Event Center was not an easy venue for a Democrat. This area was solidly Republican, and Rebecca was determined to win them over. There were a lot of protestors outside the arena when Wyatt pulled the Mustang into the VIP parking lot. They were loud, but they were orderly and didn't cause any trouble. Rebecca was prepared and capable and received enthusiastic support inside. In all, she felt like it was a successful event.

Wyatt whisked Rebecca away to the Broadmoor, one of America's most famous resort hotels. The Broadmoor's original building was constructed in 1918 at the base of Cheyenne Mountain. It was painted a muted pink to blend with the surrounding mountains. Additional buildings were built over the years and they all connected in a semi-circle around Cheyenne Lake. It was an elegant resort, patterned after European hotels.

Rebecca loved the high ceilings in her luxury suite. Wyatt opened the sage green framed French doors to the balcony which had a curved iron railing on three sides. He looked out over the lake, watching the water sparkle in the late afternoon sun.

"Are you ready?" Wyatt turned to Rebecca. She had put on a black one-piece swimsuit cut high on the legs.

"Of course, I am!" Wyatt picked her up and laid her on the king-sized bed. He pushed the sage green and gold pillows onto the floor and started kissing her.

Rebecca giggled. "That's not what I meant! You need to get into your swim trunks. I reserved the spa for us for an hour, remember?"

Wyatt reluctantly got up and pulled Rebecca to her feet. "Do I need trunks?"

"Yes, you do."

They put on the Turkish cotton robes the hotel provided and went downstairs to the full-service spa. They sat in the warmth of the hot tub, allowing the therapeutic jets to ease the tensions of the day. They were thankful for the bubbles which hid their bodies from any attendants that might walk by. Rebecca's foot found Wyatt's cock, playfully teasing him and encouraging an erection. She pressed along his shaft, sliding up and down in a slow massage. She curled her toes over the tip and playfully pulsed it away from his body. Her impish smile brought a look of barely-contained lust to Wyatt's eyes.

"Becky, darlin, you might want to stop what you're doing. We could end up with a situation we would have a hard time explaining."

Rebecca laughed and suggested, "Perhaps we should go up to our room and finish this properly."

Wyatt nodded in agreement. "Just give me a couple minutes to compose myself."

Rebecca climbed the steps out of the spa and grabbed her robe. She turned to Wyatt and said, "I'll be waiting in our room. Hurry."

Forty

Rebecca returned to Colorado the Sunday before election night. It was cool that fourth day in November. The foothills had yet to have their first covering of snow for the season and were in sharp relief against the sky. It was so clear you could count eight ridges back from the front range. From her childhood until now, the only constant has been the majesty of the Rockies. Rebecca had told her campaign managers that she wanted to make one last, very important speech. It was early afternoon, and she was poised and confident as she stood at the podium at Clement Park in Littleton. It's a spacious area with ball fields, picnic pavilions, playgrounds and a man-made lake. The lawns were still a lush green and the aspens were showing off their gold leaves. Clement Park is on shared grounds with Columbine High School. The memorial to those slain was behind the stage. With a strong, unwavering voice, Rebecca reaffirmed her promise to do all she could to aid in the prevention of more mass murders in schools. Her speech concluded and she made her way to the white Chrysler 300 that was waiting to take her downtown to her hotel. She settled back against the soft, tan leather of the seat. She closed her eyes. *That's it. I hope it was enough.*

Forty-One

Election night and Rebecca took the stage in the ballroom of the famous Brown Palace Hotel in downtown Denver. Her blue eyes sparkled with excitement and her smile was radiant. She was ready to win this. Senator Paul Michaels was there with her, but Vyshali sent her regrets, and her best wishes. Wyatt was at Rebecca's side, his arm around her waist, holding her tight to him. All eyes were on the television monitors watching the final returns come in. Senator Michaels' phone rang. He turned the phone towards Wyatt and Rebecca and they could see Vyshali's smiling face. Rebecca was so happy she could be there, if only on Facetime.

Vyshali called to her. "Rebecca, look!" Vyshali turned her phone to a beautiful black-haired boy with a faded scar on his face.

"Rebecca! Dr. Benjamin! I can see you!" Imay declared. Rebecca and Wyatt were shocked and thrilled to see Imay, his eyes shining bright.

"May I have your phone, Senator? I want to take a closer look at him," Wyatt said. He took the phone and walked a few steps away.

"How did this happen? How did you find him?" Rebecca asked Senator Michaels.

"Vyshali could never stop thinking about Imay. After she heard that Wyatt couldn't find him, she was determined to. She has had people searching for him and his family for months," he explained. "They were located a week ago in Bhutan, a district to the east of Kathmandu. Vyshali flew there."

Wyatt brought the phone over to Rebecca. "Vyshali, Imay, you could not have given me a more precious gift," Rebecca cried.

Just then, Mary Ellen Moore stepped to the microphone. "Ladies and gentlemen. Our new Senator for the state of Colorado, Rebecca Andrews!" The crowd erupted in cheers, and balloons and confetti fell from the ceiling. Wyatt grabbed Rebecca and spun her in a circle.

"Congratulations, darlin'. I am so proud of you." He kissed her quickly and whispered, "We'll celebrate later, Senator Andrews."

Epilogue

Rebecca laid her hand gently against Wyatt's chest, feeling the steady rise and fall of his breathing. He raised his hand to capture her fingers, his hand warm and strong over hers. Beneath her palm she felt the beat of his heart increase its tempo. He took in a deep breath. "Touch me," he urged with an insistent whisper. She smoothed her hand over his rib cage, tracing each line that was formed, feeling the taut muscles. Ever lower she moved across his abdomen with a soft, exploring touch. He let out a soft moan.

"Becky, please!"

She straddled him, positioning herself over his erection and lowering herself onto him. He placed his hands on either side of her hips and held her down hard against him.

"Open your pretty eyes and look at me, darlin'." Rebecca smiled at this man who captured her heart with those words in Kathmandu and still held it. They enjoyed a slow, sensual journey, unhurried, uninterrupted, with no thoughts except the pleasure they gave to each other.

She shuddered through her climax and felt him release into her.

Wyatt pulled her close against his chest and the heated length of his body.

"No matter how busy we get, Mrs. Benjamin, never lose sight of my love," he whispered.

The End

A special acknowledgement to:

Ophthalmologists everywhere who give the gift of sight.

Himalayan Cataract Project
cureblindness.org

American Red Cross

Doctors Without Borders

THE SPINSTER OF INDIA

-A BOUNDLESS SHORT STORY-

HUNTER JAMES LUCK

-Dedicated to my Grandmother M.E.Giguere-
&
-Mother Terri E. Luck-

About the Author:

Just a young kid learning about life.
-Hunter James Luck

Chapter One

-Dante-

Enduring a life with adulation towards yourself and only yourself one would presume is an isolated, cold, and selfish life. Nevertheless, they would be mistaken. Only a fool would open up their being to another for the petty affiliation of love. Humanity is flawed; the corruption of betrayal easily manipulates us. It is in our innate instinct to destroy each other and take what is pure away from those who deem to be proper. For one to take a road that detaches from love is a higher level of righteousness. In doing so, they would save themselves from the pain of abortion and heartache when their so-called "love" reveals their authentic appearance.

- Spinster of India

Tangling vines draped across the sky of foliage as behemoth elephants ventured through the thickening jungle of India. Hunter green leaves scattered the forest's floor. Crackling blades terminated their existence under the hooves of the trotting elephants that passed through the shadows of sleeping trees.

To Dante, this part of the world was a cocoon, chlorophyll in color. He was used to the harsh winds and dry heat of his homeland. There, deserts of swallowing pits of quicksand devoured all life outside of his city.

It was a relief when he inherited news of Queen Babylon's diplomatic assignment. Out of her six ambassadors, he was always the first to volunteer. His penchant for travel over foreign seas and shores was a way for him to escape. He had no esteem for the barren badlands of the World's Middle (once known as the Middle East, but that name had been long misremembered), yet he was still loyal to the cathedra of his Queen.

As the Religious Crusade came to its end, the Babylonian Empire scrambled to attain new alliances. Jerusalem, another superpower of the New World, marked its gaze on the sinful and lustful nation of pleasure. Where no religion dwells, his homeland was open to any immoral wanderers. For an atheist empire like Babylon and a Hindu nation like India, they were beacons of defiance in the Pope's eyes.

Israel, newly formed into the superpower for Catholicism, will no longer stand for such insubordination. Therefore, as an ambassador of a corrupt government, Dante's task was simple. He had to make new allegiances for his nation, by any means necessary. For the wicked shall share a bed and sleep in death. Lost in thought, Dante was dragged back to the assignment at hand when his elephant abruptly halted.

"Easy Boy!" he said as he was knocked around.

The elephant let out a toot and began to drop a load before his widening watch. The manure skidded down its back leg like a caterpillar climbing down a tree. Oozing and rolling forth like a pus-like wound, the chunks of stern flopped to the ground.

Dante quickly pulled on the elephant's reins.

"No... Stop it, obese creature!"

His escorts from the port city of Surat, burst out in laughter. Shortly behind the hilarity, murmurs of sly jokes in a foreign language animated.

"What's so funny? An animal has to shit; it has to shit, right?" Dante looked around for an echo.

A woman in leather bands and silk pants called out to Dante.

"We laugh because your elephant is a girl. She... like you like to say... *shits* because she feels disrespected."

"Is that so?" Dante gazed down at the elephant's profile.

Her eye, large with a piercing glare, scowled back in agreement.

"Forgive me, little one."

He apologized before looking back at the woman who spoke. "So you commend the reins on this excursion?"

"I do. Does that surprise you?" She said as she redirected her gaze forward.

"Should it?"

"If it's because I'm a woman, then I am..."

"A woman? In this godless world, what does that have to do with anything?" Dante infringed. "Have you not heard of the transcendent nation of Babylon? A woman dictates it. Her merit eclipses all. So tell me why your genitalia has weight? Aren't I engaging with your ruler soon? If my readings were correct, *she* is of female sex is she not?"

Silence rode on the heels of the warrior.

The winds of the foreign sky swept through the thickening jungle of Banyan. For what might have been a few ticks on a sundial, seemed an eternity to Dante as he rode in stillness.

The warm breath of the decrepit elephants fumed Dante's nostrils and clouded his palate for fresh blossoms. Dante couldn't help but admire the woman's influential demeanor. That twinkle in her oculus as she spoke, that wry smile as she scorned him. Her long-braided hair as black as gloom and her fair brown complexion.

Midway in their journey, the warrior spoke once more.

"Godless world?"

Taking a few thoughts to understand if that question's intent was for him, or another, he pulled forth his prior conversation to memory and answered. "Forgive me; I meant no offense. It's just where I come; mankind governs this planet. Not a mythos of an age that has been long dead."

"Tell me, has your Queen just sent you here to dishonor our way of life or were you not sent here to be a diplomat in a time of war?"

"I'm sorry if transgression was taken. I meant no harm. Do not ask me to lie; our way of life is our way of life. I will not sugarcoat who we are. If your Queen is easily offended like you, then, by all means, I should turn around. There is no hope for our people after all." Dante stopped his elephant.

She looked down at Dante's waistband. Wrapped around his waist, a golden blade dangled in the light of the sun, its red gems flashed through the air. She gave the eye to her comrades.

"Let us hunt." She ordered as she dismounted.

In a session, her colleague of confidants detached from their rides and began to arm themselves with bows.

"As much as I would love to drown myself in your culture, I feel the Queen would be most displeased if my arrival was late," Dante said to the dictator.

"She would be provoked if we didn't come back with a trophy, young Dante." The devilish woman said.

"Who speaks to me?" Dante yearned for her name.

The combatant stepped into the thickening jungle with a spear in hand, vanishing from his gaze without a rebuttal. Alone in a barbaric jungle encompassed by seven elephants and enclosed by a growing stillness in the air, Dante dismounted and followed pursuit. Clutching the nearest spear, he entered the wilderness.

Growing thicker with every step, the jungle embraced his form. Mother Earth reached out with her twigs of fingers to caress the corners and crevices of his flesh. Twisting and coiling against his sharp jawline, her thorny nails drew blood.

The roar of the elephants sent shockwaves through the heavens. Turning in circles, he wandered farther into the remote evergreens.

Before his spying observation, a tiger as orange as the setting sun was hovering over the female warrior. As the man-eater's paws clasped the boulder he was perched upon; his drool began to downpour upon her physique.

She waved her spear tensely about the sky.

Before Dante was able to intervene, the tigress lunged forth, pawing away her weapon. The spear flung to the dirt and the cat pounced on top of her.

Rolling to her chest, the fighter tried to claw her way to her survival-tool. With momentum, the tiger dug its nails into her back, splitting skin from bone. She cried out in pain; the tiger cried out in heat.

Dante jumped to attacking position. He drew his spear, aimed and fired. With his athletic build, he sent ripples of pure energy through the air.

A wailing of unimaginable pain cascaded out of the tiger. Clawing and biting at the spear in its side, it turned its glower on Dante. Disarmed and defenseless, Dante dragged his feet backward, distancing himself from the demon.

The abnormality harvested its claws into the sand as fire began to awake in its peepers. The tiger looked at Dante's blade.

The tiger dashed towards him and pinned him against a tree. The daring warrior sprung to her feet, wrapped her finger around the handle of her spear and jabbed the tip of the spear into the heart of the beast. The battle was over before Dante was able to draw his blade.

The hunter became the hunted, the tiger-cat laid limp with tongue swaying in the gale.

Perspiration perforated from the skin of Dante as he knocked the feline to the floor. He moved quickly to the damsel in distress to aid any assistance to her, but she was fine. With his kind gesture, he only received a brush from her shoulder.

"I'm sorry, I just saved your life." he spat.

"More like you spoiled a good hunt," she pulled out a hidden blade from her belt, "And it was *I* who saved you. The heart of a tiger is worth more than any gold you can find, and you forced my hand. It's soiled now."

Dante couldn't help but grin as she reached for her spear, even though every part of him deemed she was a self-centered tyrant. Her demeanor and brass pulled forth a chemical reaction that molded within his stomach. An attraction formed at that moment.

"Why are you smiling, young Dante?"

"I just can't help but wonder your name."

"You almost got mauled to paradise by the king of the jungle, and you are still inquiring about my name?"

"I am afraid so."

"Clear that blush from your face; we have no time of this. The Queen awaits. We will take the tiger as our trophy; its meat shall not go to waste."

She whimpered in pain.

"Your back?"

"It's nothing. I will clean it after we get you to the Queen. Do as I say."

Dante said nothing; he followed suit.

As she guided him back to the elephants, he surveyed the claw marks on her back. Blood drained ever so slowly down her olive skin. *Drip. Drip. Drip.*

The repetition of the sound sent Dante into a hypnotic state of mind. He couldn't stop thinking about her, and how she aroused him. *This is not part of the mission* he said over and over to himself. *Don't involve your heart with a foreigner. Stay focused; your Queen depends on you.*

Traveling the remaining few miles to Amer Fort, the capital of India, Dante rode neck and neck with the woman who made butterflies dance in his breadbasket. Pondering over her dominance and not her beauty, he couldn't help but pry into her life. Dante was not blind to her grace, but the way she held her posture created a yearning inside of his soul.

"Tell me, warrior of the Queen, why does she title herself as The Spinster of India? Is she not fair like you? Does she shroud herself with robes of silk to cover her hag-ish complexion? Or does she prefer the company of her own sex?" Dante waited for an answer.

"In due time, all will come to light."

"Grant me this knowledge I need to know, for my Queen wishes me to woo her."

"Then woo if you must. Woo away."

"I fear it will be hard for me though..." Dante looked away.

"You are a charming man, I suppose. You have a jawline that lasts for days. Have no fear."

Dante didn't speak his mind. He didn't tell her what truly troubled him. He sat there in silence until Amer Fort arose from the jungle of Ranthambore. The forest was made small in the shadow of the enormous fort. Perching on top a large hill of stone the winding path was made clear to him.

"Incredible," he said to himself.

They rode their elephants across Maota Lake and up the ramparts of the palace. As Dante traveled over the cobbled paths and through a series of gates, he couldn't help but admire the artistic Hindu fashion elements carved into the construct.

In the eastern part of Rajasthan, Amer Fort endures as the capital of India. Erected out of crimson marble and sandstone, the opulent dwelling held an abundance of copiousness wealth. Even the Pope would sell a part of his soul to see an ounce of this palace. It's majestic carved paths led from one courtyard to the next. Four levels with four constructs stacked on top of one another as one makes their way to the summit.

In courtyard one, Diwan-i-Aam "Hall of Public Audience" stands welcoming the citizens of India. Built in the second courtyard, Diwan-i-Khas "Hall of Private Audience" is endorsed to overlook the plaza before. This was where Dante intended to meet the Queen.

Within the third gate and third courtyard, the gleaming Sheesh Mahal "Mirror Palace" reflects the light of the sun. Finally, at the pinnacle of the fort where the Queen rests her head, Sukh Niwas stood above all. With gusts sweeping transversely over cascades of water, a serene climate is artificially produced within the gardens of the palace.

Two imposing wooden doors, plated in gold, swung open as Dante arrived at the second plaza. The elephants trotted around in circles within the courtyard until they drew to a rest. Dismounting, the warrior flung to her feet, and began to unpack the tiger from the elephant. Dante descended to his heels and unstrapped his mount.

"This is where our paths diverge, young Dante." She said, looking over her shoulder.

"I will see you again, I will demand it of your Queen."

She grinned and departed. Dante scrutinized the crusted claw marks on her back.

After a few moments watching her wander off, he gathered his belonging. Two of his advocates detached a golden trunk from the end of an elephant beside him. They began to carry it behind Dante's ever-growing pace into Diwan-i-Khas. One of the Babylonians limped behind; a warped face was plastered upon his glaring stare.

Surely that man is one of mine? He dresses the part. Yet how can I forget a face like his?

"This way." One of the royal guards waved his hand towards the entrance of the Hall of Private Audience.

Dante nodded.

The man reached his hand out. "Your dagger, Ambassador."

Dante unclasped his blade and handed it to the man dubiously.

With chest puffed, hair straightened, and fingers locked across his breasts, he began his advance into the hall.

High silk fabrics swayed through the spiced scented air. Roaring fires blazed the hall. Lining the walking path, royal houses dressed in fine silk eyed the foreigner's approach. Their soft shoes shuffled about the tile floor, making way for Dante and his traveling party.

Before Dante's viewpoint, an auric throne elevated itself above the floor. Draped in shrouds of curtains, rainbow in color, it stood majestically but, to Dante's disappointment, sitting in the high throne of radiance was air. The Queen's presence was not before him.

"Where is your majesty?" Dante asked.

A man, short in stature and a rolled back, stepped forth. A noble purple headdress bobbled about his summit. "The Spinster of India has been waiting a long time for you. So you must now wait for her."

Dante bit his lip and nodded.

For what seemed like an eternity, Dante waited and waited. Resting on the extensive golden box, he twiddled his thumbs about. The room was silent as the Indian Royal Court stood ogling.

What is taking her so long? What game is she playing?

A group of women and men stepped out from a branching corridor and approached the side of the throne.

The bobbling purple headdress spoke, "The Queen."

The whole room knelt to the floor and rested their foreheads on the warm tiled ground. Dante followed suit.

"Rise."

There, perched on the throne of gold, was their Queen. Enshrouded in white silks and decorated in a bleached dress, her face and hands were masked off from the world.

Censorship filled the chamber. Dante couldn't tell what form of a woman she was for she was unreadable. He stood still waiting for her next move.

The man spoke once more, "Behold, Queen of Spice, Ruler of Men, Lover of None, and The Spinster of India. Show your value."

Dante stepped forth.

"I am Dante Aligh, Ambassador of the Babylonian Empire, and I bring forth the treasure of our future."

Waving his hand, he called for his men to move the chest closer to the throne's steps.

"That is far enough!" Barked the Advisor.

"Let us see." A soft voice perfumed the air.

Dante kept an eagle eye on the Queen; *her shrouds are lifting.*

Dante walked around the box and reached for the top of the lid. "Behold our future." He yanked the lid away, and the walls of the crate tumbled to the floor.

The room shrieked with abhorrence.

"What form of mockery is this?" The Advisor screeched.

"None of any kind," Dante assessed the empty crate, "I come with the truth. If our nations do not align, *this* is our future."

"Arrest this man. He brings dishonor to our Queen." The Advisor squealed.

"No. Let him speak." Ordered the Queen.

As the Advisor took a step back, Dante peered into the fool's soul as if a vulture.

"The power in the West grows with every day. Backed by a God, they enforce a belief in their people that empowers their will to crush anyone who opposes them. I tell you when Babylon falls; you are next."

Dante looked around the room.

"I do not just bring you an empty crate; I have brought you the full might of Babylon. All my Queen asks is for a marriage between nations."

"Marriage? I marry no one. No nation. No man. This diplomatic assembly is over; you may rest your head in my abode. But as day breaks at week's end, you will set your sails home to your dying desert."

Dante's lips formed to mouth words but he was cut off.

"I will not hear it, young Dante. You may take your leave."

Dante left the hall with his guild of men.

Clasping his knife back to his belt, he spoke, "You there! Write to Babylon. Tell the Queen it has begun," Dante looked at his shriveled comrade. "Do I know you?" he continued.

"Of course, Ambassador. I am Dix, the Queen's trusty blade." he smiled crookedly.

"Very well, write to her and tell her I will not fail… this time."

"You better not, or else I will be taking your head, as promised," the man smiled off-center.

Dante's eyes narrowed.

They both gazed at a bulky brown hawk nipping a cage.

Chapter Two

-Spinster of India-

That dark hour, my remembrance transmundane with desire. Metamorphosis takes root. My thoughts form into a connoisseur for passion. Like a turophile hunting for the finest cheese, so do I quest for that warrior's admiration. Love pollutes my intent and my reason for being here. Blighted I have become. Damned like the fables of fiends in hell. Why must this thirst be quenched? What may come of thy? Do I query the seas questioning and yearning for the unknown? Or do I resist the hellhounds in my mind? I dare not know the outcome of my quest; I freeze at its end. Oh Aphrodite, Eros, Hathor, clear my appetite and set me loose.

-Dante

The Spinster of India sat eating her breakfast within the open air of her terrace. Jubilant rows of fresh fruit piled high on her plate. Steam rose from rolls of sourdough before her eyes, and dainty golden-ware lay freshly polished by her teacup.

Subtle stirs of spicy air showered the Queen's snout. Tastes of tart taffy tantalized her tongue. Shrouded in secrecy still, she sat sternly. With gawking and gazing eyes, she observed the garden grounds below. Growing greenery gleamed with zestful zeal.

Overlooking the Untouchables trimming her fields of passion, she approached the railing. *How minute their lives are in the grand scheme of things. Yet without them, nothing would be what it is.*

Tapping her fingers on the lip of the stone wall, she began to ponder over the Ambassador's bold showcase of yesterday's eve. *What to do, what to do?*

Hearing a disturbance in the air, she peered over her shoulder and leered at Dante's approach.

"I was dismayed when the wind carried the news of your desire to treat with me. I was about to withdraw, your sovereignty," Dante stood alongside.

Peering through her drapes of concealment, she examined his features: chestnut in the shavings, cerulean in optics, bronze in the coat. Dante was dressed in a Sherwani, the iconic fashion of nobility for men. The quality of the reflective light of the fabric was the shade of a white man's flesh. With trims of burgundy and gold outlining the shoulders and lapel, the foreigner's clothing complemented his muscular physique. Placed upon his waist was a gold knife, hilted in rubies.

Does he mean to slit my throat, hear and now?

Attractive he was no doubt, but his voice was so clear, clear as ice. With every word of his, tremors were sent down her spine. Fearing if it was a pull of temptation or a warning, she stepped away.

"Forgive my actions of the day before today. Your 'term' does not sit easily in my ears."

"I spoke in metaphors, nothing else." His voice was silk.

That wrinkle between his brow, how it toiles with me. What form of sorcery has been cast upon my soul?

Dante leaned over the banister and watched the waterfalls emitting streams of prisms across the court.

"Answer me one thing, Ambassador." The Queen of Spice necessitated.

"Entreat away."

"How can I trust a man who doesn't put his anchor in a God?"

"Or in your case, Gods?"

She waited for him to continue. However, he took an awfully long pause. *What is he thinking? Why does he seem as if he has discovered something? Does he know?*

"I put my church in Love now," He was breathing softly with a faint smile, "Nevertheless, I once believed in a God if you do care to comprehend, long ago it seems now, the year was."

The Queen detected behind his eyes of glass, shame and a guilty conscience, perhaps regret dug deep into his soul.

"If one does not wish to pursue down this road, we can turn back and shadow Love."

What is even love to a man?

"No, I will answer your question. Hopefully to win allegiance with India."

"Nix promises." She relaxed at her table.

"Youthful I was, baptized in the Glory of God I had become. In the time of my eighteenth year of breath, I stumbled upon a boy skipping in a baptismal font. His cranium had become wedged in its marble conduits. Unable to extract himself, I feared immediate drowning for this naïve child. I took it upon myself to shatter its casket," Dante paused and then continued, "You would think the Bishop would honor me? But no, in his sight I performed Sacrilege, a sin punished in the Eighth Circle of Hell."

The Spinster of India sat still, peering into his eyes of doe. Never has she ever thought she could find anyone more attractive than she, let alone a man. Perhaps it wasn't until she saw the soul of a boy in the tent of a man, that she could understand the building blocks of love.

"So I lost my faith that hour, unable to renew it like a Phoenix. I packed my belongings and headed east." Dante finished.

"The Eastern Lands are now below your feet." She said pridefully.

"Farthest one can go now, without entering deaths walls..." he paused, "my home is in Babylon, where I must now withdraw."

"Please me for a little longer. Tell me what form of a man you are?" The Queen softly spoke as she looked through her mask.

"I believe I should tell you about my country, not of me. Surely that would help sway you? Babylon stands as the pinnacle of the new world. Our nation's forces are stronger than ever, we stretch to the northern borders of Constantinople, and our roots dig deep into the southern realms of Africa, all the way to Black Gold Bay. All we ask is your alliance, and your Eastern might..."

"Bite your tongue!" The Queen's voice enraged with flame, "Is this the form of a man you are? One who does not obey a command?"

"Forgiveness, grant me. To solve your puzzle, I am equivalent to any other man, in most fashions, I would presume. But some aspects I outshine in." Dante gaped the Queen with a smirk; his intent made clear.

Dante approached the table and pulled out a chair, he scanned the silhouette of the Lover of None. She nodded, and he sat.

"Kamadeva? Tell me about this church of weakness. Does a man claim to love, for merely sex?"

"Nix! What clichés of men clatter about your brain. I am no fool of pleasure and the feeling of orgasmic passion. But that is not my centrifugal force for life, only a mere safari." Dante leaned in to examine the female behind the white cloth.

"How about a beloved, or youngsters, do they sit cradled at home?"

"None. I am a free man. If you are asking for my hand, all you need is to remove your veil." He jocularly laughed.

She found no amusement in his jokes. How she loathed the narrow-minded views of men: sexuality, domination, and selfishness, even if this one professes to be unconventional. *What a foolish reproduction; thinking all you need is a man to sweep you off of your feet and marry you. What is more foolish, the man's quest or the woman's surrender?*

"My heart does yearn for another if one must know," Dante said as if fishing. He raised his lowered gaze.

"Do you not pursue?" *I will feed into his ambition, just a little longer. Then become rid of him.*

"My path lies somewhere else. Besides, I know not where to look. For my seeing peepers are confused."

The Spinster tempered her voice to only a whisper, "Does one give up so easily?"

The Queen reached for his leg and grazed her fingers across his thigh. Even though she would normally cringe inside at the mere touch of a man not because she did not find them attractive, but because their souls repulsed her she did not with Dante. Somehow Dante was different. She continued to play her little game fearing not the outcome.

"Such honor is granted to me, first your presence, now your touch. My country is overjoyed with amazement."

"And you?" She leaned in.

"Rivaling temptation has never been a man's strong suit. But I fear I must veto."

"What a pity." The Spinster pouted under her shrouds.

Send him away now, free yourself of his presence.

As she was about to dismiss him, Dante spoke.

"Where are your guards, Goddess of India? Surely that warrior who escorted me from Surat would be by your side. I do wish to continue my conversation with her, in due time. She was fair like you."

"We are done here." She rose to her feet.

"Is that all? Evidently, I failed." Dante's face filled with sadness.

"Nix, walk with me to my gardens below."

The heavens saddened themselves with a dusky gloom on the distant horizon. Tears of sorrow sprinkled in the withdrawn somber valley.

The Spinster and Dante walked through the nursery. White frangipanis burst with jaundiced-looking central nuclei. The flame of the forest, butea monosperma, burned with their cardinal tassels of vengeance. Fairy-like wings of amethyst ascocenda covered the man-made walls of limestone. Like cores of suns and branches of love, ponds of lotus flowers bounced in the splashing waves of swimming fish. Appearing like snow, jasmine flowered the walking path of the venturers. Rosemallows sweetened the air as gusts of wind blew its petals through the spacey air.

The Spinster admired her garden. Indian rosewood stretched to the heavens as if waking from a deep sleep. Mango saplings colorized the green thicket of timber, and curry trees swayed their feather-like arms in a dance while Ashoka seedlings line the towering walls of Amer Fort.

They reached a fountain of transformation and stopped. A stone butterfly with its wings spread had casting waters transcending down its form.

Dante examined the Queen with a smile as if knowing something.

"Young Dante, I admire your boldness."

"Gratitude I send your way for such words. Is there anything you wish from Babylon in order to sign the dotted line?"

"I must dwell on it a little longer."

"Fair enough, take your time. For I am beginning to enjoy my stay within your country. Beautiful people, plant life, and animals are scattered throughout your land. I would not mind staying here a bit longer, as long as I do not reencounter a tiger, you surely would recall?" Dante laughed.

"A tiger." She paused.

"Yes, do you not remember?"

"What implications do you apply on me? I remember no tiger." She spat in defense as if being accused.

"Forgive me, my gift must have offended you. I hunted a tiger with your warriors, surely the leader of your pack gave you its soul?"

The Spinster relaxed and replied, "Oh, yes. The tiger, I recall now."

She surveyed Dante, and Dante surveyed her.

His face was forested in a thin layer of hair, freshly trimmed. How his ocular of blue felt like daggers in her heart. *Did the Gods grant him the vision into my soul? Such a wicked thing to do.*

Sitting on the lip of the fountain, she fanned her white dress out and gazed away.

The Untouchables, dressed in rags and sandals, scurried away and out of sight. For they know that their presence are a dishonor to their Queen. Low on the mountainside sat the small village of the Untouchables; its dome sheds of clay garbage the sloping hill. Their mere existence is strictly to labor though the day and night. Each family is allowed one child, no more, no less. Otherwise if caught, they are banished to the east of East.

"May I have a seat?" Dante settled his palm on her shoulder blade.

The Queen shrieked in anguish. His touch was venom.

"Your hand! Snake or flesh?" She cried out and tore away.

"Merely a gesture of courtesy." Dante scanned her with a puzzling face and drew speechless.

Under her shrouds she spoke, "My scars are there, why would one touch?"

Dante stood still and studied her.

"It is true." He said beneath his breath.

"What did you speak? What is?"

The Queen cultivated in fear. Her heart pulsated like a drum. *Has my masquerade fallen so quickly?*

Dante cornered The Spinster of India.

"What is your name?" He stretched out and shredded her shawl from her face.

Screeching in embarrassment, the Queen cowled to the floor. Dropping from her heals, she scuffed the stone slabs with her limbs. Anger and madness fumed her face. Switching from day to night, her emotions colorized her complexion.

Dante took a step back and peered into her eyes for the second time.

The warrior who'd escorted him from Surat and the same warrior who saved him from the jungle lay before him in robes of white. The strap of her dress rolled off of her shoulder, exposing three claw marks on her back.

"I thought it was impossible, but I had to know. Why does one conceal themselves when beauty is granted upon them? " Dante leaned in with a helping hand.

Spitting on his fingers, the Queen then rose to her feet.

"I have toyed with my emotions long enough. I will send for my guards. They will take you to your ship."

"Do not transfer me away. I simply wanted to lay sight on the woman who have rattled my mind for days. Your beauty has pumped my blood. I am awake with joy, not regret."

"Lies! You mock my kingdom, from your very first breath. No man can understand the struggles I have had to endure to get here. No man can ever know the pain or sacrifices I had to make!"

"That has nothing to do with the theme at hand, you are babbling like a demon from Hell. Besides I am not like most men!" Dante pleaded with her.

He placed his hand on his hilt.

"You are." She shed a tear.

Dante kept approaching her, and she kept retreating. *He means to strike me now.*

"I tell you this, and I will take my leave. I saw in your eyes the gates of heaven again. Love drives my soul, and your face clouds my actions. I care not our country's outcome. Sign... or do not, I do not worry. Just have my hand, and dine with me tonight."

The Spinster tried to form words.

"Do not speak. I will stay till night. If one has an ounce of love in their heart for another besides themselves, then meet me at your

Palace of Mirrors. Feast with me as the sun sets on your empire. If not, then I will disappear." Dante said and turned away leaving the Spinster alone.

That spine of a man cowers and flees. He has the audacity to come into my abode and profess his love! What a goat, I am the Queen of India, Queen of Spice, Ruler of Man, Lover of None, and The Spinster of India! I need no man. I want no man. These feelings that sprouted to light were merely Kali's form of trickery. I expel them from my soul and out of my sight, as I expel Dante and any Babylonian.

Fire may course through my veins, but my heart is now iced. Love only weakens one's beings, a vulnerability I cannot afford. I banish love as if it was blood, for Nepal once forced their women out of their homes twelve times a year, so will I.

The Spinster sat on the lip of the fountain once more. Tears of pain shivered down her bruised cheeks. She placed her palms freshly on her lids of sight. Torrential hurricanes split her insides as she moaned.

Clean yourself from weakness, you are a Queen. Only the sky may cry. Empower yourself with your beauty. Peer into the reflection of this pond. See into this mirror and recognize that you need none.

The Lover of None bent down and watched her reflection dance across the ripples of the fishpond as if it was a ballet. Her brown hair curled like the waves of the sea. Her optics as green as fields of grass gazed back into her soul.

This is love.

Placing her hand upon her thigh, she began to slide her fingers across her flesh. Inching their way closer and closer to her groin of pleasure, she rolled her eyes back and began to moan with a soft pant.

Quickening her pace, friction flamed between her legs, like bronze over coal, like a witch at the stake, and like a celestial being crashing into the sun.

Faster. Faster.

Not fearing to be caught she continued her pursuit of self-indulgence.

Groans of spasms converged between her petalled lips as her two fingers slide in and out of her legs.

Lying on the rim of the fountain, her white dress darkened with mud as its weight flung itself into the water. Arching her leg and head she pursued her quest.

With effleurage fingers, she tickled her groin. Like a cat pumping its mother, or a butterfly landing on a tree, she softened her speed. Silent gasps of air cried out from her mouth.

Finally, after three orgasmic releases, she laid there motionless. Salty sweat poured down her brow. Dipping her hands into the pond of fish, she washed her fingers and cleansed her sin away.

What's so wrong with love? After all I have my own flesh.

A man with panting breath approached The Spinster of India, "Your majesty! Your majesty!"

"Pause. Then speak clear."

"We intercepted a letter, its intent was for one of Dante's comrades." The man waved about a yellow envelope.

She snatched the message, "From who?"

A wax raven in color was broken. The seal of The Black Bell of Jerusalem was imprinted upon the envelope.

"His Pope." the man claimed.

Chapter Three
-Dante-

I do not know who I am anymore. These twirling cosmoses of tender devotions fog my senses as umbrae casually oscillate in the tempests of my soul. I appeal for someone to shake me from this illusion. I have surmounted ranges to obtain my throne, relinquished everything, and if that did not terrify me then, this feeling of attachment certainly does now. I lie alone in the cryptic shadows, reflecting back at what you uttered. That abyss stretches darker and darker with every word of yours yet a light shines ever so faint at its bottom. Do I roll the dice? Do I try and remake my universe? Do I abandon that cliff's edge and plummet?
- *Spinster of India*

Dreams of divine light cast rays into the heavens as the Mirror Palace glowed with candlelight. In the remote night sky of the east, fuming flames of fog toppled over each other as a wall of shadow stretched forth. Branching like fingers from a demon, the roaring storm clouds dimmed the drifting stars. Aquarius hung itself low on the horizon of starlight. However, the dark heaven directly over Amer Fort was as still as an abandoned pond. No cries from animals sung in the air, no bats took flight, and no wind whispered names of the dead.

Relaxing on the balcony of the palace was Dante. With his legs crossed, he sat at a rounded table dressed for a festival. He inspected his surroundings; meager candles were strewn about, some covering the furniture around him, others on the railing of the platform, as well as hundreds more assembled on the floor.

The building glowed brightly as the light ricocheted from wall to dome. For each surface was made out of a mosaic of miniature glass mirrors. As the candlelight shone its rays into a single mirror, its beams then bounced forth into the air, finding hundreds of other reflective discs to repeat the process.

Dante eyed the moonlit lake. It rippled like navy silk blowing in a soft breeze. Haunting waters chilled the air, as its mist worked

its way u[...]
of perspir[...]

Dante [...]
were sterl[...]
his seat, e[...]
trimmed h[...]
was cut a[...]
noble diam[...]

Around [...]
shining in [...]
black rock [...]
small engr[...]

*Will she [...]
does she d[...]
heart with [...]*

Dante sa[...]
Queen's en[...]
clogging a [...]
on the cut[...]
bounced wi[...]
for a glass of wine.

"It is over, she wishes not to treat with [...] breath of flame on his voice.

"You know your fate when you st[...] Dante Aligh. I am the one who is [...] task. If you leave now, you will d[...]

"Silence worm, I know m[...] ride to the sea."

Dante hopped on th[...] other imposing mou[...] comrade, Dix, wit[...] Traveling o[...] was not a s[...] now app[...] tombs[...] ind[...]

Time passed, and it took away his nerves. After finishing three glasses of wine, Dante's stiff posture began to slope into his chair made from Vicuna Wool. Dante rested his hand on the wooden handle of the chair and began to tap his fingers in a repetitive pattern, over and over again.

Finishing the pitcher of wine, Dante rose to his feet. Hearing a sound, he turned towards the exit. There before him in the dark archway was the still void, taunting him with a smile. He was forever alone in this room.

She never came.

Dante picked up an ornamented box from the table and left the chamber.

Dante was packing his trunks on the back of his elephant as Dix approached with a cockeyed face.

"We cannot leave now, our Queen commands it."

s," Dante said with a

 ep back in the Grand City, ranted with such an honorable e. You must stay!"

 y outcome. Let it be. For now, we

 back of his elephant and took off. Two ts followed his march out of the city. His the scowling face, rode ever so close to Dante. t of the city of light and into the heart of darkness mple ride for Dante, the once evergreen forest of life eared as if a graveyard. Its trees were as gray as ones, its bark peeled away like bleeding scabs. The ntations of the wood gave the illusion as if epitaphs were carved into their trunks. Charcoal spikes of grass transformed into iron fences. The once sweetening air soured itself with rotting flesh. Every step of the elephants was felt with a crackle of pain, for the dried grass was made more of bone than earth that night.

Hours and hours went about the night sky.

With every step, my heart grows heavy with sadness. Oh, Lover of None why could you not find a spark within yourself to love me? Why are you so cold? Now I must roam life alone, and every woman henceforth will be a dim flicking candle when compared to you, my sun. I will walk my remaining short life not even knowing your true name. What is your name? Tell me your name, nameless one. The cleaver of judgment waits for me in the Court of Babylon for I have neglected my Queen; unable to complete the task she so entrusted upon me. Do I flee now, or do I carry on down this road of death? I shall carry on, for death shall be my only reward.

The still air hummed in Dante's ear. All life was at rest six feet under the surface.

His comrade stopped his mount suddenly.

"Something is out of place..."

With a whisper, Dante spoke, "What do you see, Dix?"

Breathing softly and gazing into the thickening darkness, the man did not reply.

"Blow out the torches. Now." Dante ordered.

"Something approaches..." the crooked man said as if a ghost.

Two raptor-like monsters toppled over the plant life, long webbed legs rapidly approached. Thick, feathery backs fluttered the air, creating a whirlwind of drafts around them. Long giraffe-like necks towered the sky with monster-like beaks crowning their tops. Two men rode their backs, with black harnesses wrapping around their mouths. These ostriches were colored like Yin and Yang.

A man with a commanding voice spoke, "Halt. Dante, we are taking you in."

"What is the meaning of this? You have no right!" spat Dix.

"It is all right. If their Queen wishes it, so be it."

"Nix. The diplomatic meeting is over; your Queen has wasted too much of our time as it is. She has made a mockery of Babylon; we are leaving now."

The man on the ostrich eyed the shriveled snake. "Bite your tongue or I will sever it from your mouth. You are in the country of India; *we* govern these lands, not you. Besides we are not asking. Come with your own free will or face the consequences here and now."

The man drew his sword.

"There needs to be no violence. I will go with you. As for you, my Babylonians, head home. Tell the true Queen what has transpired this night."

"Very well." Dix adjusted his mount.

"Do not take me for a fool, Dix, surely you would stay with me. Your task is simple, is it not? You either bring my head home or a signed treaty, was that not your mission?"

Dix hesitated, "I suppose... However, I can..."

The Indian guard interrupted, "The Queen has asked for the presence of *both* of you."

"I... I..." Dix stumbled over his words.

"Let us proceed back to the fort," Dante rested his hand on his dagger and spoke calmly to Dix.

The magisterial palace erected out of the thick jungle, its glowing red stone shone like a bleeding thorn from a rose. Dante traveled up the ramparts of Amer Fort and was escorted into Sheesh Mahal. The Mirror Palace was dimly lit, only a few remaining candles curled their lights about.

Before his eyes was a woman so radiant and so pure that Gods would pour libations in honor of her for eras.

The Spinster, dressed in black, walked forth with clicking heels of authority. Golden necklaces dangled around her neck, and gilded bracelets draped around her wrists. Her lace dress revealed her bare olive skin underneath.

"So one does give up so easily" she galled Dante and Dix as she spoke. "You may be wondering why I have called you back in the hour of twilight." She rested her locked hands below her hip.

Dante stood in censorship waiting for her to make her point. She moved around them with her clicking heels.

"Guards, leave us."

"Majesty...?" they questioned.

She raised one of her eyebrows; they left without another word.

"Bend the knee."

Dix watched Dante as he lowered himself to the ground. He followed suit with shifting eyes.

"Amongst us is a traitor of the crown." The Queen of Spice threw a yellow envelope at Dante's feet.

"Read it." She barked.

Dante picked up the envelope and examined the black seal. His eyes narrowed as he scanned the paper. With darting eyes, his face grew in rage as he peered over its text.

"I see." He whispered to himself.

With an impulse of hatred, Dante jumped to his feet quickly. He drew his golden dagger and charged towards Dix. Wrapping his blade around his throat, he halted and glanced up at the Spinster.

"Give me the command."

"Easy now, Dante, not yet."

"No... Stop this; there must be a mistake..." Dix stuttered forth.

"No, there is none, Dix of Jerusalem," The Queen lowered her face towards Dix, "*You* were sent here to kill me, you thought by leaving those snakes in my vanity that I would fall into your trap?

You thought Babylon would be accused of the act? What a foolish child, do you not know the art of war."

"You will *all* die!" Dix spat in her face with hatred.

Wiping off his saliva, she waved her hand, "Let him crawl back to his Pope. Tell him India will join Babylon in the war against you. Tell him; I *am* coming for his head."

Dante lowered his blade, and Dix crawled out of the room like a wounded snake.

"You set him..." Dante tried to form a sentence.

"Hush, we will hear no more of this. Dine with me."

The Spinster of India neared the table that Dante dressed for the two of them. He extracted her chair; she nodded with a smile. As she sat, Dante scooted her into place.

Finally.

"Would you like a drink?"

He attempted to pour wine into her glass, but she planted her hand over the lip.

"Very well, more for me." He chuckled softly.

Sitting down, he moved for his glass and the pitcher. However, it was empty.

"I neglected my memory; I previously finished the wine. Allow me to fetch..."

"Do not bother, my Untouchables will fill it for you," she said delicately with a snap of her fingers. "In the meantime, tell me about yourself. What does Dante Aligh yearn for?"

"Besides you?" he chortled, "My biggest longing in life is to govern a small port town. Truly. Hopefully settle down with my family next to the sea in a quaint castle. Wake up to the sun on the horizon and the smell of salt in my nostrils..."

The Queen's Untouchables approached. They filled Dante's glass and split.

"Really? The mighty Ambassador of Babylon wants a meek lifestyle? With rainbows and flowers?" She raised her eyebrow.

Dante laughed, "No."

He paused, "I want everything."

"The world?"

"Yes! Everything that surrounds you and I. Everything beneath Apollo and everything beyond the Crescent."

"How will you apprehend such a quest?"

Dante leaned into her, "By loving."

"You naïve child, Love is not a weapon."

"You are wrong; Love is the greatest weapon known to mankind. We fight for our loved ones; we die for them. Love drives every action... you have to crack yourself open, so you can learn that without Love, life is trivial."

The Ruler of Men consumed her food before him. Her red lips softly slid across her fork with such luxury.

"I have met many monsters in this world and all of them have undergone love. Demons love more than angels I would say."

The Spinster studied Dante, "That is a striking declaration."

"I speak the truth. Now, will you excuse me for a moment, Queen of India? I have a gift for you."

Dante rose from his seat and left the room. Quickly returning he held a small chest covered in gems.

"Gifts? We have not even had our sweets yet, and you shower me already."

Dante placed the item before her.

"Open it. I promise this chest is not empty." He smiled.

The Lover of None stood from her chair and stretched for the box. She sheltered her ringed fingers around its rippled exterior. Lifting the lid, her foci expanded with sensations of marvel.

"What form of trickery is this?" She took the item out of the case.

Situated in her hand was a tiger's heart, bleeding crimson blood.

"Here is the heart I stole from you in saving my life. Just know you took mine that day, I do not ask for it back."

The Queen of India wandered over to the balcony with the hemorrhagic heart in her hand. She weighed its virtue as the moon's luminosity glowed in the reflective skin of its core.

"You have brought honor to your people, Dante. How did you obtain one at such an hour?"

"The moment after my departure from your beds of flowers I went into the jungle in an exploration to find a king. I abolished it with the guidance of this blade." Dante rested his hand on his knife.

She shifted and contemplated beyond the boundary of the sky. Dante observed with lustful eyes a deep slit in the back of her dress, stretching from shoulders to crack it displayed her fair olive skin. Three sizable slashes carved into her shoulder blade.

With liquid courage running through his stream, he approached with softening steps. Gently resting his hand around her hip, he closed the distance between them. Her cold skin chilled his warm palm as their cells touched for the first time. Dante's heart rattled in his chest posthaste.

The Spinster looked up at his soothing appearance and blushed.

"I really want to kiss you presently." He whispered in her ear.

"What are you waiting for?"

Dante bent down and kissed her. Their lips collided with the energy of a comet crashing into the moon and with the force of a butterfly fluttering its wing in the breeze. He gently wrapped his hands around her body, lightly kissing her skin with his fingers.

She dropped the heart to the floor and began to drape her hands around his broad torso. With every touch, Dante felt her exploring his surface of skin like a miner digging for gold.

Drawing her in closer, Dante lost his fingers in the silky webs of her hair. Twirling tornados of spinning yarn surrounded his fingers. Lost in the Queen's thick black trellis of locks, he tugged at her hair softly.

The Queen of Spice nudged herself away.

"Strip." She demanded.

Dante grew with excitement.

He gradually unbuttoned his Sherwani. With every pin undone, more and more of his bare chest became visible.

"Slower." She ordered, watching.

Dante gently wrapped his fingers around the diamond studs. As he finished undoing the last button, he peered up at the Queen with a glowing face. Dante softly grasped the coat with his hands. He plucked it off of himself with teasing eyes; the fabric fell to the floor.

The Spinster examined his exposed chest; subtle indentations of muscle chiseled itself throughout his skin. Gifted with stunning pectoral muscles and rows of abs, the Lover of None smiled with delight.

"All of it." She directed.

Dante unclasped his belt, his dagger crashed to the floor. He then coiled his fingers around his waistband. Loosening the loops of his trousers they fell to his ankles. His flesh was made bare. The Queens's eyes grew with pleasure as she glimpsed down at his manhood, freely hanging before her. A faint trim of hair traveled from his bellybutton to his groin.

Leaning in, The Spinster of India sheltered herself in his warmth. Dante kissed her with his soft lips over and over. He made his way down her neck and across her breasts.

"May I make love to you?" he asked.

"Yes." She softly said with a moan.

Dante lifted her up off of the ground and carried her across the room. She wrapped her legs around his stripped ass and hugged him tightly.

Traveling into the dimly lit suite of reflecting mirrors, Dante placed the Queen down on a thick fur rug. With his ivories, he slowly untied the knotted lace down her breasts. As every bow was undone with his teeth, a moan of delight was let out of her. Farther and farther he traveled down her body until he undid them all. Dante ripped her dress off and revealed her nude figure to the Gods.

Thin-waisted her small frame became eclipsed, for his body shadowed her bronze skin. Her glossy skin glittered like gold. Intimate touches of soft tickles enticed her pallet.

Cupping her small perky breasts in his hands, he kissed her over and over again.

Dante removed his weight from her and began to stare into her eyes fiercely. In the eyes of his lover, constellations of emerald stars palpitated with luminous gyrations.

He wrapped his hand around his manhood and gave it a few strokes until he decided to guide it into her.

The Queen arched her back and dug her hands into the fur; moans of passion and romance filled the room. Seizures of erotic spasms vented through her body as if a herd of horses were released into the wild for the first time. Bursts of fuming thrusts pounded one another like two horned rams clashing heads. Groans vibrated the air. With fulminating explosions of love and piercing cries of pleasure, the Queen pushed Dante off of her.

"No more... no more." She faintly moaned.

Dante rolled over to his back and exposed himself to the heavens. The Spinster turned over to her side and rested in the curves of his chest.

With glancing eyes, she gazed up at him as she effleuraged his ribs.

"I will sign. Give me the document and our nations will work as one." She said to him.

"I am most pleased." Dante sat up.

"Do not leave this bed, not yet." She encased her hand around his manhood.

Dante's eyes rolled back into his skull and moaned with pleasure. He laid back down eagerly wishing for more.

The sun softly peeked through the open terrace. Its rays blanketed their nude bodies with a warming embrace. Orange succulent beams reflected from the walls as eddying mists balmily danced through the air. The linen drapes moved rhythmically as the hazy breeze dampened the draft. The fur of the rug enveloped the corners and crevices of their flesh with its dark chocolate fibers.

Dante kissed the Queen on her forehead, and then rose to his feet. He walked over to a table and uncovered a scroll with a wax seal melted on it. The seal was of a red tower (The Tower of Babylon). Dante opened it.

"Come to me." He softly called as if a phantom.

The Ruler of Men stood upright and wrapped the blanket of fur around herself. She reached for a quill and signed the document.

"It is done." She said.

Dante rolled it up and walked over to his coat on the floor and started to get dressed. He quickly slid his trousers around his bare cheeks. He tossed the elegant coat on as the Lover of None watched with saddening eyes.

Dante made for the door without fully buttoning his clothes. The Spinster watched as his chiseled chest cast harsh shadows across his ribs in the rising eye of the sun, shining its rays of lights upon his skin.

"Why are you in such a rush? Stay awhile, lay with me for another night."

"My Queen awaits my return."

"Send another in your place!"

"It must be me." He said.

The Spinster stood her ground; she did not run to him, she did not shed a tear.

As Dante erected himself in the archway of the room, she called out, "Dante."

He turned and eyed her as the shadows of the abyss surrounded him in the arch. A deleted expression was plastered upon his gazing face as his thoughts were whited out.

Her voice called out like a vampiric siren.

"My name is Pallavi."

Impasse

A Uniform & Lace Romance Novella

Tina Maurine

Dedication

To my sweet T. & K.

You kiddos rock!
Thanks for the joy you bring me every day...
I love you bigger than the universe.

To B.

How did I ever get so lucky?
With you, the world makes sense...
I love you forever.

To Mom

For being the kind of mom I strive to be everyday.
For being my best-friend... since forever.
I love you Momma!

-PROLOGUE-

"Miss Renyols, the President and First Lady are ready to see you now."

I stood confidently and smoothed my hands over any creases that may have formed on the plain, conservative suit all of us in the security detail wore.

"Thank you, Ollie." I smiled warmly at Mr. Marsh, the President's personal assistant as he opened the door to the Oval Office and gestured for me to enter before him. I approached Ethan and Kaitlyn West, who were seated on sofas gathered in an informal sitting arrangement in this office of such high prestige.

"Vette," the first lady rose and extended her hands out towards me, "both Ethan and I are so glad that you could find the time in your busy schedule to fit us in."

I took both of Kait's hands in mine and held them in friendly greeting. "Anytime either of you needs me, you know I'm here for you." I smiled largely and with the genuine warmth I felt for both her and the president.

"Miss Renyols, please take a seat. Kait always thinks I have all the time in the world, and although I make time to prioritize my family, I really haven't any to spare."

I nodded to the president and took a seat across from him and next to Ollie, who sat poised and ready to take notes on the legal pad he had open on his lap. I watched as President Ethan West took his wife Kait's hand in his. His eyes met hers in quiet support and provision. He nodded gently before they both turned their attention toward me.

"Vette," she began in a wavering voice, "I will have to be cutting back on the myriad of duties, projects, and commitments I've been pouring myself into these past years. You've worked for us as head of our son Davien's security detail for just under a year, and I…"

"We," the president interrupted her, "will be having you take on added duties with regard to Davien."

"Yes," Kait went on, "what Ethan is trying to say... is that I'm sick."

"Very sick," the president added.

"We have interviewed for nannies we thought Davien might respect and click with, but even amongst the best applicants, we found fault." She shook her head and the two of them caught each other's eyes before she continued. "Vette, I have stage four cancer, and although we are going to fight this with the best treatments from the best doctors, my prognosis is grave."

"Don't say that bab... err, Kaitlyn. You can beat this. You know I'll spare no expense."

"Shh, Ethan my love. Now's not the time to rehash this..." she briefly looked over at me as she squeezed his hand, "we have company." They held each other's gaze for a time, before the president diverted his attention to me.

"Miss Renyols, we—Kait and I—feel that because Davien is nearly seventeen, and because you are with him practically every minute of every day anyways... that perhaps you'd consider being his pseudo-nanny, so to speak?"

"Mrs. West..."

"Kait, *please*," she said with quiet adamancy.

I nodded, "Kait, I can't be..."

"You can," the president interjected gruffly, "and will if you'd like to keep this assignment."

I watched as the first lady shot her husband one of her *looks*.

"Please, Vette. I'd... we'd feel much better knowing that someone who already has his best interests at heart, someone who already knows the... shall we say, weaknesses in character and behavioral traits," she chuckled, "would be looking after him in my absence."

I stood and walked to the window in quiet reflection. *How the fuck am I supposed to make her understand that I am NOT mom material? I can't be watching after him! Davien no less! He's NOT an easy charge. Besides, I'm too messed up to deal with anyone else's shit.* I crossed my arms as thoughts of my own childhood bombarded my mind, each more painful and harder to reflect on than the last. *I can't do it. I was never meant to be a mom, and after Iraq, I just... I can't.* I turned slowly and walked back to where they were sitting, "Mr. President, Kait, I really think after careful consideration, that both of you, Davien, …for all parties involved, I'd best serve your family by remaining as *only* head of his security detail."

"*THAT'S* not an option."

"Ethan, please." She looked at him pointedly, then patted his leg in a quiet, *I've got this* gesture.

"Respectfully, I am NOT mom material." I could feel my heart begin to race and my anxiety was climbing at the thought that I'd either be fired or forced to take on these extra duties that I most certainly did *not* want.

"Ethan and I are not asking you to be Davien's *mom*." The harshness with which she spat 'mom' indicated I'd clearly offended her sensibilities. "You know he's mostly grown. We just need someone to be there for him; someone he can come to or talk to… You already shadow him and keep him out of trouble."

"Please forgive me for using the term mom. I only meant I'm not a nurturer. It goes without saying that you ARE and forever will be, Davien's only mother. It's just… and please don't take any offense, but I am not interested in taking on this level of responsibility and with it, the added stress and anxiety it would cause me." I hurriedly added, "I hope you understand."

"I hate to say this, but I told you so."

"However do you mean, Ethan? Told me what?"

"That we'd be taking a risk by hiring her for this detail. She's clearly not the person that we banked on her being."

"I'm sorry…" I butted in with no regard to the fact that the president was speaking to his first lady. "What do you mean I'm not who you counted on me being?" my voice broke. "I've worked 24-7 for you guys, followed Davien to the ends of the map and then some…" I laughed. *If only they'd known the places and situations I'd pulled him out of.* "How am I *not* who you thought you'd hired."

The president spoke first, "Your military history clearly outlines the trauma you've suffered and the resulting PTSD. I felt it was a deal-breaker. Seems I was right."

"Ethan…" Kait shook her head, then looked at me before continuing. "Vette, if it were a deal-breaker, you wouldn't be here.

I loved your file and how you've rebounded from a past riddled with tribulations… it IS, after all, our pasts who make us who we are today."

I nodded and smiled at her.

"Please reconsider." Again, her voice waivered. "I'm going to die, Vette. Please don't let me worry for the next few weeks or months about who my son will have to go to if he needs an ear, or a friend he can count on in my leave. Your job detail really won't change much, except for if he needs anything outside of your current job duties, they'd fall under the pseudo-nanny detail… if that makes any sense?" She quickly added, "He's not a child, so it wouldn't be for much longer."

I nodded again and stood, quietly absorbing what I'd just heard. I did love Kait and her family… "In that case," I said heavily and with audible uncertainty, "it would be my pleasure to attend to Davien and *all* his needs, not just the ones pertaining to his security." I heard the president grumble under his breath, but Kait jumped up and embraced me in a tight hug.

"Oh thank you, Vette! Thank you so much for caring after my baby. You have no idea what this means to me." her voice broke and she released a quiet sob.

"Kait," I whispered as we held each other, "so long as I'm here looking after Davien, you have *nothing* to worry about."

-ONE-

I shifted uncomfortably on the hard clinic couch, moving the bone-ivory pillow from behind my back and settling against the gold wool.

"Vette, why do you think President West hired you to run the security detail for his son?"

I shrugged. "I'm guessing he received my file from the CIA—honestly, I've never given it much thought… although to say I was surprised would be a lie. I was an INTEL officer with the ISA." I paused, waiting for her to acknowledge the accomplishment. *Nothing.* "It is the highest division of intelligence for the US military…" *Still nothing from her. What the fuck?*

"Dr. Thorne, following my military service, I was at the top of my game. As a result, one of the top private military companies—one that is contracted with the US government—hired me as a private security contractor, a mercenary. With them, I completed missions that officially never existed. I have a top security clearance, tactical training, vigor and brazenness. I am fully qualified—overqualified—to run after a punk kid."

I watched as my president-mandated therapist, Belle Thorne, scratched on her pad, making notes for my bi-annual review. "So, you feel qualified for the position?"

"I do."

"In spite of your clinical diagnosis of PTSD?"

"Belle…"

She interrupted me. "Dr. Thorne, please."

I watched her make a few more scratch marks on her notepad.

"Belle, we've done this since Kaitlyn passed from ovarian cancer. Many times in the past months. Can we possibly just call it good today?"

"Officer Renyols, you know what would make it a good day? You not fighting me. You respecting that, while *you* may feel fine, it remains up to me and my professional opinion whether I sign off if you're fit for duty."

"I was merely saying…"

"I'm saying, respectfully *LET ME* do my job. Upsetting me will not garner the results you desire."

I nodded, resigned.

"Tell me; how do you feel about the first lady's passing?"

I sighed. *This is such an incredible waste of time.* "Kait was educated, eloquent, and kind. It was her kindness that softened the public—and her husband. She did more for her humanitarian causes than most do in their lifetime."

"Tell me about this; is this why you don't mind the dual roles as Davien's head of security and his pseudo-nanny?"

"She had always been inordinately kind to me. She had found out—I guess from my file—what happened in Iraq. At first, I was irked that she knew the details of that day," I paused to draw in a long, cleansing breath, "the day the terrorists infiltrated our base." I shuddered involuntarily, noticing Thorne having a field-day of this in her notepad. "But, once I saw her humanitarian efforts, I just innately knew she was one of the kindest people I'd ever had the pleasure of working for." I laughed. "Although that doesn't say a lot, considering the motley crews I've worked with."

I took a long draw from tall glass tumbler she'd placed on the table beside the couch. Ever since I'd asked for a glass of water that first visit with her, she'd had one sitting there for me. It had taken a year of going first bi-monthly, then monthly and now every six months for me to appreciate the kind gesture. "Kait's efforts were international in their spread and varied. She saw a need for sanitary women's products in numerous third-world countries and got them what they needed. She personally fitted kids and adults in Ecuador with hearing aids. She saw the need for schools in Kenya and made sure they were built. Infants needed shots in Uganda—she had them shipped."

I took a moment to reflect on her question: *How do I feel about caring for all things Davien? All things, especially outside of my title as Head of Security.* "You know, when Ethan and Kait hired me, it was because she had so many commitments regarding her humanitarian efforts, and she needed a hand in watching over Davien in her absence." I paused, shifting my weight on the couch.

"As terrible as it was—her passing—to me it is was not a surprise. When you're that sick, and working that hard, something has to give. She literally gave her life trying to do right by as many people as possible. So I guess I felt like, because she did so much for everyone else, the least I could do was care for her son in her absence."

Thorne flipped through her notes, "You mentioned a few sessions back that your best friend from childhood had the same form of cancer. How's she doing with her treatment?"

"You know," I went on, deep in thought, ignoring the question. "Kaitlyn West's death rocked the White House. She blew in like a hurricane, upending the old, classical décor, making it modern and warm. It's impossible to walk through the halls or wander through the rooms of their personal residence and not feel her presence in every one of them. Sad, really. She is so greatly missed."

"Vette? Vette."

I blinked, startled to find that she was questioning me.

"We're almost out of time, and I have to say—off the record—that your PTSD seems to have been re-triggered." She set her notepad down. "How do you feel working for such a hard-hitting man as President Ethan West?"

"Well," I stated in a deadpan voice, "he's easily 6'4" tall, broad-shouldered and his stature commands the same presence as his attitude. He is the Commander in Chief, and 'commander' fits his personality to a tee. He commands respect and is official in all of his dealings—personal and relating to the public office he holds so dearly. That is, except when it came to the first lady." I shifted my weight again, trying to get comfortable on the hard, wool couch, leaning forward, my elbows on my pantsuit-clad thighs.

"Around Kait, he was a whole different man; that is, when he wasn't in front of his adoring public. He won by a landslide, which I'm sure you know—the biggest in history—and not from a sleazy election either. People just believed in his abilities, and with his military experience to back it, and with Kait at his side, the American people rallied behind him. It's hard not to. Rally behind him I mean." I clasped my hands together and took another cleansing breath. I greatly disliked talking about Kait—and pretty much all things—with people like Thorne.

I looked her dead in the eyes, "So, to answer your question, I am honored to be working for the president. True soldiers are found in the trenches with their men, and I know President West is fighting the good fight… that's all I can ask of him and my team."

Dr. Belle Thorne nodded. She sat with her hands grasping each other as she rubbed the knuckles. Picking up her notebook, she unfolded a piece of paper and scrawled her name at the bottom. "I am clearing you for continued duty, Officer Renyols, but I want to see you back in here at the beginning of next month."

She opened her calendar, "Let's say the week after you get back from Davien's little birthday shindig—sound like a plan?"

I nodded.

"But during the interim, I want you to journal."

Fuck me. "I'm sorry, what was that?"

She eyed me keenly, her eyebrow cocked.

"Sorry, but really? You want me to fucking journal? How often?"

"Ideally at the end of each day."

I laughed, and a snort escaped. "Well, that's *NOT* going to happen. I can tell you that much."

She didn't budge an inch. "I'd like for you to try."

"Thorne, I am all too well aware that President Ethan West hired me to run the security detail for his son. I know the role I was hired to fill was more than simply a personal bodyguard; I was hired to *care* for his son." I stood to leave. "He hired me knowing my history; the same history that was in my file, which hasn't changed, and neither has my mission or assignment. I was capable then and am no less capable now." I glanced at my watch. "I really do need to be getting back. If you'll excuse me?"

Dr. Belle Thorne sighed and stood resolutely, smoothing her hands down her suit-like shift. "Vette, you're obviously one of the best in your field; otherwise, President West wouldn't have retained your services. However, you need to know that continuing to push the past under that façade you front will only work for a measured length of time. Eventually, even the best façades crack without care."

I nodded and extended my hand, "Thanks for your professional opinion, but I'm fine. Really." I shook her hand and smiled, then confidently strode towards the door. *Fuck. There's an hour of my life I'll never get back.*

"Officer Renyols?"

My eyes lifted from my steno-notepad, aka journal, as I laid my Parker fountain pen down on the page. It had been a gift from Ethan soon after Kait's death, to help me remember her by. He'd said Kait had developed a love of writing after first receiving a similar pen. He'd hoped I'd develop the same love for writing, and he'd suggested I'd have lots of time on my hands, waiting around on his son. I'd found it sweet that he'd known how close she and I had become during her fight.

"Yes?" I asked Foster Black, a member of my security staff.

"Davien has requested to go out."

"It's 2:30 in the morning. Where's he think he's going this late?" I grumbled.

Black shrugged his shoulders. "Damn kid. Maybe you can talk some sense into him. God knows I've spent the last ten minutes trying, and the arrogant little shit told me to take a hike... to get you." He laughed sardonically.

I nodded as I stood, tightening the satin sash of my favorite robe. "Thanks, Foster. I'll handle him. There's no way I'm going out this late, especially since we fly out in a few hours." I smiled warmly at him. "Go get a few hours of sleep. I'll need you ready and roaring first thing in the morning."

"Rodger that. Vette."

I cringed inwardly. Usually, my name didn't garner that response from me anymore, but when Foster used it, something about the way he said it stirred up memories of my dad. *My father. He was a hard one, just like Ethan was around everyone except Kait. He's harder than most with Davien.* I shook my head. *The only thing my dad had a soft spot for was his Corvette collection. Too bad he named me after them. They became a constant reminder that they were the apple of his eye, instead of me, his daughter.*

I walked silently through the corridors. Eerie light shone through the Venetian and other large-paned windows as I passed them, my feet padding softly on the eclectic collection of Persian rugs, some new, and some old, which populated the herringbone wooden floors. I nodded casually to the members of my staff who roamed the passageways on their twice-hourly security checks. Only those who lived within these walls knew the schedule.

I looked regretfully as I passed the door to the Treaty Room, which President West had redone for me as my private suite. Oh, how I wished I was ensconced in my down comforter instead of this shit-storm I was walking into.

I paused in front of the Lincoln Bedroom—Davien's apartment—right next door to my suite. I raised my deceivingly delicate hand—I could lay any grown man out, with only the use of my hands and the Eastern martial art skills I'd become an expert in—to rap lightly on the impressive door, just as it swung open.

"Jeezus, Davien! Give me a fucking heart attack why don't you?" *Before my tour in Iraq, I was never this jumpy...*

He laughed maniacally, stepping aside to allow me entrance.

"How'd you know I was there," I inquired as I stepped inside his bedroom.

"I ordered Officer Cruz to inform me when he saw you, and I just received the call."

Later, I'll have to remind Cruz who he takes orders from.

He winked. "So, Foster told you I wanted to go out?"

I leaned my shoulder against the wall by the impressive double doors, my face blank.

"So," he snapped, "why the fuck aren't you ready?"

I smirked arrogantly. *No* way *am I going out this late.* "Davien," I replied, trying to sound firm but unable to suppress a sigh, "it's too late."

He opened his mouth to argue, but I didn't give him a chance.

"Your father hired me to watch over you..."

"You're not my mom," he interjected angrily, *and drunkenly,* I noted. "Do your fucking job and take me out." He swerved toward me haphazardly, bumping his hip on a decorative table along the wall and cursing under his breath.

I watched with mild amusement and annoyance. *At thirty-four I'm too fucking old to be babysitting. What was I thinking when I accepted this assignment? Oh yeah; it would've been career suicide to turn down First Family security detail. Hindsight's 20/20 though. I wish I'd considered how sorry for myself I'd feel three years in...*

"You're right. I'm not your mom, but I am in charge of your safety, and so I've decided going out is not in your best interest."

He stood barely two feet in front of me, his sea-blue eyes glaring at me indignantly. I challenged him back, pulling on my sash in a decisive, final manner.

"Do you have any idea how beautiful you are?"

His comment upended me; I couldn't have been any more startled than if he'd jumped out of a dark corner at me. "Davien..."

"No, really, Cori." He advanced on me so suddenly that short of pushing him on his ass, I had no way to make an evasive move. "Cori," he hummed it as it rolled provocatively off his lips, "I like it so much better than Officer Renyols." His body was close enough to mine that I could feel his warmth.

"Davien," I warned.

He leaned in, bending his head so his lips fell at my temple. "Cori," he whispered, "I think it fits you better than Vette. I always have." His eyes locked onto mine, "Vette is too severe." He took my hands and held them out to my sides, so he could appraise me in my satin robe—clearly the wrong choice to visit my drunken charge in. "There's nothing beneath that robe that's as tough as Vette implies." He smiled flirtatiously.

I needed to put an end to this—this *thing*—before it went any farther. *How did I ever let it get this far?!* "Davien, your father hired me to watch out for your best interests..." I protested, uncomfortable and cornered. I could feel that all too familiar panic response setting in.

He interrupted me. "*This*, what you do to me... *IS* in my best interest." He pressed his six-foot two-inch frame against my five-foot six-inch athletic one. His firm, muscular chest pressed against my ample curves. "Cori," he moaned, desire lacing the syllable, "as of three hours ago, I'm officially a year past being a child."

I cleared my throat and writhed in an attempt to get out from between this sexy, virile nineteen-year-old and the heavy door at my back. "Davien, please!" My voice sounded desperate, nearly pleading. My heart was pounding, and my hands had grown sweaty. *I NEED to get out of here.* I looked toward the other exit, "I'm practically your mother," I argued, searched for a reason that he'd relate to. "I'm old enough to be your mother!"

"No, you're not," he stated arrogantly, "but even if you were… that would make you fifteen when you had me… and that's fucking sexy as hell."

"Jeezus, fuck…" the explicative fell out of my mouth. *What am I going to do with this kid?* This sexy as fuck, hard-bodied, aroused sex-machine who turned nineteen as of three hours ago, this kid—who wasn't much of a *kid* anymore—was doing things to me. I needed for it to stop. I tried pushing him away, but his sturdy frame held me captive against the door, and short of dropping him to his knees, which I didn't want to do on his birthday, I couldn't think of a way out.

My body jerked when he took his hand and placed it at my nape, gently tugging my black-violet hair to tilt my head up towards his. I tore my jade eyes from his mesmerizing, clear blue ones. *They're even more beautiful now that they're heated with passion… wait, no! What am I thinking?* "Davien," I pleaded again, "I'm, I'm…" I stuttered breathlessly, "I'm practically…"

"No. No, you're not," he rasped raggedly. "There's no way I'd do this to my mother." His lips descended. His hot, dry lips pressed against mine, encouraging me to allow his exploration. The hand at the base of my neck held me firmly. He dominated me, although not in the slightest bit offensively. His other hand sent a shudder through me as it cupped my ass, hiking my apex into his impressive arousal.

My hands, which had been arrested against his chest in a half-hearted, frozen push, snaked up around his neck and found refuge in his sun-highlighted, sandy brown waves. I pulled him deeper into me, as my body folded into his. My mouth parted, welcoming in his scotch-flavored tongue. He skillfully explored, lancing and diving into my depths, before retreating and grazing my lips with his, nipping and biting before delving back in. Our lips danced to the beat of our pounding hearts. Our bodies swayed scandalously to the rhythm thrumming deep within our chests.

When he eventually released his hold on me, my neck, my ass, my lips felt desolate. Cold. Vacant. He backed up a bit, and for the briefest of moments, a fleeting expression of awe and shock, as intense as I was feeling, swept across his face, before an arrogant smirk chased it away.

"Fuck me," he marveled.

I met his gaze unabashedly as the dizzying effect of the kiss left my senses.

"I'll be damned…" he muttered.

The crack of my hand connecting with his cheek resounded off the walls of his cavernous room. My hand smarted. "Don't," I grated evenly, "ever try that again." I pierced his eyes with a finality I somehow mustered, despite how my core fluttered. My apex had grown moist and ached for his touch, not to mention the heaving of my chest and erratic beat of my heart. *What's wrong with me? Maybe I should write this one down in my "journal" for Thorne to use in her psychoanalysis of me…*

I turned from him and opened the door. "Go. To. Bed, Davien." I gave him one final once-over, my eyes lingering a second too long on his pronounced, heavy desire, easily distinguishable as it, strained between the textured fabric of his low-waisted cords and his muscular thigh. *Sweet Jeezus.*

I pulled the door closed with a click, walked hastily across the hallway to my bedroom, opened the door and closed it. I leaned against it, sliding to the floor, my head hanging, to rest heavily on my knees. The unwanted image of an arrogant Davien stood there. His eyes danced impishly, and swollen lips smiled as I'd all but stared at his erection. The image refused to leave my eyes. *Fuck me. What have I gotten myself into?*

-TWO-

I stood outside the Oval Study, the large yellow room framed by the Truman Balcony. President West used it as an informal work space and meeting area. He was currently inside with Senator Gordon and her son, Connor, and of course the birthday boy, Davien. I didn't have to be there to know that the president was giving Davien the rules for the trip we were about to embark on, and that Senator Gordon was dishing them out to Connor in like fashion. The two boys had been hellions from the time they met around the age of eight or nine, at least from what I've heard, and very little has changed. Without exception, every time they 'hung out' together, there was trouble.

The door opened and Ollie Marsh, Mr. President's personal assistant, smiled my way. I could tell he had a thing for me, but he was too ordinary, to dignified and bland, to arouse me in any way. I mean, sure, we'd had a glass of wine here and there, but to see him as more than just a friend would be nearly impossible. He was not my type… just too, *nice.*

"Officer Renyols, President West requests your presence."

I smiled and nodded as I walked through the door he held open for me. In passing, I noted the two upholstered sofas. If memory serves, Laura Bush redesigned the room during her term in the White House. The senator and her son were on the sofa to my right. I sat down opposite President West and Ollie, joining Davien. The little shit had his legs splayed wide, slouched as he rested the back of his head on the sofa cushion nonchalantly.

I hope that hangover hurts… bet you don't even remember last night. I shrugged it off, but the thought of him not remembering our kiss stung a little. It would take me awhile to get past the feelings he stirred deep within me.

"Officer Renyols?"

My eyes snapped in the direction the voice had come from. *Fuck!* I looked from the president, to the senator, back to the president and on to Ollie. I sought the assistant's eyes, imploring for help.

Ollie nodded in my direction. "President West asked you if you needed a larger security detail to cover both boys, as the original travel plan didn't have Connor in it."

"Oh, yes. Of course." I paused, took a deep breath and turned to look at Davien, who sat there in smug, arrogant silence, smirking at my lack of focus. I narrowed my eyes at him ever so slightly before redirecting my attention to the matters at hand. "On second thought, Mr. President, I am confident with the security plan we have in place. We've background checked the staff at the Coco Bodu Hithi Resort, and this morning, I have confirmation that the Coco Residence, where we'll be staying, has been completely swept and any vacationers have been background checked as well. There is no immediate threat. As of two hours ago, the plane's flight plan has been approved and the plane prepped for the flight to the Maldives."

"That's wonderful, Vette," the president addressed me again by my cringe-worthy name. "That's why you're in the position you're in—you're fully capable and carry the tiniest detail out to completion."

I smiled at him and extended my hand in response to his outstretched one. He grasped it warmly, taking it in both hands.

His voice softened, "Take care of my boy. He's the only family I've got left."

"Yes, and who else is there to take over your legacy?" Senator Gordon chirped playfully. I smiled as I glanced from her to President West and saw definite chemistry there. *I wonder...*

I turned to my charge, "Get up, Davien. Have you packed yet?"

"Do you realize you haven't even wished me a happy birthday yet?" He eyed me mischievously.

"Happy Birthday, Davien." I cast him a haughty smirk of my own; not professional, but I was granted some leeway, seeing as how, for all intents and purposes, I also held the role of his nanny.

I paused from any further conversation with Davien until only he, Ollie and I remained in the room. "Have you packed yet?"

"No."

"Don't you think that's something that you should do?"

"Not really. All I need is what I'm wearing and a swimsuit… unless I chose to wear just my birthday suit? You'd like that wouldn't you… Cori?"

My eyes shot to Ollie, and his pointedly measured mine. "Davien, that's the complete *opposite* of what I'd like. Get up. Now, *please*." Frustration edged my voice and I could feel heat creeping up my cheeks. I'd never make a good mother. I hated dealing with this obstinate, bullshit behavior.

"Or *what*?" Davien crossed his legs defiantly and crossed his hands behind his head as though he meant to camp there for a while. "Do you plan to *smack* me, cause I have to say, from experience, I'd much prefer a good *spanking*."

Ollie choked as I heard him set his coffee mug down.

"Get your ass up. Now!"

"Okay, okay. Sheesh, boss. You could learn to have a little fun." He stood from the sofa, towering over me. Leaning in near to my ear, he whispered, "…about those birthday spankings?"

I pointed to the door. "Go pack. Now!"

I swear I heard him breathe me in as though he were smelling me, before he stood to his full height, ran his tongue provocatively over his bottom lip and winked at me. "Ribbed or lambskin?"

"I swear on my mother's grave…"

"I'm going." He strode toward the open door, pausing before he stepped into the passageway. Turning his head toward me, he shouted, "How about if I just pack both? That way we won't run out." I could hear him laughing as he headed to his apartment.

Condoms? Really? Little shit!

-THREE-

We pulled out in a modest motorcade and headed to the president's plane; it wasn't Airforce One. President Ethan West was not a poor man by any stretch of the imagination and owned his own Gulfstream G650 jet. It was rumored that it had cost him, or his family—not sure of the specifics there—north of sixty-five million dollars, new.

Traffic was light between the morning and noontime rush hours, so we made it to the airport in record time and boarded the plane with zero unforeseen problems.

The plane engines were already starting, and after getting my charge situated, I took my seat in the forward cabin in one of the four club-arranged seats. I preferred this space to the mid-cabin, where the movie screen was always on. Here, I had my own table, 21-inch screen, and power-reclining leather seat. I also generally had my own flight attendant, as one worked the front and one the rear of the plane.

"Mind if I join you?"

I lifted my head, nodded and smiled at Officer Adrian Rogue. He took his seat across from me.

He and I had been stationed in Iraq together until my enlistment had ended. Then I had signed-on with a crew of independent security contractors for the US government. We'd always been close, and I have to admit, I wish more had happened than the one or two sizzling make-out sessions that still played through my mind when I wanted to satisfy myself. *Fuck. He was one hell of a kisser... and those hands... the size of his... erection.*

When I was hired by President West, he'd let me choose my security team, and I'd sought, and found, Adrian... who was currently dating one of Ollie's assistants.

"It's going to be a long week. Dav," he nodded toward the aft of the plane, "seems to be in rare form."

"Yeah, no kidding—the form of the devil incarnate." I laughed as another member from my team, Foster Black, joined us, taking a seat across the aisle, and the flight attendant began her safety spiel. I turned my devices to in-flight mode and crammed my ear buds into my ears, ready to hunker down for the nearly 15-hour flight to Dubai. We'd refuel there and continue on another two hours to the Maldives.

I glanced at Adrian, and, catching him watching me, flashed him a killer smile. I turned up the volume on my phone, letting the cool sounds of James Bay's song "Let it go," wash over me, and let my mind drift.

Oh, how his hands splayed against my back. His hard erection ground against my intimates. I returned his kiss, deeply, passionately. Thoughts of the man who sat across from me flooded in. *Adrian was everything I wanted from a lover; attentive, adoring, and ardent. He was courageous, sexy, masculine... he was ALL MAN. He oozed sex appeal in the way he carried his strong, lean, muscular build, and in the way he commanded respect when he gave orders.* My best friend Adrian, the *one* man I'd do anything for... filled my thoughts as I drifted off to sleep listening to Tom Walker's ballad, "Fly Away with Me."

I rubbed my eyes; they were sore from tracking the satellite images—suspected terrorist targets—I'd been closely watching for the past eight hours on one screen and a Predator drone live feed video on another.

I stretched, repositioning the headphones I'd been using to listen to the Arabic, Pashto and Farsi chatter on the internet and in hacker forums. I needed a break, but since I was covering for Officer Julien Rowe, I just had to "embrace the suck;" the motto around here and accepted standard.

I'd returned from a tactical mission not even forty-eight hours ago, and immediately went in to debrief with the CO. My role in the ISA— Intelligence Support Activity Group—was to collect

INTEL crucial to carrying out missions. Crucial to the Army's Delta Force and the Naval Special Warfare Development Group, since officially, SEAL Team 6, doesn't exist. They're the best and the brightest counterterrorism units around.

I had literally just made it back to my team's bunk when I'd been called in to cover for Rowe. Food poisoning. Just my luck. I'd staggered in, sleep deprived, filthy, and mentally exhausted.

"Officer Renyols, front and center, soldier."

I looked up, thrilled to have a reason to move from my station. Moving through the darkened tent past tables of computers, maps and light-tables with photos strewn across them, I reached the large table at the center of the room.

"Sir?" I responded.

And, that's when I saw him. Or rather, felt his energy...

How could anyone not? He was amped on adrenaline and testosterone—clearly jazzed about how well his team had carried out the mission. I stood front and center listening to him as he debriefed our commander. I faced this soldier, watching how he radiated masculinity and vibrated with energy. I was mesmerized. I wanted— needed—to know him. Intimately. I'd never been so drawn to someone I didn't know before.

Later that night I wandered into the base bar—if you could call a rough slew of tables and chairs haphazardly strewn on the desert sand, covered by a massive parachute—a bar. The speakers were blaring, card games were going on and everyone was drinking, except for him and me.

I studied his breathtaking good looks and felt the electric pull of his energy. I wanted Adrian and I'd be damned if it was going to happen while I was drunk. I discretely watched him, as he nursed his one Jack & Coke for most of the hour. I was surprised as hard as everyone else was throwing down.

He stood behind his second; Tanner Lyons, another hottie, watching the poker game. This table had to comprise one of the finest examples of masculinity—both in looks and military skill. These special ops guys were rugged, commanding, strong, and oozed raw sex appeal.

It took me several well-calculated minutes to make my way discretely to him. Now, under the guise of watching the game, I stood directly behind him. I took a deep breath and slid my hand from the sinewy muscles at his upper back, down the taut ridges of his back. My delicate, slim fingers continued making their way down to the hard lines of his fine ass. He instantly stiffened. Every muscle in his body tightened, fight or flight, ready to spring.

"Hi," I whispered, more timidly than I'd imagined I'd sound. "I'm Vette."

He looked out the corner of his eye, taking me in, a sly smile etched on his handsome face. Reaching for me, suddenly pulling me from behind his shoulder, he wrapped his heavy, muscular arm around my athletic frame. I never wished harder than I did at this moment that I was sexy, if only to feel like I deserved his attention.

"You were in the TOC tent today." It wasn't a question. I nodded. "You were watching me." I nodded again, feeling stupid; however, when he looked down from his impressive six foot plus height, my insecurities all went away. His eyes, warm chestnut pools of honey, weren't mocking or condescending. They shone with attraction.

"You know how I knew that?"

Shit! He'd noticed me as I'd all but undressed him with my eyes earlier!

"I noticed you," he rasped, as he gave me a squeeze, "your head bent over your work, the moment I walked in."

My attraction deepened, my jade eyes falling deeper into his honey depths. "Your raven-black hair shone nearly midnight violet, and when you looked up... fuck me," he admitted unabashedly, "I thought maybe the green-screen had reflected off your eyes, but now I can see they're just an amazing shade of green," he paused, studying me, "like the most perfect emeralds..." he uttered more to himself than to me as his voice softened and faded.

I was dumbfounded. I stood there awestruck, like an idiot. Do something, SAY SOMETHING I chastised myself, but nothing came to mind, except I blurted out, "Damn."

He'd laughed good-naturedly, "You can say that again. Hey, want to get out of here?" He squeezed me tighter to him as he began backing us around the crowd that gathered at the card table. It was as though he was my liege, and I followed him trustingly through the riotous midnight throngs.

We walked through the base, past the TOC and supply tents, past the infirmary and mess tents, on up the hill past the barrack tents until we'd reached the quieter, more secluded side of the base, where the special ops teams bunked. He led me to a wooden picnic table in front of a tent I presumed was his quarters, and climbed up on it, motioning me to join him.

"So, you're going to have to tell me more about yourself. You made, I'm sure you'd agree, a pretty brazen move." He paused while I situated myself next to him. Our knees touched as we faced each other. "But, you haven't said nearly a word. You're quite the paradox." He reached up and ran his hand through his dark waves, down across the *whiskers on his jaw, and over his chin to his neck. Stroking his short beard, he cogitated, "Brazen and shy. Quite the anomaly around here."*

"I, I..."

"Vette, right?" He didn't wait for me to confirm. "You know, I'm not going to bite." He smiled in the moonlight and the tension eased from my shoulders. I nodded.

"I don't usually—I don't EVER do that," I corrected myself.

"So, then," he paused as though searching for the right words, "why did you? I mean, if I weren't such a nice guy, that forward of a move—not to mention following me out here blindly like this—could've landed you in deep water." He chuckled. "Cause, and please don't take this the wrong way, but it certainly SEEMED like you've pulled off that kind of move before."

I smiled at him, relaxed now, knowing he wasn't going to pounce on me immediately, even if it was what I wanted. "I don't know what came over me; I mean, I don't even know your name. It's like, Petty Officer Rouse, or something?"

He burst out in loud laughter. "Rouse? Shit. I'd never hear the end of it if my parents had cursed me by bearing a last name like that. It's Adrian Rogue. First Class Adrian Rogue."

"Well, I'm Vette Renyols, and before you ask, yes, like Corvette. My dad collected them, loved them actually. So, naturally, when I was born, he named me after his most loved collection—his Corvettes." I shrugged and shifted myself more closely to him. My knee now lay across his right upper thigh.

"So," he cleared his throat and set his hand on my thigh, above my left knee, where it rested on his, "you grabbed my ass, remember? I'm still asking myself why a shy, mild-mannered girl such

as yourself would do such a thing to a hardened war veteran like me." He chuckled. *"I must be losing my edge."*

"Shit, I'm not coming off *that* mousy, am I?"
"ABSOLUTELY."

I didn't expect him to say yes! What a slap in the face. Maybe I just need to go for it and show him he's wrong. That he doesn't have my number. *I drew in a deep breath for courage... Fuck it!*

I leaned in, reaching up behind his head and pulling him to me until I grazed his lips with mine. "I guess," I whispered nervously, *"I finally saw something I wanted badly enough to go after it."*

Adrian's eyes narrowed slightly, then darkened with desire. He took his right hand, his large, strong hand, and snaked it under my hair, finding its home at the base of my neck where he applied pressure, bringing me masterfully toward him. His lips met mine with hungry passion. He kissed me deftly, as his left arm reached around my back and pulled me in one swift move until I straddled him. I gasped through our kiss as I felt the hardness of his erection press firmly against the rear seam of my jeans. My knees fell over his hips on either side as the tops of my feet rested on the picnic table.

His hands skillfully skimmed up my sides. My skin drew taut and goose-bumped instantly, as his palms felt the weight of my breasts through my thin t-shirt. His hands were manic, moving masterfully across my breast, to my neck, while he deepened our kiss. His hands massaged their way down my back, one splaying across it, the other gripping my hip as his hard, pronounced arousal ground intimately against me.

"Vee?" I felt a strong calloused hand brush the hair from my cheek. "Vee, wake up."

My brain snapped from its deep contemplation. Lucidity flooded back through my consciousness, pulling me from my dream. *The same fucking dream; my agonizing memories, replayed in my mind like a broken record.*

I slowly opened my eyelids and stared into the honey-brown eyes of my best friend. "Adrian." I cleared my throat and shifted, uncomfortably aware of how close he was, afraid he'd see right through to my heart if I looked into his any longer.

"I figured I'd better wake you up before you said anything more incriminating in your sleep."

"No!" I gasped. "What did I say?"

"Well," he chuckled uncomfortably, "it wasn't so much *what* you were saying, but you were groaning and writhing quite a bit." His lips curved upward just slightly, as red crept up his cheeks.

"Oh my God." I paled and quickly closed my mouth.

He leaned in close, his lips mockingly flirtatious against my ear. "You weren't dreaming of me... were you?" He joked as he straightened and took the seat across the table from me.

"Hell no!" I hoped the vigor in my response didn't betray me.

"Well, that's too bad." He winked at me, knowing that I'd never take him seriously.

This is now how Adrian and I were. *Flirts.*

We'd made out that first night we'd met in Iraq, talking until sun broke over the horizon, and then he'd been sent on a covert op two days later. His mission turned into weeks, then before long it was months since I'd seen him. I'll never forget though, one night I ran into him after he'd returned.

"Remember me?" I'd asked more timidly than I'd envisioned sounding. In an effort to redeem myself and appear more brazen, I ran my hands from his shoulders down to his ass, as he stood overlooking a card game in the crowded base bar, Oasis. I immediately felt him tense, like the first night. I fought a strong feeling of déjà vu. "I thought either you'd transferred or become a casualty of war, it's been so long since I've seen you," I joked playfully, although it was in bad taste. I tried to keep my cool, but what I really wanted to ask was, "Where have you been? Are you okay. Did you think of me at all?"

Adrian stood, steadfast. Unbudging. Seeming completely, and entirely disinterested. So, doing what any tossed chic in my position would do, I snugged up close to his form. "Adrian," I breathed into his ear, "I want you to *fuck* me."

That did the trick. No sooner had the words left my mouth than he'd grabbed my hand and led me briskly away from the loud music, darting off between two tents. Ensconced in the shadows, his lips hungrily met mine. His hands devoured the surface of my skin—roaming. Seeking and finding my sexy curves, he consumed me, taking liberties I'd dreamt these past long months he'd take.

It was dangerous how well he made my body crave him. His tongue delved into my mouth, tasting and teasing. His lips traced searing hot trails across my neck and collarbone, but his arousal. *Fuck.* His cock goaded me, seeing if I'd make good on my earlier tease. I reveled in the attention. *Adrian's attention.* I teased his dick through his camis, relishing the feel of its hardness, his steel rod and pronounced helmet. All I wanted was him in my mouth, where I could savor the feel of him, revel in his musk.

His lips retraced their exploration to my mouth and he kissed me deeply, roughly, lustfully before he froze. With a nearly painful sounding groan, he crammed his hands into his pockets and took a step back from me.

"Damn it, Vee! See what you do to me? Goddamn it!" He hung his head and I watched him kick at a mound of dirt. Then, clearing his throat harshly, he looked back up at me. "You and me. This is a mistake. Sorry." He waved his hands between us. "I know you were just flirting, this isn't who you are, and I took advantage of the bogus invitation." He sighed, "Jeezus, Vee. I haven't seen you in months, but I want you as badly as the first night we met… which is why *we* don't work."

"What do you mean we don't work? You were just *HERE* with me, right?" I could feel my insecurities surfacing, but anger pushed them aside.

"We can be friends…"

I interrupted him, "Friends is bullshit and you know it."

He shook his head and turned to leave.

"Wait!" my voice cracked from the emotion I as feeling and expressing so poorly.

"*This,*" he gesticulated in the air between us "is why we can't be more than friends. Emotions get you killed out in the field. Caring for *someone* more than the mission will compromise it and my men." He moved toward me with conviction, sliding his arms around my waist and pulling my body against his hard lines. "I already care too much for you," he whispered painfully. "Nights when I was freezing in the Afghan mountains were only bearable because thoughts of you warmed my heart."

Fuck me.

"I don't even fucking know you—" he chided himself. "How ridiculous is that?"

"But you do. We shared so much… you know more about who I truly am than some of the friends I've had through high school."

"Vee, it's simple really," he said pushing me gently away, putting distance between us. "I'm already falling for you and that *cannot* happen while I am here on this set of orders." He was being honest, but I could tell it hurt him to shut me out. "You already mean more to me than I'd even believe was possible five months ago, and because of that, I can't draw you into the dark depths of my own vile reality. You'd get hurt in these hellish pits. You're too good, too pure, to exist down here with me. You deserve to be coveted, worshipped, and to do that would eventually ruin me."

"It doesn't have to be that way," I sobbed. "We're made for one another. I know you feel it too!" my voice hitched, seeking confirmation.

He shook his head adamantly. "To love you, Vee, would take me out of the head-space I need to be in every time I leave this base to carry out a covert op. I'd be too worried I wouldn't return to you. It would take my head out of the game." He pressed his palms to his temples, holding his head. "*Fuck…* this wasn't the plan. I wasn't supposed to meet you. Not now."

I heard him mumble something about knowing these were the rules before he took these orders, then he closed the distance he'd put between us, his head dipping so that his perfect lips met mine. He kissed me with such intensity, such caged passion that it stole the air from my lungs. His body molded to mine, his steel frame partnering with my subtle one. I felt his erection growing harder than I thought possible, pressing hungrily for its release, as his hands cupped my ass, then rested at my nape, driving our kiss. I fought for us, for life giving air, for him to realize we didn't need to be over before we began.

It was no use. He backed away from me, robbing me of my future. "Goddamn it, Vee. No more. God help my soul, to love you is to keep you from me. Mark my words, that's the last time I'll ever kiss you." He turned heel and strode off into the darkness between the tents.

I'd wandered, choking back silent sobs, swiping messily at the tears that streamed down my face, until I'd found myself at *our* picnic table. I lay down on it, staring up at the inky blackness above, only the brilliance of the stars to soothe me. I lay in the darkness and listened to the deep, stark sounds of silence. The thrumming of my heart was my only surety, my only comfort. As I listened to the rhythm, I nearly forgot that I'd died watching him walk away.

For months, I couldn't bear to see him. I'd spent my time meeting others for a random hook-up here or there, but even kissing them left me missing Adrian more, so I figured, what was the point? I'd made a point of staying away from his hangouts, and from the side of the base where his tent was.

Eventually, enough time passed and the raw cut he'd made had scabbed over. I'd made it into the base bar and had joined a poker game with Adrian's second and close friend, Tanner Lyons. Not long after, Adrian joined us at the next buy-in. The game had been the vehicle that had steered us back onto the path for a close friendship that I still held dear to my heart. Someday, *someday* I still believed the stars would align themselves and we'd end up together… somehow.

Adrian thrummed on the table until I looked up at him in annoyance, my daydream shattered. "Yes?"

"I don't know, you seem… *off* somehow." He eyed me suspiciously. "Is everything ok?"

You mean besides not being able to get you off my mind? I shrugged.

"Come on now, you know you can talk to me, right, Vee?"

"I guess." I looked behind me to make sure no one was coming and nodded over to Foster, whose head slumped to one side while his chest rose and fell in deep, even breaths. "How long has he been out?"

"I don't know, maybe two or three hours. Why?"

I leaned in. "Cause, nobody, and I mean *NOBODY* can hear about this or I could lose my job."

Adrian raised an inquisitive eyebrow and leaned in, resting his elbows on the teak table between us. "You know, at least *you should know* with everything we've been through, that you can tell me anything, and I'd have your back."

I placed my head in my hands and shook it gently, "Oh Ade, it's bad. I don't know what I was thinking."

"Jeezus, Vee, what is it? You're starting to worry me." His eyes were shrouded, my trouble mirrored in his expression.

"Well, last night, Foster came and got me around 0230 to talk Davien out of wanting to go out." I looked out from my hands. Adrian was intently focused on me.

"And?"

"And, he made an advance."

Adrian sprang up from his seat, interrupting me. "That little piece of shit!"

"NO! No, it's not what you think."

"*Oh really?* Sure as fuck sounds like it."

"Okay, well at first it was…"

He cut me off again, "At first? Jeezus, Vee, what did you do?" He swiveled his chair and plopped down heavily.

"Well, he made an advance—pinned me against the door—and I don't know what he was thinking, or why, but then he kissed me." I reflected. "I was in a state of panic… you know how stressful situations can trigger me. I wasn't thinking…"

"And you let him?" Adrian interjected in loud disbelief.

"Jeezus, lower your voice!" I leaned back, cracked my neck and shook out my shoulders. "He said I was beautiful," I lowered my voice even more, "and sexy." I shrugged, "It's been a long, *long* time Adrian, since…"

"He's a kid, Vee. He's the *PRESIDENT'S KID.*"

"I know." I sighed heavily. "He's not *exactly* a *kid,* but I know. I did smack him, though. I told him never to do that again."

"Well, that's at least something, but where's your head at? This is a prestigious assignment, caring for and protecting the presidential family. If you betray their trust, and word gets out, you'll never work in this field again... *anywhere.*"

"I know. Trust me, I know. I feel terrible, but..."

"There's a but?" he interrupted, leaning in and taking my hands, pulling me across the table until my chest was forcefully against the edge. "It's a good thing you're this security team's captain, because if I were in charge, this would be enough to..."

I eyed him, threateningly. "You'd fire me over this?" My eyes narrowed, and I seethed with anger. "Don't fucking push me, Adrian. We've been through a lot. You're a good soldier, but there's only so much *you* can deny me of... and wouldn't you say that you exceeded that limit back in Iraq?"

At that accusation, or maybe from the memory of any future *us* that he'd ended against my will so abruptly, he released my hands. I massaged my armpits. "And if you ever threaten me again, or use force with me," I spat at him, "Adrian, you'll be the one without a job."

He shook his head as he stood from the table. "We're not done with this conversation," he leaned in on the table, close to where I was sitting, "and bringing up Iraq isn't fair. It's beneath you." He put his hand on my shoulder and eyed me, hurt lingering in his expression, before he strode from the forward cabin.

"Officer Renyols?"

I turned my head as I swiveled my chair to see who was addressing me. Connor was walking into the forward cabin, looking expectantly at me. I turned back around and began searching for my earbuds. After my heated discussion with Adrian, the last thing I wanted to do was talk to Davien's entitled, snobby friend... or that's at least how he'd always acted around me.

"Mind if I join you?"

I looked up at him, studying him really, before nodding. "Sure," I said sarcastically, "why not?"

He smiled at me, then ordered a ginger ale—using his manners, which surprised me greatly.

"Got a minute?" He sounded concerned. "It's about Davien... he's sleeping right now, and I know after we reach Dubai, he'll probably be up at least twenty-four hours before he needs to recharge—unless he passes out sooner," he joked easily.

The flight attendant walked in, and he turned to her, reaching for his drink. "Thanks, this is exactly what the doctor ordered," and smiled at her politely.

So, he DOES have manners. Maybe I was wrong about him...

I crossed my hands in front of me. "So, Connor, you sound like you have something on your mind. What's up?" I smiled to encourage him, hoping he was one of those kids who could communicate clearly what he meant to say. It was selfish of me, but I was in no mood to try to decipher what he meant.

"Well, it's about Davien."

I nodded, waiting.

"Okay, I guess the easiest way to say it, is to just say it. Right?"

Again, I nodded. "Let me guess; when Davien comes to the Coco Bodu Hithi Resort, he has a casual hook-up he sees every time, and he wanted you to warn me that he'd be off schedule and not to worry." I looked at him smugly and cocked an eyebrow. "Am I right?"

"No... *not at all.*" Connor sat back in his leather café-lounge chair, flagging the flight attendant down.

"Can I help you?"

"Sorry to bother you again, but I'd like two shots of Jose Cuervo, please," he requested, looking the flight attendant in her eyes.

"Two for me as well. Please." I smiled at her and mouthed 'Thank you.'

"You know, he was totally right." He sat back in his chair and swiveled from side to side, pensively.

"Oh? Who? About what?"

"Davien." He paused, still gliding his leather seat meditatively from side to side. "Well, he said that you didn't think very highly of him, even after knowing him these past three years, and that you thought he was... how'd he put it?" He accepted his two single bottles, cracked one at the same time as I did, and we toasted in the air before each of us slammed a shot back. "He said that you considered him to be a kid and thought he was an 'arrogant little shit'.

I sat back, stunned as I would've been if he'd gut-punched me. "I've never told him that."

"Does it really matter if you've said it? He still knows it, Cori... you don't mind if I call you, Cori, do you? Dav feels Vette sounds far too harsh for you, and I tend to agree."

"Actually, I'd prefer Vee." I leaned back in my chair, crossing my legs casually. "I've only ever let Davien call me Cori." My admission sounded feeble, even to my ears, so I added, "It's just something special he calls me; it would be strange if you used it is all."

Connor nodded, but scrunched his eyebrows in confusion. "So, if it's special, then you also feel like there's something *special* there? Cause... well, I mean, from what Dav's said, he's got it bad for you."

I shook my head slightly as I leaned forward, motioning for him to do the same. "Connor, it doesn't matter what, *if any*, personal feelings I have toward Davien, President West or anyone else he employs. He hired me to be Davien's personal bodyguard and pseudo-nanny. To confuse my personal feelings with my professional responsibilities would be... irresponsible, to say the least."

"The very least," he agreed. "Okay, but it's like this. You know Dav... he's not exactly the committing type. I mean, you can't *not* know this, right?" I nodded. "You know he pretty much gets any girl that he decides he wants—always has, but especially now that he's *President West's* son." He leaned in even farther. "But, have you noticed that he hasn't been going out the past few months, he's had me over and he's been—hanging out at home—with you? I mean, come on. It's the summer after his senior year, before he hits Columbia up in New York this September, and he's been staying home to watch movies. Which, coincidentally you watch with him." He opened his hands, as though presenting a gourmet meal. "Boom. In your face, right?"

I must have looked stunned, and I was. I slowly leaned back in my lounge chair, searching for words to say, but none came to me. Finally, I sat up, swiveling my chair to see if anyone was around. Once again, Foster looked dead asleep, which was a good thing, because I'd assign him to Davien for the next twenty-four hours while the rest of us slept. Everyone else was settled in the mid-cabin or the aft, possibly resting. "What has Davien told you?"

"He said last summer, when you all went to the Hamptons for his birthday, you wore some white swimsuit with white netting…"

"Mesh." I corrected him.

"Whatever. He said that you were this 'dark-haired, tan-skinned goddess.'"

I chuckled. "He didn't!"

"Yup, he did. He admitted that before that, he was really annoyed by your hovering and not letting him fuck around… but after he saw you in that swimsuit, you were it for him."

"What about Halsey?"

"What about her? Senator Nash just wants his daughter to marry someone rich. I'm sure you're aware that the West family will never, *ever* run out of money, even if Davien tried to spend it all." He chuckled at that one, cracked open his other shot and held it out, urging me to get mine ready. When I had, we toasted again before slamming them back. Truth be told, the way this conversation was going, and after the one I'd just had with Adrian… fuck, I could use a fifth of Cuervo instead of these paltry one-hitters.

I settled more comfortably into my chair and looked at my watch; it read a little after one in the morning. "I figure we'll hit Dubai around two, or a little before."

"What time is it?"

"Ten after one. I don't turn my clock forward the ten hours until after we land in *Malé*."

"*Uggh. We need to just get there already!*" he lamented and shifted uncomfortably. "*Listen, the whole reason he wanted to come here was to spend time with you. I wasn't even part of his plan, but my mom and his dad got this wild idea that he'd have* more fun with me tagging along. Oh yay! It will be so much fun being the third wheel... but it's not like I could tell them that. Besides, between you and me, we think our parents just want to get it on without Dav or me around."

"Well, that could be, but there's still tons of personnel and security staff at the White House. I just brought my skeleton crew."

As the silence between us grew, I felt the long day's fatigue washing down me from my head to my toes. I plugged my earbuds into the armrest and looked up off-handedly at Connor.

"He told me you smacked him after fucking his mouth with your tongue."

I choked. "He said what?" The incredulity was tangible in my voice. I dropped my earbuds.

"Yeah. He said you were both pretty into it... I mean," he leaned in close, "you weren't at first, but then when you got all into it, well, it wound him up pretty tight." He shifted, looking at Foster, then motioning to me.

I looked over, but Foster was still breathing heavily, his head still slumped to the side, so I relaxed some.

"He said that you grabbed his hair, fucked his mouth, and were into it when he grabbed your ass and ground his dick into you." He choked on the last part.

Serves you right! You shouldn't have heard about this and sure as hell shouldn't be telling me you did.

"Did you kiss him back, or is this another of his bullshit stories?" he paused, reflecting—studying the horror on my face. "Oh, fuck, it is huh? He always gets me!"

I let him assume Davien had spun a thread and settled into my seat, ready to forget the whole thing.

"I just can't seem to get the details out of my mind," he said more to himself than to me. "I mean, why would he say all those things if..."

I interrupted him, "It doesn't matter, Connor."

"Was he crazy thinking you *were* into it? I mean, he said it felt like you were, that you kissed him back, and that it could've gone farther... I mean before you freaked out and smacked him."

"Connor, this is really none of your business, it's not something I feel comfortable discussing with you."

He winked, nodding that he understood, "I'll take that as a *yes*." He stood and walked up to me. "He needs this, ya know. He needs to love someone and feel excited about life again. You could really be good for him." Leaving it at that, he strode from my view.

I tried resting the remainder of the flight to Dubai, during our 6000-gallon refueling spree, and the remaining two hours to *Malé, Maldives. It wasn't until I felt warm breath at my ear, and heard "Cori, we're here," that I pried my eyelids open.*

-FOUR-

As planned, once we'd swept the property, had settled in and unpacked, I assigned Officer Foster Black to Davien and Connor, while the rest of us got some much-needed shut-eye.

When I opened my eyes, dim moonlight poured into my overwater bungalow. I could see the private pool and chaise lounges out on the deck, and past it, the calm ocean waters. The sky was dark, except for the sliver of moon and bright stars. They were one of the main reasons I enjoyed travelling—to places like Turkey, Iraq, Afghanistan, Fiji, New Zealand, and here, the Maldives—the night sky, or rather, the stars. They never seemed as brightly lit as when I was in dark, wide-open spaces, away from cities, bright lights and bustle. The quieter side of the world knew the night's beauty intimately; it was what us Westerners were missing—at least in my opinion. The inky blackness brought such an intense peace and quiet that it was overwhelming at times. Sometimes, I was merely breathless, but on nights like tonight, I lay mesmerized by the raw beauty.

My eyes adjusted to the dim light and I took a look around the bungalow. Mine was one of the largest. Granted, it was Davien's, but I had an attached room. It was the only way President West would allow Davien to go alone. Adrian was with Connor and I was bunking with Davien.

"Stunning."

I jumped at hearing his voice and fought to see him in the shadows that hugged the corners. There, by the door that adjoined mine to his, he stood still, watching me quietly.

"Where's Foster? What time is it?"

"Around one. You've been out about nine hours."

"Where's Foster?"

"Reading. I went out the living room slider. I told him I wanted to take some 'me time' out on the deck, under the stars."

"And he bought that crap?" I laughed as I pulled myself up, straightening the comforter.

"Why wouldn't he?"

I shrugged. What am I going to say? Because you've never needed 'you time' since I was hired three years ago? Seriously?

Davien walked out of the shadows, wearing only his board shorts. I inhaled sharply. He'd most certainly grown up since last summer. His abdomen was etched, an eight-pack clearly defined, and the 'V' disappeared into his low-slung shorts. I noted the strings were laced but not tied. His pecs were cut, and his shoulders and arms ripped. I mean, I'd been to the gym tons of times on security detail for him, but he hadn't looked like this afterward... when had he grown into a man? When did I start seeing him as a man?

"Swim with me?" The eagerness and hopefulness in his question, caused his voice to hitch. "I mean, we don't have to go in the ocean. The infinity pool would be just as cool."

Against my better judgment, I agreed. "Give me a minute—why don't you go ahead and get in?" He nodded and strode toward the open sliding wall. I dug around in my suitcase until I found my white suit—the same one Connor had mentioned—and headed to the bathroom to put it on.

Satisfied with my loose chignon and the tendrils that cascaded around my face, I hoisted my 'girls' back in place. I gave myself a final once-over before turning off the light and stepping back into the darkness that shrouded my bedroom. I padded softly across the bamboo floor and out the open slider. My feet never made a sound as I closed in on the pool.

"I was wondering if you'd changed your mind." Davien looked up at me and flashed one of his sexy smiles.

Jeezus, I'm so going to regret this later, but I need to get my mind off Adrian. So long as nobody knows, what's the harm in a little dip to relax?

I stepped down the stairs into the pool, its salty warmth enveloping me like a baby floating in its momma's womb. It was so comforting. Any tension I'd felt before entering the water immediately left my weary muscles and wary mind.

"Mmm," I hummed, dipping my shoulders down into the water. "This is heavenly, such a great idea, Davien. Thanks for suggesting it—I wouldn't have gotten in if you hadn't invited me." Flashing him a genuine smile, I headed over to the edge closest to the ocean and rested my forearms in the channel that ran along the entire edge of the pool.

The stars glistened off the top of the waves, light dancing up and down on their crests. I could hear the waves as they rolled in, softly breaking below us against the bungalow's supports.

"Magical, isn't it?"

I startled at the husky voice behind me. Davien glided up. His arm brushed mine as he raised it to hug the side of the pool like I was. Oddly, the simple, accidental touch electrified my skin. *What is wrong with me?* I figured my reaction had more to do with the intimate conversation that I'd had with Adrian earlier than with Davien brushing his arm against mine.

"It's hard to believe we left D.C. almost two days ago already."

"Yeah," I breathed, "the time change nearly accounts for half a day."

"Okay, Ms. Technical," he razzed me and bumped my hip with his own.

"No, I was just saying..." I stopped myself. After all, what was the point? "You know, Dav..." I paused, turning and reaching for his arm. He jumped when my cool hand came to rest on his warm skin. "We don't always have to do this... tension thing."

He cocked his head, his eyes measuring mine, his face pensive and thoughtful. "Do we? I mean, our dynamic, is it always tense?" He chuckled, "Well, maybe there's some tension, I'll give you that... but there's different kinds."

"I don't know. It just always seems like you fight me on everything. I don't want that. I'd rather be your friend than nanny."

"Well then stop, being my nanny, I mean. And before you go off on how Dad hired you and kept you on to take care of me in the absence of my mom, know that while I needed that two years ago, I don't need it now. My needs have... changed."

My eyes flickered to his. A blush crept up my neck and spread across my cheeks. "Davien, I run your security detail. It's not practical for me to satisfy your other needs. I'd find myself in need of a job." I laughed and slid my hand from his shoulder, down his muscular arm, before resting it on my other one.

We stared out over the ocean, entranced by the stars' reflections and the gentle lapping of the waves. My body gravitated towards his, and before long, we were hip to hip, shoulder to shoulder.

"Can I ask you something, Cori?" I felt his intense, clear blue eyes measuring me, willing me to look at him. But, in order to do that, I'd be mere inches from his soft, kissable lips, so I continued to stare off toward the ocean's horizon.

"Depends," I prevaricated. "I may not answer if I don't like the question." It was hard not to feel close to him, given as much time as I'd spent with him over the past three years.

"Fair enough." I felt him shift; now his thigh and knee grazed mine. He sighed deeply, as if mustering up courage to ask. "Our kiss, the night before we left…"

Fuck, this again?

He waited, as if hoping I'd jump in and save him from this awkwardness. I maintained my silence. "I mean, it wasn't just me, right? Like, you felt it too, didn't you? I didn't imagine your hands in my hair or your body molding to mine? What happened?"

I turned toward him, just as he ran his fingers through his wet hair. "So, what exactly are you asking me, Dav?"

"Why did you slap me?"

I turned toward him. My arm still rested on the edge of the pool as I gently splashed warm water over my neck and chest. "It really doesn't matter, does it?"

"Yeah, to me it kinda does. I mean, sure, I know you're older than me, and that if we started something, you might lose interest in me, thinking I'm still a fucking kid or whatever, but…"

I interrupted him. "You startled me, okay?" I lowered my voice and looked toward the living room slider. The coast was still clear. "When you kissed me, I fought it. I did." It sounded more like I was trying to convince myself than Davien of this fact. "But my mind and body went numb. I couldn't move." *And I panicked…* I thought back to Iraq and how I never responded under pressure, the way I'd been trained since…

I swallowed. "My body tingled and fired off in all the right places," I sighed, "and all the wrong places. It wasn't something I expected. Kissing you back was not something I was supposed to do." I leaned in toward Davien. "My response to you when you kissed me," I moaned, but went for it, since I was already in this deep, "well, let's just say that I haven't felt that in a *really, REALLY,* long time. So, I slapped you. It was the only way I knew to regain control of the situation."

Before I could move or put up any resistance, Davien had pulled me between him and the tiled wall. His lips met mine with an intensity that stole my breath away and robbed any willpower I had—should I have tried to muster any. His lips seared mine with their heat and ferocity. The kiss was passionately savage and brutal; my lips would feel bruised in the morning.

His teeth grazed my jawline and branded the skin on my neck as he nipped and kissed a hot trail to my shoulder, before returning to my lips, which were slightly parted as I panted with desire. A strong hand drove our kiss, navigating it from my nape, where it had woven in my now loose tresses. His other remained respectful, steering clear of my heaving breasts, but pulling my frame to his with the strong hold he had against my back.

I kissed him with abandon. At first, I'd poured all my pent-up feelings from my earlier dealings with Adrian into this kiss; however, Davien stole every conscious thought from my head once I felt his raging erection against my abdomen. At that moment, it became all about him. *ONLY HIM.*

"Cori," he breathed, "I've wanted this for so long." He nuzzled his mouth into my neck, breathing raggedly into it. I could feel his heart thrumming out of his chest, against the beat of my own.

"This feels so… wrong," I admitted warily.

"Not to me," he mumbled into my neck as he held me tightly, his erection noticeably present against my own pulsating intimates.

"I want to, but we just…" I paused, trying to catch my breath, willing my heart and raging hormones to quit their wild assault on my senses, "…can't."

"Damn it, Cori, I want you so bad." Frustration laced his words. "You can't tease me like this and then pretend it means nothing… like last time." His voice hitched in his throat, indicating real emotion lay behind his words.

I rested my forehead on his strong shoulder, "I just don't know…"

Davien pulled back from me, so that the warm salty water now created a barrier between our two energies; two energies that were pulling toward each other, in spite of the moral war I was waging within myself.

"Jeezus, *fuck*," he growled, exasperated. "What is there to know? What more do you need to feel to know that what we'd have, would be fucking amazing?"

"It's not that simple for me. I'm not the president's kid—I don't have an instant get out of jail free card. For me, it's not just about how I feel. I was hired to do a job…"

Davien interrupted me. "Excuses, excuses. Forgive me if it all sounds like bullshit."

"You're nineteen. I wouldn't expect you to understand."

"Low blow playing the age card… Jeezus, Cori. FUCK!"

"Is everything all right out here?"

I looked past Davien and saw Officer Foster Black standing at the lip of the living room slider, eyeing us suspiciously.

"Absolutely! The water's fine. Want to join us?"

"Davien being difficult? Need a break?"

"Nah," I hedged, "he's my charge; it's just a regular day in the office for me."

"Alright, if you say so. Hey, if you've got it, I'd like to get some shuteye?"

"What time is it?"

"Just after 0200."

"Absolutely, Foster. See you back on the clock at 1000?"

"Eight hours." I could hear him sigh from where I was in the pool, even with the waves breaking softly under the bungalow. "If you say so, boss-lady." I could hear the smile in his voice, though, so I wouldn't push the attitude I'd perceived a moment before.

"Call me on your cell. I'll give you your assignment then."

"Rodger that."

I watched him turn from the open-wall slider and head inside.

"How's it feel to be the one in charge, never taking orders and always giving them?"

I laughed in disbelief. *"Trust me,"* I muttered sarcastically, "I take orders." Before he could ask me who, I added, "Your *dad*, President Ethan West, has given me strict orders. Why the fuck else do you think I haven't jumped your bones already?"

"I don't know, to be honest, cause with the fucking chemistry we have, it should be a no-brainer... in spite of the fact that my dad's president, or that I'm nineteen. And honestly, it really shouldn't matter if you're head of my security, cause I'd never be safer than when I'd be buried deep inside you.

Holy fuck. This kid, this man, strikes a chord with me. I don't know how much longer I can do this.

Davien closed the gap between us, his warm body so near I could feel him without him actually touching me. He leaned in, his breath hot at my ear, and still, no part of him touched me. My skin was aware, and the small hairs stood on end, just waiting for him to break that invisible barrier between us. "Cori," he hummed, "can't you just imagine how I'd feel sliding into your slick sweetness? How hard I'd be against your velvet softness?"

Where the fuck did you learn to talk like this? Who talks like this? A slight moan escaped from my parted lips, waiting for the kiss I prayed was inevitable.

"I'd worship every inch of your skin, touch all the right spots, even the elusive ones inside you. You'd want for nothing. I'd make you beg for me to make you come and once you did, I'd make you come again and again."

"How did... Where did..." I croaked. "I mean, I've been watching you for the last three years. How did you learn...? God," I groaned. "Never mind. I sound like an idiot."

"At prep-school mostly, during practice, after games, at friend's houses, with friends' mothers, even at the movies. Some of the officers you put in charge... One of them... what was his name, Officer Duggar? He was the easiest, always on his phone and if I said I needed to go do something for fifteen minutes, he let me. No questions asked."

"No shit?" I was glad I'd fired him, but not nearly so glad that I'd changed the subject, because my core still ached, and I still pulsed from the promises he'd made. My lips still begged silently to be kissed. "Hey, Dav, it's getting late. I really need to think about winding this down."

At this, he placed his large palms on my shoulders, sliding them down until he encircled my wrists, cuffing me. He closed the minuscule distance between us, pressing his hard lines into my softer ones. Leaning in, his lips grazed my ear. "Cori…" He lowered himself in the water just enough so my intimates were line up with his stout erection, which jutted substantially from inside the front of his shorts. "Are you sure," he purred, "I can't change your mind?"

To this, he slid the full length of himself from the entry of my core, all the way until I felt his hardness at my abdomen. His mouth kissed and nipped at my neck. I writhed, struggled to break free from his hold, but there was also something incredibly sexy about being controlled; about NOT being in charge for a change. He took his powerful hips and ground them into me, digging and grinding into my suited intimates until I couldn't take it anymore. "Please," I breathed, "please…" The plea fell from my lips, shameless, hungry and wanton.

Davien released my left hand, which I threw up around his neck and entangled in his waves, crushing my body more fully into his.

"Cori, may I?" he questioned, seeking my permission, which I answered by pulling his mouth down to mine for a deep kiss. His fingers deftly slid my suit aside, palming me fully before entering me with first his index, and then both his index and middle fingers. I am not sure if it was him or me who moaned, but a deep throaty groan came from somewhere deep, somewhere that needed what the other was offering.

I was mad with desire. I no longer felt the wind on my back, or heard the waves breaking. I resided in a world where only he and I existed. That is, until I heard my security phone chiming.

I tore my lips from his, ragged and battle-worn from our intensely passionate endeavor. "I *HAVE* to get that. It's either President West or one of my team." I fought to get my gumby-like body to work for me, but my muscles lacked muscle memory, still drunk from our kiss, and well… my body… *Fuck*. It was all over on that front. My core still fluttered from what he had stirred inside me, and my apex still vibrated—on the verge of finding its release. To put it simply, I was a fucking mess. I fought through the liquid prison that had so recently been my sanctuary, until I reached the stairs. I fumbled climbing them—*Why the fuck won't my body work, damn it?!*

I dashed inside, just as my phone quit ringing. I recognized the number and dialed it in a heartbeat, concerned that there had been a security breech as late as it was. "Adrian, talk to me. Is everything alright?"

"Yes?" He drew out the syllable as though it was weird for me to be asking him that. "Are *you* okay?"

I rolled my eyes, *I would've been more than okay...* "I am but let me get back with you. I just heard something on the other side. Give me ten." I hung up and drew in a deep, cleansing breath. I'd just bought myself ten minutes to compose myself, get my story straight, and get Davien squared away for the night.

I turned back toward the slider and jumped. Davien was standing there. *Goddamn it! Doesn't he know it's dangerous sneaking up on a former soldier like this? Especially one as... messed up as me.*

"Guess that means the night's over?" His voice was hopeful, but he'd clearly heard my brief conversation with Adrian.

"It is. Honestly, it should've been when you'd asked me to join you in the pool. I knew what you were really asking and accepted the invitation anyways." I walked up to him and wrapped my chilly arms around his waist. "Thanks for tonight."

"So, what? That's it? You're acting like we're over, like what just happened never took place. What the fuck, Cori?"

I placed my palms on his cheeks, angling his arrogant face down at me so I could look into his striking, clear blue eyes, which looked more like stormy waters than clear seas. "I'm *not* saying that, Davien. What I *am* saying is that right now, at this very moment, I have a job to do. I cannot make you any promises, except one. If I don't call Officer Rogue back when my ten minutes are up, he will be here in a hot second, assuming there's a security breech. What I need is for you to *please*, go to your side and crawl into bed. Watch TV, or act like you're sleeping. It's immaterial, but I need you gone. Now."

He nodded—thankfully getting the message I was sending him—and bent down, brushing a kiss on my forehead before exiting my room through our adjoining doors.

I flew to the slider and pulled the wall panels closed, dragging the heavy blackout curtain across it. Running into the bathroom, I grabbed my thrashed boot camp sweats from my open suitcase. Rushing to put them on, I only paused for a second to look in the mirror. I was flushed. I looked alive. *Maybe Davien is good for me after all...*

I opened the door between my suite and the bungalow and ran to the living room slider. I struggled a bit to get the panels to slide closed, but when I had, the room felt secure. Safe and enclosed. I jogged over to the front door and checked that it had been locked behind Foster. It had been. Lastly, I knocked on Davien's door and quietly opened it. He smiled at me and went back to watching some local TV variety show. I quietly walked back to my room, closing my doors behind me. Grabbing my work phone, I picked it up to text Adrian.

-False Alarm. All secure here.

-9.5 minutes.
On time as usual. ☺

-Thanks 4 checking in.
I meant 2 earlier.
I'm jet-lagging bad.

-Get some rest.
I can cover the morning shift?

-Nah. It's my job 2 lead my team.
I will just suck it up.

-Always the dutiful soldier.
2 tired for a night-cap?

-It's 0235!

-Perfect!
It's Happy Hour back home!

-IDK Ade…

-We have a few things we need 2 address…
That conversation we weren't done having.

-Waaay 2 tired for that. ☹

-2 tired 4 company?
Had U on my mind since the flight.
Would really like 2 C U?

-Meet me @ the front door.
Don't knock.

-Rodger meet you at the front door.
Don't knock. ☺

I set my phone down beside my bed and shuffled toward my bedroom door. *What have I gotten myself into now?* In less than a minute I was standing on the wooden walkway that led up to my bungalow. I saw Adrian leave his residence and stride toward me. When he reached me, I turned, and he followed me inside. I shut the door, and we walked in silence to my room.

I closed the door and headed for my bed. "I warned you I was tired, but you wanted to talk. So, talk, on my terms." I smiled at him pleasantly, climbing under the covers, still in my thrashed boot camp sweats.

"I'm sure I don't need to ask, but who's watching Connor?"

"I called Officer Cruz. He wasn't any too happy I was waking him up, but I spun a thread about how you needed me to go over tomorrow's deets. Anthony's already messaged me that he's posted there." He smiled as he rounded my side of the bed. "No worries. It's *all* taken care of."

"Well, kick your shoes off and climb in then." I patted the bed beside me, encouraging my best friend to take a load off. "So, what did you want to *discuss* exactly?" I jested. "Cause if it's a lecture, you can walk your silly ass back out my door."

Adrian did exactly as I'd encouraged him to do and settled in. He snuggled up next to me and wrapped his muscular arm around me.

He and Davien were such polar opposites. Where Davien was *mostly* proper and groomed for politics, Adrian couldn't care less about propriety and decorum, and you sure as hell wouldn't see him running for any type of political position. Davien was obviously younger, and with it, he lacked maturity—or call it life experience. In contrast, Adrian was hewn from the cloth of life. He was mature, responsible and the most dependable person I knew. I could count on him with my life, and his past experiences were reflected in how he handled all situations with ease. I guess, after being shot at, the rest of the shit life threw at him must have seemed pretty easy to take. I know similar experiences have forever changed me.

The men were close to the same size, but I'd never felt as secure and protected as when I was in Adrian's arms. He was ripped, muscular and fit. Not one of those sausage-beefcakes you see pumping iron at the gym, although I'm sure his Adonis-like physique wasn't just from rock climbing, hiking, biking and all the other sports he did.

Davien's body though, was just that—sure, he swam, and his shoulders showed it, but the rest... well, that was from hours in the gym. He was lean and fit too, but somehow, his frame lacked the strength Adrian's had. Not that I was complaining about either—fuck, what kind of girl would I be if I did? It's just, Davien was somehow... softer. *It's because he doesn't have 'killing' eyes... the eyes of a war-torn soldier who's taken lives. Much, unfortunately, like my own.* I sighed heavily.

"Where's your head at, Vee?" He squeezed me for good measure.

"I don't know, just thinking about stuff."

He chuckled, "Shit, when aren't you?"

I looked up at his warm, chestnut eyes, and butterflies exploded in my gut. *Fuck.* "Life's just crazy, right? I mean like with us. Who would've ever thought that after our past in Iraq…" I exhaled.

"Vee, I'd rather leave that chapter buried."

Instantly, my bodied hardened against his side. "Sure, fine. Whatever." I sat up and tried to find more space between our bodies. "Why did you want to come over so badly, Ade? I'm tired, and moody, badly jet lagging… I thought you wanted to talk about our conversation on the plane?"

"I'm concerned about you getting entangled in President West's web."

"Oh?" This sounded interesting.

"Connor's been talking my goddamn ear off; you know, he wants you and the *kid* together. I think he's hoping that if Ethan is fixated on the affair between you two, then he won't be as focused on his mom… at least that's what I've gathered."

"How would Ethan find out? There'd be no way the president would know unless… *oh…*," It hit me with the force of a head-on collision. "Connor is going to say something."

"It sounds that way, Vee. Like I said earlier, if you get blacklisted by the president, you aren't working for anyone in D.C." He pulled me in tighter to him. "I don't know what it is," he breathed softly, "but being this close to you has always made me feel—*centered*. At home." He shook his head, as though to snap out of the spell I was unknowingly spinning. "Anyways," he cleared his throat, "I just think you really need to be careful when it comes to Davien. He comes with a whole boatload of bullshit, and suppose you guys hit it off, where would it go? What future do you see with him?"

I shrugged. "I haven't gotten that far."

"You!?" His shock registered in his voice. "The girl who overthinks everything? Besides, remember Tanner Lyons? My second in Iraq? He's been pestering the shit out of me to put a bug in your ear. He wants in."

I laughed, still shaken by Adrian's earlier confession. *Somewhere in that big head of his, I still do it for him!* "Oh yeah, great. That's the last thing I need, hooking up with your guy best friend. Then we'd be locked into a weird triangle forever."

"Triangle?" And then it dawned on him, as if he didn't already know. "Vee, I'm seeing Natalie."

"I know, but it isn't serious; at least, I didn't think it was."

"Well, it's not, but you and I work together every day."

"So? I'd be working every day with Tanner, too."

He squeezed me, "You've got me there." He sighed. "It's just, I don't know, I thought we'd moved on to being *just* friends."

I looked up at him, searching his warm, honey depths for any sign of encouragement.

"Fuck, Vee," he grated. "Your damn eyes… your goddamn green eyes still do it for me."

His mouth collided with mine, as though we were two magnets who'd been instantly flipped, our attractions now pulled toward the other instead of pushing. His tongue ran across my lips, and I parted them, inviting him in. He aggressively sought mine, and we engaged in a match; spearing and jousting, nipping and biting. Instantly, I grew wet with need, a need that had been long denied, a thirst that only Adrian could quench.

With the skill of a lover who knows what he's doing, he slid his hand off my shoulder to my hip. He seized the other and spun me effortlessly onto his lap, so that I straddled him. His large, strong hands gripped my hips possessively. Memories of our nights together in Iraq flooded back to me as I felt his engorged erection at my clothed apex.

His left hand clenched my loose tresses as his right grasped my hip tighter, guiding it in a salacious dance. He rocked me back and forward as he thrust, his movements restrained, but did nothing to disguise the passion that had been belayed for far too long.

"Jeezus, Ade…" I struggled for the words to convey what this meant, how good this felt. "God, I've wanted this for…"

"…ever." He rasped, finishing my sentence through clenched teeth.

I could only nod as my mouth danced with his, my emotions too tumultuous to express. His hand went from being entangled in my hair, to tenderly touching my face, and then back to my nape, guiding the cadence of our kiss. Our passion was all over the board, first fervent and needy, then passionate, then soft and tender, and last... back to lustful and shameless. His hand on my hip elicited more moans from me as he rocked me on his erection. Our clothes did nothing to hide our need, or my readiness for him.

Then, as suddenly as our licentious affair began, it ended. His hand slid from my hair, to my shoulder, and from my hip, to rest quietly on my thigh. He pulled back, abandoning my lips. The sound of our labored breaths echoed off the walls of my room.

"Damn it," Adrian grumbled as he lifted me off his lap, simultaneously shifting out of my way. He rolled off the opposite side of my bed and adjusted himself.

"Ade? Adrian?"

"Give me a minute," he grumbled.

It stung. *How can he be so cold now, so emotionally vacant? Did I do something wrong?* I slid off the bed, grabbed a pair of leggings and took them to the bathroom to change.

When I came out, I noticed my curtains had been opened and soft, incandescent light streamed in through the closed slider. Adrian stood there, pensive, looking out at the black ocean. He must have sensed I was there, because without even looking at me he began to talk, in a pained voice, "I'm sorry, Vee."

I walked up to him, placing my hand tenderly on his shoulder. He stiffened, so I let it slide off.

"You're my superior; it was unprofessional that I took the liberties that I did..."

I cut him off angrily, "Is that what this is about? Cause I don't give a damn about being your boss right now." I moved toward the slider, turning so I could see his face. I looked him in the eyes. "What is going on? Did I do something wrong? Why are you always shutting me out?"

Adrian looked down at me, his chestnut eyes lacking their usual luster and zest for life. "I thought I'd moved past this. Sorry."

"Will you quit apologizing? What's really going on?"

He stood there for a time, cold as steel. I decided it was best not to push him. I could see it was more of the same, more of Iraq, and I didn't want to go months this time without my best friend.

Work would be awkward, and the last thing I wanted was for him to put in for a transfer.

Finally, he slapped his palms on the glass, resting them there as he leaned his forehead between them. He shook his head sadly. "I can't. I just can't do this with you."

"Adrian?" I reached for him, but my hand fell short. "Ade, I don't understand. Don't do this again. Please, at least give me something, some reason why…" my voice quivered, constricted by the confusion, fear and so many more emotions balled up inside me. Silent tears travelled down my face.

"Vee, it's nothing personal." I opened my mouth to protest, but he continued. "It's me. We're just not good for each other." At that quiet disclosure, he pushed away from the slider and headed toward my bedroom door.

"The hell we're not!" I snarled, pissed.

"Vee, I'm not… you're not going to do this. I'm seeing Natalie. Maybe it works out for us and maybe not, but I'm not being fair to her. You also need to consider Davien's feelings in all of this."

"What about being fair to me, or don't I count?"

He sighed heavily. "Of course you count, but I don't want to ruin what you and I have. You're my best friend, and I don't want to lose that."

"What makes you think this won't work?"

"Trust me, I know me. With you, I'm not myself. I feel too…" he sighed, his composure wavering a brief moment before the walls slammed back up. "Trust me, it just won't." He headed with finality toward my door, "I'll let myself out." His words were icy, cold, unfeeling. He opened my door. "See you tomorrow."

That was it. He walked away from me. The sound of the door clicking was like a knife to my heart. A million thoughts ran through my mind but one stood out—*he hates the vulnerability I bring out in him.*

-FIVE-

I settled into the couch at the aft of the cabin with my fountain pen and journal—*I guess I'd better do as the good doctor prescribed and get some of this shit out of my head.* The pen began to glide effortlessly across the page...

> *If it hadn't been for Davien, I never would've made it through this past week. Thankfully, though, he and I have grown closer. It eased the pain of losing Adrian... again.* I wiped angrily at a single renegade tear.
>
> *After Adrian left my room that first night, Davien came in and found me curled into a ball, crying.*
>
> *"You two have a past." It wasn't a question. It was all he said, as though he'd understood the pain I was in and decided not to be an ass about it. He matured in my eyes and gained my respect as he nursed me through the night, and next couple of days.*
>
> *Adrian and I? Well, fuck. Where to start?*
>
> *We just went back to as normal as possible. He acted like nothing happened, and I've tried my damnedest to keep it professional. I've done pretty well, I think.*
>
> *So far today, we all had lunch on the beach, splashed in the clear waters the Maldives are famous for, and even swam with stingrays and turtles. It's been a good day.*
>
> *Adrian joined Davien and me in our motorcade to the airport earlier, and even that went off without a hitch. We all visited and jested with each other. It appeared as though Adrian and I were back to being best friends again, which to Davien's credit, he's been handling like a pro.*

I felt a light touch on my shoulder and looked up from my journaling, into a hypnotizing set of clear blue eyes that were quickly becoming my favorite. Davien motioned for me to remove my earplugs. "What's up?" I said sunnily, flashing him a big, genuine smile. I'd found that so long as I wasn't around Adrian, being happy was relatively easy; otherwise, it was a chore.

"The captain just announced we need to prepare for landing." He offered his hand to me, which I gladly accepted. He pulled me up from the clutches of the couch I'd been lying on for the past hour or so, while writing about the past week.

We walked from the rear of the plane, through the mid-cabin, to the café-lounge seats in the front cabin. I nodded to Adrian and Foster before taking the seat Davien—ever the gentleman—had swiveled for me. Adrian would've just plopped down across from me. Like I'd noted on fifty if not a hundred occasions, these two men were polar opposites. Davien buckled into the leather seat across the teak table from me, and without pause, took my hand in his. Reality seeped in that we needed to reprise our roles, and I pulled mine out from under his.

-SIX-

Sliding into a seat across from a stern, all business President Ethan West, I watched as he signed a document that his assistant had brought him. "Thank you, Ollie. That will be all for now."

Ollie nodded politely at his dismissal. I followed him with my eyes as he strode confidently from the Oval Office. My gaze returned to the president. He sat there, his hands clasped, studying me. I felt my back straighten as I subconsciously squared up my shoulders.

"Officer Renyols?" He paused for effect.

I waited for him to say something else, but he just sat there glowering at me. His scowl unnerved me. "Sir?" I prodded as I fought to keep panic under lock and key.

"I'm sure you have surmised why I have called you in here." He dropped his clasped hands onto a manila folder that lay on his desk. He opened it and removed a document, which he began to read from.

"Officer Vette Renyols, when you were asked if you have engaged in vaginal/penal sexual intercourse with my son; you answered no. The test confirmed that was the truth. When you were asked if you had engaged in any form of anal penetration; you answered no. The test confirmed that was the truth. When you were asked if you had engaged in cunnilingus, you answered no. The test confirmed that was the truth. When you were asked if you had engaged in fellatio, you answered yes. The test confirmed that was the truth. When asked if my son had placed objects; fingers, vibrators, phallic toys inside your vagina; you answered yes. The test confirmed that was the truth." He closed the folder, clearing his throat uncomfortably. "Do I need to continue?"

I struggled to hear him past the loud beating of my heart, and shallow breaths I fought to suck in. "No, sir."

"I'm sorry, but I didn't hear you." His eyes remained steely and fixed squarely on me. I squirmed under his intense scrutiny, my clammy hands tightly folded over the chair armrests.

I cleared my throat and hedging my trembling, I held onto what little self-respect I had left, "No. Sir."

"So, then... after reviewing the lie-detector results, I have determined that you were being forthcoming and honest with me earlier when I had questioned you about the nature of yours and Davien's relations." At this, his gaze softened a hair as he leaned back in his chair. "I am not in the habit of apologizing, but I'm doing exactly that. It was wrong of me to accuse you of lying." He sighed. "Vette, can I just talk to you as a father to his... his, son's girlfriend?"

My eyes grew wide, as I gently shook my head from side to side in disbelief, some of my panic subsiding. "Yes, Mr. President. I would like that very much."

"Well, then call me Ethan."

"Sir... err, Ethan." My heart still beat erratically.

"Vette, Kait and I welcomed you into our home over three years ago when my son was a strapping sixteen-year-old in love with his high school sweetheart, Amity. We took a risk on you. Your personnel file was strong. You'd proven yourself in your military career, and again while working for Academi. Your references were glowing and your conduct impeccable. You received the highest level of security clearance and have maintained it through the duration of your career... I mean, we took all of these things into account."

He leaned forward, placing his elbows on his mahogany desk. "The one thing that gave me pause—the bombing and terrorist incident in Iraq— Kait glossed over, commenting that many contributing members of society had PTSD and pasts they could not escape from, and who were we to deny you your history for a future with us?" His eyes moistened, and his voice grew suddenly soft. His gentleness did nothing to prevent the terrible memories from welling up, restarting my panicked pulse. *Iraq. That fateful day. The terrorist. The gunfire. The explosion. The pain...*

"Kait adored you from the get-go and was convinced that having you in Davien's life was the right move. She wanted you to give Amity a run for her money, be there for Dav when she wasn't... It was as though she looked right into the future and had this all mapped out."

"Sir." I cleared my throat, trying to speak through my frozen vocal cords. "I NEVER had any intention of this happening."

"Well, that's good because *THIS* isn't going to happen. Your relations with Davien ended the moment you walked into this room. Is that clear?"

My heart shuddered as it slammed shut, denying me the freedom to decide what was in my best interest. I'd known this was coming, but it didn't make the finality of it all any easier. I willed away tears, but they welled up in spite of my efforts to keep them at bay. "Yes, Mr. President. Crystal," I croaked. I hadn't admitted it, but Davien had made me forget Adrian, even if just for a brief time... and I'd been happy these past few weeks.

"Exactly how did it happen, if you don't mind me asking?"

"Of course." I took a deep breath, willing, praying my nerves and panic response would just *fucking* stop. "I entered his apartment one night at his request to go out... if memory serves it was nearing 0300. Davien had been drinking and came on to me. I shut that down immediately, but it planted a seed, which grew under all of his flirtatious attentions towards me on his birthday trip. He knows what he wants and makes sure he gets it."

A genuine smile of pride spread across the president's face, "I'll be damned. I wondered... Just between you and me, that's how I finally got my Kait." He chuckled softly. "I guess the apple doesn't fall far from the tree."

"No, Mr. President, it would appear that it doesn't."

"Ethan."

"Ethan, I recognize my gross lapse in judgement, taking your trust for granted. For that I am gravely sorry."

President Ethan West sat back up, straight in his chair, resuming his role as Head of State. "Yes, well, trust is a curious thing. As it turns out, you've redeemed yourself by being so honest, which is why I am not going to blacklist you in D.C. or fire you; however, you will not be head of Davien's security anymore."

I nodded as I drew in a shaky breath, "I understand, Sir."

He buzzed Ollie and the door immediately opened. "Take Officer Renyols and debrief her on the opportunities I am affording her."

"Yes, Mr. President."

I rose, nodding to Ethan, and followed Ollie from the Oval Office as three men in suits came in at that same time.

I glanced at my watch, 0137. I walked through the empty corridors of the executive quarters, closing doors and turning off lights. I walked past my room, pausing in front of Davien's. I hesitated before knocking. He needed his sleep since he was scheduled to fly out today in a few hours, but the desire to say goodbye on my own terms encouraged me to rap softly on his door.

We've grown so close these past few weeks since getting home from his birthday trip. I wonder how he's going to take this news?

I struggled to calm my pounding heart. The surge of adrenaline from my earlier confrontation with the president made me uncomfortable as it brought back the same bodily responses from that fateful day. I leaned against the door, my breathing shallow, panic threatening to consume me.

The door creaked softly on its hinges as Davien cracked it, then held it wider for me to slip in. He embraced me before the door clicked in its jamb. I collapsed into his arms.

"Jeezus, Cori. Are you okay?" His tone was concerned, and he held me tightly as he stroked my hair. I just trembled in his arms, my façade down, vulnerable. "Man, Cori, I've missed you. Please, tell me you're okay. Is everything alright? What's wrong?"

I nuzzled into his chest. He smelled of sandalwood and spicy vanilla. It wouldn't work on everyone, but Davien smelled good; a little spicy and sweet. It was a heady concoction when mixed with his pheromones, and I swam in his scent. He held me tightly. His hand held my head to his chest as he laid kisses on my crown, the other drew me tightly to his hard body.

"Are you going to miss this place? I know I am," he mumbled softly against my head. "I can't wait until it's just you and me up at Columbia."

I squeezed him around his trim waist, then glided my clammy, trembling hands up his chest to his neck, pulling his lips down to mine. I grazed his soft, full ones, gently kissing him, waiting for my invitation to be accepted. When he parted his lips, I slid my tongue into his eager mouth. Shudders rippled through me as soon as our tongues touched. My mouth coupled with his, as his tenderly caressed mine. He trailed kisses along my jawline, to my neck, sending another shockwave coursing through my body.

"Mmm, you like that, don't you?" he growled huskily, his voice laden with pent up passion. He backed me against the wainscoted wall. Like the first time we'd kissed, he hitched my leg up over his hip. His arousal pressed against my intimate places. He kissed me deeply, his ardor becoming more fervent and eager. I responded to his enthusiastic kiss with as much passion and welcomed his tempestuous touches as they became more demanding against my ass. His hand slid from my rear, up my abdomen, dropping my leg. He found my bra clasp and released my breast into his strong hand, while his other went to work fumbling with the button on the front of my jeans.

I shook my head, willing myself to clear the intoxication from my senses. "Davien, wait," I whispered against his lips. "Wait. Not like this. We can't."

His hands froze their pursuit, and he brought them up to my face, holding it endearingly. "You're right. We've waited this long; you deserve a bed." He laughed throatily, his tenor edged with heavy lust and mischievousness.

"No, I mean... we *can't*."

His sparkling, clear blue eyes met mine with an iciness that surprised me.

"Of course not," he grumbled under his breath, as he went to work adjusting his belt buckle and hard erection in his jeans.

I reattached my bra and straightened my shirt, hanging my head guiltily. *Davien deserves better than me. I shouldn't have let it get this far; not tonight, not ever.*

"Davien," I breathed, still fighting my thrumming heart and the lusty hormones flowing rampant in me, "this isn't easy for me, either." I looked up at him, reaching for his hand. "Please, let's talk?"

He begrudgingly took the hand I offered and followed me to his leather couch. I sat down, facing him, and placed my hand on his knee, as much for his benefit as mine. I hoped it would still my nerves.

"The President," I began nervously, "I mean Ethan... err, your dad called me into the Oval Office today."

"Shit." He and I both knew that being called in there was a big deal.

"Yes, you could say that." I took in a deep, cleansing breath to steady my nerves. "He said it had come to his attention recently that you and I have entered into a 'less than appropriate' relationship." I ran my fingers through my long black hair. "Dav, he's sending you to Columbia without me." I watched Davien, as his whole demeanor crumpled.

I squeezed Davien's thigh. "He asked me how far it has gone. I had to tell him, Dav. He said, based on his intel, that I was lying. Can you believe he had me take a lie detector test?" A slight sob escaped past my lips. "It was so degrading. He had *his* head security officer, Daniel Cook, hook me up and conduct the test." I shivered from the uncomfortable memory. "He asked me intimate details, Dav... even went through a list of items and body parts that you may have *put* in me."

"Goddamn it! He has no right! So what if he's the fucking president; he's not God." I sobbed again at his outburst. The last thing I'd wanted was to come between them. My pulse was racing, and familiar panic was beginning to take its stronghold.

Davien pulled me into his warm embrace. "Sorry, Cori. Dad can be a real asshole, but really, what can I do about it? Image and all. I can't ruin his career..."

It was suddenly all so clear how right Adrian had been. How wrong I'd been. I'd been enjoying the attentions of my charge to drown out the pain my best friend had caused. He'd called it exactly, how this would all play out, and that there was no future between Davien and myself.

I knew there was no future between Dav and I deep down; I'd just wanted to prove Adrian wrong for the sake of being right. I hate that he knew Davien and I had no future... uncanny how he'd said the same thing about him and me. I shook my head at the striking parallels.

"Well, thankfully we haven't had intercourse." I shook my head. "My conversation with your dad could've gone a lot worse... Adrian told me this would happen."

"Fuck Adrian. What's Dad's plan for you?"

I pulled back and wiped the tears from my cheeks. "He's considering a possible new position for me, but I may request a transfer from the Executive Residence to the grounds... or I may accept an offer from the private military company Constellis, who acquired Academi." I sighed. "I owe a lot to Academi, and it's why the CIA even looked at my resume for this position." I fidgeted uneasily. "I received a call from Lucas Maxwell of Constellis today, and there's a few openings..."

He interrupted. "Let me guess, for you and *Adrian*." It was a sarcastic statement, which he didn't even bother to disguise as a question.

"And Tanner Lyons," I added. "He's recruiting us because we all served together in Iraq. I have the intelligence analysis and paramilitary skills he's looking for, and of course, they're all military trained special ops guys."

"Of course," he said flatly. "So then, who's heading up security at Columbia, or don't I matter to him anymore?"

I drew in a slow breath. "Senator Powell's team. Amity is back from her senior year in Italy and has decided to pursue a degree there in the performing arts." I hurried on about Davien's first crush. "From what I've heard, she's quite an artful dancer."

"Ami's going to be there?" I could hear his shock in his voice. He'd shared that he'd lost his virginity to Amity when they were fifteen and had dated right up to when Kait had passed away. Her last request of her son, as he told it, was to find a *better*, more virtuous girl than his love for the past three years. So, Amity had left the state, and eventually the country, heading to Italy with her older brother for school... and ultimately a break from Davien.

I stood up and pulled him to me, embracing him as a friend now. "See," I spoke softly into his chest, "this could be a good thing. You've shared how deeply you cared for her, and I suspect, if you give it a chance, those feelings you still carry could be rekindled."

"I'm so fucking tired of Dad controlling me." I could hear the anger in his voice. "I've fucking had it, Cori." He broke our embrace and stormed towards his closet like a tornado. I watched as he pulled out his backpack and threw some clothes and necessities into it.

As he approached me, I could see that red had crept up his cheeks and tears streamed down them. He threw his pack down on the couch beside me, reaching out for me. I allowed myself to be pulled into his arms. He squeezed me and, looking down at me with his sparkling blue eyes, planted a soft, endearing kiss on my forehead. "I'm gonna miss the hell out of ya, Cori. You're an amazing woman and you've taught me a lot in the past few weeks. I feel like I've grown up so much, just so I could keep up with you."

"You've matured a lot, Dav."

"Well, I had to, to try to prove I was worth your time," he kidded. "But I'm definitely going to miss the way you smell, and those jade green eyes of yours and…" he added jokingly, "that *fucking* sexy as all hell white swimsuit of yours. The one with mesh sides."

"The netting?" I ribbed him back and flashed him a big smile… referencing one of our inside jokes. "Mmm, I'm sure going to miss you, Davien," I admitted, squeezing him one final time. "Thanks for being everything I needed when I had no one."

I gazed up at him. Our eyes connected, his expression mixed with anger toward his dad and excitement at the possibilities of a future away from here, away from the controlling heavy hand of his father, and mine stormy, my future undecided. He placed his hand on the small of my back and walked me to the door, opening it for me. I stepped into the hall.

"Hey, you've got this. If anyone can recover from Dad's bullying, it's you. Who knows; maybe something can happen now with you and *Officer* Adrian Rogue?"

Yeah, maybe something can… if he can ever get over his damned, misplaced nobility and superior attitude.

I shrugged and smiled. "Bye, Davien." Squeezing him one last time, I found it hard to walk away. I looked back up to his eyes. "You've got this. I'm really proud of you for standing up for what you believe and demanding the freedom to live your life your way. You'd better take care of yourself. Don't get caught leaving by your dad's security staff, and keep me updated. I can only give you a sixty-minute head start before I need to report you're missing." I confided, as I released him.

"I will, I promise… bye, Cori."

"Bye."

The door closed with heavy finality, just like this chapter of my life…

-THE END-

A Promise Kept

Mary Darlene Messina

The late-morning sky ablaze with the sun edging toward high noon canopied Francesca as she drove along the narrow dirt road looking for '70 Mirror Lake Drive'. Her eyes spied '70' on the mailbox but it was the faded '70' embedded in the gnarly tree that more strongly identified what was waiting beyond. Alongside the number, a lamplight, hanging a tad crooked and with old spots of rust pitting the black tin, proudly stood sentinel.

Francesca turned into the narrow drive lined with apple trees, pines and an acre or two of goldenrod interspersed with daisies...all lazily waving in the slight breeze. As the house came into view, she was unprepared for the charming cottage nestled under the towering spruce trees. The modern homes splashed with wide porches and shiny tin roofs with solar panels, all neatly tucked in among the trees that lined Mirror Lake Drive, led her to believe the Formichella house would mimic these summer get-a-ways. She pulled in front of the old cottage sitting at the end of the dirt driveway. The sun cavorted on the old shakes, giving the house varying shades of gray tones, from dark hues on the side shadowed by the trees to the soft blue-gray roof soaking in the rays of brilliant sun. Wavy blue patches of Mirror Lake played peek-a-boo between the massive tree trunks and bushes.

Francesca sighed with a long-lost feeling of pure contentment tempered with growing peace. "Well, girl. Time to get your mind off yourself and onto someone else." She tried not to think of the last three months...disbelief, shock, sadness, anger and then the realization that being mad at God and blaming Him for her husband's death wasn't healthy. She had held fast to the word 'Faith' that she and Liam had adopted to boost their spirits when their marriage roller-coasted spiritually, financially and medically. They believed when the day is the darkest, that's when God tests your faith and asks you to trust Him to bring you through the grayness and into the sun's light. Facing the world while Liam was dying from a fast-paced cancer and then stepping into the world alone had stolen her ability to even have an iota of faith. She couldn't even remember what their word came to symbolize; the bitterness and the disappointment in God had taken over her heart. The cozy house, the woods, the lake and fresh air seemed to beckon her heart to walk the road of renewed faith. She sensed a new hope for peace tickling her soul.

Grabbing her purse from the front car seat, she walked up the handicap ramp and onto the narrow porch where a rustic bench was nestled under a window. A battered pail and faded 'Welcome' sign leaned against a wall covered with delicately spun spider webs. Her knock was answered by a woman who looked totally frazzled but wore a welcoming smile.

"Hi. I'm Francesca. You must be Athena."

"Come in, come in. Yes, I'm Athena and you've arrived to a mess. Marian just spilled a full bowl of chowder; she's glad it landed on the floor and not on her lap. But, she's so upset because her favorite bowl broke and I'm trying to get the pieces gathered before she gets cut."

Francesca followed Athena into a small kitchen and through a good-sized living room. They walked down a small ramp into an all-season porch enveloped with a wall of slider windows. Drapes guarded the room against the bright sunlight. The scent of fresh flowers mixed with the fragrance of clam chowder. A tiny woman with an upset look on her face was sitting on an old sofa.

"Mom, this is Francesca. She is going to help me clean up the spill and then we'll get you a fresh bowl of chowder."

Francesca gently took Marian's hand and spoke softly. "Looks like you need a little help; guess I arrived just in time. We'll have this cleaned up in a jiffy and then grab you some more soup."

Marian smiled at her and in a barely audible voice said, "I don't know what happened. All of a sudden the bowl seemed to jump off the table. It broke when it hit the floor. What a mess!"

Francesca smiled at her and assured Marian it was no big thing; accidents happen.

Marian looked grateful as the mess was cleaned up and a fresh bowl of chowder was set before her on the small desk serving as a table.

Francesca chatted with Athena as Marian finished her chowder. Then she helped pile up the dishes, carrying them into the kitchen. After loading the dishwasher, Athena offered to show Francesca around the house while Marian was watching the news. "Down this hallway is your bedroom. The twin-bedded room across the hall is for family when they come to visit".

The two bedrooms were outfitted with old but sturdy beds and dressers. The pine paneling reflected the tastes of yesteryear…back into the 50's when the cottage had been built. Homemade curtains of cream muslin edged with fringe balls gave each room a cozy air. Colorful quilts dressed each bed. Athena told Francesca that if she needed more pillows or bedding, the wooden blanket chest held plenty. A claw-foot dresser complemented the décor like a page from an old Yankee magazine depicting the life in an Adirondack camp. A small but functional closet hugged the wall across from the bed. Wire hangers bent from years of clothes hanging on them hung from the iron clothes bar. The bathroom, small but functional, had a knotty pine tall cabinet that held bath and beach towels as well containers of bath supplies.

They walked down the hall and back into the living room. Against the far wall, a fireplace invited you to sit in the cozy rocker and read while the fire kept away the chill from a winter's night. Pictures of Marian's family – parents, grandparents and great-grandparents as well as newer wedding pictures of her sons, their wives and children – were displayed on antique end tables and hung on every available inch on the pine boarded walls. Hand-me-down items from bygone days filled the room, maybe leaning towards clutter in another home but it all looked so natural in that cozy room.

Delicate bone teacups, teapots and a set of English china were attractively displayed in a large enclosed glass cabinet that kept the antiques safe behind a stunning oval door. Even though the old carpet needed a good cleaning, the overall look bespoke a cozy feeling leaning more towards old-fashioned and homey rather than shabby. An old student desk from the early '30s stood against the kitchen counter; a tiny chair was pushed against the opening. Dusty ancient silver goblets, plates, bowls and pitchers were perched on the old breakfront and on a shelf above the mirrored coat-tree. The air was a tad on the stale side, but wisps of fresh air sailed in through an open window.

Athena told Francesca she needed to get ready for the drive back to New Jersey. She invited her to go outside and enjoy the view while she packed her and Ed's suitcases.

As she stepped onto the deck, Francesca noticed the weeds fighting for control of the narrow pathway; the summer breeze tossing them to and fro. As she walked toward the bobbing dock, Francesca mentally clipped the weeds and tamed the overgrown lawn. Hopefully, the yard could be trimmed up and restored to its quaint cottage look of wild flowers and perennials.

The lake's surface reflected the white clouds that resembled bits of cotton strewn across an endless run of blue fabric. A small sailboat meandered across the far end of the lake; the boater oblivious to the ducklings that followed the wake. The very picture of a perfect summer's day.

Suddenly, as her eyes took in the peaceful view, the feeling of being watched set goosebumps tingling on her bare arms. She looked back at the house, but all drapes still were tightly closed against the sun. She saw no neighbors peering at her. Shivering slightly, Francesca turned back and entered the house. Athena was settling Marian down for a nap in her bedroom. The feeling had not subsided as Francesca came back into the house. In fact, it had only grown stronger. She began attributing the feeling to being tired from her long drive. She carried her suitcase and bags to her bedroom. Athena joined her and said she had some ice tea ready and invited her to sit and chat on the porch while Marian napped.

Athena gave Francesca a quick overview of the family dynamics. Athena's husband, Ed, was a surveyor in New Jersey and was currently in Wolfeboro running errands. Ed's brother, David, and his wife, Ann, lived in Wolfeboro but were not able to move in and care for Marian. Jobs and family obligations kept them pretty busy. With Athena and Ed living in New Jersey and having demanding jobs, they couldn't even consider relocating to Mirror Lake. When Marian needed 24/7 caregiving and refused to move into a nursing facility, a mutual friend had suggested a live-in; and they called Francesca. "You came highly recommended. So, here you are".

Al, Marian's late husband, had gone to be with the Lord nine years ago. After he took an early retirement from his school career, he built this cottage on Mirror Lake for their permanent residence. The two sons were in their late teens and stayed with Marian's sister, Barbara, in New Jersey to finish out their year of high school. Ed, older by a year, was a senior and David was taking the early senior step-up program to graduate with his brother. Ed attended college to continue with his love of surveying while David had joined the electrical apprenticeship program with a Wolfeboro contractor. Al had always dabbled in his local New Jersey politics and became immersed in the dominant party in Wolfeboro. His dedication to local programs that would benefit the citizens of Wolfeboro led to his election as mayor. For over ten years, he served in that position and the little village bloomed under his leadership. His crowning glory was the Hope House for the families that were homeless and striving to stay together. That program provided housing for ten families in a renovated apartment complex. Men and women were able to have professional counseling to help obtain steady employment leading to a stable living environment.

The fight for Hope House lasted four tedious years and kept the local politicians seriously involved with countless town meetings. Many Wolfeboro residents either fought for or against having homeless families nearby. Sadly, drug addiction haunted many of the homeless and the locals believed that providing housing would enable the families to retain a negative life style. Al's constituents were able to convince the town that Hope House was for a 'hand up', not a permanent 'hand-out'. Sadly, he had to step down as Mayor due to his declining health. His avid involvement with local and state politicians dwindled down to attendance at occasional fundraisers or sitting on his deck with his old cronies debating hot political issues of the day. Marian had loved to invite friends over for dinner and cards and was known for her tasty meals, especially lasagna, Al's favorite.

Athena rattled off names of grandchildren who would be stopping by to visit Marian. She gave Francesca a notebook with the names and numbers of local businesses. A few adult granddaughters would be available to care for Marian when

Francesca needed to run errands and Marian wasn't up to accompanying her. Francesca would have every Friday from 8 am until Saturday at 8pm to leave the house for a break. Athena had arranged for someone to stay with Marian during that time.

They heard Marian gently snoring over the baby monitor kept next to the couch. Athena asked if Francesca had any questions as Ed was back and they needed to head for New Jersey. At the moment, she could not think of any. Athena said if she ever had questions or situations came up, to call her any time.

After Athena and Ed left, Francesca checked on the sleeping Marian. She decided to make a simple soup from the leftover roasted chicken Athena had pointed out earlier. Soon a fragrant aroma of celery, garlic and parsley wafted throughout the house. She gave Marian a cat bath when she awoke from her nap.

Marian was quite chatty during supper speaking about various family members, past events and her days as a physical education teacher. She told Francesca that in the early 40's, she was working at a high school in NJ when she met her future husband, Al, who was the sports coach for the boys. He proudly wore the feather of golf pro in his multi-faceted cap. The Golf Team was NJ High School champions for ten straight years. The couple worked at the school until their retirement to the lake thirty-five years ago.

Marian spoke proudly of Al's interest in local politics and his election as Mayor of the small town. Not one to sit quietly, she told Francesca how she organized fundraisers for Wolfeboro that aided the families who struggled with the necessities of life. Al's insight to get the New Hampshire powers-that-be to assist with getting State funds channeled to Wolfeboro gave residents much-needed public service programs, good roads and renovations in their little corner of their world. The businesses in town thrived to where half of them were able to close during the winter months when their owners relocated to warmer climes. Marian spoke of one favorite restaurant where a fellow golfer was a waitress. Nolan's had the most delicious pizza and wings, her favorite. She said that they would soon go there for lunch.

Marian's usual night time routine of Andy Griffith, Wheel of Fortune, Jeopardy and a Hallmark movie was followed by Francesca giving her a cup of tea and tucking her into bed.

Hearing aid out, glasses off, emergency alert button in place, tissues at hand, right eye drops in and her old-fashion teacher's bell close by...Marian was settled down for the night. Making sure the baby monitor was on, Francesca gave her a kiss on her forehead and bid Marian a good night's sleep.

As Francesca settled herself on the porch couch to review the log book, she again had the feeling of someone watching her. Of course there was no one other than Marian in the house. "Funny," she said, talking to herself, "I'm not scared, just curious about why I'm feeling this way." It was as if there was an invisible security guard hovering nearby.

The night proved peaceful; Marian woke only twice to use the bathroom. Morning dawned sunny and warm; the weatherman had predicted a day in the high 80's. Marian woke at ten for her morning meds, eye drops and enjoyed what would become her favorite breakfast of poached eggs over toast, fruit cup, cranberry-peach juice and crispy bacon. Steaming hot tea was always a given.

After breakfast, Francesca and Marian enjoyed a chat that led into talk of yesteryear with Marian talking about the day Al died. His heart had been giving him problems and she'd had to call an ambulance to take him to the local hospital. After the doctor examined Al and told him his heart was "shorting out," she said he demanded to be taken home. "No way in hell am I staying at this place!" he'd ranted and raved. However, he was so weak that the doctor said even if he went home on a stretcher in an ambulance, he would not survive the fifteen-minute ride. He couldn't even promise that Al would see a new dawn. With that said, Marian had asked everyone to give her and Al some privacy.

When the room emptied, Al whispered in her ear; she smiled and whispered something back. Then with the softest look of love, Al closed his eyes and took his last breath. Bowing her head in prayer, Marian sobbed quietly as the doctor and nurses ran in, responding to the resounding alarm bell of his heart monitor. "Let him go in peace, Dr. Lewis. No CPR, just let him go." Since there was already a DNR on the wall, the medical team nodded and walked out of the room, leaving her be. Marian gently kissed Al on the lips, tucked the blankets to his chin, and patted his head as she had always done just before they settled down to sleep. Whispering, "God Bless you, my love; sleep tight," she walked out to their children waiting in the hallway.

Francesca felt as though she was there in the hospital room as Marian described Al's stepping into Eternity. The feeling of their love was so overwhelming she could just about envision their last moments together. Turning to Marian, she said, "Have you told anyone what he whispered to you or what your answer was?"

"Oh, no," Marian softly said. "That was only between us...for now."

The days caring for Marian turned into a comfortable routine. With permission from Ed and Athena who controlled the funds, she hired a lawn company to initially tame the exterior disorder of the greenery. Once it was identifiable as individual shrubs, plants and lawn area, she was able to keep up with the care herself. Marian loved sitting on the deck, watching as Francesca tenderly cared for the flowers, all the while keeping conversation lively and interesting.

When the weather wasn't too hot, they enjoyed lunching on the deck while watching the pesky squirrels scampering through the yard. With Marian's input, she was able to organize the closets in the bedrooms and gather bags of good but outgrown or outdated clothes for the local Christian school's ongoing project for fundraising. Last year enough used clothing and household items were swapped for cash at the Saver's Center in Portsmouth to put a new floor in the school's gym. Marian was happy that she could help out with the project. There was never a lack of "nitty-gritties" as Marian loved to call the little chores that filled their days.

Days slipped into weeks that churned into the New Year's Eve...Marian's birthday. Francesca felt like an adopted member of the family. They, in turn, trusted her judgement and care for Marian. The feeling that someone was watching from the wings was less during the day with the sunny rays of Old Sol. It was more like a sense that all was well with their little world as long as the daylight was there. As soon as the sun began setting and the dusk descended on the cottage, Francesca began sensing the unseen presence of 'the guardian' – the name given to that unknown entity.

As the second summer floated in on the rays of the shimmering sun, Francesca casually asked Athena if she had ever felt what she was feeling. Athena smiled and said, "Truthfully, yes. But, since it seemed to be just after Al died, I felt that he was somehow watching over Marian whenever it got dark. You see, Marian always was uneasy when daylight gave way to night ever since she and Al began spending their life "in the wild" as Marian called the cottage site. While she loved being here, at heart she was always a city gal who was afraid of the dark and the critters that could be lurking in the shadows, just outside the skirt of lights. She depended on Al to keep the unknown terrors of the night at bay. Sometimes I could sense his presence during the daytime, but it was usually when a storm was brewing and darkness would be coming to shroud the lake earlier than usual".

She thanked Athena for the information and reassurance. From then on, Francesca welcomed the unseen sentry and would actually carry on a conversation with 'him' if she herself became spooked. "Now, Al. You know I'm taking good care of Marian and you don't need to worry. No need for you to make those noises in the house while we are trying to sleep. It can be pretty unnerving, you know." And oddly enough the noises would stop, as if Al had actually heard her words.

Francesca's own family lived nearby and had become cozy with Marian. They often visited to the delight of Marian whose own grandchildren lived a distance and weren't able to often visit. Marion loved attending Francesca's family parties and other activities as an adopted grandmother.

It worked out well when neighbors and family members came to stay with Marian whenever Francesca needed to run errands or simply "recharge her own batteries". Marian loved having her family visit and delighted in the antics of her "grand-dogs" who loved swimming in Mirror Lake. In particular, Onyx, an old black lab, and Kobe, a mix of American Staffordshire terrier and Pitbull, loved to settle in on the couch beside her, snoring up a storm. Marian always insisted that their nose noises didn't bother her; she loved having their heads on her lap.

In the beginning of the third fall of caregiving, Marian began having increased restless nights, talking more in her sleep and often waking Francesca to relate dreams that both frightened and soothed her. Francesca would hear her moaning, tossing and turning and talking in her sleep over the baby monitor. Sometimes she could understand what Marian was saying; other times it was just a mess of mumbling. Francesca would go to Marian, gently awaken her, and get her a hot cup of tea. These 'night programs', as Marian called them, were mostly about her life with Al...how they met...how her family didn't approve of him at first because he was from a different culture and didn't come from "old money." They warned her that he had better work diligently, be a good husband and always be a good support to her and any children they may have.

Often when Francesca entered the bedroom to check on Marian, she would find that sweet little lady staring at the curtained sliders with a worried look on her face. Whenever she asked Marian what was wrong, she would reply, "I know Al is coming but I can't see him". During one particularly unsettling night when Marian was awake almost every hour, she whispered to Francesca, "He asked me to wait for him here at the lake, no matter how long it took. I promised him I would." "Ah ha," thought Francesca. "The truth comes out."

The very next morning, Marian slipped from bed, hit her head and Francesca had to call 911. She insisted on returning home as soon as the doctor stitched her forehead even against the doctor's wish to keep her overnight. "No!" she had emphatically cried. "I have to be home. I have to be ready." She became so agitated that the medical team released her and sent her back to the cottage on the lake.

From that day, Marian's spirits were down, her appetite diminished and the look of worry forever on her face. Francesca felt that it might be good for Marian if her NJ family came for a visit. She called Athena and Ed who drove up from New Jersey, bringing Marian's little sister, Bobbi, to visit. Barbara or 'Bobbi,' was five years younger than Marian. They would laugh as they related how Bobbi was known as 'the pest' because she always wanted to tag along with her big sister. But as the years passed, they became very close confidants and shared many great adventures as sisters.

The visit to the lake went well but, as usual, was too short for both sisters. Old friends stopped by for lunch, tea and chatter. Bobbi's month long stay made for more work for Francesca, but she was happy to see the sisters enjoying each other's company.

Francesca took Marian on rides to view the changing of the leaves. Their stops to farmers' stands for the harvested fruits and vegetables often were the highlight of their rides. All too soon, the beautiful scene of the potpourri of colors dissolved into the nakedness of the trees because of the fast approaching winter. Francesca had become quite the expert at making a warm and cozy fire in the stone fireplace. She and Marian would sit for hours sipping tea and leafing through magazines.

One brisk November morning, they noticed the lake had frozen overnight, much earlier than usual. Early December welcomed the first snow of the season coating the trees and bushes with sparkles of white.

Marian became obsessed with wanting to go Christmas shopping so she could put gifts under the tree. For many years previously, she just slipped money into Christmas cards and handed them to the family as they visited. Her mind had slipped back into the years when she would spend weeks finding the perfect gift for each family member. So, on a day when there was no snow forecast, Francesca took Marian to a shopping mall an hour away. It was an unsettling and stressed day. Despite suggestions for gifts, Marian came away empty handed, she couldn't make up her mind about what to buy. Francesca decided to do the shopping on her own. She gift wrapped scarves for the females in the family and winter hats for the men and put the gifts under the tree. Marian was delighted when she saw the piles of gifts wearing festive bows and beautiful paper. She seemed to forget she hadn't actually purchased and wrapped each one herself.

The restless nights that robbed Marian of a good sleep became the norm. She insisted on getting up by ten every morning even though she said she felt tired…that she hadn't slept well. Shortly after a snack each noon, she would close her eyes for a catnap that turned into a solid two or three hours of sleep.

For most of her married life, Marian had outdone herself in making Christmas Eve very special for her family. Though she wanted to do the same this year, she agreed that it was time "for the children to take over." The traditional Christmas Eve preparation was handled by her adult children and grown grandchildren who made the lasagna, prepped the giant shrimp and cut cheese to go with a variety of crackers. The Granny Smith apples weren't forgotten; Marian insisted they were needed to go with the appetizers. Francesca made the apple pies that Marian always prepared for the feast. Neighbors dropped off plates of homemade cookies, reflections of the cookies Marian had always gifted them with for years.

After a delicious dinner, the family unwrapped the festive gifts, exclaiming how perfect the scarf or hat was. They presented Marian with her favorite chocolates and a beautiful fuzzy blanket to ward off the chill of the winter nights. As the day came to an end she seemed to be more tired than usual and did not object to Francesca getting her into bed before the family left. Each one, however, came into her bedroom to say "goodnight" and give her a hug and a kiss. Marian was sound asleep before the last grandchild quietly shut the front door.

Francesca sat out on the porch and watched the soft snowflakes slipping into the mounds of whiteness on the lake. She wondered if Marian would want to sleep late because she was so exhausted.

About 2 am, Francesca woke to hear a small commotion over the baby monitor. At first, she thought Marian was simply talking in her sleep. As the noise became louder, she hurried down the hall and into Marian's bedroom. The bedroom was ice cold. Francesca ran to the slider that was wide open. A cold wind was angrily blowing into the room and Marian was sound asleep. Francesca closed the door and checked the lock. All seemed okay but as she turned away from the slider, it slammed open again and then slid back closed. This scared Francesca who, with a racing heart, now quickly closed the heavy drapes and checked Marian who was softly moaning in her sleep. She decided to stay in the bedroom and sat in the chair by the closet. Watching Marian for an hour, Francesca's eyes grew heavy and she drifted off to sleep.

In the quiet hours when dawn had just begun thinking about starting a new morning, Francesca was startled from sleep by voices speaking softly. As she became fully awake, she gasped when she saw a shadow standing by the bed. She watched as Marian opened her eyes and lifted her arms towards the shadowy figure. Francesca's heart pounded as the mist cleared and she saw Al, looking healthy and smiling as he was in pictures taken before he became ill. It was like she was watching an old movie. Francesca couldn't move…so caught was she in the spell of a real-life ghost story.

The smile on Marian's face seemed to be beaming from her heart. As Francesca sat like a captive tied to a chair and spellbound by the scene before her, Marian floated to her feet, her hand grasped ever so gently by Al's hands. Without a trace of noise or effort, they both floated just inches above the floor, over to the slider that had reopened and became one with the night.

As Francesca's startled eyes watched, Al and Marian ascended into the night sky that enveloped the frozen lake. The brilliance of the stars was just beginning to wane with the coming dawn. The soft twinkling of their light was just bright enough to guide Al and Marian into Eternity.

Francesca sat quietly until they had disappeared into the blanket of sky that enveloped Mirror Lake. Still in disbelief at what had just happened, she turned to look at the bed. Francesca was totally surprised to see Marian tucked under her covers with a peaceful smile and closed eyes.

Getting up from the chair, Francesca went over to Marian and tried to find a heartbeat. Her body was still; there was no pulse. Francesca realized that Marian's wait was over. Al had come for her at their lake, just like he promised. As in the years he had given her shelter from the dark, he was there with her to protect her, to love her and to take her on that final journey into Eternity.

Time doesn't erase endearing words that echo for years in a lonely and hurting heart. Precious love keeps pace with the minutes, days and years that separate two people who have loved each other more than life itself. It was her time, and it was his time to come to take her hand.

Al's last words to Marian had come full circle. "I'll come for you at the lake. Please wait for me." With a gentle kiss, Marian had promised, "I will".

DEDICATION

This story of a promise kept is dedicated to Marian "Mamie" Formichella…who is the little lady on Mirror Lake who came into my life as a "client" and remained there as a most precious "friend". Regulations cannot dictate to one's heart that it must remain neutral and not have feelings of love, compassion and tenderness. Mamie has become a heartstring lovingly perched on my family tree. God bless her and God bless her family. My heart reached out and found peace and love.

Also, I want to thank my team; Debbie, Robin, Karen, Candace, Lori and Peggy for the friendship, support, love and caring they gave me while we were a team caring for, loving and going the extra mile in our hearts for Mamie, a dear, dear friend to us.

River
Jude Ouvrard

Prologue

As I sit at my desk where hundreds if not thousands of people dream to be, I realize that I'm fucking bored. Not just bored of the day, more like bored of my life. I'm thirty. I haven't travelled much for pleasure. I have that trademark conservative haircut politicians have, and I wear a plain old tie every day. Even on weekends.

This isn't what I thought I would do with my life, I'm an artist. Politics aren't really me but it's what my father lived and breathed.

Is this life mine?

Absolutely not.

My parents planned it and now, I feel like standing up for myself. I don't need my job, and I certainly don't like it. I have a girlfriend who acts like we've been married for thirty years. She matches her outfit with mine and her teeth are so white, they blind me in the sun. I don't need this woman by my side. We share nothing but fake smiles over newspapers and magazine articles. In fact, there isn't much about her that isn't fake.

I shake my head, ruminating again on why I am even with her. "Enough is enough," I mutter under my breath as I flip the photo of her face down on my desk.

Removing my tie, I shook out my boring hairstyle. Pulling my shirt out of my pants on the way to my father's office, I pause. Shit, what am I going to say?

Hearing my mother's laughter as I step into his office, I know the situation might take another turn.

I clear my throat to get his attention, "Dad, can we talk?"

He looks over at me, "Son, are you okay?" concern etched on his face. "Were you attacked?"

"No." I frown not realizing the impression my hair, shirt and tie gave off. "I've never been better."

"You're drunk then?" He turned to my mother, "Amelia, would you take a look at him? We need an intervention."

I close my eyes at the stupidity of the situation. "I'm not drunk or stoned. No need to alarm the nation." I pause to think about how to announce my retirement to my sixty-eight-year-old father who has no plan to stop working. I take a deep breath, "This isn't me."

"Amelia?" For a president, he can be quite dramatic.

"What's the matter, John," she sounds concerned.

He narrows his eyes on me.

"Dawson, what's happened? Were you attacked? Is security on their way?" He looks back to my mother, "Amelia, get security on the line stat!"

"Dad, enough!"

I glance at mom, her face is white and from the look of it, she might pass out.

Dawson, just say it, I chide myself. "I need vacation." I snap. "I'd like a forty-year long vacation." From the blank looks on their faces, I can see that I'm getting nowhere... *Maybe I should phrase it differently?*

I clear my throat and roll my shoulders back, taking on an authoritative stance, just like I'd been taught to do when I wanted to be taken seriously. "Mom, Dad, I quit. This life isn't for me."

John swaggers to his chair, sitting down heavily. He slumps back into the chair holding his head with his two hands. "What?" disbelief palpable in his tenor.

"Well, I've been thinking about this for a while. My decision is made. I'm done with politics."

"What about your dreams?" Mom points out, "You're almost at the top."

I shrug, "They aren't my dreams, they're yours."

"How dare you talk to your mother like that?"

Seriously?

"I'm thirty years old; I can make this decision for myself." I hold out my hand, "Here are my access cards and passwords."

"Dawson." They said in unison, incredulity in their tone.

"Yup, I'll keep in touch."

I high-tail it out of the Oval Office, and practically run to mine. I've never been the center of attention, but all eyes are on me now. Every White House staff member I pass, looks at me like I've grown a second head. Grabbing my wallet and car keys, I leave my necktie on my desk. Goodbye old life.

First order of business now that my life is mine—shave off my hair or dye it blue. I haven't decided yet.

Second on the docket, my new wardrobe. Dressy shoes, tailored suits, white Oxford shirts, and monochromatic ties are a thing of the past. I want a real wardrobe, one that shows my personality.

I make it to my car, unlock it and slide into the comfortable black leather seat. I'm thrilled that I've resigned from politics, from my life.

I leave the White House through the back gate, with loud metal music roaring out of the speakers; waving at the security guards, who probably got the memo that I'm having a breakdown. But I'm free and fucking happy. Finally!

Where should I go? Home to change? I have no damn clue. No agenda. No assistant. This is the good life.

My reverie is interrupted when my phone rings. I glance over at it.

Melissa.

Oh, HELL NO. She isn't breaking my mood now, no fucking way. I'll deal with her later—she's probably heard anyways. Knowing my parents, they called hers the moment I'd left his office, to tell them I was losing it. After all, Melissa's father is my father's right-hand man. I was losing my mind.

What they don't understand, is that I'm not having a breakdown, I'm acting this way because I feel good. *Amazing.*

After checking on my phone for the nearest non-conservative sounding barber shop, I locate The Rogue Barber. It's in the trendier, hipper side of D.C., plug the address into my GPS navigator, and settle back for the drive. I luck out and find parking only a block away. Walking the long block and pull open the heavy glass and mahogany door—ROGUE—etched deeply into the glass. It was impressive looking, as was the décor inside. There were antique craftsman wooden benches by the door, and along the full length of the wall were floor to ceiling mirrors framed in heavy mahogany frames. The barber-shoppe style chairs and high-polished black and white checkerboard tiled floor gave it a feel from days past, but that is where the nostalgia ended.

The barbers were tattooed, most were bearded and sported quiffs, pompadours, faux hawks and slick-backs. There was nothing old-fashioned about what they were wearing either a feel from days past, but that is where the nostalgia ended.

"Who do we have here?" A tall guy in his thirties approaches me, smiling, tatted, and groomed like the rest.

"Dawson Rhodes."

The man repeats my name with airs, like I'm someone.

"Yeah, and you are?" I proffer my hand in greeting.

"Raymond James." He takes my hand and we shake.

I've shaken so many hands in my life, it has become natural, easy. I can see Raymond knows who I am, and it makes him a bit edgy… I can feel his nervous energy. I'm used to it and can generally make people comfortable around me.

"Nice meeting you, Raymond. Do you have time for a quick haircut?" I look around and the shoppe is bustling.

"Of course, you can follow me." He leads me back to a private VIP room with only three seats, but I'm the only one back there, although it could be because it's Monday.

"What can I do for you today?" He takes his brush and starts brushing my hair.

"I need a 2007 Britney Spears breakdown special." I try not to laugh but I'm failing.

He frowns looking at me. "Are you okay?"

"Oh yeah, I want my hair short, very short." *That much I know.*

"Okay." He clips a towel around my shoulders and leads me to a copper sink. "No problem Mr. Rhodes."

"It's just Dawson."

"Of course, Dawson, let's get started."

I held it together during the wash, but it was impossible to keep serious when Raymond buzzed the first line with his clippers. It looks so weird already, but hey, it's the beginning of the new me.

Fuck politics and on with life.

Chapter One

"Melissa." I rub my forehead trying to find a way to get me out of this quickly.

The poor woman looks shattered, which I didn't expect. I'm still wondering if she's acting or something... I mean, hell, we had about as much chemistry as two toothbrushes in a glass

"Why don't you love me?" She cries, tears streaming down her face. The more she cries and rubs her eyes, the more she transforms into the joker. I feel like a total ass that I'm thinking of her this way, and I'm super bummed that this is how she's reacting.

Damn, *this isn't going to be easy* like I thought it would be. After all, why would I have ever expected her to take it this hard? We don't live together, I can't say that we're very active, and I'm not talking about tennis. So, what's her deal? We'd started dating when our parents decided it was time a few years back. There was nothing romantic or cute about how we started dating. We didn't have a great story to tell like most people, it was an arrangement. Plain and simple.

"Melissa, there was no love between us. It was a fake relationship; simply an arrangement between our two families. Come on, you know that."

"I can't believe this! Amelia was right, you've lost your mind. I mean, look at you...you cut your hair and dress like a slob. I deserve better than that." She lifts her chin up and humphs at me.

Okay, *I kind of deserve that.*

For such a smart woman, she just doesn't get it, that there's more to life than fake smiles, fancy trips, expensive things, and approval ratings. One day she'll understand. Hopefully, it's before she's married and has four kids with a shell of a man. She deserves to be with a man who will love her back; I want Melissa happy... just not with me.

"I haven't lost my mind, I'm just stepping up to live the life I've always dreamed of. One that I make for myself and that isn't planned out by the hour for me."

Disbelief is written across her face. "I don't get you Dawson but, *whatever*. Don't call me when you come back crawling and begging to your dad, because I'll be gone."

I wave my hand goodbye, dismissing her. "Don't worry sweets. That's never going to happen." *Shit, I didn't mean it like that.* Well, kind of...Sorry, NOT sorry.

"Arghh! You're such an ASS!" she groans in frustration and slams her bedroom door in my face.

"Hey, Mel, I'm sorry, okay?"

"I *hate* you." She yells from the other side of the door.

In this situation, hate is better than love. She'll move on eventually. Right?

I walk back to my graphite grey, Bugatti, feeling restored, like a weight has been lifted from my shoulders. It's crazy how great you feel when you are doing what you want and love. Melissa hates me now, but one day, after she finds her true happiness, she'll understand. I can't say that I feel good about what I did to her but there was no love between us. She knew that.

I speed back to my studio—my getaway—my refuge where I went when I needed to get away from my 24-7 job and executive quarters at the White House. Packing everything I want to bring with me takes a handful of minutes, I won't be staying in D.C. much longer. I leave my ties and suits behind and bring my most normal clothes. The ones that doesn't scream BORING. Something that matches my age and is comfortable. That's what I want in my life now, to be comfortable and to do what I want. *Doing what I want... sounds amazing.* I merge onto the Capital Beltway from I-66, heading back to my place to pack the clothes that fit my new life. I've decided to head to New York City. Why? Because the person who made me reconsider my whole life is there and I want to see her again. *Khloe.* It's been years since I last saw her in person. Keeping in touch through emails is great but I want to see Khloe's face again like the good old days.

I've missed my old New Yorker life a lot lately. This new adventure is going to be fun. I'm not going back for business either, this is purely for me. It shouldn't feel weird to do something for myself, but it does.

I blast my music as I put more miles between D.C. and the Big Apple; I feel like I'm in a movie. You know when the main character is so happy, and everything is about to crash, well, I'm that kind of happy except there won't be any crashes. Not in my movie. *Hell no.* I sing to the top of my lungs and let go of all the craziness I've locked inside of me throughout the years: Metallica, Deftones, U2, System of a Down—all of the music that I listened to during my dark and rebellious phase. I miss those days. At least, I was doing something for myself. *Kind of.*

It takes me four hours to reach my penthouse downtown, smack dab in the middle of the Manhattan district, and the city's lights shine brightly all around me. I love the hustle and bustle of the big city and navigate the traffic, pulling up to the building's posh front entrance. I take one look at the valet and choose instead to give my car gas. *Valet isn't me anymore—it's Dawson.* I park on level three of the building's parking structure, grab my bags and lock the car with a loud chirp that echoes off the walls of the immense garage.

I stride to the elevator and after fumbling for my lock key, insert it, and wait for the doors to open. Once I'm inside and on my way up to the penthouse, I have time to think about how my evening is going to go. I'm on one of the biggest damn highs lives ever thrown my way and there's only one thing I can do.

Well, more than one thing.

Let Khloe know I'm back in town.

Shower and change.

Eat because I'm starving—it has to be junk food.

Party in the city that never sleeps.

The elevator doors open to reveal an open floor plan, my kitchen, living and dining rooms in one place—great for parties—and the floor to ceiling windows offer an unsurpassed view of the city. I toss my keys on the counter and am relieved to find everything in place. *Mrs. Lane must still be coming weekly to tidy up...* I make my way to the master suite, tastefully decorated in deep wood tones, drop my bag and pull out my phone.

Khloe, so many things happened today. First, I stepped away from politics and second, I'm in New York. Do you want to hang out? River

It feels good to be back to River. I'm only Dawson to my family and the political world, I've always been River to my friends and at school. There's something about keeping my River identity private. My Dawson identity—*fuck*—he can take a nap... *a dirty nap for all I care.*

I cross off the first thing to do on my list, before showering and changing into comfortable jeans and a t-shirt. That alone, wearing *my* clothes and not the political uniform I've been wearing, is the greatest feeling. I find an old college pair of black converse that I've kept here in my wardrobe and put them on. I catch my reflection in the vanity—*that'll do for tonight.*

I run my fingers through my new cut as I walk back into the main-living area. There's nothing like a home that doesn't feel like a home at all, nothing personal, no family pictures on the walls, absolutely nothing could make this place warm. It's cold. It was decorated by an expensive designer chosen by my mother and her assistant. This is the first place I got to call mine when I was in college, and yet, it had Melissa's touch everywhere. It's never felt like mine. Today's been so overwhelming that I haven't figured out what I'll do with my life and where I'll stay. When I make up my mind, this place will need a major makeover.

I glance at my phone, still nothing from Khloe. While it bugs me, there's nothing I can do about it but wait.

I leave the penthouse and start walking the couple of miles from Upper East Side, toward Times Square, in hope of finding the junk food I've been craving for my late-night dinner.

Cars, city lights, and people are in every direction I look. Some of them are looking at me, probably recognizing me, but I'm not giving them the opportunity to approach me. I'm on a mission.

I need food. *Greasy, yummy, fattening junk food... lots of it. And fast.*

The alert on my phone notifies me of a new message.

River, what the hell is going on? I'm at a concert. Can we talk later?

I nod even though she can't see me I type out a quick response, **Sure.** I hit send.

We need to hang out, I'll get back to you as soon as the concert ends.

That little heart of mine has started beating again. Khloe's the first woman I've ever shed tears for. Her long curly light brown hair, bronzed skin, and smile... I've never forgotten her smile. *How could I?* Or the small R tattooed on her hip bone. I still can't believe she got a tattoo for me.

It stopped eight years ago when Khloe left for Costa-Rica mid-semester to care for her sick grandmother. Her mother is from Costa Rica and father's American. She lives her life between the two countries and has been loving it, at least was the last time we'd talked.

Two weeks ago, she asked me a simple question, "Where do you think you will be in five years?"

Of course, my first thought was by my father's side, one step closer to working on my own campaign.

"So, you really want to be the president of the United States one day?" her concern apparent in her tone.

It was a simple question that I should have answered yes to without hesitation, but I said no. "It's a family thing, you know? I was raised to think and prepare for it. Kind of like the Bush family legacy. Father and son. But it's not my passion, it's what I'll have to do."

"Don't you think it's crazy?" she asked warily. "We live in a country praising freedom and you can't even do what you want. If doing what you do now makes you unhappy, how do you think it'll be when you sit in your father's chair?"

"A disaster." I sighed. "I'm good at it. I have a mindset built for this, but deep down, I don't want to follow through with what I was groomed to do. It won't make me happy."

"You're thirty years old, don't wait until it's too late to take control of your life. You can still do it now." Khloe pointed out.

Her words had resonated with me. I could take control, and I did. Of course, her words have been on my mind all this time. Now that I've quit, I feel relieved, but I don't know where the fuck I'm going with my life. It'll take time for me to figure out my future, but right now, I think I deserve a break. I'll take my long overdue vacation. *You know, I DO have to live a little.* Be crazy. Act my age.

The crunch of the French fry, and the greasy juice exploding in my mouth is orgasmic. I haven't had a bite of the Grande Bacon Spicy burger yet, but I know it will be as good. *Maybe better.* I've been eating clean and healthy food for as long as I remember. Too busy to cook and think about grocery shopping, I always had someone doing all the work for me. I'm thankful I've had the luxury of help, but I like having the option of eating something I'm craving, which I've never had. *The small things I've been missing out on blows my mind.* The large fries, a burger so thick it's like having two, and a tall strawberry milkshake. Delicious. Heaven.

With a full belly, I venture outside, still on a high and nervous as fuck that I'll see her tonight. Khloe. I can't believe it.

The timing between us eight years ago had been terrible. Khloe and I were both attending Colombia University. I was there for political science but minoring in art and so was she. As soon as Khloe walked into our classroom, I wanted to get to know her. My father was deep into his campaign and it didn't stand to play-out well for me. I'd stayed in my corner, but always kept an eye on her—kind of creepy—I can admit it.

One day, we had to do a team pottery project, and as luck would have it, she picked me. ME. One of the best days of my life; she brought so much light into my life like a star brings to the night sky. She has so many talents that we always had something to do. Photography, jewelry making, pottery, painting, every type of art, we've tried them all. We got closer the more time we spent together, we kissed, made love more than humanly possible, and then—she was gone. One day we were together and the next, there was no trace of her. Her family in Costa Rica had needed help, and she couldn't stay despite us.

It broke me.

When she came back, I was deep into my dad's world. Congress after congress, meet and greet, schedules and responsibility. The timing was always off and then, Melissa happened, and I started living my life as I was told to. Pleasing my parents to the point of forgetting who I was, became my way of living.

Meh, enough about the past.

I pay my bill. The waiter recognizes me, I can see it in his eyes.

"Thank you, Mr. Rhodes." he says cordially as he reaches for the payment.

"Dawson's fine. It sounds like you are talking to my father." I quip, shorter than I'd intended. So, I offer a friendly smile.

He looks downs to his feet. "Sorry."

"Hey, no worries. You have a good night."

I leave him a good tip and head out. Checking my phone every few minutes to see if Khloe has sent me a message, I'm disappointed because she still hasn't.

Patience is all I need for but I'm getting tired. I want to hear her voice again or see her. It has been so long since we were together.

Khloe, I type. **Maybe I can meet you there.** I don't want to be pushy, but I want to see her.

This incredible day is starting to weigh me down. Facing my parents with what I had to tell them, well, that alone equals more stress than I've ever been through. I can give speeches to a crowd of thousands but the two of them, they're a tough crowd. They're loving parents but also very stubborn and not so open minded when it comes to me. I've come to find it's their way or the highway… and so I took the latter.

At this point, I have lost track of time. I know it's late, but I don't want to look at my phone. Not until it rings.

I sit on a bench at the entrance of the Central Park Zoo and I wait.

I wait forever. When I hear the morning, birds chirping and see the sun rising over the horizon, I know it won't happen—Khloe texting me. How stupid am I to wait that long? I walk the couple of miles home, hurt and alone.

Well, that sucked, I think, as I drift off to sleep.

Chapter Two

I'm having breakfast with my old friend, Simon. I can't say that I have much appetite left after eating like a pig again. Banana pancakes and maple syrup, the real deal not a maple flavored syrup. I could eat this every day of my life.

"I don't understand how you can eat that much and not be obese."

I have no idea either. "I don't normally eat like this, are you checking me out, man?" I joke.

He flips me the finger. "Did you let Khloe know you were in town?" I knew he would ask. He's the one who had to deal with the aftermath of her departure.

I nod, "First thing I did."

"So, you guys are still talking?" he asks.

"We are, every few weeks we email or call each other."

He frowns, "I saw her last week."

"Oh yeah, where?"

"At work." Simon is an obstetrician at the hospital, he sees a lot of people.

Why was she at the hospital? "Did she look sick?"

"No, she looked fine." He smiles, "Do you have plans on seeing her soon?"

I shrug, my pride is a little bit hurt that she bailed on me last night. "I was supposed to talk to her or see her last night, but she never got back to me. She left me hanging."

"That sucks. I'm sorry."

"Me too."

We're silent for a few minutes before Simon breaks the silence. "We've all changed in eight years, you know?"

"What do you mean?"

He shakes his head as if he regrets saying that. "You were working at the White House while she finished her degree, and has been trying to survive."

"Survive?"

"She's had it rough... it's as though she's cursed."

What is he talking about? She never mentioned anything like that to me. She always made it sound like she was doing fine. "She's never shared any of this with me."

"I think she is nervous to see you, to disappoint you."

"She shouldn't. I'm the same guy, I haven't changed."

Simon laughs aloud, "You can say that as much as you want, but when your old crush is seen across the world with his father, Mr. President, it's hard to believe that you are the same old River that we met back then."

I hate to admit it but he's right. My career path can be intimidating. "So, what should I do now?"

Simon shrugs, "I don't know. Give her time, maybe try to dig in a little, talk to her."

A ghost of a smile forms on my lips. "All these years, I never forgotten her and never lied." I shake my head, "It seems as though she hasn't been as honest with me."

"Don't be too hard on her, Riv." he says, nudging my shoulder.

The way I feel now is far from the high I was on yesterday.

"So, what happened with your girlfriend, Melissa?"

"Oh man, that was terrible. I want to laugh, even now, but I'm not a dickhead so I won't. Let's just say she didn't take me breaking up with her well."

He raises an eyebrow at me. "Are you surprised?" Simon chuckles.

"I know, to me, you've always been River but... to them, you were the young politician Dawson Rhodes travelling around the world with your father's entourage. You were the next politician to rise high, above it all. You changed a lot of things for the kids' well-being in America with your free backpack and school supplies and fuck man, they clearly didn't think you would be here today with me talking about what you left behind. Are you really, sure about this? You didn't quit a job at a supermarket or car dealership, you left something you've worked very hard for and made lots of compromises to achieve."

"What you said is true. I've done all of that, and I'm proud of myself. But damn, I don't have a passion for it. Not anymore. I don't want to be stuck sitting in the White House dealing with the next war coming, or the rich and poor. I've seen my father working through day and night, growing much older than his age. I'm a smart man; I can do something else with my life. This isn't it for me."

"Well, okay. You've obviously given it some thought, maybe you know what you're doing after all."

"Of course, I know. Isn't it obvious? It is to me." I rubbed my neck, feeling the knots from the stress of the last twenty-four hours. "When it comes to Khloe though, I don't know what I'm doing. I'm at a lost as to how to proceed, and I don't want to scare her." Before Simon mentioned it, it had never crossed my mind that my career, or how I was living my life could be construed as intimidating.

"I'm going to take a break, a vacation to clear my head. I need to find my way." I wiped my mouth and pushed the plate back from the edge of the table, giving me more room. "Thanks, man, you gave me a lot to consider."

"Don't be too hard on yourself, and about Khloe, try to find out more about her. Who she is now; I think there's a lot you don't know." *He knows more than I do, and that's frustrating.*

I hate the predicament that we're in, but I think he's right. Today, I will try to reach her again and show her that beside the political side of my life, I'm the same old guy she knew. Yes, I may look all serious and business-like when I'm working but with my friends, I'm just me. I wish she knew that.

"I have to get to work, but we should do this again later this week. It's good to have you back."

"Yeah, most definitely." I say as we stand and shake hands.

Simon has worked so hard to be where he is today. He's a good man, someone I look up to.

Alone again, my thoughts are running wild. *What is going on with Khloe?* I wonder cluelessly as I leave the , following shortly behind Simon, having no idea of where I'm going. New York is a great city, but it's hard not to feel lonely when I'm walking by myself with no point B in mind.

I hurriedly reach for my phone as it comes to life in my jeans pocket. *Khloe.* I can't mess this up.

"Hey Khloe." I say with apprehension in my voice.

"River, I'm sorry about last night."

"No worries." I shrug offhandedly.

"When the concert ended it was late, and I wasn't feeling well."

"Are you feeling okay now?" I try to keep the concern from my voice.

I can hear the surprise in hers. "Yeah. Yeah, I'm good. I think I'm getting too old for the late- night concert scene."

"Yeah, I get it. I don't think I can stay awake pass 10pm. Old age sucks." I joke. She laughs, and I like it.

"I should have called, and for that I'm sorry."

"Yeah, a call would've been nice, but I understand. What are you up to today?" hope edging into my voice.

"I'm heading to my day job in a bit."

Great, she's unavailable... again. "Day job? Do you have a day, and a night job?"

"Yup, I haven't won the lottery yet... so I have to work two jobs for now."

"Khloe, really?" I want to help her out. No one works two jobs unless they have financial issues.

"That's my reality, River." That feels like a punch in the face.

"About that, I had breakfast with Simon today and he said something that got me thinking..."

"About what?"

"He said that there were a lot of things I didn't know about you. Are you keeping secrets?"

She is still on the line because I can hear her breathing, but she remains quiet. "Maybe."

I sigh. "I'm not mad, but do you mind me asking why?" My intentions aren't to start a fight or make her feel badly, my goal is to understand her better. I've always been a gentleman with her and that isn't going to change. "Khloe, Simon said something to me earlier and it got me thinking." I paused, drawing in a deep breath, "My life has been intense and filled with trips across the world and meeting important people, but that isn't real. It's work. Most of the time, I would much rather lay low and do simple things. I'm grateful for the countries I've visited but I'm done with that. Life doesn't need to be all about politics, not anymore."

I came to the corner and stood waiting for the walk signal to flash, "Trust me, I was intimidated more times than I can count, Khloe. But to me that was work. I left it all behind yesterday. I need something that will make me feel alive, something that isn't predestined without my consent... you know? Sharing my experiences with you through the years wasn't to show off how good my life was or how important I thought I was, I shared with you because *you* kept me grounded. *You* are one of the people in this world that matters to me more than all of that."

"River." She whispered. "I've told you many times already how sorry I am that I had to leave back then. It was the hardest thing I've ever had to do and it's a decision I've regretted the most."

I should be taking baby steps and go slowly with Khloe, but we are always so intense, I'm losing control. "I'm still there for you."

"What about Melissa? She made me feel out of your league from day one and then, you were with her." she sighed, "I've always hated her."

Fucking Melissa, I knew it would bite me in the ass eventually. "Babe," *OH Shit*... "I mean, Khloe, you know our parents are involved in this. Love was never part of the deal. Let's be clear on that." My tone left no room for her to question how I felt about the whole arrangement.

"What makes you think you can walk back into my life?" Her words gut me, leaving me speechless. "River, you've been gone for years, living the good-life while I've been struggling to put food on the table." She fervidly exerts into the phone. "I'm sorry, I didn't mean to come off so passionate about it, but while you had a good life, mine has gone to shit. I really didn't feel like bringing my shitty life and its details into our conversations. I might have a degree and make good money, but New York rent, and sending my sick mother money, hasn't made it easy for me." I hear her voice waver as she chokes back sobs. "Seeing you with Melissa by your side hurt. Even if you say that it wasn't love, I still had to watch you with her when it should have been..." Her voice breaks as the emotions finally take over, pushing her off the emotional precipice she'd been struggling to hold on to.

"You." I rasp on exhaled breath. "It should have been *you* from day one. I freed myself from this world and I'm here for you."

"Life happened, River, and you'll see inside my world and you'll run away."

"No. I don't believe your world's as dire as you're saying. You can't scare me away, running isn't an option this time. You've given me the courage to leave everything behind and start over. You are in this with me... *With me, Khloe.*" *God, I wish I was I could take her into my arms... I'd kill to be with her. TOGETHER.*

"I have to go now, or I'll be late to work."

"Okay but this conversation isn't over."

"Bye, River." The line went dead, and I'm not sure what to think. Khloe admitted what Simon said, that she kept secrets from me.

All of this sucks, but we're going to figure it out this time around. I've lost her once, it won't happen twice. I should've asked where she works, that way, I could've brought her a surprise lunch. *She'd have loved that.*

I reach the impressive entry to my building and head inside to the bank of elevators. On the ride up, I decide texting Simon to fish more information out of him on Khloe, is my best chance to find out more about her. I want to know every little detail about her. I've missed so much.

Maybe I should ask Khloe first... **Where do you work? I'll meet you for lunch.**

River, please. I've got to keep it ***together at work.***

Okay. *To fuck with okay—this is bullshit.* I'm stubborn and I want to see her. Simon might be my only hope after all.

Simon, I want to bring Khloe lunch. Can you tell me where she works?

You're putting me in a sticky situation. I don't think Khloe would want me to tell you.

Why not? I just want to bring her food.

Mansfield & Clarkson, she works there.

Thanks man, I owe you.

It's a start, right? I google it on my phone and find the address in two clicks. I call to find out when Khloe's scheduled to take lunch; I know I'm stepping over her boundary lines, but I needed to do this.

I step off the elevator and look at the vastness of my Livingroom—it's empty—too empty. Khloe's laughter would fill the room. Thinking of her adds a heaviness to my heart; a feeling that I'd forgotten was so complete, so total. *God, I miss her. I've got to get her back...*

I head back to my bedroom and strip off my shirt and collapse on my California King. I had just over three hours before I got to see her again, just enough time for a quick nap. A two-hour nap will help me think clearly, I can't offend her by saying something stupid. I need s clear mind and an open heart. *Damn, what is with me? She makes me all lovey dovey.*

I set my alarm for two hours from now. I have my change of clothes ready. *I've got this. Hell yes! Bring it Khloe...*

With warm macaroni and cheese, and manicotti take out in my hands, I walk to her office building. I'm nervous as fuck; stomach's in knots and my hands are clammy. That's how much I care about her. I go to the mezzanine where the cafeteria is, and I search through the crowd.

There.

Stepping out of the elevator, her long brown, curly hair almost reaches her waist, her natural tanned skin as I remember. My eyes appreciatively comb over every part of her body, she hasn't changed. *Has she?*

Involuntarily, I shiver at the sight of her, as I try to get my head together. I want her to see me so bad because I don't have the will to move. *I'm so damn weak. Maybe I should be channeling Dawson and his courage.*

She navigates her way through the throngs of people. Walking toward me, I know she is only moment's breath from seeing me. I count the seconds in my head. *One, two, three, four...* and then it happens. She stops walking altogether.

"River?" She says loud enough for me to hear.

"Khloe."

She doesn't look happy. *Fuck.* "What are you doing here? How did you find out where I work?"

She moves her large purse from her side to her front and steps back. "Thanks, but I can't do this now, River."

I'm frustrated and hurt. *What the fuck's it going to take?* "Take the food, Khloe. I got it for you and I'll go." I walk up to her, handing her the bags of takeout.

As she reaches for them, her purse swings back to her side, and I see the secret she's been keeping from me, with my own eyes.

Below her breast, in her loose-fitting dress, a small bump appeared. My eyes flick back to hers. "You're pregnant."

"Good to see you still have your eyesight," she quips sarcastically. "I said I can't do this while I'm at work. Please go."

"You're with someone?" The thought of her in a relationship with someone kills me. Khloe never said anything about a man. Not recently. Over two years ago, she told me about a man she was seeing, but why not saying anything now? She's become a real goddamn mystery.

"River go."

"Take-off the rest of the day, we need to talk."

She shakes her head, in disagreement. "No, but you can pick me up at eight."

"At 8 pm? You're pregnant, Khloe, why work so late when you need to rest?"

"Where do you get off showing up all-of-a-sudden and thinking you have any say in how I run my life? My life isn't a fairy tale and the sooner you get that through your head, the better off you'll be… the better we'll get along." Her words show her strength, but her voice is weak.

Once again, I can see the difference between our lives. If my lady were pregnant, she'd be spoiled, and have the option of not working this late, hell… or at all. Not a chance. I would ever let my woman or wife work so late or at all when pregnant. Not a chance.

I acquiesce, it isn't worth the fight. "I'll be here at eight." *With my Bugatti, so she doesn't have to walk around the city.*

She nods and places the packages of food on a nearby table.

"Thanks." She motions toward the food.

"No problem." I say, approaching her to give her a hug. To be honest, I'm not sure she'll let me hug her, but I'm willing to try. Khloe doesn't budge. Wrapping my arms around her, I hold the only woman I've ever loved, close to me. I like how she lets me, but I can't deny I wish she'd hug me back. Her arms around me would do me so much good... confirm so many things, and quiet my mind.

I've got to let her go before it gets weird between us, but first, I press my lips on her forehead and kiss her.

As I let go, both of her arms slide around my waist, and my heart slams into my chest, beating so fast; it hurts.

"Still wearing Calvin Klein Escape?" She murmurs, more to herself than to me.

"I have, nine years now. I've gotten multiple bottles over the years, but you gave me the first. I've yet to find one I like better."

"River, you have to go now." She orders me unconvincingly and doesn't move away.

"If you want me to go, babe, you have to let go of me." Her hands holding my t-shirt come undone. Stepping back, out of her embrace, I see a tear on her cheek.

"I'll pick you up at eight."

She nods.

If she's with someone right now, it's odd that she held on to me like that. I don't want her to be a single mother or wish her something hurtful but deep down, I hope the father of the baby she is carrying isn't around. I will take his place without ever looking back.

I leave her office building feeling like I need to talk with Simon. I needed an explanation of some sort.

I remember that he mentioned seeing her at work, he almost told me then, but I didn't catch it.

Chapter Three

I glance up at the clock in the lobby, eight on the nose. As I wait in the lobby of Khloe's work, I find my thoughts center on the fact that I'm anxious to learn more about her. My curiosity is killing me, but also, I'm scared we won't work out again, and I can't have that.

"River, I'm here."

I turn around and there she is. Breathtaking. *Damn you do it for me—there's just something about you.*

"Hey beautiful." I say smiling brightly at her. "Is there anything you'd like to do, or anywhere specific where you'd like to go?"

"Can we just head back to your place? We have a lot of talking to do and I'd do better without any distractions."

I nod. *My place? I would've never offered because I don't want her to get the wrong idea.*

"Yes, let's go." We get to my car and it takes everything in my not to ask about the father. I keep staring at her belly like it was just a dream and it'll go away.

"I'm five months pregnant." She says in a quiet voice. "I've just found out she's a little girl, and the answer to the question I know you've been dying to ask—no—the father isn't around."

"Khloe? What happened?" I cleared my throat, conscious of how bad that sounded. "I mean, was she planned… or…"

She interrupted me, "Nothing happened other than sex. I modeled for a realistic drawing class. He was a student, who took great interest in me before, during, and after class. It started quite simply with me modeling and ended in the bathroom down the hall of that same building. My mama had passed away the week prior, and I was vulnerable. He offered me a chance to feel alive and I took it."

"I can't relate but I'm pretty sure you were heartbroken after the loss of your mom." I gave her a reassuring look before saying what was really on my mind, "So, was the chance to feel alive, worth getting pregnant for?"

If looks could kill, I'd be dead. Clearly Khloe doesn't appreciate my comment.

"When I found out I was pregnant, there had only been him. So, I went back to the art session four weeks in a row, but he never showed up again."

"Are you keeping the baby?" I shouldn't have asked it that way. *Fuck, I'm such an insensitive ass.*

"Of course, I am. I'm already five months pregnant. What kind of question is that?"

"God, I'm sorry." I say, hanging my head and I squeeze her knee for good measure. "I really, truly didn't mean anything by that. I'm new to all of this and what is okay to ask, and what is *clearly* NOT." I say flashing her an apologetic half-smile. "Forget I asked, please. I'm glad you are keeping it."

"Why are you glad? It doesn't change anything in your life."

Now, I don't know if she said that to get back to me or not, but it doesn't sit well with me. "Khloe." I try my best not to sound mad but I am. "I need a minute."

I drive in silence as she stays quiet, fidgeting with her dress.

"Okay. Let me be clear once and for all. If I'm here with you right now, it's not just for fun or to hang out. I came back to New York to be with you, as a couple. I think it is obvious that I want you back in my life. If you come with a baby, that's no issue for me, I'll raise it as my own."

"O... Okay," she stammers, "we need to talk."

"I know, Khloe."

The remainder of the ride is in silence. Khloe is looking out the window, thoughtful. I know what I've just told her is a lot to process but if she wants time, she'll get some. No issue there.

In my head, the baby doesn't even make me reconsider being with her. It doesn't change anything. I'm ready for this life.

"We're home."

"I know, I remember where you live, River."

I smile. The place hasn't changed much since the last time we were here together.

Glancing at her quickly before entering the interior parking of the building, I see her grinning.

"Is that a smile on your face?" I ask her.

"Maybe."

I park the car in my reserved spot, and get out before she does, dashing around the back of the car to open her door.

"It's good to have you back here." I say gesticulating into the open air between us. "It has been too long."

Her answer is a powerful yawn.

"Someone needs a nap." I chuckle.

"Sorry, it's been a long day."

I offer her my hand which she accepts and steps out of the car.

"You're beautiful, you know, that right?"

Red creeps across her cheeks.

We walk in silence to the elevator and ride it up to my penthouse apartment. I'm anxious to have her over, after all this time. My only issue is that I didn't expect to come home, so I have very little to offer her in the way of food or drinks. *I'll manage... always have.*

The elevator comes to a stop on my floor and we step out into my foyer.

"It hasn't changed at all." she whispers.

"You're right."

The conversation is strained and uncomfortable. I *think we're both nervous.*

She yawns again.

"I know we have a lot of talking to do but do you want to take a nap or something," I suggest warily.

Khloe is standing awkwardly, just inside the door, her arms crossed. "What are you going to tell your parents when it comes to me?" she asks timidly. "They were never fond of me."

Ugh! Okay, she asked a question and I need to answer it. I guess it's time we clear the air.

"I don't care what my parents say. Their support would be great, and I'd appreciate it, but if they can't provide that, I won't let them ruin us."

She nods accepting my answer. "If I let you, it's not just about me... it's about my daughter." I can feel the inner battle inside of

Khloe. "This can't *not* work," the conviction in her voice strong. "I can't mess…"

I interrupt her, "I'm not going anywhere." I cup her cheek with my hand. "From now on, you have to tell me the truth. Don't keep stuff from me. I need to know what's going on in your mind and heart. Okay?"

"I'm sorry," she says as she covers my hand with hers, "I was ashamed of my life compared to yours."

"My life looked like it was a beautiful gift wrapped with gold wrapping paper and fancy bows, but inside, there was only an empty box." I said shaking my head reverently. "I couldn't do it anymore. I was dying inside."

"We're back together now," she says smiling, "plus one."

I can't believe she's pregnant. I never expected that.

"I don't want to rush you into a relationship. If you want to take your time, go on dates, I'll be happy to go at your speed." I meant each of those words. I don't want to make her feel obligated to be with me. Whether we like it or not, we've changed in the last eight years.

"Don't be silly. Being with you has always felt natural. I don't want to take it slow, I want it all now. I know how great we can be together."

"Khloe." I whisper against her lips as my arms wrap her closer to me. "I'm going to kiss you now but know that it's a kiss that's been long-coming for eight years, I can't promise that it'll end."

"Okay." Her voice is small, her lips leaving warmth on my lips as they accidentally graze mine.

I bend my head, my lips first invite hers, then demand her acceptance. Our lips touch and memories come flooding back to me. The years we've spent apart has done nothing to lessen my feelings for her, or hers for me—they have only been on hold until our wires connected again.

She clings to my shirt with her fists, steading herself, keeping me close to her. So close, her baby bump rubs on my belly.

Our lips move in perfect harmony. Mine kissing hers fervently, making up for all the times I wished I would see her again. I slide my hand from her cheek to the back on her head, weaving my fingers through her thick hair, grasping it strongly, possessively. I have no plans on stopping anytime soon.

My other hand rests on the small of her back, my thumb rubbing over the fabric of her dress. *Damn I wish she wasn't wearing this dress.* My mind wanders, recalling the perfects curves of her form… her now pregnant form. Her condition makes me feel self-conscious and unsure, like a teenage boy, uncertain about the how-tos. I mean, I don't want to hurt her or the baby. I've never thought about any of this before now.

I push my thoughts aside and focus on her lips and feeling her in my arms. That's all that matters now. As I lift her, her legs entwine themselves around my waist. I walk to the couch and sit with her straddling me.

"River, I can't believe this is real. We're together again." The joy in her voice is impossible to ignore and the reason I'm smiling.

"We are, for good now." I confirm, planting butterfly kisses on her collarbone.

She giggles and nods, smiling lovingly at me.

I kiss her again, unable to stop myself; her giggles sweet against my mouth.

The sound of my cell phone ringing is an unwelcome interruption I ignore. Right now, my priorities are the woman I'm holding in my arms.

"Maybe you should take that."

"Maybe not," I rasp. "I'm busy."

She pushes away from my lips. "Please, take it."

Against my better judgment, I take the call. It's my mother.

"*Amelia.*" I grind out coldly. *Could you have picked a worse time to call?* I glance lovingly at Khloe.

"Dawson, Agent Rodriguez said you are in New York City with Ms. Palmer."

"I am."

"What about Melissa? What's going on with my *son?*" she wails. It sounds like she's been crying.

"You had your security team go after me?" My incredulity blatant in my tone.

"Dawson, we are worried about you. You acted so out of character, we don't understand what's going on with you."

I clear my throat and square my shoulders, preparing for a battle. "I'm trying to live my life as I please for once. That means Melissa had to go by the wayside, and so the career you crafted for me. I don't intend to be the next president of the United States of America. It's that simple."

"Dawson!?"

"I'm sorry, I love you, but I have to go now." I rush out unevenly.

I hang up, my eyes locked on Khloe's, trying to gage her reaction. "I'm sorry, you had to witness that."

"It's okay. I get that your parents won't be too pleased with me. I'm part of the big changes you're making that your parents don't understand."

"Don't give them another thought. It'll take time but they'll come around." *God, I hope they do.*

She cuddles on my side and I wrap my arms around her. That phone call broke the mood we had going. It's too bad, but we don't need to rush eight years into one evening anyway.

Khloe yawns for the third time and I know it's a matter of minutes before she falls asleep. I let her; she needs it. I bet my returning to New York caused her unnecessary stress. I'll take care of her from now on.

Once she is deep asleep, I leave her on the couch as I stride toward my room to fix-up her bed. I'll give her mine and I'll take the couch. I don't want to take for granted that she wants to share a bed with me already. We never discussed it and I'd rather be cautious now, than have regrets in the morning.

I stretch my arms above my head, getting in one of those toe-curling stretches before swinging my feet off the couch. They hit the floor with a thud and I groan as I sit up. Wandering into the kitchen to start the coffee, I pull open the fridge, taking a quick inventory. *Fuck.* I don't have shit. Since my refrigerator is seriously lacking in the food department, I decide to take her out for breakfast.

After Khloe and I have a leisurely morning getting dressed and having a cup of strong coffee, we ride my elevator down to the lobby. To my surprise, there are lame paparazzi's waiting outside, if I had noticed them before now, I would have taken a different exit but I'm too little too late now.

I don't pay them attention and hail a taxi as fast as I can. I open the door for Khloe, and slide in quickly behind her.

"Sorry about that. They'll find out I'm boring soon enough and they'll leave us alone." I hate lying to her, but hell, they caught me walking out of my place holding hands with a pregnant woman when I was with Melissa last week. We've just given them the best scoop they could dream of.

"I don't think they'll leave us alone, Riv." She knows the shitstorm that comes along with the paparazzi discovering us, and I hate that I'll put her through this. She doesn't need the bullshit that comes with dating me.

I don't want this to come between us. "Let's just get some breakfast for now and we'll figure out the rest later."

We're both starving. We'll have breakfast and we'll deal with whatever is thrown at us.

"I'm supposed to leave for Costa Rica soon." She blurts out all-of-a-sudden.

What the fuck... out of the blue? Why? I don't understand. What about her job? Me?

"When are you leaving exactly?" I have so many questions popping into my head, but this is the only one I can spit out.

"River, I don't want to see my face on "The Enquirer" or "Hollywood Life". I've always maintained a good, clean reputation, and I've worked hard my entire life. I don't want my child to think she's a marriage wrecker or whatever they're going to say."

"I don't want that either, so... when are we leaving?" I nudge her playfully, in the backseat of the cab. "I was getting bored of New York anyway." I try adding a dose of humor to our situation, but I know this must be hard for her.

I look over at her and see that she's biting her bottom lip, trying not to cry. "I'll have to give my notice at work." her voice is soft, filled with emotion.

I nod, patting her thigh. "You know I'll help you." I squeeze her leg gently. "I don't want money to become an issue for you."

"River, I would leave today if I could. Dealing with the press is my worst nightmare but I have to give my job a respectful notice; they gave me a chance when no one would."

"You tell me when and I'll have everything ready, ok? I'm the reason you want to run away." I paused, the gravity of the situation hitting me hard. "Are you sure you want me to go?" It kills me to ask her. *I don't want to see her go.*

"You're coming with me." She turns to me, her expression serious. *I could get lost in those eyes.* "River, I lost you once, I won't lose you twice."

Best answer ever. "Deal." I lean over, giving her a peck that deepens more than I intended.

As the taxi slows to drop us at an Italian gourmet in Soho, I pull my lips back from Khloe's. We're both out of breath, and I can't speak for her, but my heart is racing... *the things this girl does to me.* We both hop out of the cab and walk together hand-in-hand into Martinelli's.

We're both quiet, thinking about our options, and the direction our futures are going to take. I've never been one to run away but it seems like I've been doing a lot of that lately, thinking back on how I left things at the White House, and now how I plan to leave the country with Khloe. *My parents are going to seriously freak the fuck out.*

"Do you still have a home in Costa Rica?" I ask after we're seated in a quiet corner. *A trip to Costa Rica isn't ideal considering my life and hers but laying low for a while is all we can do. If the rumor–mill can't find us, they'll have nothing to say to anyone... besides, I need a serious vacation after how hard I've worked the past decade for Dad, and Costa Rica sounds nice.*

"I do. It's nothing like what we have here, but it has potential if we want to improve it a bit."

I smile at the woman who's thrown my life into a tailspin, "All we need is a roof and we'll figure out the rest."

We take a quiet minute to examine the menu, and again my thoughts wander. The server asking us for our drink order, ends the silence.

"I'll take a house red for me, and..."

Khloe interrupts me, "Water's fine, thank you." After he leaves our table, I study Khloe as she's *still* studying her menu, "What are you getting?"

"I'm not even sure I'm still hungry."

"Maybe, but you're still going to eat."

"Bossy aren't we?"

Hell, yes, I am. As long as I'm taking care of her, it's my job to make sure she eats.

"Blueberry waffles, it is with extra scrambled eggs on the side." she says sweetly, winking playfully at me.

"Now, we're talking."

The waitress comes to take our orders. I'm so distracted by my thoughts of our future that I don't remember what I've ordered the following minute. I keep looking outside scared that we were followed; New York isn't as big of a city as everyone makes it out to be.

"River quit looking for them. They didn't see where we went, or they'd already be outside," she motioned toward the restaurant's windows, "we'd see them."

"You're right, I just can't shake the feeling we were followed is all. I've never had this anonymity since Dad became president." I reached across the table and took Khloe's delicate hand in mine.

"So," she breathed, "what's the plan? You've been a million miles away, and knowing you, I'm sure you have it all figured out by now."

I smile at her, she knows me so well. "Well," I paused thinking, "after breakfast I think we should go to your place to pack your things. If it's safe to travel at this stage of your pregnancy, we'll leave as soon as we're ready." I glance at her new curves. "It is safe to travel at this stage, right?"

"I think it is, but I can always call Simon. He has been helping me with the medical side of the pregnancy. His patience with my endless questions is remarkable."

"Khloe, I'm so sorry that I wasn't there these past few years," I said sighing, "and I'm sorry that now that I'm here, our world has been flipped upside down."

"Stop apologizing. Before you came back, I was already contemplating going. I would love for my daughter to be born in Costa Rica like my mom and I. You have to keep in mind that back home, it's back to basics."

"I look forward to going back to the basics."

"Blueberry waffles and your side of eggs." The waitress places a heaping breakfast plate in front of Khloe; it looks delicious. "And the strawberry pancakes with a side of chocolate sauce for you." She gives me the look that says, '*You look familiar, I must have seen you somewhere before.*'

"Thank you." I say, avoiding eye contact.

We eat our breakfast, bite after delicious bite. Khloe keeps reaching over to steal bites of my fresh strawberries.

"I think I now know how to seduce you or keep you forever." I say grinning mischievously.

She blushes. "How?"

"Strawberries seem to do the trick."

She laughs, and her facial expression reminds me of the young Khloe I met, free from adult issues, just having a good time.

"*You* are beautiful."

She tilts her head to the side, "Thank you," she says softly.

We spend the rest of our breakfast in easy conversation, and relaxed flirtations.

"Are you ready to go?" I ask after a bit.

"Yes. Packing right?"

I nod. "I think it's better if we stay together. Pack everything you want to bring with you at your place. We'll be ready to leave for Costa Rica."

***

We could have walked to her place, but we got another taxi cab… in the hope of staying incognito longer.

As she unlocks the door of her place, I can tell she's a little hesitant to let me in. I know by the look of the building in general that it won't be anything luxurious. Khloe pushes the stiff door open, and steps inside to flip the light on. I'm surprised to see how small it is—a small studio with a bed and kitchenette—there is no way she could have raise a baby in here.

She looks at me sheepishly, "I know what you are thinking, but it was a temporary solution to save a little bit of money."

I shrug casually hoping to ease her discomfort. "It's okay, sweets. You had a roof over your head, a place to sleep and food on the table." It's far from okay, but I don't want her to feel bad about it. We all struggle at times, and Khloe's one hell of a fighter.

Khloe heads across the small space, pulls out her large suitcase and within a few minutes she's able to empty all her drawers, packing her clothes in their entirety. From her small wardrobe, she pulls out a final box where she stores her personal belongings: a frame, a few books, and her toiletries.

"Okay, I'm all done."

It takes her less than five minutes to pack her whole life.

"Okay, let's go."

I'm saddened by how she lived her life prior to my return. In the future, I want to give her more, or everything.

Chapter Four

The media made our life together, impossible in New York. My parents have also been bugging me since I told them I had no intention of coming back in the near future. I have separated myself from the politic world, but it hasn't stopped them from thinking I still belong in that world.

So, two days after being spotted at my place, we flew to Jaco Beach, Costa Rica where we could be together in peace. This place is unbelievable. The weather, the beach, the people I've met so far and even our place.

After Khloe's parents divorced, her mom moved back to Costa Rica and invested her money in the Bed & Breakfast. Since her passing, her aunt doesn't have enough time to make it work, so Khloe decided to let it close.

Now, this is where my mind is at... *Maybe we should open it up again. I haven't been able to think of a good reason why we shouldn't. Yes, the baby will be here soon, but I'm here to help and I have few months to wrap my head around the chores. We could even move to the house next door since it's on sale and operate the Bed &Breakfast as our main job. I'm sure we can do this.*

"I've been thinking," I say reaching for her hand.

"I know, I've seen your papers laying on the table and it's clear that you have a project in mind; one that seems to include the pretty house next door."

"Huh? Well, yeah." I'm bummed that it's no surprise to her. "We could reopen the Bed & Breakfast" I said with enthusiasm, "and move next door." I watched her, trying to gauge her reaction.

"River..." She says my name with a heaviness that makes me doubt she agrees with my plans. "What if you have to go back to politics for any kind of reason, or if your family needs you?"

"They're my family but I want my own family here, with you. We can build something of our own and make a life together here."

"We just got here." Her laughter hides concerns.

"I know, babe, but I think we could spend a couple of years here without a doubt. If you want to go back when the baby is ready for school, we can move back home or wherever you want to call home."

"Bed and breakfast's are a lot of work: cleaning rooms, cooking, and accounting." her voice trails off.

"I think we can do this and if we need help, we can always hire a student or someone like that. There are ways to make it work, plus, it's your Mother's."

She sighs deeply and rubs her belly. "Do we have to decide now?" The weariness is noticeable in her tone.

"I've scheduled to visit the house already, we have an hour before our appointment."

"Riv, what about taking decisions together?"

I'm the one laughing now. "We are, but from what I've seen, the house is great."

As I was formulating this plan, I checked the realtor website and I also found few minutes to check through the windows. The house next door is a lot nicer than here, it's obvious the owners invested money into renovation, and it shows. We could do the same with her mom's house; it's a great house on the beach, but it needs love and a few thousand dollars.

This project is an unexpected twist in my life, but I'm so ready to jump in and start a new journey with the love of my life.

"I love you." Those words are so real. Khloe's the only woman apart from my mother and grandmother to whom I've said those words... *I love her so much.*

"I love you." Khloe looks at me with magic in her eyes. Tears of joy perhaps?

I may be crazy, but I can really see us doing this together; I'm sure she does too. We're in love. "Are you ready for a new adventure?"

"You're crazy." She says stepping closer to me.

"About you, yes."

She makes the first step to kiss me and I respond to her needs. As soon as our lips touch, I take her in my arms and bring her to our improvised bedroom. We still have to get our things unpacked, but with the possibility of having a new home, we may not have to yet. Wearing a light summer dress, which I pull over her head, my eyes linger on every part of her. The beauty of her changing body. She owns her new curves and god, she's sexy. Pregnancy fits her well. Although it makes me nervous, I want her as much as our first time. Probably even more since I know what it's like to be with someone else... and it didn't work out well. It's her, Khloe, she's always been the one.

My pulse quickens. Our kisses remind me of hungry teenagers and how they devour every inch of each other. *What the hell is she doing to me?* She's driving me crazy and I love it.

Our fingers entwine, and our lips take a break. Passion is all over her face and I bet it's on every inch of mine. The heat between us is burning my skin and I don't care. This is the moment we're one again and forever.

"River bring me to the bed." Each word is separated by a soft kiss sending me high, closer to the edge.

"Well, I'm pretty sure we are eight years overdue." A man can keep it together only for so long.

THE END

Electing Ellie
Michelle Rene

One

Ellie

"Ellie Wallace, I'd appreciate your vote," I repeat for the hundredth time as I stand at the entrance to the Farmer's Market handing out flyers. "I cannot believe I let you all talk me into this," I grumble to my campaign manager as she stands by my side smiling and keeping me stocked with handouts.

"You could have said no," she reminds me. "We would have been disappointed, but we would have understood. We could have learned straight out of the textbooks, and possibly even retained everything you taught us. But being involved in this campaign, being hands-on during the *entire* process of an election *that* will be something we'll always remember."

"Ugh, how did you become a master of guilt trips at such a young age?" I grumble.

Giggling she replies, "Momma says it's a gift passed down from Granny Alice. Works like a charm most of the time."

And there it is, the reason I couldn't, or more accurately *didn't*, say no when my class of fifteen high school students asked me to run for mayor. Guilt. So rather than disappoint them, I negotiated that they could run my campaign as part of their American Government class.

"Oh trust me; I'm aware of how well it works."

Laughing she shakes her head, "I'm going to go check on Lincoln and Grace and then find Kayla and Cody."

Watching her walk to the exit end of the market, I shake my head. One thing is certain; these kids have bright futures ahead of them in either sales or hostage negotiations.

Living in a small town, career choices are limited. I know, I grew up here. Of course, I always knew what I wanted to do. Unlike my classmates who couldn't wait to get out of Buckhorn Wyoming, population 283, I couldn't wait to move back and teach at the same school I attended. Housed in a three story, yellow brick building, Buckhorn School runs from Kindergarten through high school. Administrative offices and the cafeteria/auditorium are on the first floor as are the elementary classrooms. The middle and high school classrooms are on the second floor and third floor. A gymnasium sits behind the school and the public library directly across the street.

Ask any teacher and they will tell you the same thing, there was that one teacher that struck a chord inside them that made learning so interesting they couldn't wait to share it with someone else. For me that teacher was Mrs. Holbrook.

It took me a little longer than expected to secure a position at Buckhorn High School. I stayed in constant contact with Principal Markham while I worked on my degree in education and even afterward. My persistence paid off. After three years of teaching in a small town outside of Casper, Principal Markham called to tell me a position had opened for a social studies teacher. I accepted immediately, and then let the school I was working at know I wouldn't be returning the next year.

Now here I am, three months into my dream job and I'm campaigning for mayor of our little town. Of course, I have no one but myself to blame because Lila is right, I could have said no. However, with the excitement they showed in being able to run the campaign, there was no way I could disappoint them.

We continued passing out flyers until traffic at the Farmer's Market began to slow. When Kayla, Cody, Lincoln and Grace joined us, Lila gathered the remaining flyers and said, "Thank you all for coming out today. If we don't see you at church tomorrow, we'll see you at school on Monday."

I bite my lip to hide my smile. Lila has amazing leadership skills; it's easy to see why we have such a good turnout for campaigning.

As Lila finishes speaking and before everyone takes off, I add, "Yes thank you, everyone. Great job today."

I watch as they begin to disperse, each going in their own direction, before turning back to Lila. "Lila, do you need a ride home?"

"No ma'am," she says, "Mom has a booth set up with vegetables today, so I'm off to help her now."

"Okay, enjoy the rest of your day. And thank you again for all your help."

Turning towards the parking lot, I walk to my car, open the hatch and put the remaining flyers inside before turning back to the market to pick up a few things for Sunday dinner.

Making my way down the aisles of booths, I've forgotten how much I love the feeling of community that Buckhorn emits. It's something I haven't felt in the time I've been away. Not that the other towns I've resided in didn't, but Buckhorn is home and the people here I've known all my life. Everyone I encounter greets me with a smile and asks about my family, even though we'll see most of them at church tomorrow. Being home creates a warmth inside me I didn't realize I was missing until I moved back.

Just ahead of me, I see a booth with fresh produce. Making my way through the crowd, I zero in on the zucchini and yellow squash stacked on the booth.

"Hi Miss Wallace."

Looking up I see Lila inside the booth.

"Hi Lila," I say smiling up at her while I inspect the produce.

"Mom, come here a second," I hear her say.

"What do you need, sweetie?"

"Mom, this is my teacher I've been telling you about, Miss Wallace."

Looking up I'm surprised to see Becky Barker standing in front of me.

"Becky?"

"Ellie?"

We laugh as we both speak at the same time.

"Wait, you two know each other?"

"Know each other? Sweetheart we practically grew up together," Becky clarifies as she drops her arm around Lila's shoulders.

"I had no idea you were Lila's mom," I admit as I look between them, the family resemblance now evident as I see them side by side.

"Well, the last name probably threw you off, but yes she's mine," she says hugging Lila to her side before Lila wiggles out of her mother's grasp to help another customer.

"Well you should be proud, you've raised quite a confident young lady."

"Thank you, Ellie, that's the greatest compliment I could receive. I was afraid she wouldn't adjust to a new town and school as quickly as she has after the divorce. Sometimes I think she's more well-adjusted than I am." Becky stares after her daughter for a few moments, then shakes her head, "So," she says effectively changing the subject and motioning towards the produce. "What can I get for you today?"

"I'll take some zucchini and yellow squash, which look amazing by the way."

"Thank you, I grew them myself," she says as she places six of each into a bag for me." "It's been nice getting my hands dirty again and gives me something to do while Lila is in school."

"I'm sure your parents are happy to have you home," I offer as I pay her for my purchase.

Smiling she replies, "They would be if they were here, but they're off traveling for a while. We're staying out on the ranch with Nate."

Butterflies immediately take flight in my stomach at the mention of Nate Barker's name.

The Barker's have owned and operated one of the most successful cattle ranches in Buckhorn for the last thirty years, all while raising three daughters and one son. Becky is the third child and the same age as my older brother Denny. Nate is the youngest, and even though he is four years older than me, I've always had a crush on him.

Quickly recovering from the thought that Nate is still in town, I take my bag and smile, "Good for them. Maybe next time they're home they can talk my parents into taking a vacation."

"They may surprise you one day," she says with a laugh. "I know mine sure did."

"That's true. They've already surprised me by letting Denny take over more of the daily operations on the farm."

"I bet he loves that. The four of us should get together soon. It will be like old times."

"I'd like that. I'll mention it to Denny and see when works for him. It was great seeing you Becky; I better let you get back to work."

"You too, Ellie, we'll talk soon."

"Can't wait."

Satisfied with my purchase I give her a wave, and head to my car. Thoughts of the times the four of us spent together going to football games, riding horses or just hanging out play through my mind and I find myself smiling at the idea of us all being together again. *Of course*, I think to myself as I pull out onto the highway and head home, *that may have more to do with seeing Nate again than anything else.* But I'll keep that to myself, for now.

Two

Nate

Tossing bales of hay from the flatbed to my most trusted ranch hand, Ken, I pause as I see a cloud of dust coming up the driveway. My sister pulls the truck to a stop, I wave as they get out. Removing my hat, I wipe the sweat from my brow before putting it back in place.

"Hi Uncle Nate," my niece calls and waves before turning toward the house.

"Hi Sweet Pea," I call back as my sister smiles over the hood of the truck before following her inside.

"Shame things happened like they did," Ken says, stopping to wave as well. "But I'm sure glad to see those two around here."

"Yeah, me too," I say as I pick up another bale of hay and begin tossing them to him again.

Nine months ago, my sister's husband, Mitch, decided he didn't want to be married any longer. Becky stayed long enough for Lila to finish out the school year then moved back home, giving them both a fresh start.

Becky moving back has helped me out tremendously. She's taken over the business side of the ranch, giving me more time to be involved in daily operations.

Finished with the hay, I thank Ken and head toward the house as Ken heads home.

Walking into the house, I hang my hat on the peg beside the door and walk into the kitchen to wash my hands.

"That didn't take long," Becky says as she looks up from the green beans she's snapping.

"Nah just ordered enough for the rest of the month. We'll start stocking up for winter next month," I say as I scrub my hands. "How'd things go at the Farmer's Market?"

"Good. Sold everything I took with me and still had plenty left over for us."

"That's good," I say as I dry my hands and turn to face her. "Just don't forget to put some up for the winter. We may not be able to get to town as often."

"I'll make sure we're well stocked. I haven't forgotten what winter can be like."

"Wasn't sure if living in Denver made you soft, so I thought I'd remind you," I tease as she throws a green bean at me, effectively hitting me in the chest.

"What about you, sweet pea, you enjoy the Farmer's Market?" I ask my niece, as I grab a bean and place it in my mouth.

"I was outside most of the time helping to campaign," she says as she too snaps green beans.

"Campaign? For who?"

"My teacher, Miss Wallace. She's running for mayor.'"

"Wallace?" I say directing my question to Becky.

"Yes, Denny Wallace's sister, Ellie, is teaching social studies at Buckhorn this year."

"Huh, I didn't realize she was back in town. And she's running for *mayor*?" Scoffing I ask, "Is she even old enough to vote?"

Looking at me crossly, Becky draws out her reply, "Yes. She's only a few years younger than you, you know."

"Yeah, I guess she is," I say as I pour myself a glass of water.

Ellie Wallace with her blonde hair and mesmerizing blue eyes was the prettiest girl around here while we were growing up. I always wanted to ask her out, but she was my best friend's sister and there are unspoken rules about that. Ever since she left for college, I've considered her the one who got away. Now that she's back in town, maybe I'll take a chance, ask her out and see if anything develops.

"There's a campaign rally Wednesday night in the gym," Lila says. "You should come Uncle Nate; you know, *support* your favorite niece and her candidate."

"I just might do that, sweet pea," I say as I head upstairs to shower.

Three

Ellie

Riding into town with my parents and brother takes me back to when we were kids. Only now, my brother rides quietly beside me instead of incessantly picking on me during the thirty-minute ride as he did when we were kids.

As we reach the edge of town, Denny's voice breaks through my concentration as I take in the scenery through the window.

"So Madame Mayor, are you ready to present yourself to the town?"

"As ready as I'll ever be," I say with a sigh. "I still can't believe I let them talk me into running for mayor."

Dad chuckles from behind the wheel, "I'm not surprised. Some of those kids can sell water during a flood."

"Don't I know it," I agree. "At least there are two other people running, so my chances of winning decrease."

Confused Mom turns in her seat to face me, "So you're not going to try to win?"

"Of course I am. Running for office is more about giving my students an inside look at the election process. But I would never disappoint them by not trying, especially considering how hard they've been working on the campaign. All I'm saying is that I am not going to be devastated if I don't win. After all," I say as Dad pulls into the parking lot, "I already have my dream job."

As we all step out of the truck, Mom wraps her arm around me and says, "Well I'm certainly glad your dream job brought you back home to us. I've missed having you around here."

"Thanks Mom, I missed you all too. It's good to be back."

"You were gone so long, even *I* was starting to miss you," Denny says as he tugs on my hair.

"You just missed having someone around to aggravate on a daily basis," I reply taking a swing at him as he dances out of my reach.

"That may or may not be true," he says as we step into the gymnasium. "But either way I'm glad you're home. Now go show them why you are the best candidate to become the next mayor of our amazing little town."

As Denny bounds up the bleachers to find a seat, the current Mayor of Buckhorn, James Holbrook, greets Mom, Dad and me. "Dennis, Marguerite," he says shaking their hands, "good to see you."

James Holbrook has been mayor of our town for as long as I can remember. Standing at just over six feet tall, his white beard and sparkling eyes give him that Santa Claus quality that draws people in.

"Good to see you too, Jim," Dad says as he shakes the mayor's hand.

Turning to me the Mayor greets me with a nod and smile, "Ellie."

"Mayor Holbrook," I return with a smile.

"You've been a constant topic around my dinner table the last few weeks." He smiles.

"All good I hope?"

Chuckling he says, "Have you met my wife? There'd be serious consequences if I'd said anything negative about her favorite student."

Mrs. Holbrook was the social studies teacher from the time I started at Buckhorn School until I returned to teach myself. She is also the one who helped me develop a love of history. Everything she did made the class interesting for me. I was honored to be taking over her position at Buckhorn when she decided to retire.

"Well I'll be sure to thank her for keeping you in line before I leave."

Laughing again he says, "You be sure to do that. Now," he says clapping his hands together, "how about we get this rally started?"

"Sounds like a good idea, before I lose my nerve," I half whisper making him laugh once again.

"Well we can't have that," he says as he motions me to the stage.

Stepping onto the stage ahead of Mayor Holbrook, I greet the other candidates, Nolan Pratt and Tim Morrison, both whom I've known all my life. Nolan Pratt and his wife own and operate one of the two restaurants in town, while Tim Morrison is the editor of our local paper.

As Mayor Holbrook steps up to the podium, he greets the crowd, "Good evening, folks! Thank you for coming out tonight. It has been my pleasure to serve as Mayor of Buckhorn for the last twenty years, but the time has come for me to pass the torch to someone else. These three brave souls," he says, turning and gesturing toward us, "have decided to throw their hats into the ring to become your next Mayor."

As the crowd applauds, my nervousness begins to rise, but Mayor Holbrook quiets them and continues. "Okay," he says raising his hands to the crowd. "Now normally we'd go alphabetically, but since I'm running the show, I say it's ladies first. Now this young woman just happens to be the most ambitious person to happen into our little town in quite a while. Not only is she a candidate for my position, she recently took over my wife's position at Buckhorn School. Please make welcome, Ellie Wallace."

Walking to the podium, I share a smile with the mayor as he moves to take a seat. Before I begin to speak, I scan the crowd to find my focal points. Locating my parents on one side, I search the other side for a familiar face. Finding Lila, I return her smile and begin.

"Thank you, Mayor Holbrook. Good evening and thank you for coming out tonight. As I look around, I can honestly say there are only a handful of faces I don't recognize. And considering I've been gone for nearly eight years, that's saying a lot. Now Mayor Holbrook said he thought I was ambitious, although gullible might be a better description. You see, while my bid for mayor started out as a way to make learning fun for my American Government class, something I learned from Mrs. Holbrook while I was a student at Buckhorn School." I say smiling in her direction before I continue. "I've been reminded just how much I love this town and the people in it. As your mayor, I will do my best to reflect the values instilled in me not only from my parents, but from all of you as well. Thank you."

As I turn to take my seat, the crowd applauds and I'm encouraged by the turnout and support the town is giving not only for me but the other candidates as well. Returning to the podium, Mayor Holbrook says, "See there, folks, I told you she was ambitious."

While the other two candidates speak, I scan the crowd watching for their reaction. When my eyes land on Lila, she gives me a wide grin and a thumbs up. The motion catches the attention of the man beside her, causing him too to turn his focus on me. My heart leaps into my throat, for staring back at me, with that sexy, crooked grin that has always made me weak in the knees, is none other than Nate Barker. Tipping his hat, he turns his attention back to the podium just as Nolan Pratt finishes speaking.

Before closing out the evening, Mayor Holbrook reminds everyone of upcoming events, stressing the need for volunteers for the Founder's Day celebration. Once he's thanked everyone for coming out, the crowd begins to disperse. Making my way from the stage, I'm caught by Mrs. Holbrook.

"Ellie," she says as she wraps me in a hug. "I am so proud of you and what you are doing for the students. I knew getting you as my replacement was the right decision."

My eyes dart around the room, hoping to catch another glimpse of Nate Barker, but my search comes up empty. Disappointed, I smile, return my focus to my former teacher and politely reply, "Thank you, Mrs. Holbrook. I just hope I can be half the teacher you were to me."

"Don't sell yourself short, Ellie dear, you're already doing more than I did just by joining the mayoral campaign. Think of the example you've already set for them, not only have you taken on one new job, but you're campaigning for mayor. That's huge Ellie, and don't you forget it," she scolds

She's right, it is huge. Thank goodness, I've already given my speech, because now my palms are sweaty and my knees are shaky. I blow out a cleansing breath, trying to calm my sudden case nerves. "Well, we'll see how it goes. Hopefully the kids won't be terribly disappointed if I don't win."

Hugging me to her side, we begin to walk toward the door. "Either way, it will be a good learning experience for them."

"Yes ma'am, I think so too."

Four

Nate

Walking up to the house, I stomp the dirt from my boots and climb the steps leading up to the back porch. Pulling open the screen door, I step into the kitchen, where Becky is making the weekly grocery list.

"Perfect timing," she says as she glances up from the table. "Need anything from the store?"

"Not that I can think of, you know I'm not picky," I reply as I walk to the sink. Turning on the faucet, I run my hands under the water and before lathering them up with a new citrus scented soap Becky has placed in the kitchen.

"I'm not going until tomorrow, so if you think of anything let me know."

Rinsing my hands I grab the towel that hangs over the cabinet door and dry my hands as I lean against the counter. "Will do. Is Lila around?"

Curious as to why I'm asking, Becky looks up from what she's doing. "Yeah she's in her room doing homework. You need help with something?"

"I have a couple of horses that need exercised, I thought she might want to ride."

A smile lights her face and I know that she's pleased I'm including Lila and encouraging her to ride. "Ask her, I'm sure she'd much rather ride than do homework."

"Sounds like someone else I know," I say as I head for the stairs, while Becky laughs.

I reach the second floor and make my way to Lila's door. Sitting cross-legged in the middle of her bed, surrounded by books and notebooks, she looks so much like Becky at that age. How Mitch could walk away from her or Becky for that matter, I'll never understand. As long as she's here, I'll spend as much time with her as possible. Before I let my anger toward him get out of control, I knock on the open door to get her attention.

Lila looks up and smiles while removing her earbuds. "Hey Uncle Nate."

"Hey sweet pea. I've got a couple of horses that need ridden, you up for it?"

"Sure," she says, excitement lighting her eyes as she moves her books off her lap. "Let me get my boots on and I'll meet you downstairs."

Once we have the horses brushed down and saddled, we head to the back section of the ranch to give them room to run.

After about twenty minutes of putting the horses through their paces, we decide to head back to the house.

"So sweet pea, how are things going at school?"

"Good," she says as she rides beside me. "It's a lot different than Denver, but I like the small classes and everyone's really nice. They never made me feel like the new kid, just kinda accepted me."

"That's good. I'm real proud of the way you've adjusted."

"Thanks," she says with a shrug. "But it's not like I had much choice. Can't stay where you're not wanted."

The sadness and disappointment I hear in her voice nearly guts me. No child should ever feel unwanted, especially by her own father. "That's true. Just remember sweet pea, you are always wanted here, and I'm more than happy to have you around."

"Thanks Uncle Nate," she says as we continue to ride toward the house.

As we ride toward the barn, once again thoughts of Ellie Wallace fill my mind. I haven't seen her since the rally, watching her take command of the crowd the way she did proved to me she was no longer little Ellie Wallace. She now a woman that know exactly what she wants. As much as I want to straight out ask Lila about her, I know better than to put her in the middle of my attraction for Ellie. Instead, I take a different route, hoping that my intuitive niece doesn't see right through me.

"How's the campaign going?"

"Good. I think Miss Wallace has a chance at winning. What did you think after seeing her at the rally?"

"I think you might be right about her winning. She seems to have charmed the entire town."

"I think Miss Wallace may have charmed you too," she teases with a grin.

If she only knew, I think to myself. Ellie charmed me years ago, but I won't share that just yet. Back then I was too nervous to ask her out, hell I still get nervous at the thought of asking her out. By the time I convinced myself to ask her out, she was gone.

"What makes you say that?"

"I saw the way you watched her at the rally. You should ask her out, you'd make a cute couple."

I can't help but chuckle at her assessment, "Is that so? So not only are you a powerhouse campaign manager you're also a matchmaker?"

"Just calling it like I see it, Uncle Nate," she says as we ride back into the barn.

Shaking my head, I laugh as I dismount and begin removing the tack from my horse. "So what you're saying is, you wouldn't mind me asking your teacher out?"

"Yeah, I would *definitely* be okay with it," Lila says as she too dismounts her horse. "Miss Wallace is my favorite teacher."

"Good to know."

"So Uncle Nate," Lila says as she begins brushing down her horse. "What can you tell me about Miss Wallace's brother?"

"Denny? He's a good guy, he's had a crush on your mom for years."

"Really?"

"Mhmm. Why do you ask?"

"Mom introduced me to him at the rally," she says with a shrug. "He's taking her to the dinner Saturday night."

"Is that so?" My question comes out laced with more animosity than I actually intend. Truth is, Denny has been my best friend for years and if I could hand pick anyone to date my sister, it would be him. "Funny your mom didn't mention that. I'll have to ask her about it at dinner. Are you okay with your mom going out with him?"

"Yeah, I think so. Mom deserves to be happy. And if Denny is as nice as Miss Wallace, I'm definitely good with it."

I shake my head; sometimes it's hard to remember that she's only fourteen. "He will be or he'll answer to me," I tell her with a wink, making her laugh.

"You're funny, Uncle Nate. I know you would defend us, but you're such a big softie, it's funny to think about."

"Don't go ruining my reputation by letting that get out," I say as I lead the horse to the stall and close the door.

"Don't worry, your secret is safe with me," she says through a giggle.

"Good. Now let's get cleaned up so we can go help your mom with supper."

Sitting down at the table, we begin to pass the food, and as we fill our plates, I start the conversation. Winking at Lila I ask, "So Becky, Lila tells me you're going to the dinner with Denny Wallace."

Her cheeks turn pink as she glances at Lila, who's trying not to laugh at her mother's embarrassment. "I am," she says. "He asked me to go last night after the rally. Why are you asking?"

"No reason," I say as I begin eating my dinner. "I like Denny. Just thought it was funny you didn't mention it is all."

She studies me for a minute, and then asks, "So you're okay with it?"

"Yeah, why wouldn't I be? Like I told Lila, Denny's a good guy, he would treat you well. Besides, you're old enough to date whoever you want, you don't need my permission."

"True, but I've been gone a while too, so a little insider information wouldn't hurt."

"I'd let you know if there were any problems, but Denny's a stand-up guy. So go out with him and enjoy yourself."

Of my three sisters, I'm closest to Becky. Being only two years apart, we spent the most time together growing up. Even as she dated Mitch, they allowed me to tag along on more than one occasion. When they married and moved to Denver, Becky visited frequently; bringing Lila with her to make sure, she had the ranch life experience, while growing up in the city. After seeing how

Mitch treated her the last few years of their marriage, she deserves a second chance at happiness.

Glancing over at Lila, she receives a nod of approval and I can see her visibly relax. Smiling she says, "You know, I think I will."

The conversation continues as we sit around the dinner table, when Lila asks, "Mom, what did you think of Miss Wallace?"

"As a candidate for mayor, I think she would be a good choice. She knows the town, and the people that live here, and like us, she has recently returned to Buckhorn and offers a fresh perspective."

"Good point," Lila says as she continues eating.

Curious, even though I know I'm going to regret asking, I do. "What are your other thoughts?"

Becky looks at me from across the table, "Nate, you've always had a little crush on Ellie, even Lila noticed how you were looking at her last night."

"You two have talked about this?"

"Well, yeah, Uncle Nate, we talk about *everything*."

"I'm learning that," I mutter more to myself than them, causing them both to laugh.

"Look, Nate," Becky says as she reaches across the table and squeezes my hand. "It's been a long time since I've seen you look at anyone the way you looked at Ellie. There's more to life than this ranch. You deserve someone to share your life with, someone to love. Do us and yourself a favor, the next time you see Ellie, ask her out."

Five

Ellie

After seeing Nate Barker at the rally last week, I spent most of the week hoping to run into him again. But Nate is a rancher, and ranchers only come to town for two reasons. Necessity and church. Unless of course it's harvest or calving season, then even church takes a backseat. Which also explains why I took extra care in choosing my attire this morning and making sure my hair and makeup were just so.

Pulling the cornflower blue dress that matches my eyes from the closet, I slip it over my head and step into navy blue pumps. Running a brush through my golden tresses, I let it fall in soft waves over my shoulders. Satisfied with my reflection, I head downstairs to join my family and ride with them to church.

Walking into the church I grew up in fills me with comfort. The exterior looks like every little white church you've seen in a movie or magazine. But the interior magnifies the warmth you feel when you walk through the doors. Rich wood panels cover the walls and vaulted ceiling, while sunlight streams through beautifully designed stained-glass windows. The wooden pews have been recovered many times over the years, and now boast a deep burgundy fabric.

Following my parents and brother down the aisle to the third row, the same row my parents have sat in since the day they began dating. It's always amused me, how where you sit in church can cause such a stir. Moving from your established family pew, can have the rumor mill running in full force, and the next thing you know someone is asking if you've set a wedding date.

Before we move into the pew, I see Denny wave to Becky, Nate's sister, making her smile and blush.

Once we've taken our seats, I tease, "Did you just make Becky Barker blush?"

"Maybe," he says with a teasing grin. "I took her out to dinner last night."

"Really?"

Denny has always carried a torch for Becky, so it really shouldn't surprise me that he would ask her out. Deep down I think Becky has always liked him as well, but she was with Mitch. Now there's nothing standing in their way, and they are free to explore their feelings for one another.

"Well by the looks of that blush, it must have gone well. Her daughter, Lila, is a sweetheart. Not to mention a heck of a campaign manager." Turning to sneak a peek over my shoulder to see if Lila's here, my eyes collide with Nate's. He gives me a wink, causing butterflies take flight in my stomach and my cheeks flame. I smile in return, before turning back to face the front.

Leaning over Denny whispers, "Looks like I'm not the only one making women blush today."

"Hush it, Denny," I whisper sternly as he straightens, still chuckling as Pastor Stafford takes the pulpit to welcome everyone.

While he speaks, my mind wanders back to the lifelong crush I've had on Nate Barker. Being four years, my senior ensured that we never had any classes together. Of course that didn't stop me from thinking he was the cutest boy around here. Since he and Denny were such good friends, Nate spent as much time at our place as Denny did at theirs. Which worked well for me, because that meant I saw him even more. I chance another glance in his direction, and smile to myself. It's good to see that some things haven't changed, he's only gotten more handsome with age.

As the service ends, I make my way down the aisle to wait outside for my parents, who have been swept up in another conversation.

"Hi Miss Wallace," Lila says as I step off the last step and onto the sidewalk.

"Hi Lila. You look very pretty today."

"Thank you," she says smiling as she looks down at her purple floral print dress.

"Miss Wallace," I hear from behind only to see James and Jeffery Norton fast approaching. "We had an idea we wanted to run by you."

Holding up my hand, I stop them. "Boys, while I appreciate your dedication, I'm afraid all campaign talk will have to wait until tomorrow. It's Sunday and if we talk politics or the campaign while standing on the church grounds, we may be risking a lightning strike. After all even, the Lord needed a day of rest. "

"Okay," they reply in unison, sounding a bit defeated.

Just as I'm about to give in to my guilt for not hearing them out, Lila steps forward and speaks up, effectively rescuing me from further discussion.

"I'd *love* to hear your idea. Let's step over there out of the way," she says offering them her brightest smile while ushering the boys to one of the picnic tables under the pavilion.

"Still a heartbreaker, I see," a rich baritone voice says next to my ear, his warm breath caresses my neck and sends a shiver down my spine, and makes me weak in the knees.

"Funny, I don't remember getting a chance to break your heart," I tease as I turn to face him.

"That's because you left for college before I got a chance to ask you out."

"Well, I'm not in college anymore," I reply, opening the door for his invitation.

Chuckling he shakes his head as he toys with the hat in his hands. "No, you're not," he states, giving my body a quick once over that should offend me but instead gives me a sense of pride that he noticed I'm no longer Denny's little sister.

"I hear you're running the family ranch now."

"I am," he replies with a nod of his head.

A moment of silence passes between us, before I say, "I, um, better go find my family before I have to walk home. It was good to see you, Nate." I was a little bit disappointed that he hadn't asked me out. Some things never changed.

"You too, Ellie," he says still fidgeting with his hat. As I turn to walk away, his voice stops me. "Ellie," he says causing me to turn back around. "Would you like to have dinner with me?"

Smiling I accept, "Yeah, I'd love to."

He nods and grins, "Friday? Pick you up at seven?"

Still smiling I nod, "See you then," I agree before I turn and go find my family.

The anticipation for my date with Nate only grew as the week progressed. After going through my closet three times, I finally decided on an off-the-shoulder chambray dress that falls just above my knee with a pair of cowboy boots. A light application of makeup and my hair loose and natural and I'm ready for my date.

Tossing a few essentials into a small handbag, I can't help but think what I would have given for a date with Nate Barker while I was in high school. Heading downstairs, I step into the living room where Denny and Dad are watching a basketball game.

Glancing up from the game he's watching, Denny says, "Wow, El, you look great. Good thing I already had a talk with Nate."

All forward motion ceases as I groan, "Please tell me you're joking?"

"Don't worry, I left the intentions talk for Dad," he says as if that makes everything all right."

Dad chuckles from his recliner, "Thanks son, I appreciate that.:

Rolling my eyes, I shake my head while trying not to laugh. "You two are impossible," I say as I hear a knock on the door.

Even though I know who is on the other side of the door before I open it, I'm still unprepared for just how handsome Nate Barker really is standing on my front porch holding a bouquet of sunflowers, which just happen to be my favorite.

Dark denim hugs his muscular thighs and a light blue button down highlights the gray flecks in his sapphire eyes. Quickly removing his ever present Stetson he says, "Good evening Ellie. You look beautiful."

"Thank you. You look very handsome too," I reply as I open the door wider for him to come in.

"These are for you," he says handing me the bouquet. "A little bird told me sunflowers were your favorite."

Accepting the flowers I smile, "Your little bird was right. Everyone is in the living room if you want to say hi. I'll just put these in some water and then we can go."

He nods and turns toward the living room, leaving me to admire the view from behind, which is equally impressive. Nate Barker is one fine sight, and tonight he's all mine.

Six

Nate

Standing in the Wallace's living room, waiting for Ellie to return, I'm surprised by my nervousness. I've known this family all my life, gone to church with them, even attended school and community functions together. But never have I been here to escort their daughter out on a date. Thankfully, Denny's presence makes me feel more comfortable and the conversation easier.

Hearing Ellie approach, I straighten form my leaning position against the doorway and turn my gaze on her as she reaches my side. She looks even more beautiful tonight than she did on Sunday. The girl I knew growing up is gone. The gorgeous woman standing in front of me replaced her and I'm the lucky bastard that will have her on my arm tonight. Long blonde hair, sapphire blue eyes and curves that my hands itch to explore.

"All set?"

"Yes, ready when you are," she replies smiling up at me.

Saying goodnight to her family, I place my hand on the small of her back, where it fits perfectly, and guide her out to my truck. Opening the door, I help her inside and close the door before making my way around to the driver's side. Sliding behind the wheel, I start the engine, pull out onto the highway and head west toward Sheridan.

"I thought we'd head over to Sheridan for dinner, and maybe catch a movie. If that's okay?"

"That sounds nice."

There's a moment of uncomfortable silence before I notice her fidgeting. Reaching over I take her hand in mine and give it a squeeze. Taking her by surprise, her eyes find mine. "I'm a little nervous too," I confess.

She giggles nervously and the sound is as beautiful as the woman beside me is. Tilting her head in disbelief she asks, "Why on earth are you nervous?"

"Because the most beautiful woman in town agreed to go out with me."

She looks down, embarrassed by my confession, even though it's true. "You're very sweet," she says. "If I were being honest, I'd tell you that I've had a crush on you since I was old enough to notice boys."

"Really? Why didn't you ever say anything?"

This time she laughs as she relaxes and turns toward me a bit, "Are you kidding? You were older than me, and I was sure you only saw me as Denny's annoying little sister."

"I had no idea. But since we're being honest," I say as I relax more resting my left hand on top of the steering wheel. Happy with how easily conversation is flowing between us, I continue with my confession. "I always wanted to ask you out."

Surprise laces her voice as she tilts her head, not sure, if she wants to believe me. "You did? What stopped you?"

"Yeah, I always enjoyed spending time with you, but I was afraid you'd turn me down." I tell her as I pull into the parking lot of the Italian restaurant and park in one of the spaces beside the building. Turning off the engine, I get out of the truck and walk around to open her door. Taking my offered hand, I help her down and close the door.

"For the record," she says as her big blue eyes meeting mine. "I wouldn't have turned you down."

Taking a step forward I eliminate some of the distance between us and say, "For the record, you were *never* annoying." Lifting her hand to my lips, I kiss the back of her hand, and then lead us into the restaurant.

Once the server takes our order, Ellie asks, "What made your parents decide to move to Florida?"

"Well technically they only spend winters in Florida, or so I've been told. They bought an RV and split their time between my other two sisters the rest of the year. They stop at the ranch along the way."

"Good for them," she says before taking a sip of water.

"What about you? Why did you come back to Buckhorn?"

"Because it's home," she says with a shrug. "Returning to Buckhorn was always part of my plan. I didn't expect it to take me three years after I graduated to do so, but it was a good learning experience for me. Besides if everyone leaves, Buckhorn will die, it's a small town. Towns have to have people in order to thrive."

"That's true. Is that why you're running for mayor, to turn Buckhorn into a thriving metropolis?"

Laughing she shakes her head, "No. I love our small town. Running for mayor wasn't my idea, that was my students' idea. I already have my dream job."

Confused I ask, "If teaching at the school is your dream job, why agree to run for mayor?"

"For the kids," she says with a shrug as if the answer is obvious. "Getting them involved in running the campaign makes studying American Government even more exciting for them. And as a bonus they get to learn about the election process."

"What happens if you win?"

"I guess we'll have to wait and find out."

Walking back to my truck after the movie, Ellie surprises me by stopping bedside the driver's side door. Looking up at me she smiles, and I can no longer resist the pull I feel towards her. Cupping her cheek with my hand, my thumb caresses her soft skin as I lean down and brush my lips across hers. Ending the kiss all too soon, her eyes flutter open, "I hope that was okay? You looked so beautiful here in the moonlight, I couldn't resist any longer."

"It was more than okay," she whispers back, her voice a bit raspy.

"Good, because I'd really like to do it again."

"I'd like that too," she says as she climbs inside my truck. Sliding to the middle of the bench seat, she tucks herself into my side as I slide behind the wheel. The heat from her leg pressed against my thigh goes straight to my groin, making my jeans uncomfortably tight. Once we are headed home, my hand finds hers and I place it on my thigh, before covering it with my own.

Pulling into her driveway, I put the truck in park and slide out of the cab. Stopping her exit, I place my hands at her waist. "I'd like to see you again, Ellie, if that's okay."

"Yeah, I'd like that."

"Tomorrow?"

"I think I can do that," she says smiling brightly. "I'm free all day, unless your niece has scheduled something I don't know about."

"Good, I'll make sure it stays that way," I tease, giving her a wink that makes her laugh. Helping her out of my truck, I keep her hand in mine and walk her to the door. "I'll pick you up at noon tomorrow, and dress to ride."

"I'll be ready," she agrees as we walk up the porch steps. "Thank you for tonight, I had a really nice time," she says as we reach the door.

I can't resist the urge to tease her just a little, hoping that I'll be blessed with the sound of her laughter once more before ending the night. "Just nice? I was shooting for incredible; I guess I'll have to up my game next time."

Granting my wish, Ellie throws back her head and laughs. "Well I'd upgrade it to amazing, but I'd rather have a second date."

I watch her cheeks turn pink and she begins to fidget, embarrassed by what she just blurted out. I lift her chin, forcing her blue eyes to look into mine. "Me too. Pick you up tomorrow at noon?"

A slow smile tips up the corners of her mouth. "Sounds perfect. Goodnight Nate," she whispers as she starts to turn for the door.

Tugging her hand, I pull her body against mine, wrap my arm around her waist and kiss her. Melting into me, I deepen the kiss until I hear her sigh, and then gently pull away and whisper, "Goodnight Ellie."

Leaving her standing on the porch, I walk back to my truck and head for home.

After cleaning the stalls with Lila this morning, I shower, dress and head into town to pick up a few things for my afternoon with Ellie.

Stopping at the Bullseye Diner I walk in, remove my hat and take a seat at the counter.

"Good morning, Nate," Doris, the longtime waitress, says as she pours me a cup of coffee.

"Morning, Doris. I need to place an order to go."

"Sure hon," she says taking out her pad of order slips. "What can I get for you?"

"I need two BLT box lunches, and two slices of apple pie."

Writing down my order she says, "Coming right up," as she tears the ticket off and places on the wheel for the cook in the kitchen.

As I sip my coffee while waiting for my order, Doris reappears with a coffee pot offering me a refill. Pouring more of the hot, strong coffee into my cup she asks, "How's Becky doing now that she's moved back?"

"She's good," I say as I lift my cup to take a cautious sip. "She's been a great help around the ranch too."

"Well you tell her if she ever gets tired of working at the ranch, I could use her around here."

Laughing I promise, "I'll let her know," just as the cook rings the bell signaling my order is ready.

Retrieving my order, Doris places it in a bag and hands it to me, as I hand her enough cash to cover my check and tip. "Thanks Doris, say hi to Hal for me."

"Will do, Nate, take care," she says as I turn for the door.

Climbing back in my truck, I head toward Ellie's to pick her up before going back to the ranch.

Pulling up to Ellie's house, I put the truck in park and walk up the same steps I walked her up just last night. Knocking on the screen door, Ellie appears looking just as beautiful in jeans, a t-shirt, and cowboy boots as she did in the dress she wore last night.

"Hi," she says smiling as she opens the door for me to step through before letting the door close behind me.

"Hi, I hope I'm not too early?"

"No, you're right on time," she says as she places her purse on her shoulder and jacket over her arm.

"Good," I say as we walk out to my truck and help her inside.

As I climb behind the wheel, "Something smells good," she says as she tries to peek inside the bag.

"I picked us up lunch, and thought we'd ride out to one of my favorite spots and have a picnic. That is if you still ride?"

"It's been a while, but I've been getting comfortable in the saddle again since I've been home."

"Good. I'll make sure to give you a gentle mare to break you in slowly."

"I appreciate that," she says with a laugh as I pull up to the barn.

Jumping out of the truck, I grab our lunch and make my way around to assist Ellie, but she meets me at the front of the truck. Taking her hand, I entwine our fingers and walk her into the barn and down to the stall of the horse, she'll be riding, a black mare named Onyx.

"This is Onyx," I say as Ellie reaches her hand out toward the mare's nose. "My sister, Kari, taught her kids to ride on this horse, so she won't buck but she's happy to run when you get comfortable with her."

"She's beautiful. I think we're going to do just fine, aren't we, Onyx?" The horse's whinny confirms what Ellie said, making her smile. "Yeah, we'll be fine."

"Okay then, let's get 'em saddled up then."

Taking the lead hanging beside the stall, Ellie opens the gate and attaches the lead to the bridle, walks her out to the corral and lightly ties her to a post. Turning back to the barn she grabs a brush hanging on the wall and then begins brushing Onyx down like it's the most natural thing in the world.

I watch her silently for a few minutes while I brush down Sarge. "For someone who hasn't ridden in a while, this seems to be old hat for you."

Smiling she looks over at me, shrugs, and moves to the other side and continues brushing. "I guess it's kind of like riding a bike, you never forget once you learn. Though I'd rather ride a horse than a bike any time."

"That makes two of us," I say as I finish brushing down my horse. "Come on, let's get you a blanket and saddle." Following me back into the barn, she hangs back up the brush and turns to take the blanket from me. "Go ahead and place the blanket, and I'll bring out the saddle."

With the blanket in place, I set the saddle, leaving Ellie to fasten the buckle while I saddle my own horse. Once my horse is ready, I check Ellie's to make sure it's tight enough before giving her a hand up. As she gets comfortable, I place the bit and hand her the reins.

"You good?"

"Yep," she says smiling down at me, "I'm ready when you are."

Grabbing our lunch, I hang the bag from the saddle horn as I walk my horse through the gate and wait for Ellie to ride through before closing and securing the gate. Climbing onto my horse, I lead us to the back section of the ranch and up a little rise to a clearing with an overlook. Over the years, I've ridden or walked every inch of this ranch, but this has always been my favorite spot. Lush green grass, a grove of trees offering just enough shade to shelter you from the sun. Now as fall approaches, the leaves are beginning to changing from shades of green to red and gold, paint the landscape.

Climbing off my horse, I remove the blanket from the back of my horse, grab our lunch and walk over to meet Ellie.

"Do we need to tie them up?" she asks.

"Nah, just drop the reins, they won't wander off," I say as I take her hand and lead her to the overlook, my favorite spot on the ranch.

Looking out over the ranch, Ellie says, "Wow, I can see why you like coming here. This view is spectacular."

"It is," I agree as I wrap my arm around her waist and pull her back against my chest. "It's where I come if I need to think or if things are stressful. I always feel recharged when I leave."

"I can see why."

We stand silently, enjoying the view until her head falls back against my shoulder. Kissing the top of her head, I spin her toward me, "Come help me spread the blanket."

Blanket in place, I lower myself to the ground and take a seat beside her.

We unpack our lunch, and before taking a bite of her sandwich, Ellie asks, "Is all this part of your ranch?"

Swallowing the bite of my sandwich, I nod. "It is. We rotate pastures with the cattle every spring and fall. We do the same with the hay fields. Now Becky has carved out a larger section behind the barn for a garden, which will probably grow next year."

"That's great! She really seems to enjoy selling them at the Farmer's Market."

"She does," I agree. "She deserves to be happy after what she's been through the past year."

Pointing out the house we passed as we rode up here, Ellie asks, "Whose house is that?"

Following her line of sight to the two-bedroom clapboard house, I once called home. "That was my house until I moved into the main house. I'm thinking of offering it up to Becky and Lila. Give them their own space."

"I'm sure they would love that."

"Yeah, and it would give us some privacy too," I say as I brush the hair back from her face.

Blue eyes meet mine and I can feel her pulse quicken as my hand cups her cheek. My eyes dart to her mouth as her tongue moistens her lips. "It would?"

"Yeah," I reply just above a whisper as I lean in my lips a breath away from hers. "It would definitely give us more privacy so I could do this more often." Eliminating the distance between us, my mouth captures hers, tasting and teasing until she opens for me. Our mouths meld together as our tongues begin a sensual dance. Lowering her to the blanket, her fingers thread into my hair and I can feel the heat from her core against my thigh. Slowly ending the kiss, my work-roughened hand caresses the flawless skin of her flushed cheek. "What are you doing to me, Ellie Wallace?"

"The same thing you're doing to me, Nate Barker," she teases using my last name like I did hers.

Chuckling I rise from the blanket and offer her my hand, "Come on, let's go take a walk or the ride home is going to be extremely uncomfortable."

"Or in my case," she mutters as I pull her to her feet, "extremely satisfying."

Pulling her to my side, I kiss the top of her head and laugh. "Well I can't have that, I want to be the one to claim that pleasure."

Seven

Ellie

The first thought on my mind when I wake up is the same as the last thought I had before I falling asleep. Nate's goodnight kiss. A kiss like that clears away any doubt I may have had as to whether he feel the undeniable pull between us. I've never had a man leave me breathless and wanting more the way Nate does each time he kisses me. If he kisses me like that again tonight, I may have to drag him under the bleachers and have my way with him.

As I make my way to the bathroom, I laugh to myself. I can see the headlines now *Buckhorn Mayor Candidate Ravages Rancher*. My opponents would have a field day with that.

After showering and dressing for the day, I head downstairs to see what Mom has planned for the day. "Good morning, Mom," I greet as I step into the kitchen and head for the coffee pot.

"Good morning, sweetheart," Mom says as she looks up from the list she is making. "You seem cheerful," she says, a smile teasing the corners of her mouth. "I guess your date went well?"

Smiling from behind my coffee cup, I answer, "Yeah, it went really well. In fact, he's taking me to the rodeo tonight. It's hard to believe we've been seeing each other for a month already."

"That's great, honey. I'm so happy for you."

"Thanks," I say as I sit down at the table to eat my breakfast. "Are Dad and Denny out and about already?"

"They are."

"What do you have planned for today," I ask before taking a bite of toast slathered in strawberry jam.

"I was just making a list of things I needed from the store, and then I need to prepare a few things for the church dinner tomorrow."

"Well," I say as I take my dishes to the sink and wash them. "I'm available, if you'd like some help."

"Are you sure you don't need to campaign today?"

"No," I say shaking my head. "Well, not until tonight anyway. Somehow Lila managed to schedule me to present trophies to the winners tonight."

"She is quite resourceful isn't she," Mom says through a laugh.

"You have no idea," I reply as I sit back down at the table.

Once Mom has her list complete, we head to town to do the shopping.

One of the best things about living in a small town is that everyone knows everyone. Of course, that's also one of the bad things about living in such a small town. Add in the fact that I'm running for mayor and that just adds a reason for every patron at Buckhorn's only grocery store to stop and talk about the upcoming election. Each one telling me how much they appreciate how I was getting the kids involved in the process, but never giving anything away as to whom will get their vote.

Finally, after getting everything we need, Mom and I make our way to the checkout line and then head home to prepare the dishes for Sunday dinner.

After three apple pies, two dozen corn muffins, one chocolate pound cake, and enough green beans to feed a small army, we finally begin to clean up. Mom and I have always worked well together in the kitchen. The last time I remember spending this, much time cooking with her was over the holidays last year. Mom has a standard list of "goodies" she makes every year, some to keep, some to giveaway, all loved by those who get to partake.

"Thanks for your help today, Ellie. I'd still be baking if you hadn't pitched in."

"My pleasure," I tell her as I place the bundt pan into the dish drainer. "I forgot how much fun it is to work with you in the kitchen."

"It *was* fun," Mom says as she dries a bowl and places it in the cabinet.

"Are you and Dad going to the rodeo tonight?"

The rodeo is a precursor for the Founder's Day celebration and gives both local amateur and professional cowboys and cowgirls a chance to shine. Of course the biggest draw is the bull riding competition"

"Wouldn't miss it," she says smiling.

"Hopefully I won't embarrass you or myself while presenting tonight."

Laughing Mom encourages, "I'm sure you'll do just fine."

"I hope you're right," I say as I dry my hands. "Well, I guess I better go get ready, Nate said he'd pick me up at six. Don't want to keep him waiting," I say giving her a wink as I head up to my room to get ready.

After taking a quick shower to rinse off the fine layer of flour I'm covered in, I dry my hair, apply my makeup and dress in a pair of dark wash jeans and a pink long sleeve blouse. Pulling on my favorite black boots, I find my denim jacket in the back of the closet and make my way downstairs just as I hear a car door slam.

As I hit the bottom step, Nate knocks on the door. "I got it," I call to keep anyone else from rushing to the door. Opening the door, I'm greeted by that sexy, crooked grin.

"Evening, Ellie," he says as his eyes rake over me. "You look beautiful," he declares before leaning in to kiss my cheek.

"Thank you," I reply opening the door wider. "Come in, I just need to get my jacket and we can go."

Pulling my jacket from the bannister, I call up the stairs, "Mom, Dad, we're leaving. See you all later."

"Okay, sweetheart," Mom calls back. "Drive safe."

Turning back to Nate I smile, "Ready?"

"Almost," he says taking two steps toward me. Pulling me to his chest, he kisses me the same way he did last night, leaving me breathless and pliable in his arms. When he pulls away he whispers, "I've been thinking about kissing you again since last night. Thought I better do it before we had a thousand eyes on us."

"I'm certainly glad you didn't wait any longer," I whisper back as I try to catch my breath.

"Me too," he says giving me another quick kiss on the lips before turning to open the door for me to walk through.

Walking to the driver's side of his truck, Nate grins as he opens the door and watches me climb inside and slide to the middle of the seat. Climbing in beside me, still grinning, Nate shakes his head.

"What?"

"Nothing," he says as he pulls onto the highway and places his arm around me. "I like having you beside me."

"Good, because I like being here."

After paying our admission, before walking through the gates to the rodeo, I turn as I hear my name called from behind me.

"Miss Wallace!"

Finding Grace in the crowd, she makes her way to me, a stack of campaign flyers in her hand. "Grace, I didn't realize you all were campaigning tonight."

Shrugging she says, "Most of us were coming tonight anyway, might as well make the most of it."

The determination and dedication to this campaign my students have shown, completely overwhelms me. They have given their all, in order to ensure a win in this election. Guilt begins to consume me as I realize my own dedication may be lacking.

"Well I'd like for you all to enjoy the rodeo tonight instead of working so hard."

She smiles and assures me that they will be doing just that. "Yes ma'am, we plan on going inside as soon as it starts."

"Okay, good. I'll see you later then," I say as I place my hand in Nate's then turn to make my way through the gate.

"Miss Wallace, wait," she says running after me.

"Yes," I say turning back to her.

"Lila wanted me to tell you to report to the announcer's booth and they'll give you instructions for tonight."

Giving her a smile I reply, "Thank you Grace, I'll head there now."

Taking my hand so we aren't separated in the crowd, Nate leads us around the arena and up into the stands. Finding an open spot to sit, Nate says, "I'll wait here unless you want me to go with you."

Smiling up at him I reply, "Thanks, but I'll be fine. It shouldn't take long at all. Save me a seat?"

"I can do that," he says giving me a wink before moving in to row to take a seat.

Proceeding up the steps to the announcer's booth, I knock as I enter and introduce myself. "Hi, I'm Ellie Wallace. I was told to come here for instructions for the presentation tonight."

"Yes, Miss Wallace, thanks for joining us tonight," an older man in full cowboy attire says as he stands and makes his way to me. "Wes Adams," he says offering his hand, which I accept. "I'm the representative for the rodeo association."

"Nice to meet you, Mr. Adams. What can you tell me about the presentation?"

Having all the information I need, I make my way back into the stands and down the stairs to Nate's side. "Hey handsome, is this seat taken?"

"Nope, saved it just for you," he says giving me a kiss as I take a seat beside him.

"What did I miss?"

"Not much, just the presentation of riders and a few clowns to get the crowd warmed up."

"Good, I'd hate to miss anything, even though I'll probably be hiding my eyes during the bull riding."

The bull riding competition is always the main attraction at the annual rodeo. I can't imagine the adrenaline rush the cowboys must have trying to hold on until that eight second buzzer sounds. I'm certain I wouldn't last one let alone eight. Not to mention how terrifying the idea of being in the ring with a raging two-thousand-pound bull is to me.

Threading his fingers with mine, Nate bumps my shoulder, "Never fear Ellie, I'll protect you," he teases, but his eyes shine with sincerity and I know in my heart he would.

Eight

Nate

Ellie didn't hide her eyes nearly as much as I expected her to during the bull riding competition. I tried to contain my laughter as someone behind us asked why the cowboys walked funny after their ride, but the look on Ellie's face when she heard the question was too much, causing me to erupt into laughter right along with her.

"Seriously? Did they really just ask that?"

"I'm afraid so," I say through a chuckle.

"Obviously as teachers, we're failing in the health section of the curriculum," she mutters low enough for only me to hear.

"I think common sense may be lacking as well," I whisper back.

As the last competitor leaves the arena, the clown troupe enters. "Ladies and gentlemen," the announcer says, "please give a warm round of applause for tonight's rodeo clowns!" The crowd gives a small smattering of applause goes up from the crowd. "Ahh come on, folks," the announcer chastises, "you can do better than that. Remember the rider's safety is the priority of the rodeo clown." With that, the crowd stands and cheers the last of the antics going on in the ring.

"Well, that's my cue," Ellie says as she rises from her seat and I do likewise.

"I'll walk down with you and wait for you by the gate," I tell her as I place my hand on the small of her back as we descend the stairs. Standing at the rail, I watch as Ellie meets the other presenters. Walking out to the center of the arena, Ellie waits alongside Mr. Adams as the winning names are announced. As each rider comes forward, Ellie shakes their hand and congratulates them before Mr. Adams presents their prize.

A commotion around the bullpen catches my attention, as cowboys scramble up the rails and out of the way of the bull making his presence known. Turning my focus back to Ellie, I watch as yet another cowboy tips his hat, smiles, and shakes her hand. What happens next sends my heart racing and everything else into slow motion.

Wooden rails splinter and fly into the arena, as an angry bull spins back out into the open space putting Ellie and the rodeo delegation in danger. Without thinking, I climb the rails and sprint toward Ellie, reaching her just as she catches the bull's attention. "Ellie!"

She turns to look at me as the bull snorts and stomps trying to decide which one he wants to charge at first. Finally reaching her, I wrap my arm around her waist as we run together to the railing. Helping Ellie up the rails, I clear the top rail seconds before the bull slams into the side of the arena. Placing my hands on her shoulders, I turn her to face me.

My gaze travels over her checking for any trauma, "Ellie, are you okay?"

I can feel her shaking under my hands as she nods, stuttering her reply. "Y-yes, I'm okay."

Pulling her to my chest, I wrap my arms around her and hold her. Both of our hearts are beating uncontrollably, so much so it's hard to tell which one is hers and which is mine. In the short time we've been dating, this woman has become so important to me that the thought of losing her is unimaginable. When I feel her begin to calm, I run my hands up her back, until they reach her shoulders. Taking her face in my hands my thumbs stroke her cheeks as I confess, "I was afraid I wouldn't get to you in time. I don't know what I would have done if something would have happened to you." Closing my eyes against the horrific thought, I rest my forehead against hers.

"Hey," she says, laying her hand on my cheek, causing my eyes to find hers. "But you did, and I'm fine."

Caught up in the moment, my hands slide into her hair as I slam my mouth to hers, forgetting everything and everyone around us, kissing her and claiming her in front of all in attendance. The sound of the cheering crowd breaks through our bubble, bringing us back to reality and reminding us of exactly where we are. Tipping my head towards the crowd, I say, "Maybe you should give them a wave and let them know you are okay and I wasn't giving you mouth to mouth resuscitation."

Smiling while turning three shades of red, Ellie takes a couple of steps back and waves causing the crowd to applaud again. "I guess I better see if we're going to continue with the presentations."

"Okay, but you're not going back into that ring until all the bulls are secure," I tell her as I follow her over to where the rodeo man, Mr. Adams, stands.

"One," she says with a laugh and a look back over her shoulder. "You're not the boss of me. And two, I hadn't planned on it. Being close to death once today is enough for me."

"That may be true but I did save your life and, in some cultures, that would mean you are indebted to me."

"Ha, dream on, cowboy," she sasses as she tosses me a wink as we reach the gate. "Wait here, I'll find out what's going on."

Chuckling as she walks away, I watch the sway of her hips, tempting me with every step she takes. Resting my arms on the rail, I study her as she speaks with Mr. Adams. The time we've spent together has been casual and relaxed, but tonight I got to witness, her professional side. There's no doubt in my mind she would make an excellent mayor and would represent our town to the best of her ability. Reaching out, Mr. Adams shakes her hand thanking her for her participation. She smiles and waves to someone in the stands, before making her way back to me.

"You're in luck, cowboy; you only get to rescue me once today," she teases as I fall into step beside her.

Wrapping my arm around her waist, I lean in close to her ear, "That's too bad; I was looking forward to practicing my CPR skills,"

"Oh, I never said you couldn't practice," she teases back as she nips at my jaw.

Weekends are usually spent with Lila cleaning out the stalls, but considering she had a late night at the rodeo last night, I thought I'd let her sleep in this morning. Opening each stall I lead the horses out to the corral, placing feedbags along the top rail, watching to make sure the horses begin eating before I head back inside the barn.

Halfway through mucking the stalls, I hear the screen door bang indicating that someone other than me is awake on the ranch. As I step out of the stall to load the wheelbarrow, I catch sight of Lila headed towards the barn. Hearing her boots hit the wood floor of the barn, I call over my shoulder, "Morning, Sweet Pea," as I step back into the stall to continue my work.

Stopping in front of the stall I'm working in she fumes, "Don't you *sweet pea* me, Uncle Nate! How could you do this to me? Do you have any idea how hard I've worked on this, and now everything is ruined!" Pacing back in forth in front of the stall, she continues her rant, even though I have no clue as to what she is going on about.

"Hey, whoa there, swee…, um I mean, *Lila*," I correct myself after receiving a glare. "How about you take a breath and tell me what's got you so riled up this morning."

Closing her eyes, she does exactly as I instruct, and then says, "My phone started blowing up this morning with messages from my classmates wondering what we were going to do about what has just posted on The Standard's website." Her anxiety begins to build again, and before I can ask what article she is talking about, rant number two begins. "And now we have to do damage control, and I had to call Miss Wallace and wake her up to tell her what was going on, and if you could've just kept your hands to yourself we wouldn't have anything to worry about, but nooo, you just…"

Stepping in front of her to stop her pacing, I demand, "Wait, what did you say? How am I to blame for all this?"

Sighing in frustration, Lila rolls her eyes and says, "Uncle Nate, haven't you been paying attention? Here, let me show you," she says as she unlocks her phone and then turns it to face me.

There, in full color, is the source of my niece's stress and anxiety. A picture of Ellie and me from last night locked in a passionate kiss after saving her from a raging bull. A smile tugs the corner of my mouth at the memory of that kiss, until I see the headline.

Swinging the Vote? Is this the reward for candidate endorsement?

Taking the phone from Lila, I read the brief article attached to the photo.

Catching mayoral candidate Ellie Wallace and local rancher Nate Barker in this compromising position has this reporter wondering if this is the proper thank you for endorsement.

"Son of a bitch," I mutter as I shove the phone back in Lila's direction and head for my truck.

Chasing after me Lila calls, "Uncle Nate, where are you going?"

"To take care of this. Finish the stalls, I'll be back," I call as I open my truck door.

"But Uncle Nate," she starts only to have me interrupt her.

"Just do it, Sweet Pea," I demand as I close my truck door and turn it toward town.

Nine

Ellie

Nothing scares you more, or wakes you from a dead sleep faster than a ringing phone. Hearing the voice of my campaign manager, Lila Robbins, on the other end had me instantly on alert. Lila prides herself in being able to run the team, so hearing her voice on the other end of the line only affirmed that there must be an issue too large for them to handle on their own. The issue being explained to me was definitely in need of an intervention.

Getting ready as quickly as possible, I jump into my car and head to town. Pulling into the parking lot of The Standard, I pull up the article and read through it again, while I wait for someone to arrive. As I begin reading, I think *it's not so bad*, and then it is. Right there, in black and white for the entire town to see, including my parents and students, is the most frustrating part of the article, the part that insinuates that I'd trade sexual favors for votes.

Growling in frustration, I let my head fall back onto the headrest. How could I have let this happen? Maybe it was the adrenaline rush of almost being trampled by a bull, maybe it was something else, I don't know. Don't get me wrong, I don't regret the kiss, it was amazing. I spent years dreaming about being kissed by Nate Barker, and believe me, he did not disappoint, but I should have remembered where I was.

The glow of light from inside The Standard office catches my attention. Turning off the ignition, I exit my vehicle, tuck my phone into my pocket and head for the door. Making my way inside, I march confidently down the hallway to the editor's office, stopping only long enough to knock on the open door to announce my arrival.

Looking up from his desk, a knowing smirk firmly in place, Tim Morrison says, "Good morning, Ellie. I wondered how long it would take you to show up this morning."

"That's *Miss Wallace* to you, Mr. Morrison," I say as I move further into his office, jaw clenched trying to rein in my anger and display it all at once. "While I appreciate your willingness to give me free press, I don't take kindly to you insinuating that I trade sexual favors for votes. Buckhorn is a small town, Mr. Morrison, and it is well known to *everyone* that I have been seeing Nate Barker for over a month. So might I suggest that you find something more worthwhile to report, and leave the mudslinging to the boys on Saturday night."

With a roll of his eyes, Mr. Morrison sighs and looks over my shoulder. "Mr. Barker, I suppose you're here to defend Miss Wallace as well?"

"No," Nate says as he reaches my side, hat in hand. "Miss Wallace seems to be doing a fine job of stating her case all on her own. I'm here because I have a devastated teenage girl at home, who can't believe that our local paper and fellow candidate would print such garbage." Glancing at me, Nate nods before he says, "Now Miss Wallace may be too nice to demand an apology, but I'm not. And I expect to hear from my niece by the time I get home that the current post has been removed and replaced with not only an apology to Miss Wallace but to the kids who have worked tirelessly on her campaign."

Mr. Morrison looks between Nate and me, as I stand with my arms over folded over my chest, brow raised in challenge, until he concedes. "Fine, I'll retract the article and post an apology."

"Today?"

"Yes, *Miss Wallace*, it will be posted by the time you get home. You have my word."

"Thank you," I say before I turn toward the door to leave, only to turn back and ask one more question before I go. "Mr. Morrison? Just out of curiosity, were you at the rodeo last night?"

Narrowing his eyes at me, he tries to figure out where I'm going with my question. "Of course, I haven't missed one in years."

"Then you are well aware of the circumstances around that photo. So why post it with such an implication?"

Shrugging he smiles smugly, "Consider it a test, Miss Wallace. One that both you and your campaign staff passed, by the way."

"A test?"

"Yes, your students got to handle a minor scandal, and the town got to find out how you'll handle situations." Leaning back in his chair, he says, "And from what I can see, you'll be tackling situations head on. You didn't waste time going here or there to get the matter cleared up, you went straight to the source. Well done, Miss Wallace."

You've got to be kidding me! This guy actually has the audacity to praise me, while trying to justify his actions. Nice try Mr. Morrison, but I don't think so.

"Mr. Morrison, you seemed to be confused. You see I don't need to be tested by you or anyone else to prove my integrity to this town. I can do that all by myself by walking the walk and talking the talk, as they say. So the next time *you* decide *my* students need taught a lesson, I suggest you remember which one of us is *actually* the teacher and leave the lesson planning to me."

Turning on my heel, I leave the office, Nate following closely behind. Making it to my car, Nate calls my name stopping me before I get inside.

"Ellie, wait!"

"What Nate," I say as I round on him. "Kissing me last night in front of the entire town wasn't enough? I know, let's just climb up in the bed of your truck and really give them a show!"

"Ellie," he starts, but I interrupt him.

"No Nate, I can't do this right now," I say turning back toward my car.

"Fine, then get in my truck and we can talk about this," he says raising his voice and sweeping his arm toward his truck.

Shaking my head, I turn back to face him, "It's not just this conversation, Nate." I say holding up my hand and then motioning between us. "I can't do this, us. This election is too important to the kids, I won't be the reason they are disappointed."

Nate takes a step toward me, his voice softening. "What about what you want, Ellie? Isn't what we have important?"

"Of course it's important Nate," I say as I wipe away a tear that is making its way down my cheek. "I've been in love with you since the third grade, and now that I have you, I have to let you go because I can't focus when you are around."

"Is that such a bad thing," he says as a smile teases the corner of his mouth and he reaches out to wipe away another traitorous tear.

"It is if we are going to end up on the front page of The Standard."

Eyes locked on mine, Nate closes the distance between us, his calloused hand cupping my cheek. "Was the kiss really that bad, Ellie?"

Sighing I lean into his touch and close my eyes. "No," I answer honestly. "It was an *amazing* kiss. The kind of kiss I've always dreamed of sharing with you. But I made a promise to those kids and I won't let them down. I'm sorry, Nate."

Pulling his hand away, Nate takes a step back. "I'd never ask you to break a promise, Ellie, especially one involving my niece."

I have to admit, I'm a little taken aback by his words, I expected more of a fight. "So you understand why I can't do this right now?"

"I do. It doesn't mean I like it, but I understand."

Looking down as I begin to feel tears sting my eyes, I kick at a rock in front of me. "Yeah, it's not exactly the ending I was hoping for either, but it's for the best." Taking a step forward, I step up on my toes and place a lingering kiss on his cheek. "Goodbye, Nate."

"Bye Ellie," he says softly as I turn toward my car.

Climbing into my car, I start the engine and pull out of the parking lot. Tears silently stream down my face as I watch Nate disappear in my rearview mirror. There has to be a way to work this out, but right now, there's too much at stake and walking away is my only option.

Ten

Nate

Standing in the parking lot, watching her taillights fade away, I know letting her go was the right thing to do. But I honestly never expected to feel this empty as I watch her drive away.

Even though we've known each other all our lives, meeting Ellie was the best thing that has happened to me in a long time. Hearing her say she was in love with me trumped that by a million times. And the funny thing is, I'm not even sure she realized she said it. But she did, and I heard her loud and clear.

That's why I let her go.

She's right, she needs to concentrate on the election, and I'll give her that. But there are a few things I need to take care of while I'm giving her space.

Climbing into my truck, I grab my phone off the seat and call Denny as I drive home. The last thing I need is him showing up wanting to kick my ass for hurting his sister.

"Hello," He says as he answers the call.

"Denny, it's Nate."

"Hey man, how's it going?"

"Been better, that's why I'm calling."

"Okay," he says, "what's going on?"

"I just saw Ellie, and well, we decided not to see each other right now. I need you to know that it was a mutual decision and as far as I'm concerned a temporary one, until after the election."

"Let me get this straight. You're calling to tell me that you and my sister broke up and you're giving me a heads up so I don't come over and kick your ass for hurting her. Do I have that right?"

"In a nutshell, yeah that's right."

"But you are only giving her until after the election and then you are planning on getting her back?"

"That's the plan," I say confidently.

"Mind if I ask how you intend to do that?"

"By asking her to marry me."

"And you think she'll say yes?"

God I hope so. The thought of not having her in my life, is enough to make me want to jump in my truck, chase her down and beg her not to end this. As much as I want to do exactly that, I know I can't. She needs time to focus on the election and as hard as it is, I need to respect that.

I can hear the skepticism in his voice, and it doesn't sit well with me. "Look Denny, the only reason I let Ellie walk away today is because she admitted that she's in love with me. The *only* reason I didn't say it back is because she doesn't need the added stress during the election. But I can promise you this, Denny, once the votes are counted and the winner has been announced, win *or* lose, I *will* be there on bended knee asking Ellie to marry me."

"Well damn if that ain't the most romantic thing I've ever heard."

Chuckling at his response, I admit, "I may have been roped into one too many chick flicks with Becky and Lila."

"Nice to see you've been paying attention," he says with a teasing laugh.

"I'll be by this week to talk to your dad, so I appreciate this staying between us for now."

"You have my word."

"Thanks, Denny."

Ending the call as I pull in the driveway, Lila appears on the porch just seconds after I close my truck door, and begins firing off questions.

"Uncle Nate, is everything okay? Did you get everything straightened out? Can I tell Miss Wallace that the crisis has been averted?"

"Whoa there, Sweet Pea," I say as I drop my arm around her shoulder and pull her to my side.

"Miss Wallace beat me there, and had already started demanding the article be removed. Morrison promised an apology would be posted by the time I got home."

"Awesome," Lila says. "I knew Miss Wallace could be a badass when she wanted to be."

"Hey, watch your mouth, young lady," I sternly scold.

"Sorry, Uncle Nate," she shyly replies.

"It's okay," I say kissing the top of her head. "Just watch it, last thing I need is your mom jumping all over me."

Giggling she teases, "You're not scared of her, are you, Uncle Nate?"

"Maybe just a little," I freely admit. "And you should be too. Now go on upstairs and make sure that article has been taken down and the apology is posted."

"Yes sir," she says as she opens the screen door before stopping in the doorway. "Thanks again, Uncle Nate."

"You're welcome, Sweet Pea."

Kicking the dust off my boots, I pull open the door, hang my hat by the door, step into the kitchen and pour myself a cup of coffee.

Sitting at the table, nursing her cup of coffee, Becky looks up from the magazine she's reading. "Get everything taken care of?"

"For the most part," I offer as I take a seat at the table and take a drink from my cup.

"What's that supposed to mean," she presses.

"It means everything with the campaign is on track, but I won't be seeing Ellie for a while."

"What! Why?"

"She needs to concentrate on the campaign without distractions."

Becky huffs as she leans back in her chair, arms crossed over her chest. "And you're a distraction?"

"No, kissing her in front of the whole town and ending up on the front page is though."

"So she dumped you," she says her voice filled with indignation.

"No," I say raising my voice more than I intend to. "I let her walk away."

"It's the same thing, Nate," she practically yells at me, while hitting the table with her hand.

It's been a long time since Becky and I have raised our voices at each other. I didn't like arguing with her when we were kids, and I like it even less now. She needs to understand I'll do whatever it takes to get Ellie back, even if that means not being with her right now.

"No, it's not. Dumping me means I have no chance of getting her back. Letting her walk away means I'm giving her time."

"What does she need time for? I thought you two were doing well together."

"We were, are," I correct. "But she needs to focus on the election."

"And you're okay with her making the election her top priority?"

Shaking my head, I rotate my coffee cup as I watch the liquid come close to spilling over. "She's not. She's making her students her top priority, and I just can't fault her for that."

"Wow," she says as she relaxes back into her chair and studies me. "You really do love her, don't you?"

"I do. I plan to show her just how much after the election. And I'm going to need your help."

"Absolutely," she says. "What do you need me to do?"

For the next two weeks, Becky and I work on fixing up my old house for her and Lila to move into over the Thanksgiving weekend. Once it's move-in ready, Becky wraps her arm around my waist and hugs me.

"Thanks for this, Nate. I know your intentions were purely selfish," she teases making me chuckle. "But this is exactly what Lila and I need… a space to call our own."

"You're right, you do. Sorry I didn't think of it sooner."

"That's okay," she says with a shrug, "you didn't have the same motivation as you do now."

"True. I just hope she says yes."

Laughing she says, "I don't think that's anything you have to worry about little brother."

The day before the election, after finishing my morning routine, I head over to the Wallace farm to speak to Ellie's dad. The nerves that I felt the night of our first date come back ten-fold as I park my truck in front of the barn.

The slam of my truck door alerts them of my arrival and Mr. Wallace steps out of the barn to greet me.

Meeting him halfway, I shake his offered hand. "Nate. Didn't expect to see you today. What can I do for you?"

"Mr. Wallace," I say with a nod. "I'm sorry to bother you, but I was hoping to talk to you about Ellie."

Confusion mars his usually pleasant expression, "Okay, but it was my understanding that you weren't seeing Ellie anymore."

"That's true, but I'm hoping to change that tomorrow night."

He places his foot on the bottom rail of the fence and rest his arms on the top. "Is that so?"

Mirroring his stance, we both stare out across the field in front of us. "Yes sir. With your blessing, I'd like to ask for Ellie's hand in marriage."

"Marriage? I don't know, Nate, you've only been dating a little over a month and haven't been seeing each other at all for the last three weeks. Don't you think this is a little soon?"

As much as I want to argue with him, he's right. We haven't been seeing each other that long, yet we've know each other all our lives. We haven't seen each other in the past three weeks, which have no doubt been the longest three weeks of my life. I need to convince him that Ellie and I belong together.

Shifting my position so I'm facing him, I plead my case. "With all due respect, sir, as far as I'm concerned it couldn't happen soon enough. I'm in love with Ellie. In fact, I've loved her for a long time, I just never told her. But win or lose tomorrow night, I plan on letting her know just how I feel about her before I ask her to marry me."

"And you think she feels the same way?"

"No sir," I say shaking my head. "I *know* she does, she said so herself the day we broke up. And with your blessing, I'll spend every day for the rest of my life proving to her just how much."

Eleven

Ellie

Hearing my alarm sound, I throw back the covers and make my way to the bathroom to begin getting ready for the day.

It's been three weeks since I've seen or heard from Nate, and in a town the size of Buckhorn, that's pretty surprising.

I cried all the way home the day I left him standing there in the parking lot of The Standard. The pain and loss I felt that day is still as raw today as it was three weeks ago. Walking away from Nate was the hardest thing I've ever had to do. My family has been nothing but supportive. And during these final weeks of the campaign, I needed all the support I could get.

Once I've showered and dressed, I head downstairs to grab some breakfast before going to work. With each step I take, my nervousness ratchets up. By the time I reach the kitchen, a pit has formed in my stomach.

Hearing me enter Mom greets me, "Good morning, sweetheart."

"Morning Mom," I reply as I head towards the coffee pot.

"So are you ready for today?"

"I'm more nervous than I expected to be," I say as I take a seat at the table. "I just hope the kids aren't too disappointed if we don't win."

"I have a feeling that a loss would only make those kids more determined to win the next time," Mom says with a laugh.

"Next time? Bite your tongue, Mom! This is a one-time thing. I don't think I can put myself through all this stress again."

Laughing Mom says, "Sorry, my mistake."

"Principal Markham is letting us await the results in the cafeteria, so I'm ordering pizza for the kids. You and Dad should join us."

"We'd love to. We can pick up the pizza for you if you'd like?"

"That would be great," I say as I wash up my breakfast dishes. "I'll let them know you are picking it up for me when I place the order. Well, I guess I better get going," I say as I gather my things. "The polls open at seven, so I can vote before classes start."

"Good luck, sweetheart," Mom says as I reach the door.
"Thanks, Mom," I call back. "See you all tonight."

As the students begin to fill the classroom, I notice how much quieter they are than usual. When the bell rings for class to begin, I stand and move in front of my desk, leaning against it as I address the class.

"Good morning, everyone. Since today is Election Day, and before anyone asks, yes I did already cast my vote..." My comment is met with smiles and soft laughter, so I continue. "I thought we would do a recap of what we learned during this past semester. Who wants to start?"

When no one volunteers, I decide to lead off with the "scandal" we had to endure. "First of all, and I know I've already thanked you hundreds of times and I'm sure you are tired of hearing it, but you have to hear it a few more times." I smile at them and they all shyly smile back. "When I went to The Standard's office, Mr. Morrison complimented you all on the way you handled the crisis we faced. And I have to agree. You *all* showed more maturity and grace than most adults do while running political campaigns. I am beyond honored to have worked with each one of you. Tonight, after the votes are counted and the winner is announced, I hope you all walk away filled with pride for the work you have done on this campaign."

Everyone is silent and then Lila raises her hand, "Miss Wallace," she says as she stands next to her desk. "I'm sure I speak for all of us, when I say thank you for allowing us to be part of this process. We all know if we hadn't begged you to run, you wouldn't have. But you did, and you taught by example, and the things we learned will stay with us always."

As she takes her seat, I blink back tears. The idea that I've touched their lives, like my teachers did for me, fills me with joy. "Now I just want to remind you that, since voting will be taking place in the gymnasium, PE class has been cancelled. Principal Markham has agreed to let us await the results in the cafeteria.

Pizza will be provided for dinner, and please, tell your parents they are welcome to join us."

When the last bell of the day rings, and most of the students begin to file out of the room to head home for the day, I'm overwhelmed by emotions. Maybe it's nerves; that the fate of my future lies in the hands of the entire town. More than likely, it's the stress of letting Nate go and the thought that when all the votes are counted, I'll have no one special to share in either my joy or sorrow. That thought alone leaves me feeling empty.

Hearing the door open, I discreetly wipe away the tears that have started to fall. Lila's voice breaks through the silence in the room. "Miss Wallace?"

"Hi Lila, did you forget something?"

"No ma'am, I, uh, just wanted to check on you before I left. You seemed a little sad by the time class ended this morning," she says with a shrug.

I can't help but smile at her concern. "You're a special girl, Lila Robbins. Thank you for checking on me. I'm sure I'll be back to normal once the election is over."

"Yeah," she says with a little smile, "it has been a little stressful."

"Just a little," I agree while measuring a small amount with my thumb and index finger.

"Okay, well I better go, I'm sure my mom is here by now."

"Okay, see you later, Lila."

Opening the door, she stops before walking through it and says, "Miss Wallace? If it helps, Uncle Nate seems sad too."

I spend some extra time in my classroom, grading papers and finalizing my lesson plan for next week, before heading down to the cafeteria to join my campaign team.

Since Mom and Dad are picking up the pizza and drinks on their way into town, I send her a quick text letting her know that the order has been placed and will be ready in an hour.

Stepping into the cafeteria, I find it fairly quiet as my students diligently work on their homework, so they can enjoy the rest of the evening.

"Hello everyone," I greet as they look up from what they are doing. "I'm glad to see you all making good use of your time. I've placed the order for pizza and it will be here in about an hour. If you need help with anything, don't hesitate to ask, otherwise I'll leave you to your homework."

A collective "Thanks Miss Wallace," is spoken as I take up residence at a table near the door.

As the students begin to finish their work, talking begins to increase, and while still nervous, the air within the room begins to shift and fill with excitement. By the time the pizza arrives, they are in full celebration mode.

My eyes continually scan the room looking for new arrivals, or one in particular, but always come up empty. There's quite a turnout of support that has gathered with us. Most are parents supporting their kids who have worked so hard on the campaign. My parents are here, as is my brother, although he may be here more for Becky than me. The thought both makes me smile and again triggers that feeling of emptiness I've experienced over the past few weeks.

As the clock on the wall approaches seven, I make my way to the front of the room. Tapping my brother on shoulder on my way, I ask him to get everyone's attention for me. Using his most ear-piercing whistle, the room falls silent as all eyes turn to me.

Smiling I wink at my brother, "Thank you, Denny," I say before turning back to the crowd. "Hello everyone. The polls will be closing in a few minutes, but I wanted to take the time to thank you all for coming out today. Whether you voted for me or one of my opponents, voting is important, and I appreciate you being an example to your children." Speaking of your children, if you were part of my campaign team, would you please stand and make your way to me."

As the students line up beside me, I continue. "This group of students talked me into to doing something I would have never even considered before. And then, not only did they volunteer to *run* my campaign, they did an outstanding job. And I think they deserve a round of applause."

Moving to the side, I applaud my team as the rest of the audience joins in giving them a standing ovation.

As the applause begin to fade, the crackle of the intercom gains our attention as Mayor Holbrook's voice comes over the speaker.

"May I have your attention please? As your current mayor, I'd like to thank each one of the candidates for providing, fair and honest campaigns. With the polls now closed and all votes counted, it is my great honor to announce the newly elected mayor of Buckhorn is…Ellie Wallace!"

Surprised that my name was announced, I can't help but exclaim, "I won!"

The entire room burst into cheers, as the students pull me into a massive group hug.

"We did it, you guys! I am so proud of each and every one of you," I say as I turn in a circle, making eye contact with each one of them. "Without you, this wouldn't have been possible."

As I finish thanking the kids for all their hard work, my skin begins to tingle and I know immediately who it is having this effect on me. Warm breath caresses the back of my neck as he says, "Congratulations Ellie."

My breath catches as I turn to face him. Clean shaven, and dressed in dark denim and a white button down shirt, black Stetson firmly in place. "Thank you, and thanks for being here. It, means a lot to me."

He takes a step closer and says, "You didn't really think I'd miss out on congratulating you, did you?"

Shrugging I answer honestly, "I really hoped you wouldn't."

He shuffles his feet a bit, then looks up at me with that crooked grin that always makes me weak in the knees. "So, Mayor Wallace, huh?"

Tilting my head I grin, "Yeah, has a nice ring to it, don't you think?"

"It does," he says as he closes some of the distance between us, making my heartbeat faster. "You know what would sound even better?"

"What," I ask, sounding a bit more breathless than I intend.

"Mayor Barker."

"You going to run against me next time, Nate?"

"No," he says tucking a strand of hair behind my ear. "I'm smart enough to know I could never beat you. But I'd always support my wife in anything she wanted to do."

"Your wife?"

"Yeah," he says as he reaches into his pocket, before dropping down to one knee and presenting me with a ring.

Gasping, my hand flies to my mouth as tears begin streaming down my face.

"Ellie, three weeks ago I did the hardest thing I could ever imagine. I let you to walk out of my life, even after you hearing you say you were in love with me. I knew that day, that I never wanted to feel the emptiness I felt as I watched you drive away. You told me then that you've been in love with me since the third grade, and to be honest, I've loved you just as long. And if you'll allow me, I'll spend every day for the rest of our lives showing just how much I love you. So Ellie Wallace, will you marry me?"

Nodding my head as I find my voice, I enthusiastically reply, "Yes! Yes! Yes!"

Sliding the ring on my finger, Nate leaps to his feet and sweeps me into his arms, kissing me with all the passion I've missed these past few weeks without him. As Nate begins to slow the kiss, the sound of applause fills the air. "You know this is going to be front page news," he whispers against my lips.

"Then let's make sure we give them plenty to write about," I challenge as I pull him in for the first of many kisses I plan to share with him over the years.

CPSIA information can be obtained
at www.ICGtesting.com
Printed in the USA
BVHW031503151218
535701BV00001B/17/P